Tree-House Comix Proudly Presents

DOG MAN
LORD OF THE FLEAS

WRITTEN AND ILLUSTRATED BY DAV PILKEY
AS GEORGE BEARD AND HAROLD HUTCHINS
WITH COLOR BY JOSE GARIBALDI

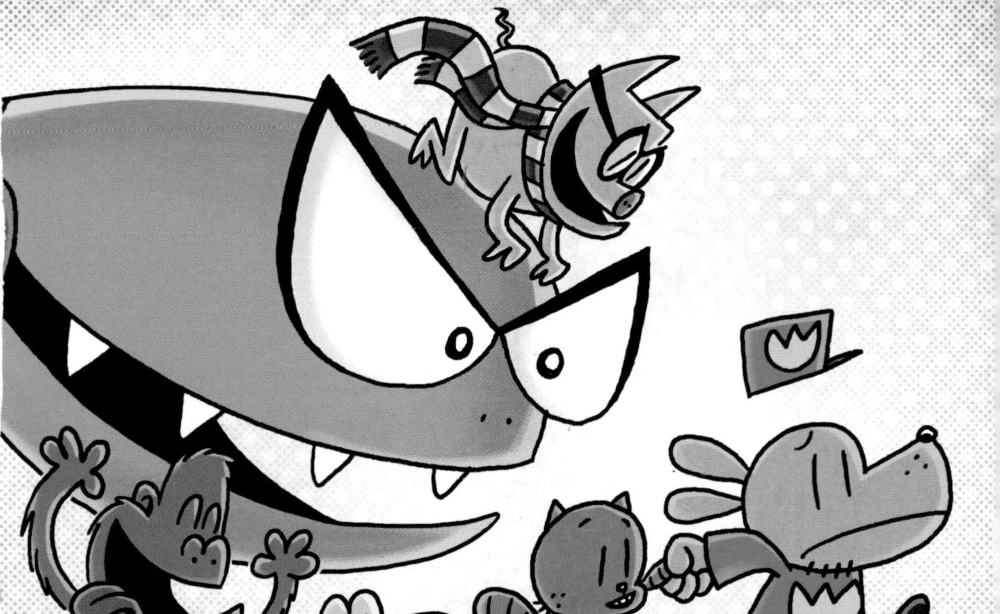

graphix
AN IMPRINT OF
SCHOLASTIC

THANK YOU TO A DEAR FRIEND, RACHEL "RAY RAY" COUN, WHO WAS THERE FROM THE START

Library of Congress Control Number 2017963497

978-1-338-74107-0 (POB)
978-1-338-29091-2 (Library)

10 9 8 7 6 5 4 3 2 1   21 22 23 24 25

Printed in China   62
This edition first printing, August 2021

Edited by Anamika Bhatnagar
Book design by Dav Pilkey and Phil Falco
Color by Jose Garibaldi
Creative Director: Phil Falco
Publisher: David Saylor

CHAPTers

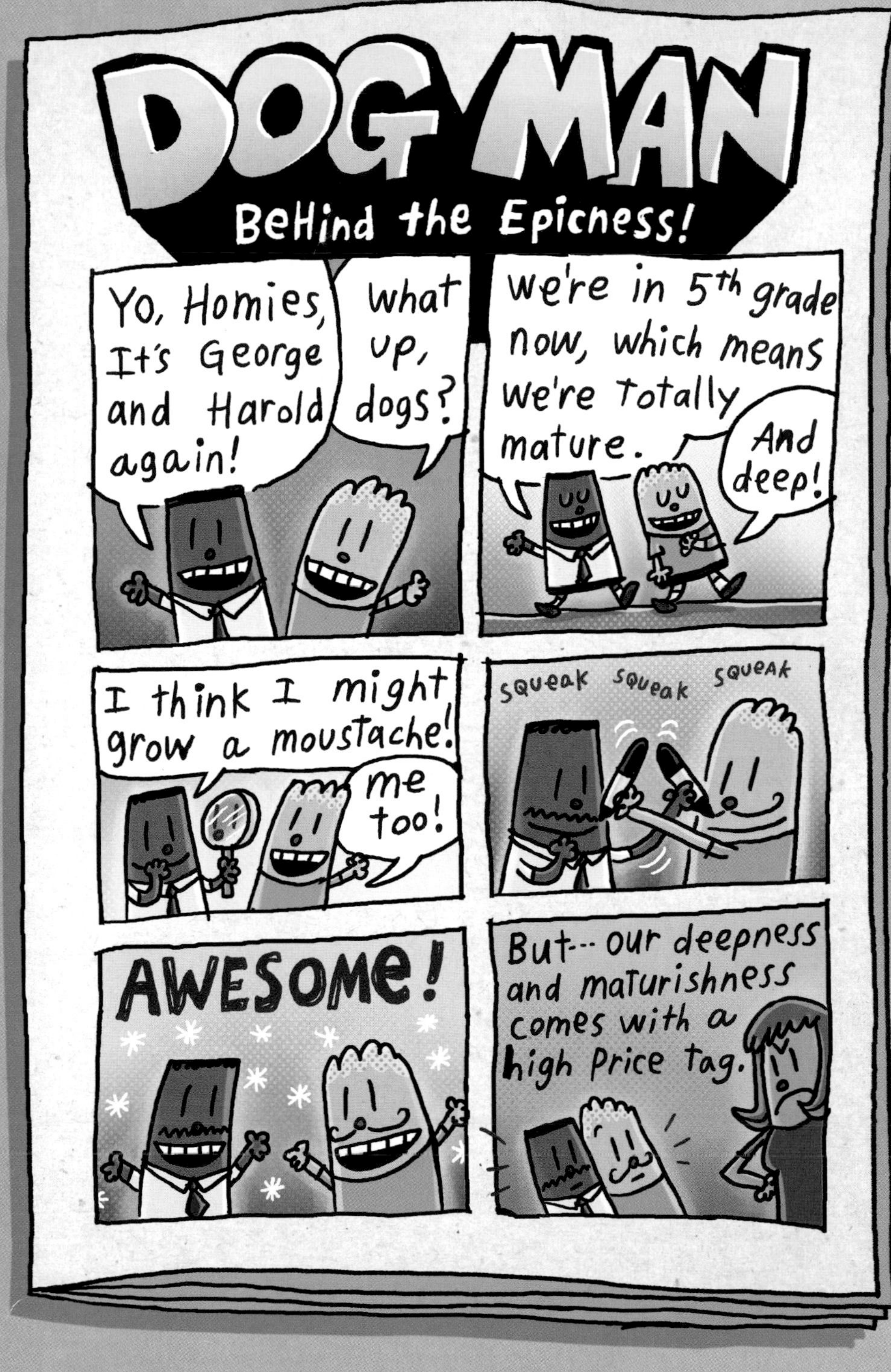
DOG MAN
Behind the Epicness!
Yo, Homies, It's George and Harold again!
What up, dogs?
We're in 5th grade now, which means we're totally mature.
And deep!
I think I might grow a moustache!
me too!
SQUEAK SQUEAK SQUEAK
AWESOME!
But... our deepness and maturishness comes with a high price tag.

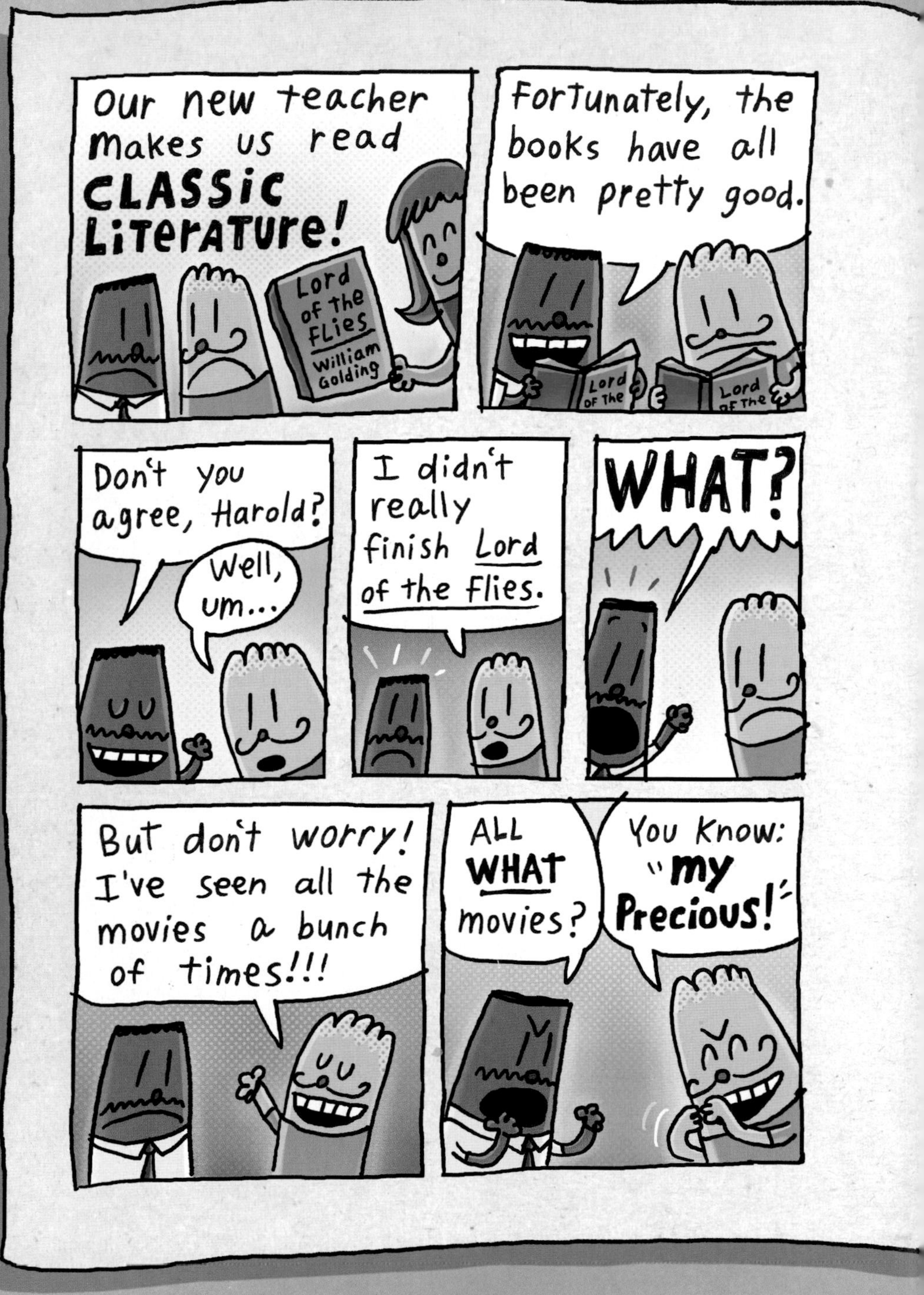
Our new teacher makes us read CLASSIC LITERATURE!
Lord of the Flies
William Golding
Fortunately, the books have all been pretty good.
Lord of The
Lord of The
Don't you agree, Harold?
Well, um...
I didn't really finish Lord of the Flies.
WHAT?
But don't worry! I've seen all the movies a bunch of times!!!
ALL WHAT movies?
You know: "my Precious!"

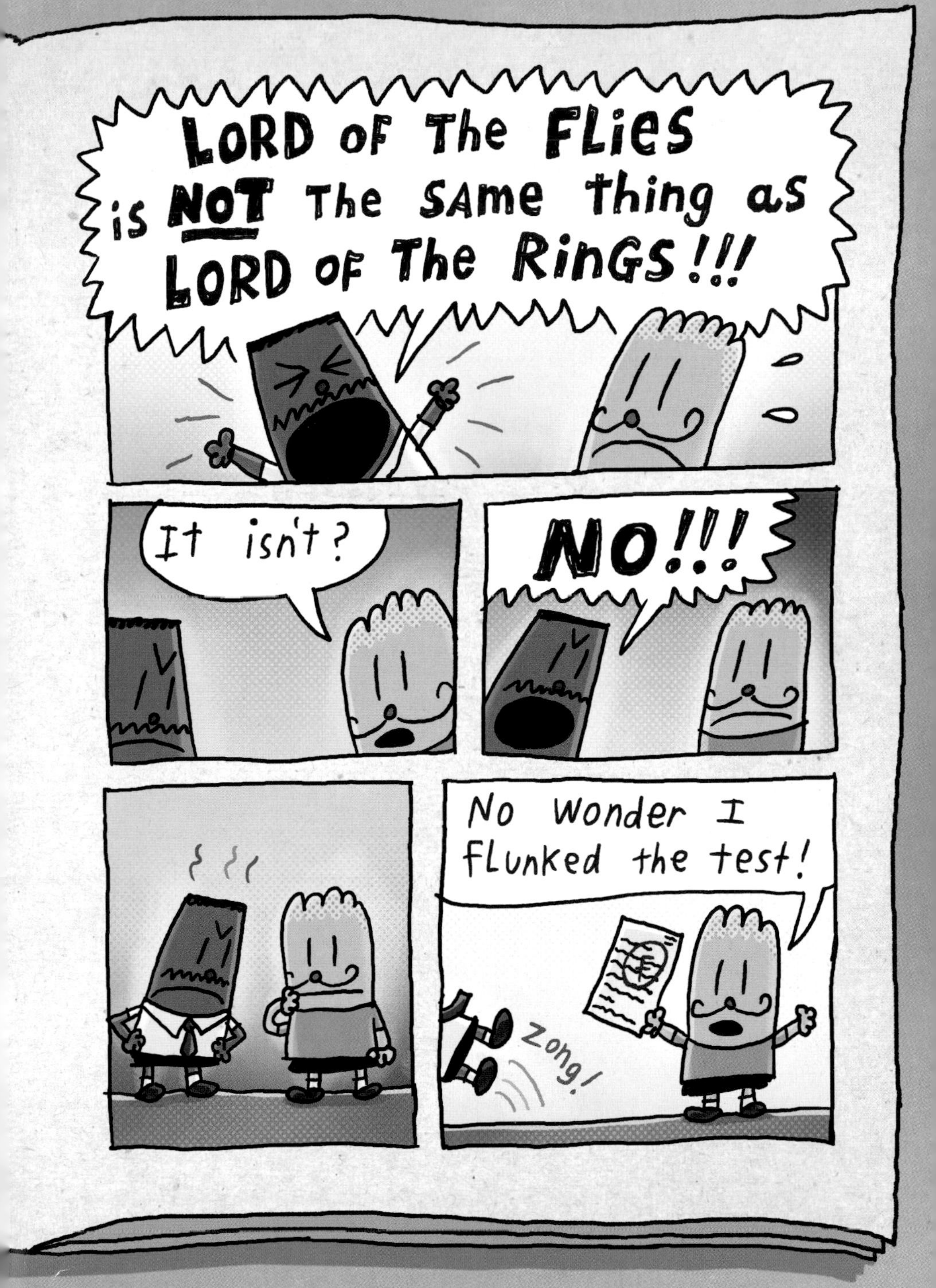

LORD OF THE FLIES is NOT THE SAME thing as LORD OF THE RINGS!!!
It isn't?
NO!!!
No Wonder I fLunked the test!
Zong!

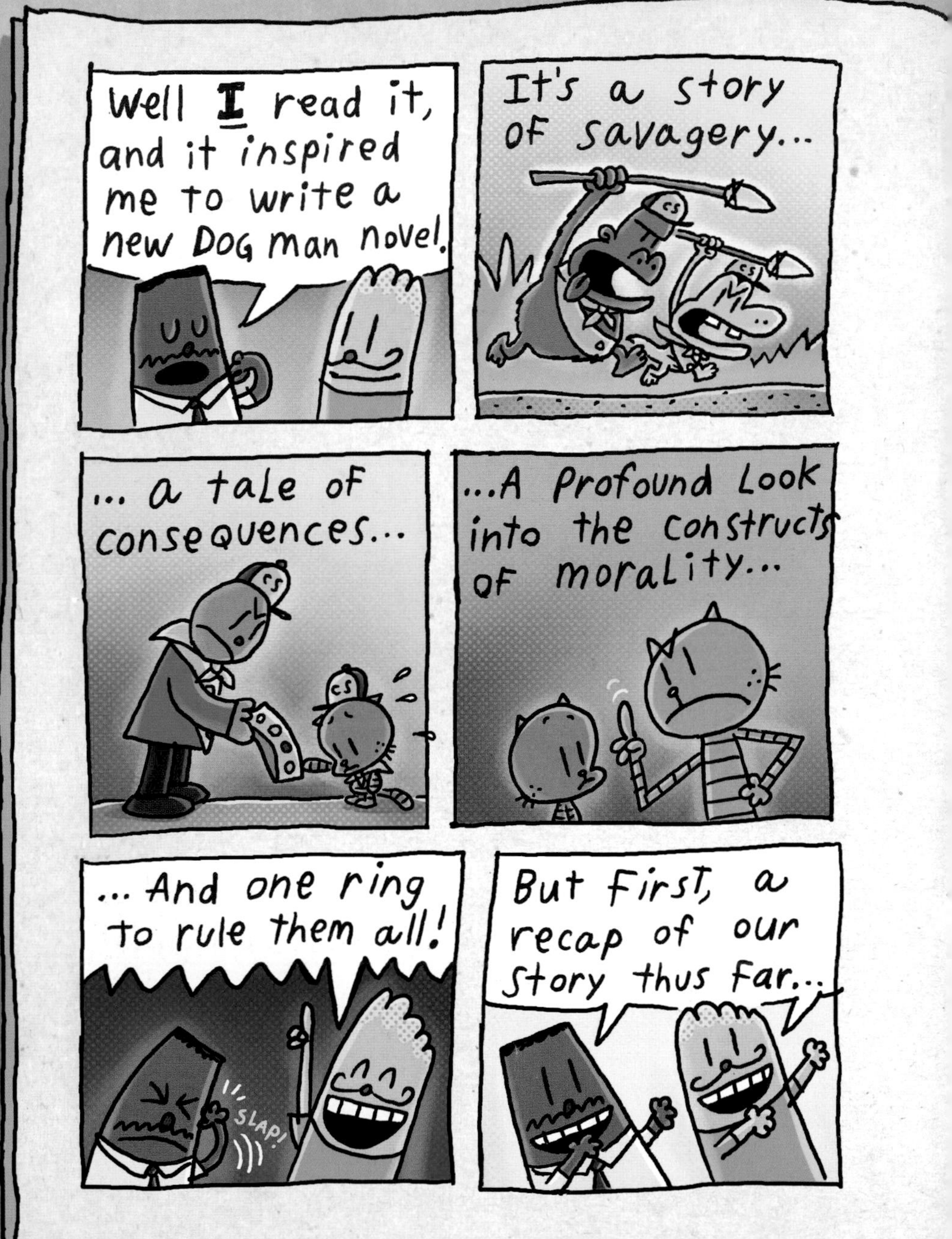
Well I read it, and it inspired me to write a new DOG MAN novel!
It's a story of savagery...
CS
CS
... a tale of consequences...
CS
CS
...A profound look into the constructs of morality...
... And one ring to rule them all!
SLAP!
But first, a recap of our story thus far...

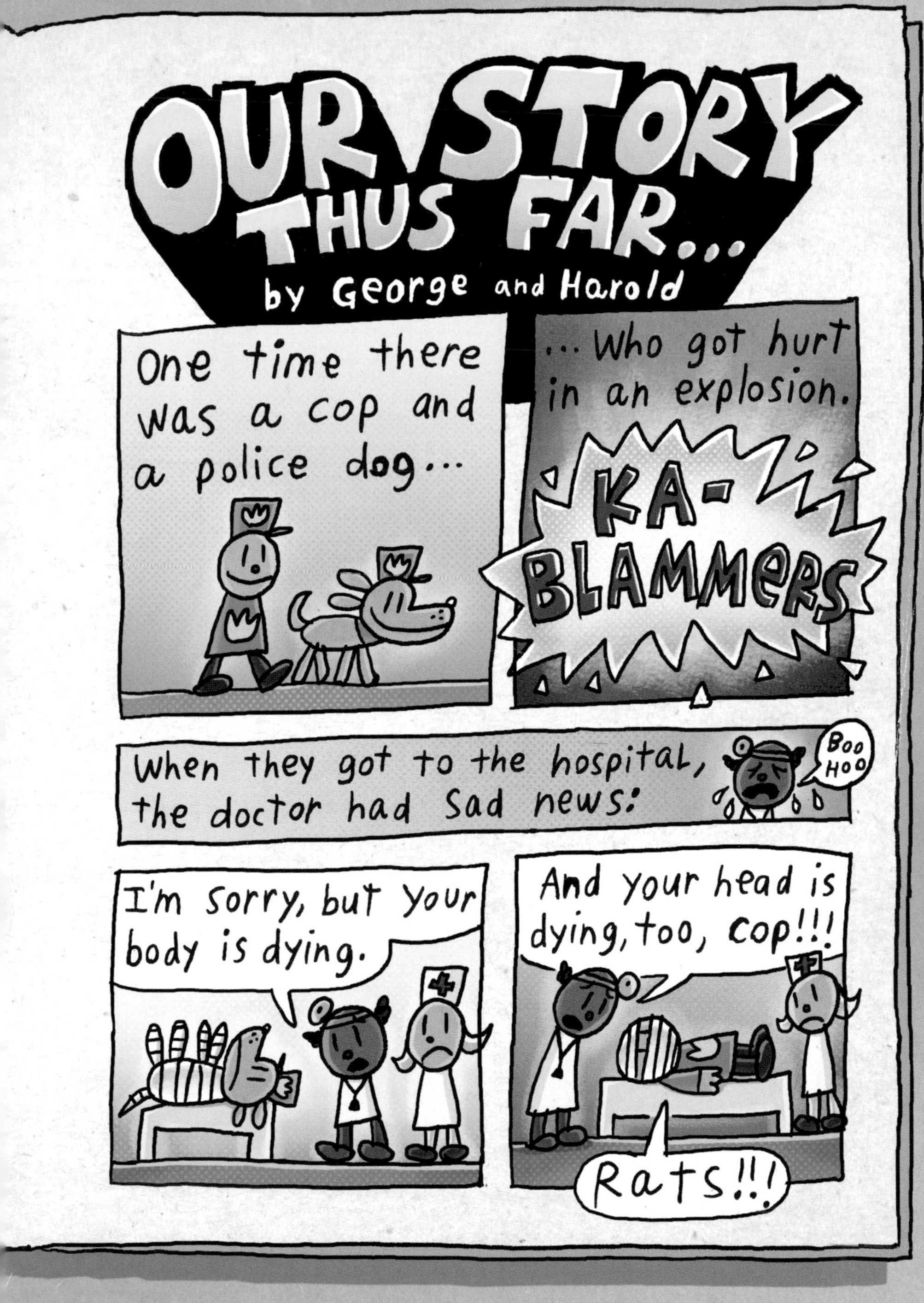
OUR STORY THUS FAR...
by George and Harold
One time there was a cop and a police dog...
...Who got hurt in an explosion.
KA-BLAMMERS
When they got to the hospital, the doctor had sad news:
BOO HOO
I'm sorry, but your body is dying.
And your head is dying, too, cop!!!
Rats!!!

But just when everything seemed hopeless, the nurse Lady got an idea.
Let's sew the dog's head onto the cop's body!
OK, nurse Lady!
So they did.
And soon, a new crime-fighting sensation was UnLeashed.
HOORAY FOR DOG MAN!

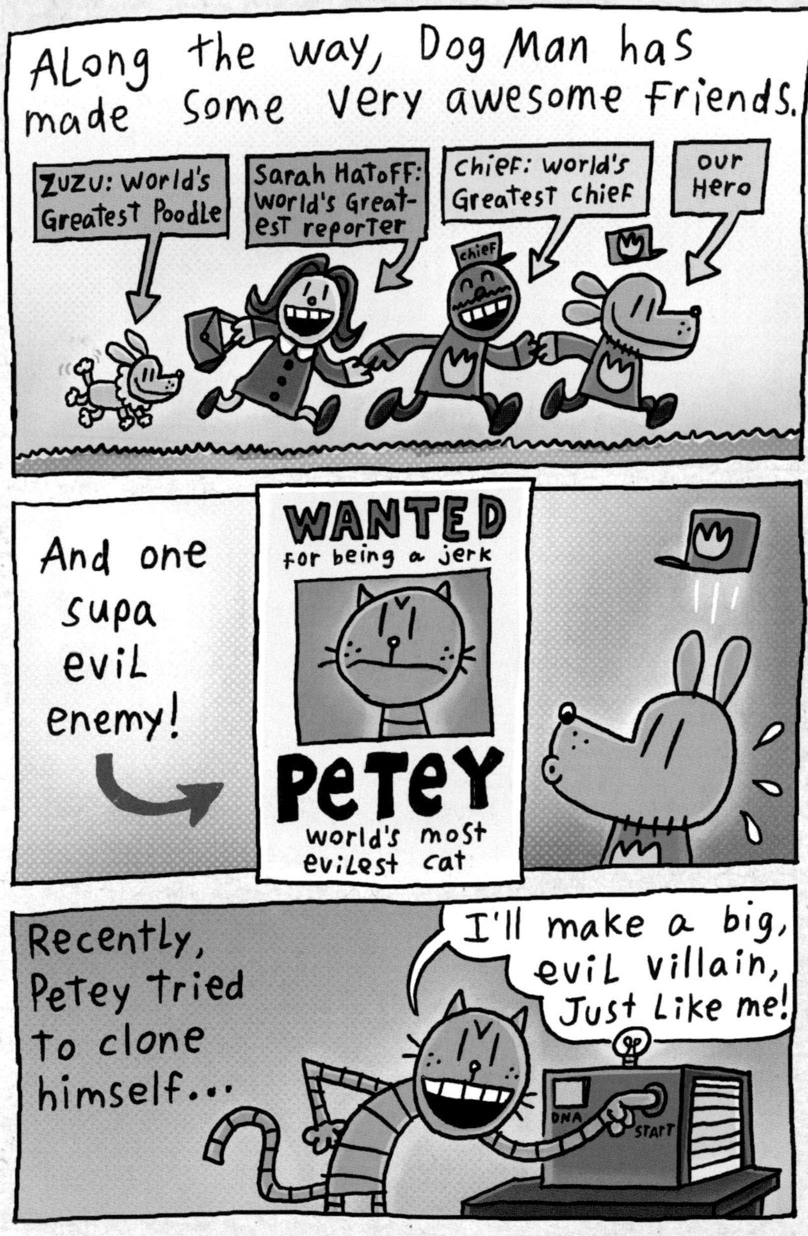

Along the way, Dog Man has made some very awesome friends.
ZUZU: World's Greatest Poodle
Sarah Hatoff: World's Greatest reporter
Chief: World's Greatest Chief
Our Hero
CHIEF
And one supa evil enemy!
WANTED
for being a jerk
PETEY
world's most evilest cat
Recently, Petey tried to clone himself...
I'll make a big, evil villain, Just like me!
DNA
START

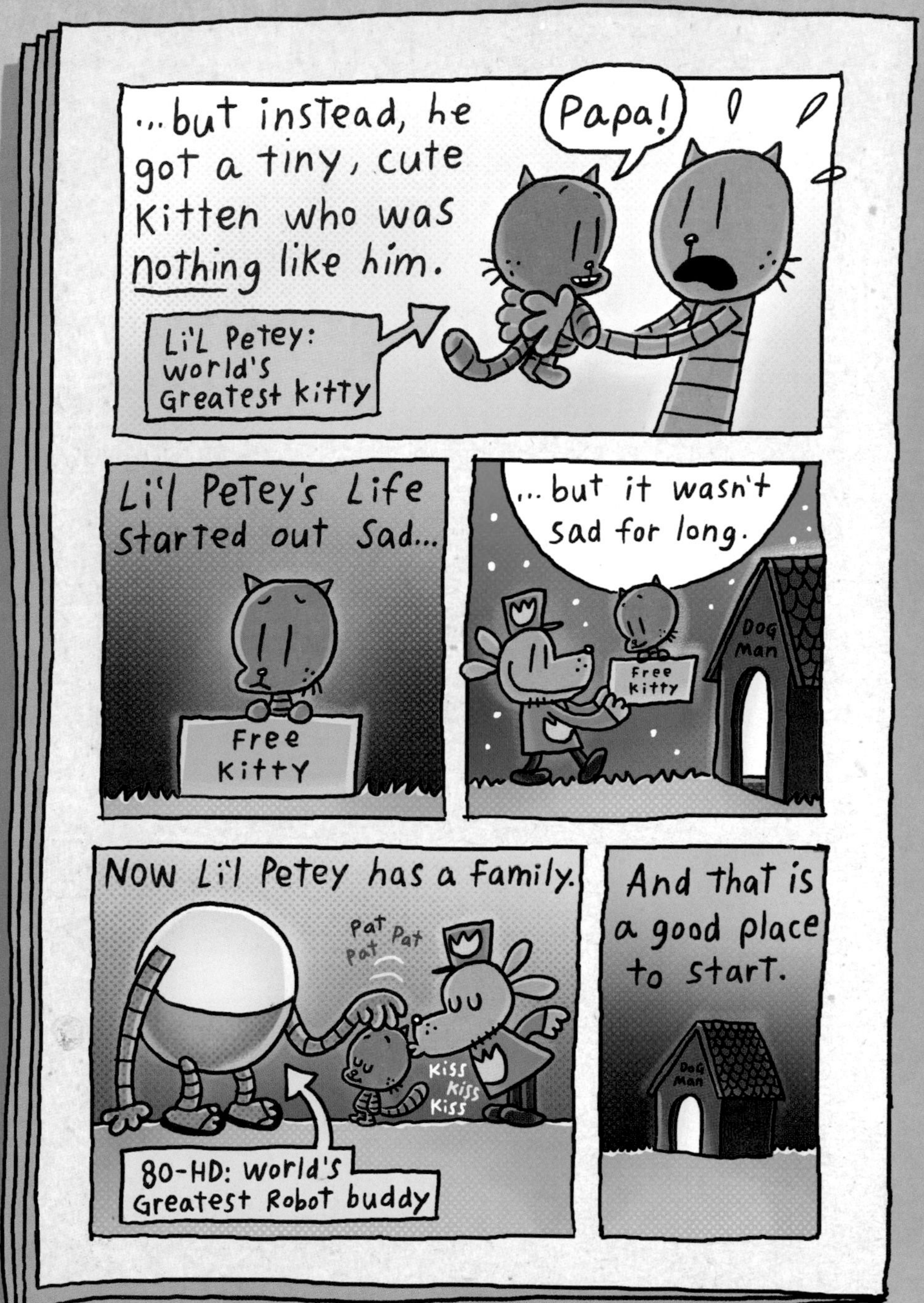
...but instead, he got a tiny, cute Kitten who was nothing like him.
Papa!
Li'L Petey: world's Greatest kitty
Li'l Petey's Life started out Sad...
Free Kitty
...but it wasn't sad for long.
DOG Man
Free Kitty
Now Li'l Petey has a family.
Pat Pat Pat
Kiss Kiss Kiss
80-HD: World's Greatest Robot buddy
And that is a good place to start.
DOG Man

Tree-
House
coMix
Proudly
Presents

CHapter 1

A visit from
Kitty
Protective
Services

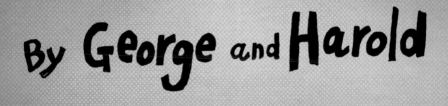

DOG
Man

By George and Harold

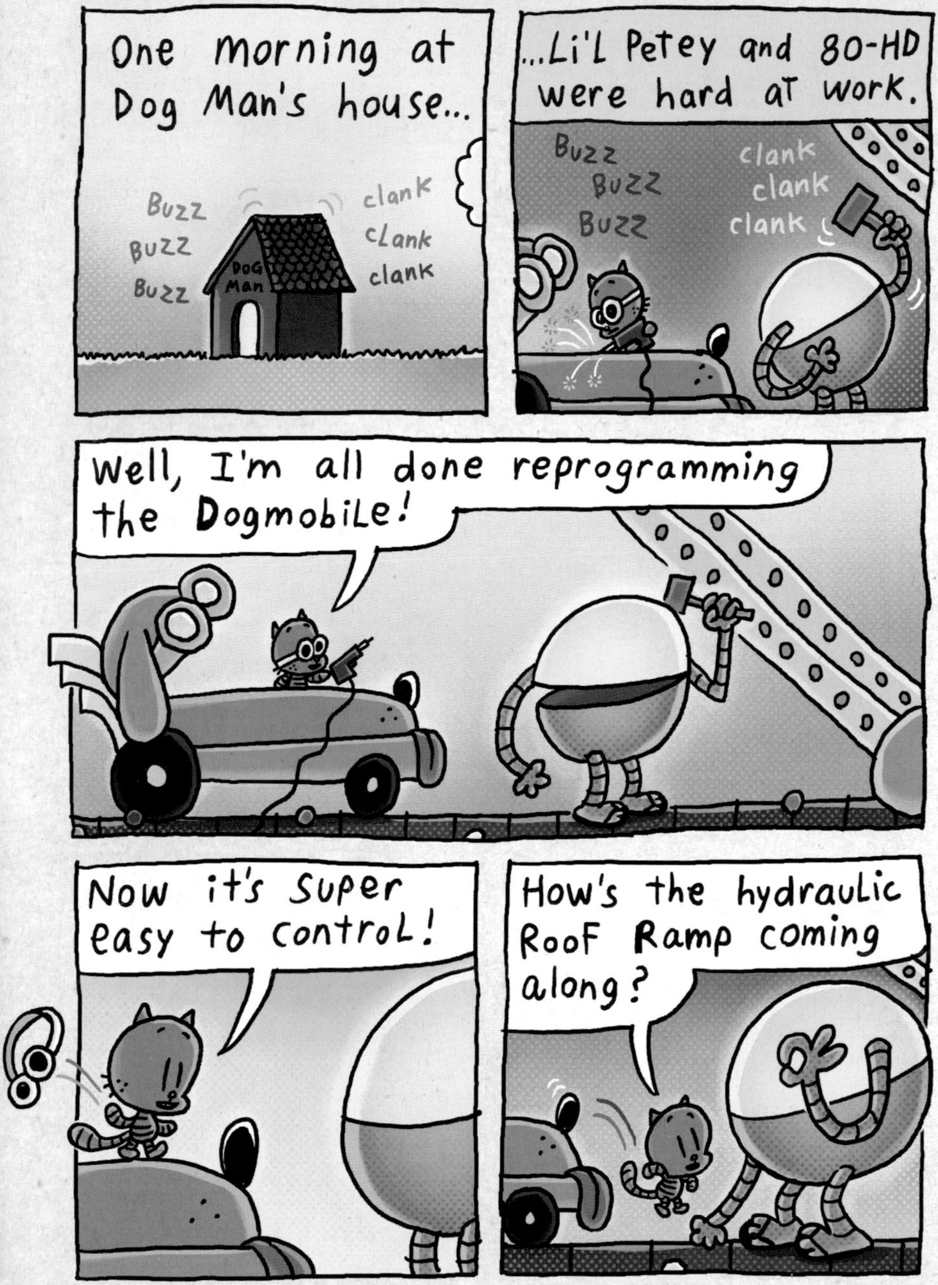
One morning at Dog Man's house...
Buzz
Buzz
Buzz
DOG MAN
clank
clank
clank
...Li'L Petey and 80-HD were hard at work.
Buzz
Buzz
Buzz
clank
clank
clank
Well, I'm all done reprogramming the Dogmobile!
Now it's super easy to control!
How's the hydraulic Roof Ramp coming along?

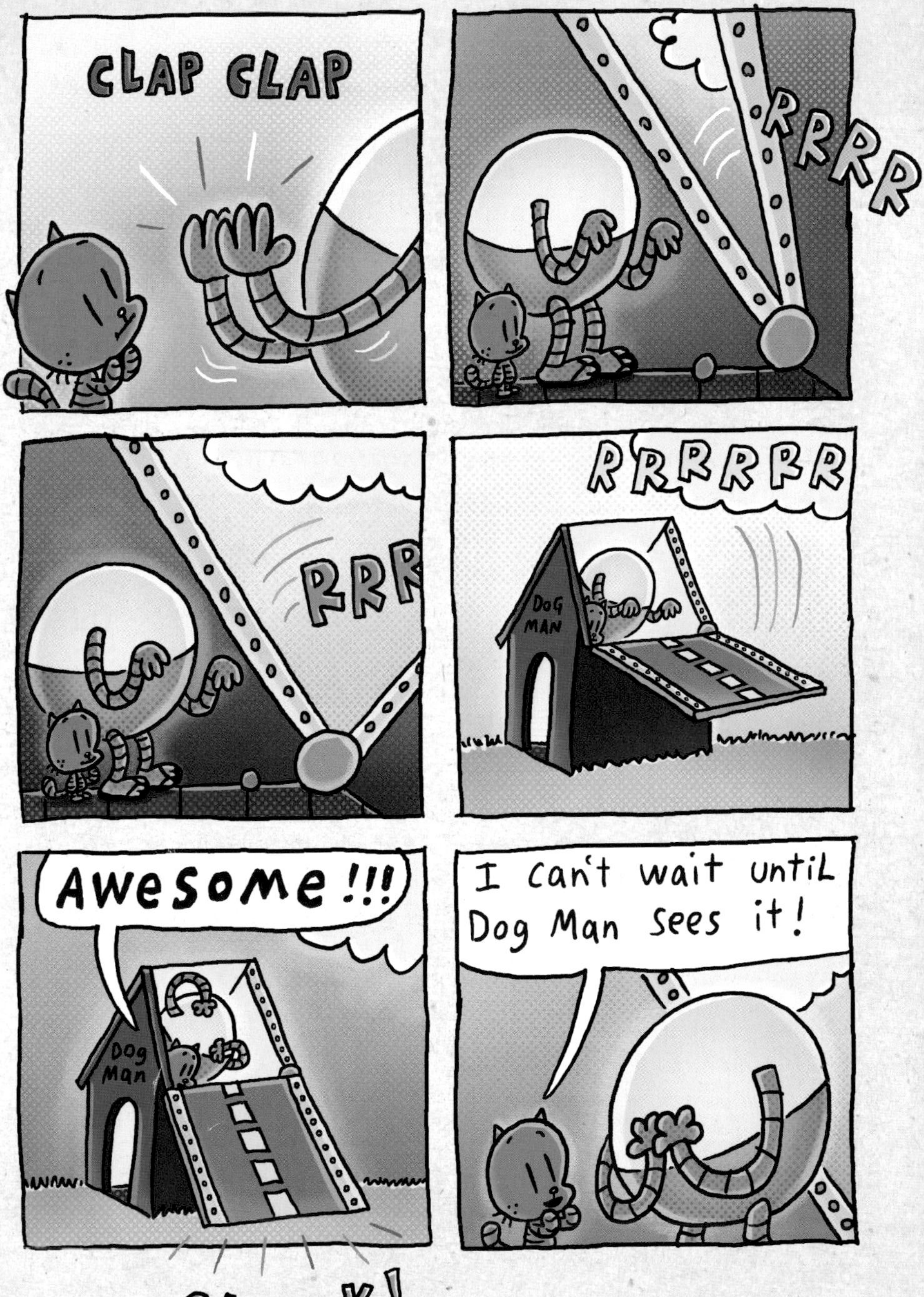
CLAP CLAP
RRRRR
RRR
RRRRRR
AWESOME!!!
CLUNK!
I can't wait until Dog Man sees it!

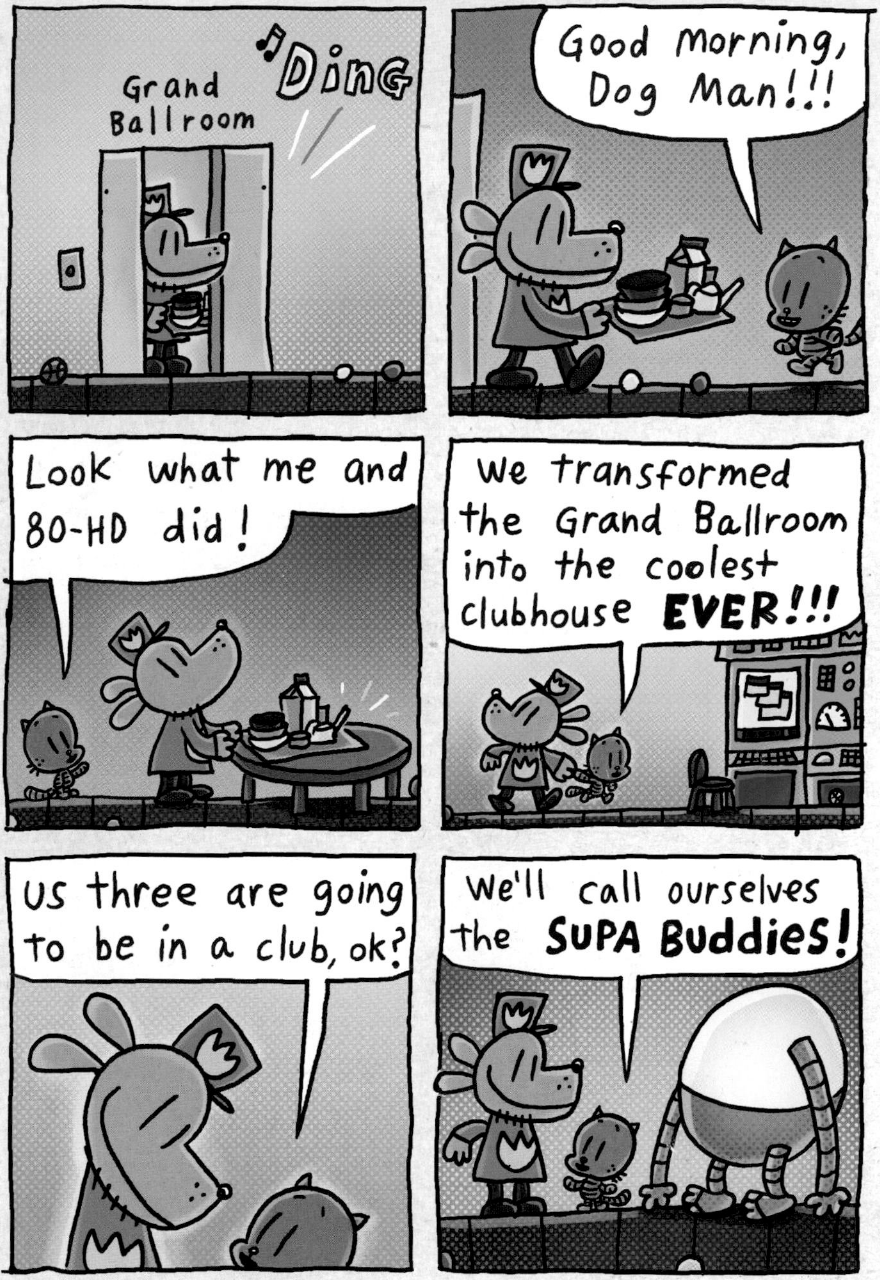
Grand Ballroom
DING
Good Morning, Dog Man!!!
Look what me and 80-HD did!
We transformed the Grand Ballroom into the coolest clubhouse EVER!!!
Us three are going to be in a club, ok?
We'll call ourselves the SUPA BUDDIES!

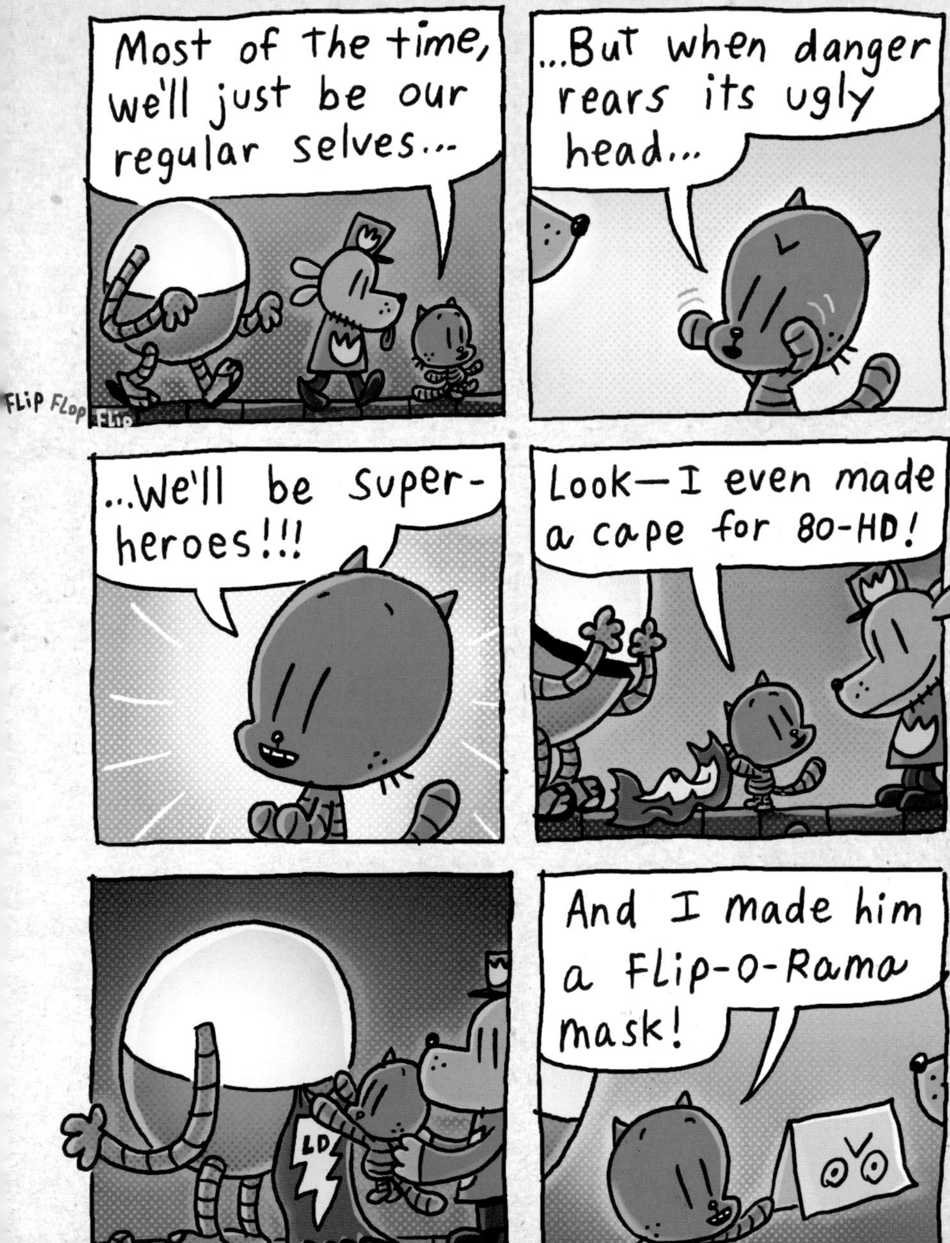
Most of the time, we'll just be our regular selves...
FLIP FLOP
FLIP
...But when danger rears its ugly head...
...We'll be super-heroes!!!
Look—I even made a cape for 80-HD!
LD
And I made him a Flip-O-Rama mask!

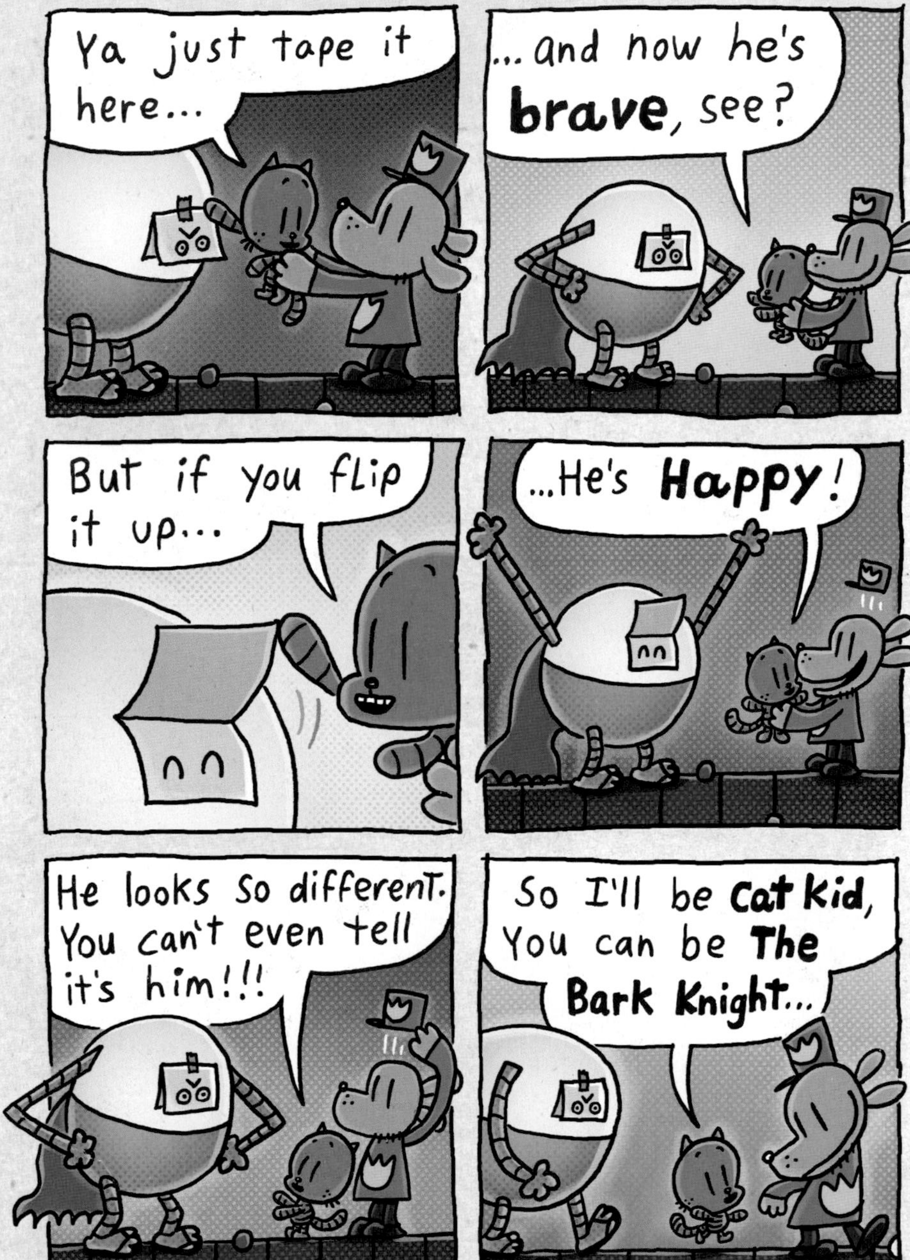
Ya just tape it here...
...and now he's brave, see?
But if you flip it up...
...He's Happy!
He looks so different. You can't even tell it's him!!!
So I'll be Cat Kid, You can be The Bark Knight...
FLIP FLOP FLIP

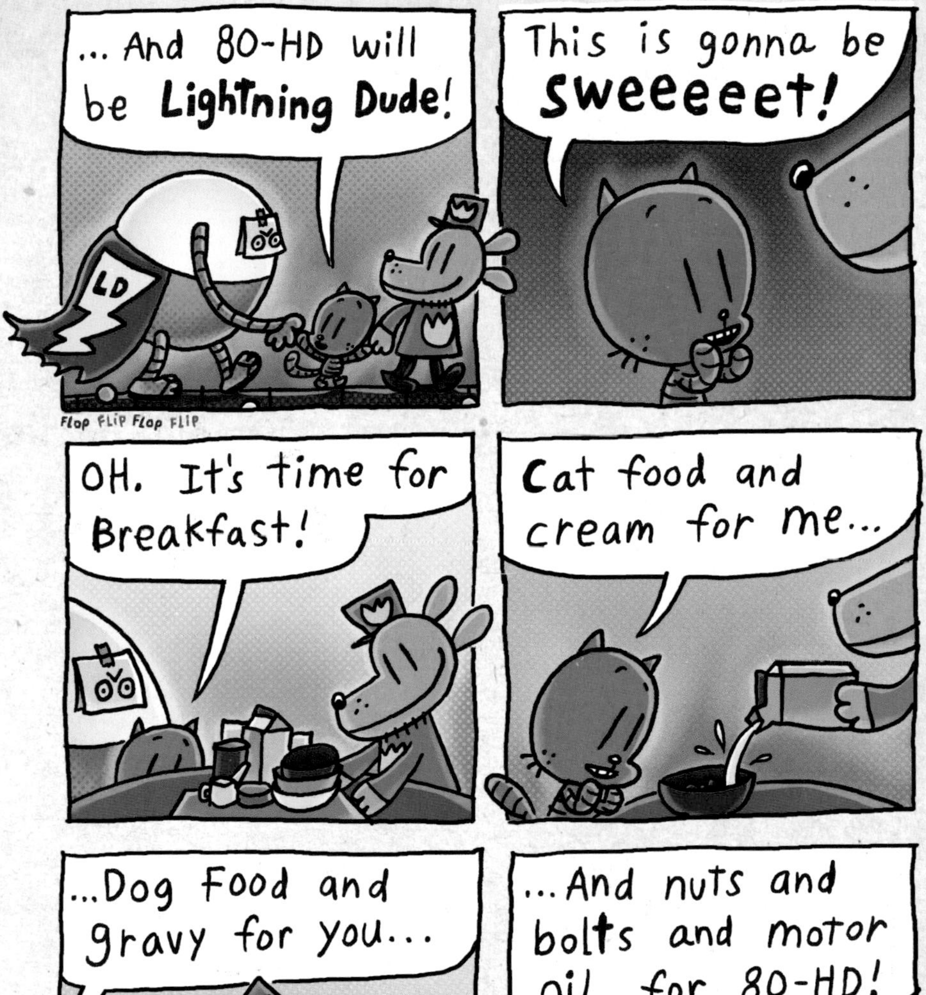

...And 80-HD will be Lightning Dude!
FLOP FLIP FLOP FLIP
This is gonna be SWEEEEET!
OH. It's time for Breakfast!
Cat food and cream for me...
...Dog Food and gravy for you...
...And nuts and bolts and motor oil for 80-HD!
Grape nuts + Bolts
OIL

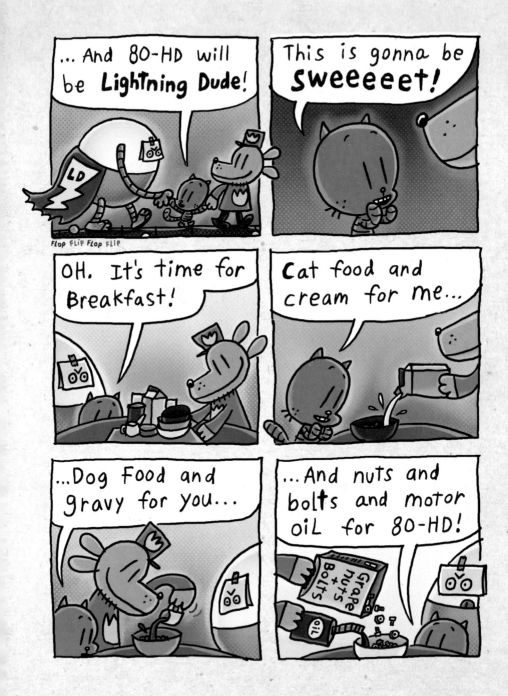

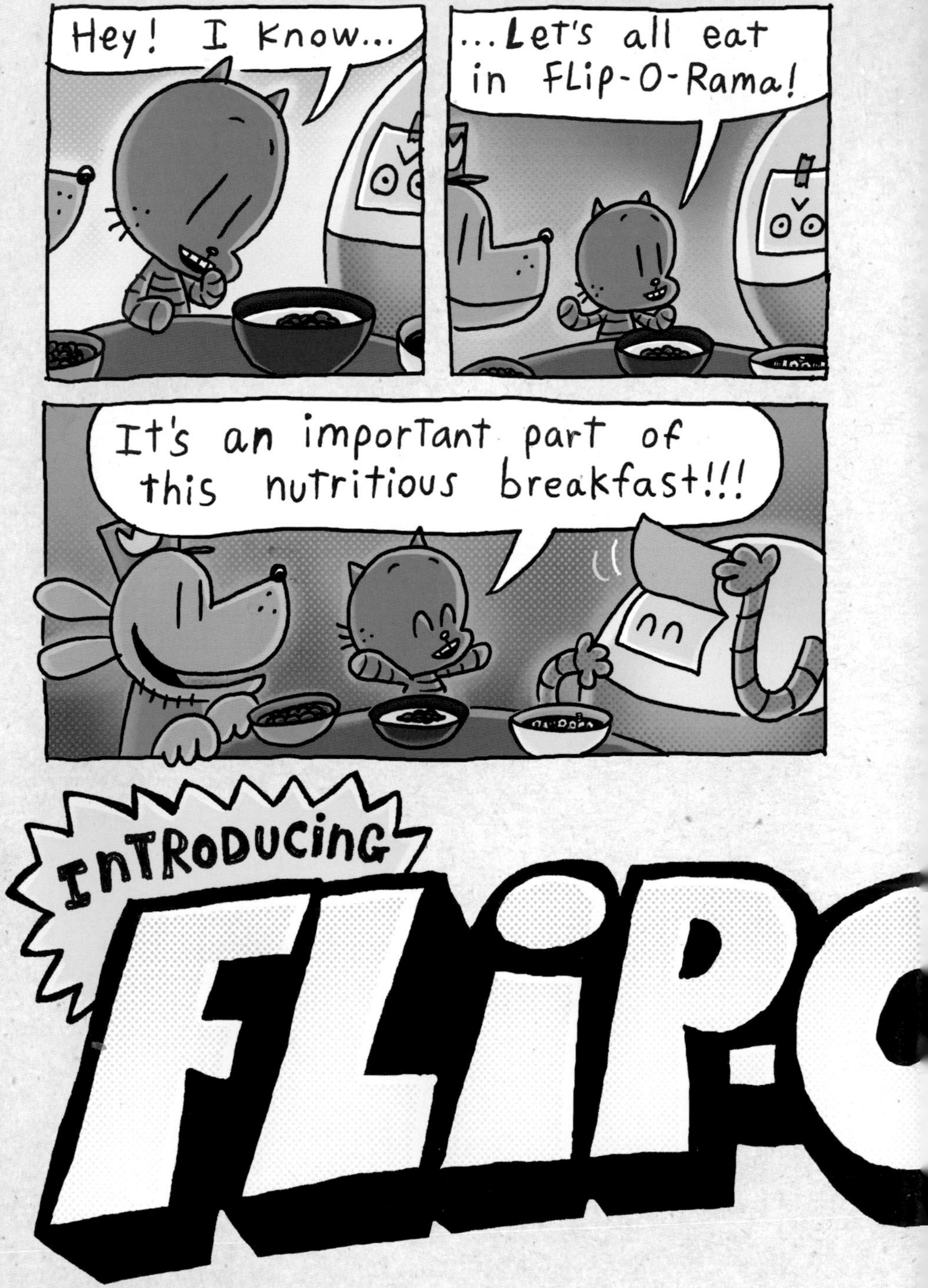
Hey! I know...
...Let's all eat in FLIP-O-Rama!
It's an important part of this nutritious breakfast!!!
INTRODUCING
FLIP

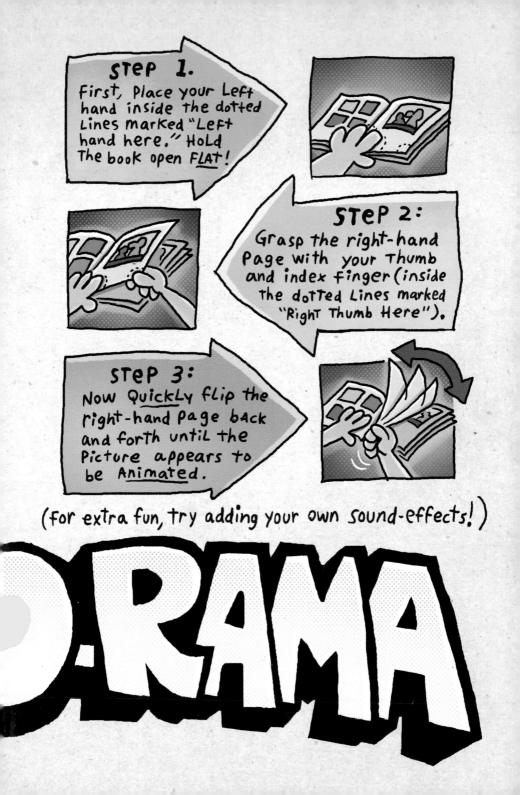

STEP 1.

First, Place your Left hand inside the dotted Lines marked "Left hand here." HoLd The book open FLAT!

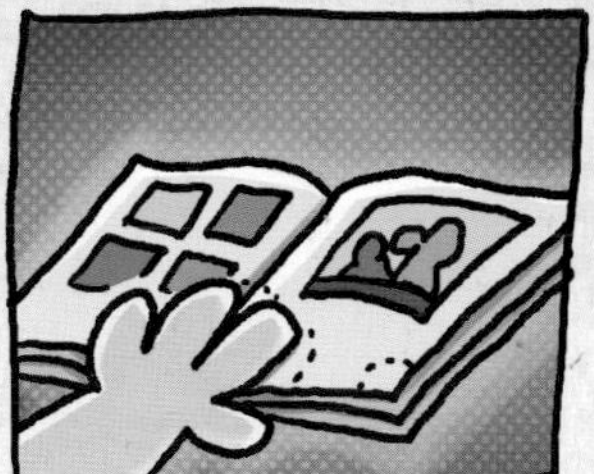

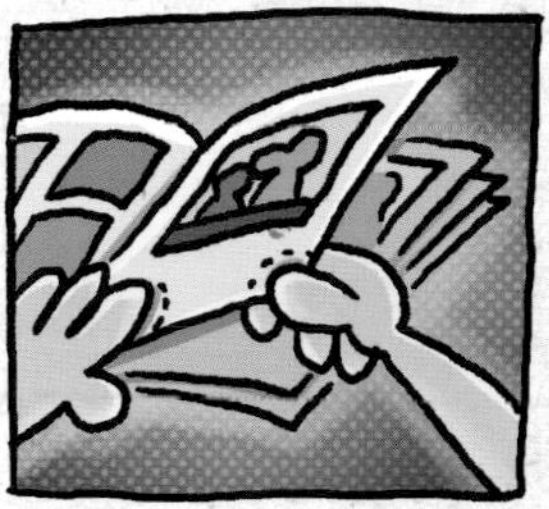

STEP 2:

Grasp the right-hand Page with your Thumb and index finger (inside the dotted Lines marked "Right Thumb Here").

STEP 3:

Now QuickLy fLip the right-hand Page back and forth until the Picture appears to be Animated.

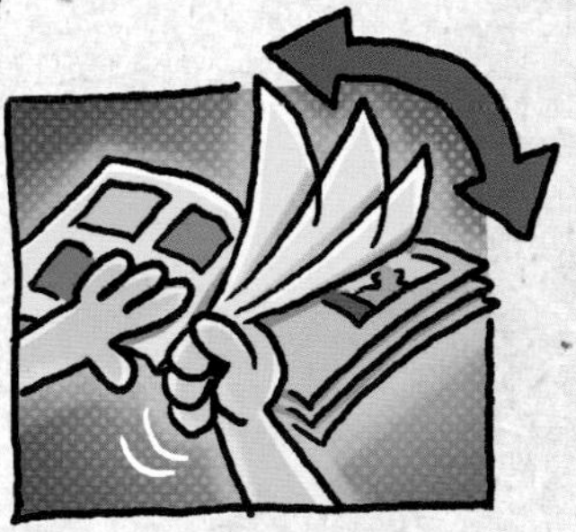

(For extra fun, try adding your own sound-effects!)

RAMA

Remember,

while you are flipping,
be sure you can see
the image on page 23
AND the image on page 25.

If you flip quickly,
the two pictures will
start to look like
one **ANimated** cartoon!

Don't forget to
add your own
sound-effects!

Left
hand here.

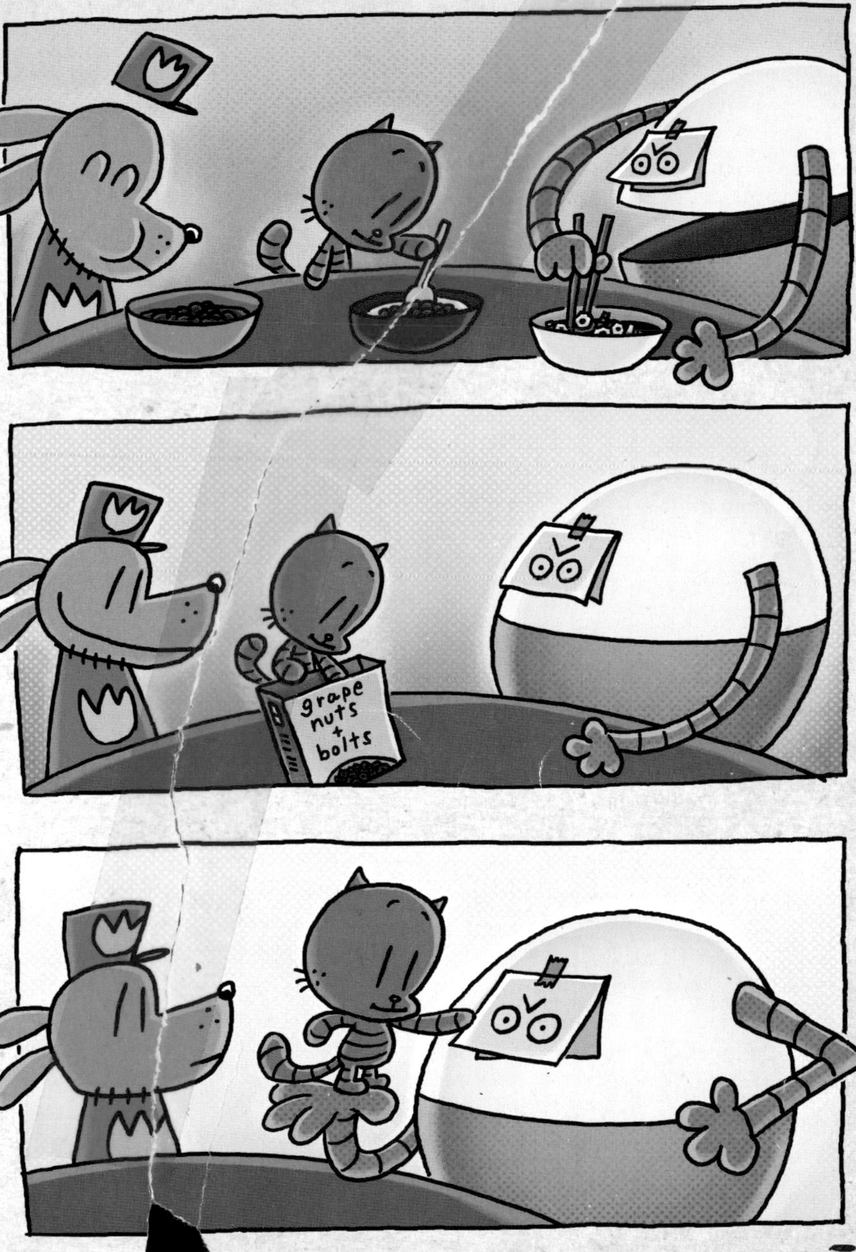
grape nuts + bolts

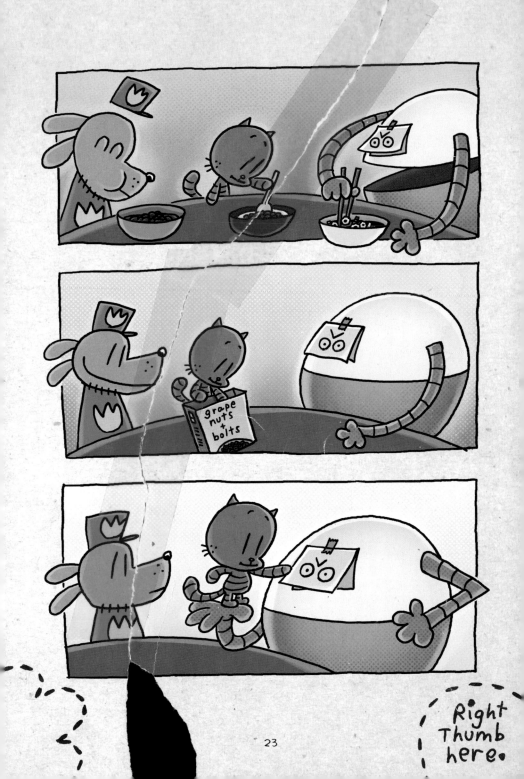

Right Thumb here.

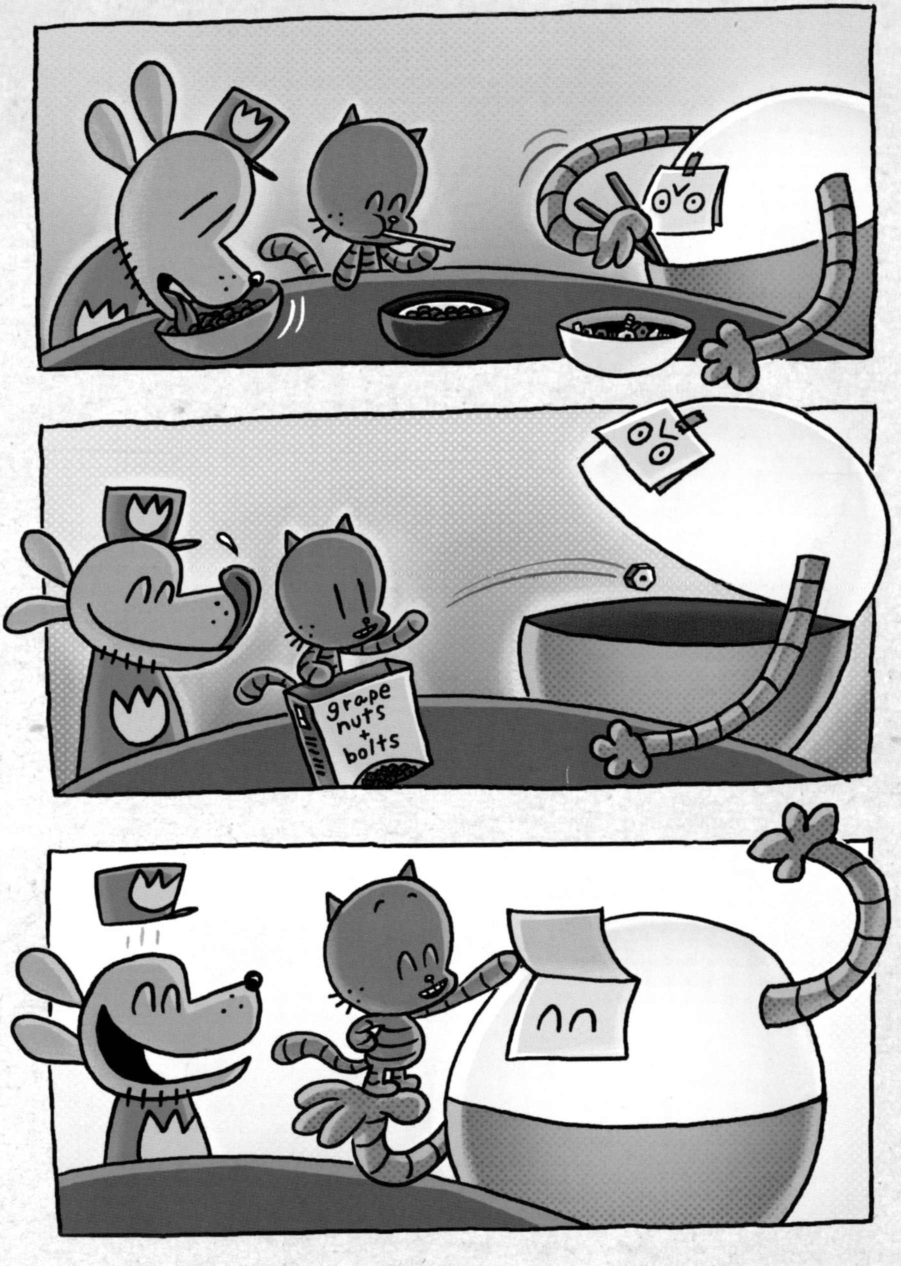
grape
nuts
+
bolts

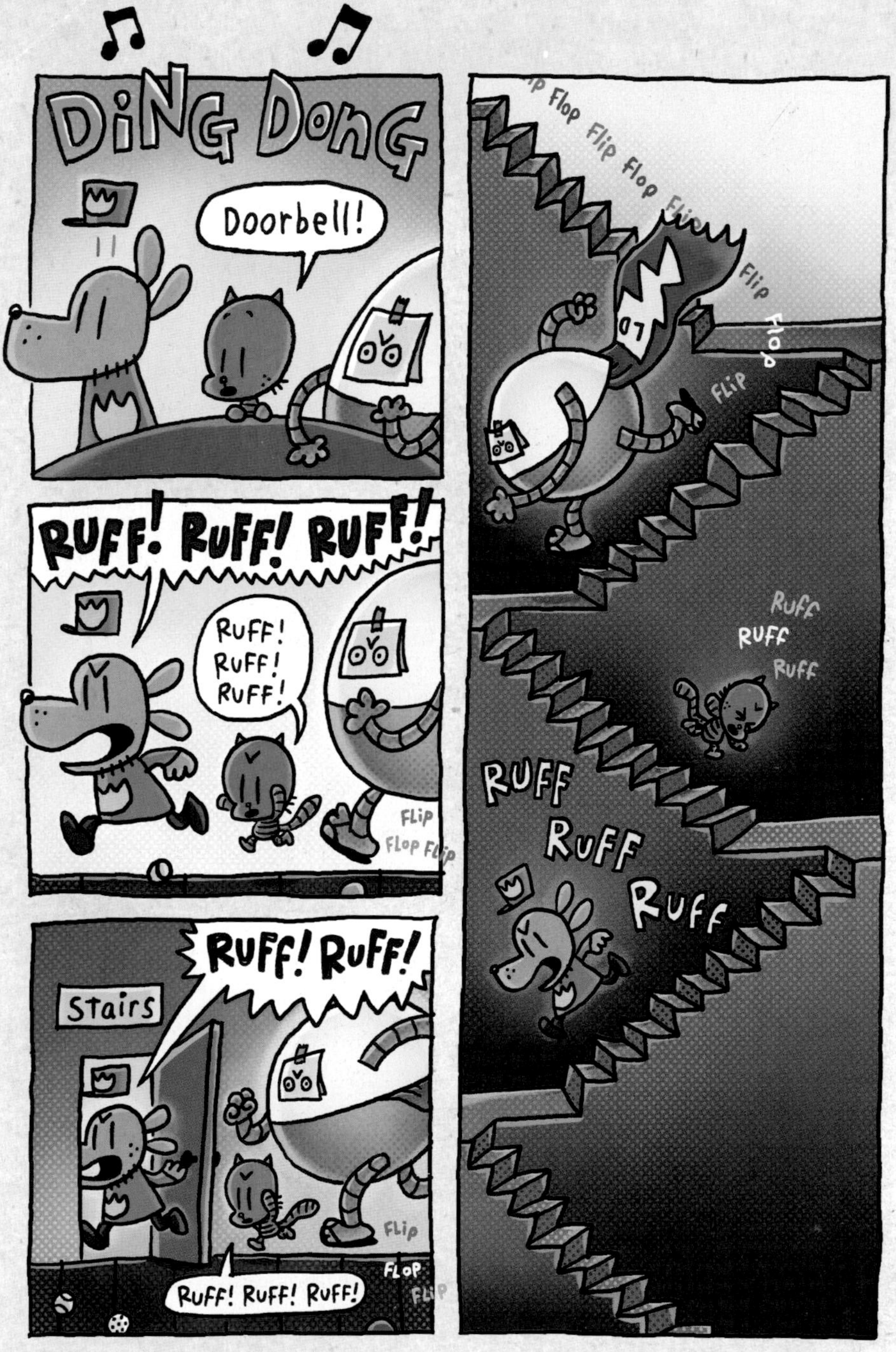

DiNG DONG
Doorbell!
RUFF! RUFF! RUFF!
RUFF! RUFF! RUFF!
FLIP FLOP FLIP
Stairs
RUFF! RUFF!
FLIP
RUFF! RUFF! RUFF!
FLOP
FLIP
Flop
Flip
Flop
Flip
Flop
FLIP
Ruff
Ruff
Ruff
RUFF
RUFF
RUFF

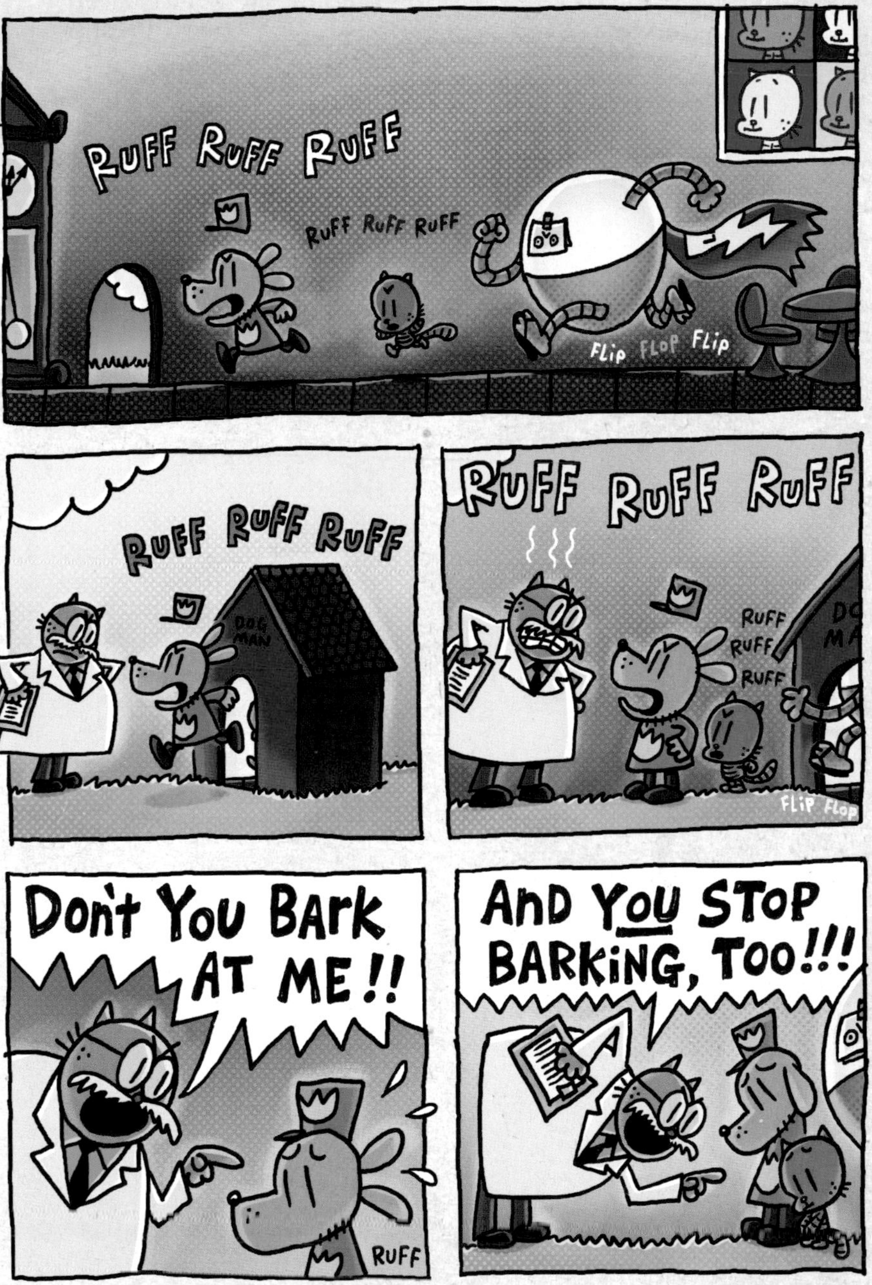

RUFF RUFF RUFF
RUFF RUFF RUFF
FLIP FLOP FLIP
RUFF RUFF RUFF
DOG MAN
RUFF RUFF RUFF
RUFF
RUFF
RUFF
FLIP FLOP
Don't You Bark AT ME!!
RUFF
AND YOU STOP BARKING, TOO!!!

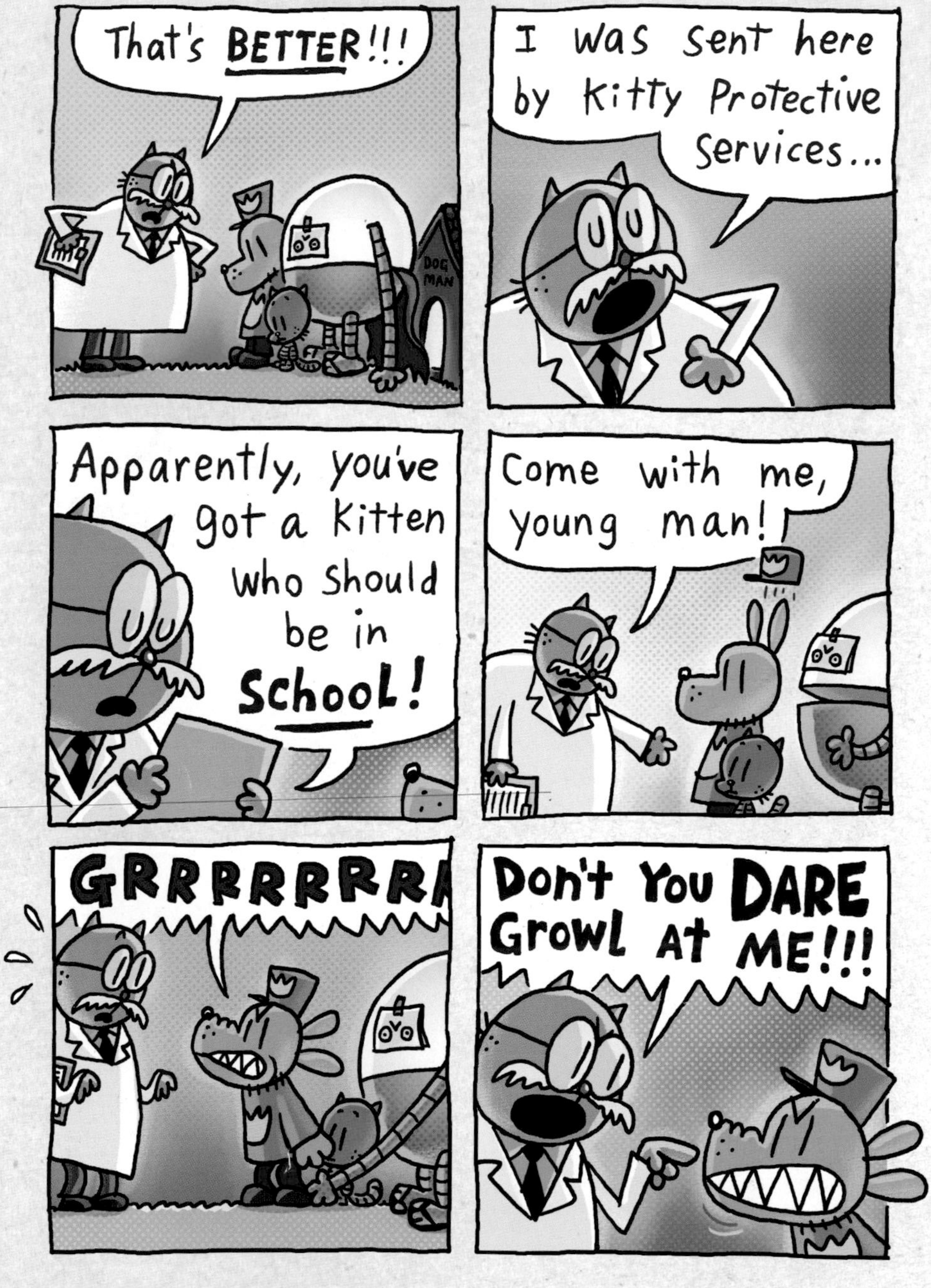
That's BETTER!!!
I was sent here by Kitty Protective Services...
Apparently, you've got a Kitten who should be in SCHOOL!
Come with me, young man!
GRRRRRRRR
Don't You DARE Growl At ME!!!

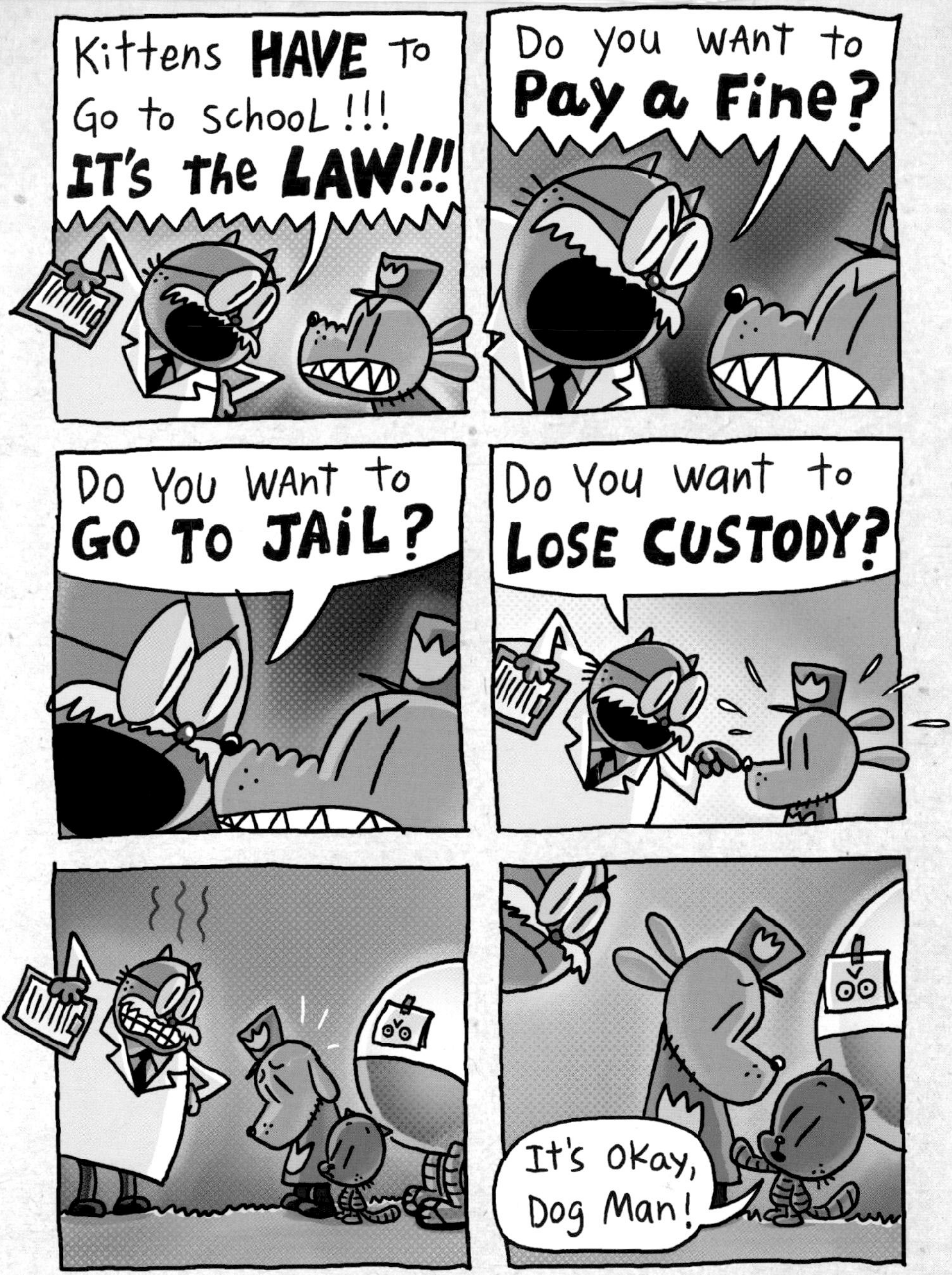
Kittens HAVE To Go to school!!! IT'S the LAW!!!
Do you WANT to Pay a Fine?
Do You WANT to GO TO JAiL?
Do You want to LOSE CUSTODY?
It's Okay, Dog Man!

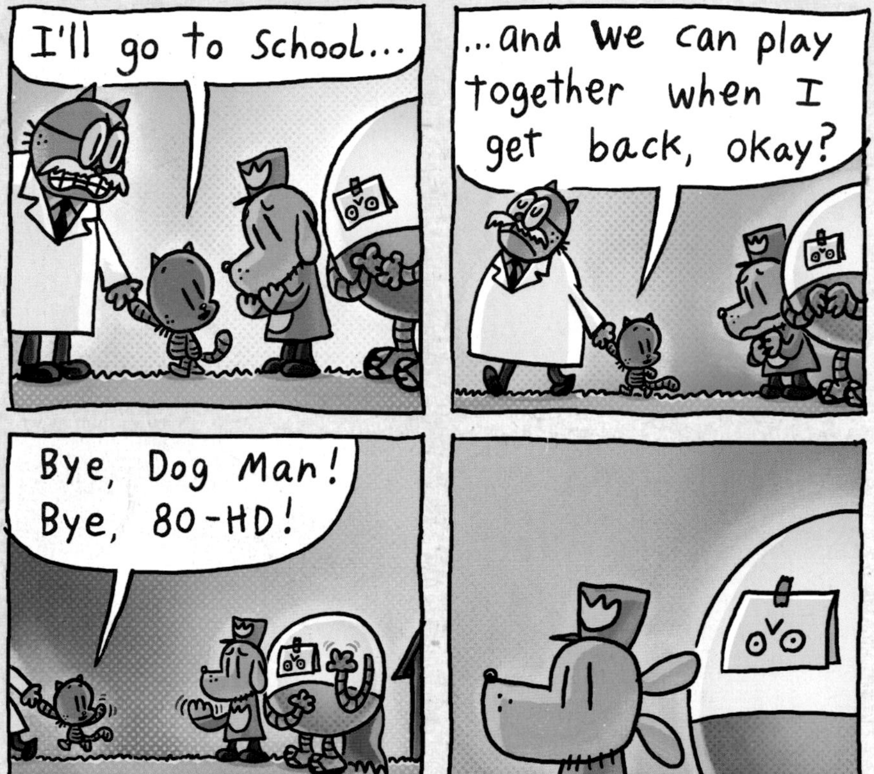
I'll go to School...
...and we can play together when I get back, okay?
Bye, Dog Man! Bye, 80-HD!

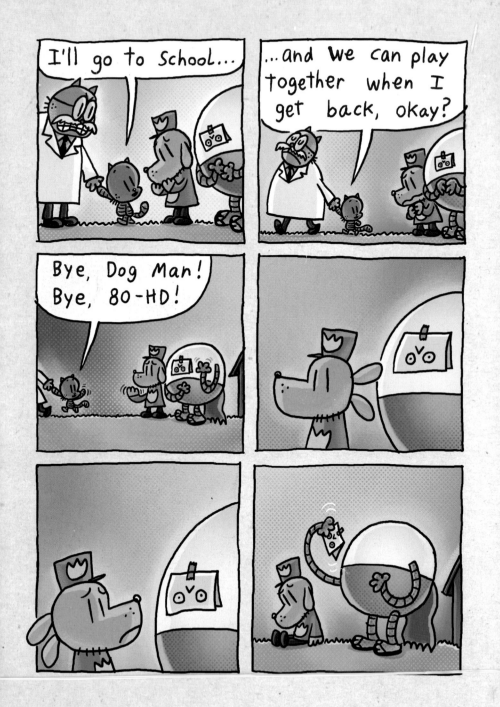

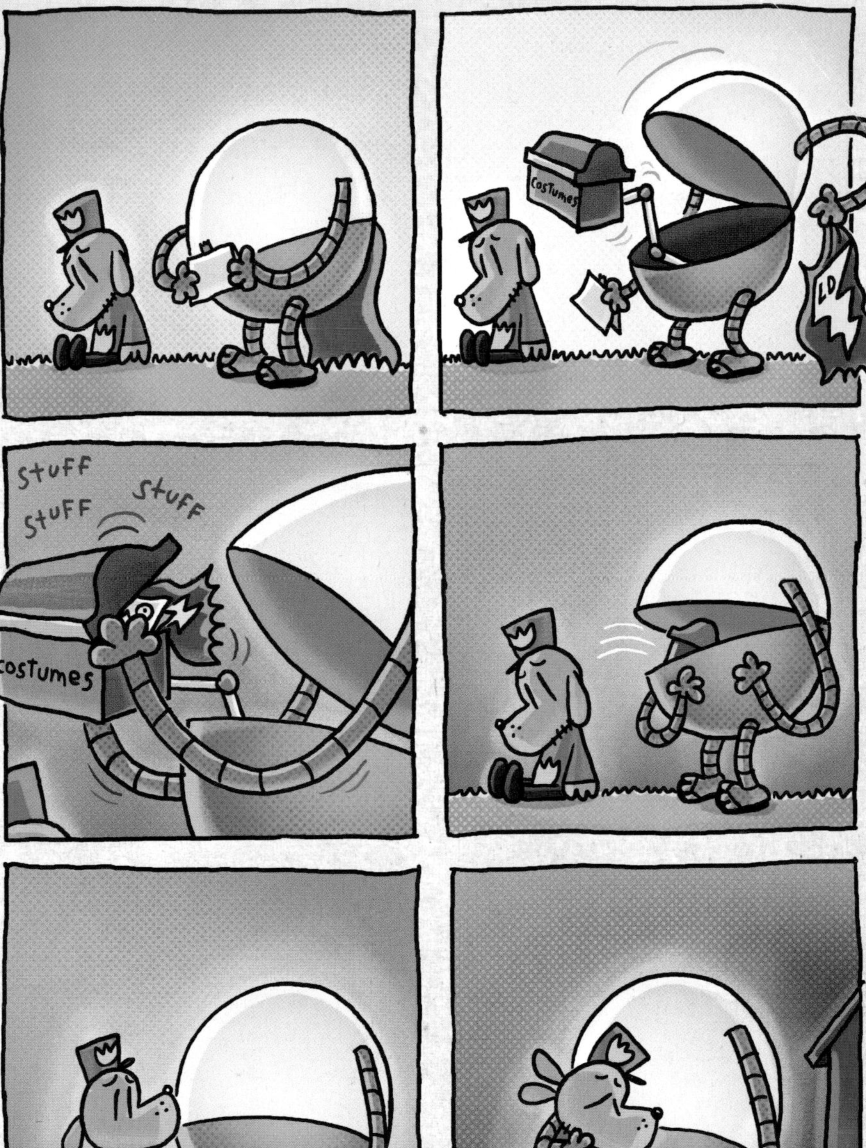
Costumes
LD
STUFF
STUFF
STUFF
costumes

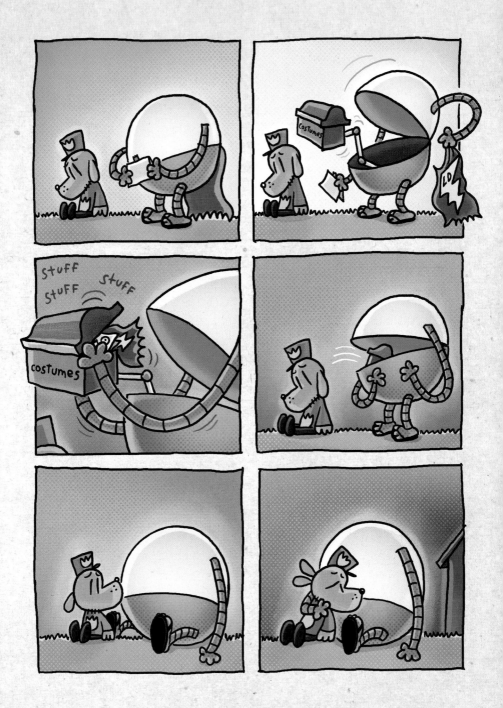

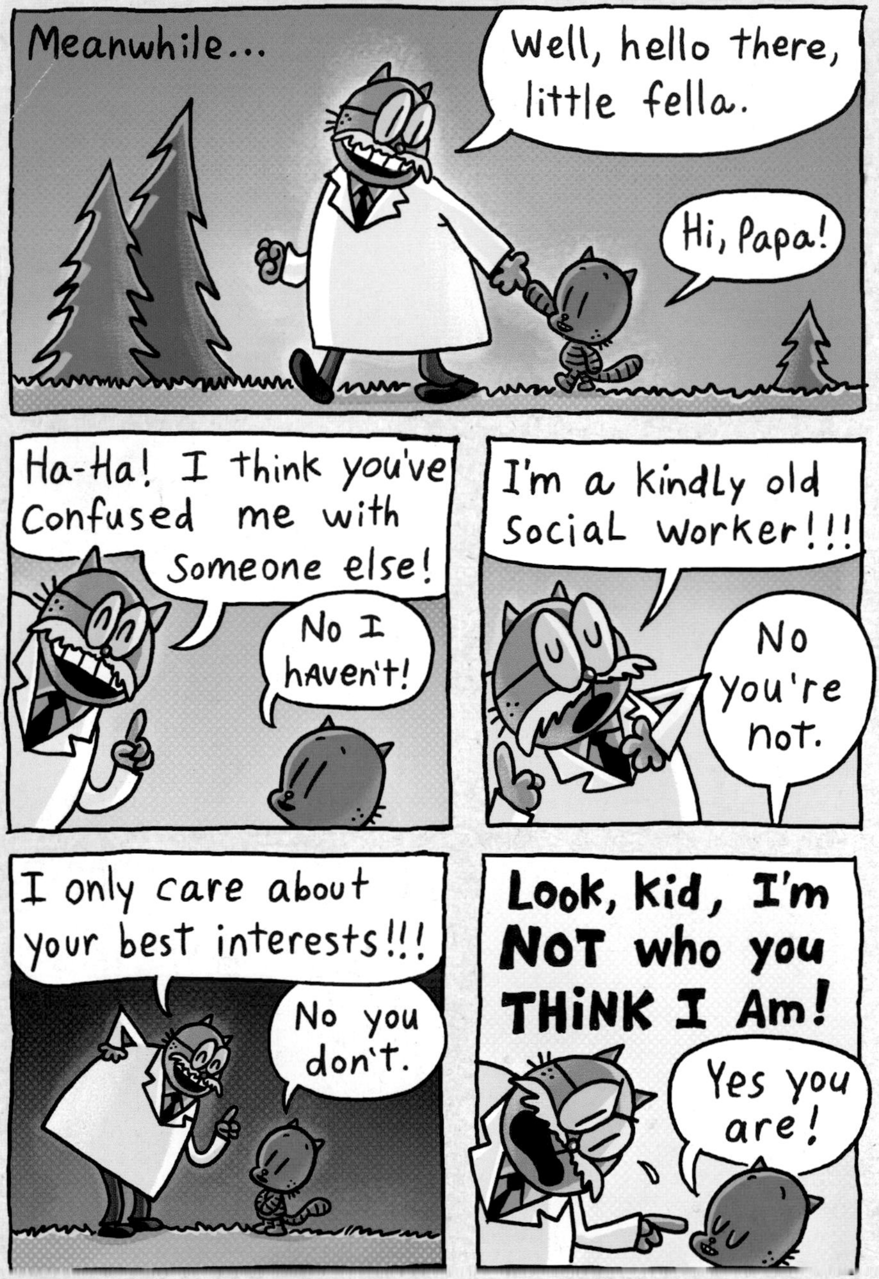
Meanwhile...
Well, hello there, little fella.
Hi, Papa!
Ha-Ha! I think you've Confused me with Someone else!
No I haven't!
I'm a Kindly old Social worker!!!
No you're not.
I only care about your best interests!!!
No you don't.
Look, kid, I'm NOT who you THINK I Am!
Yes you are!

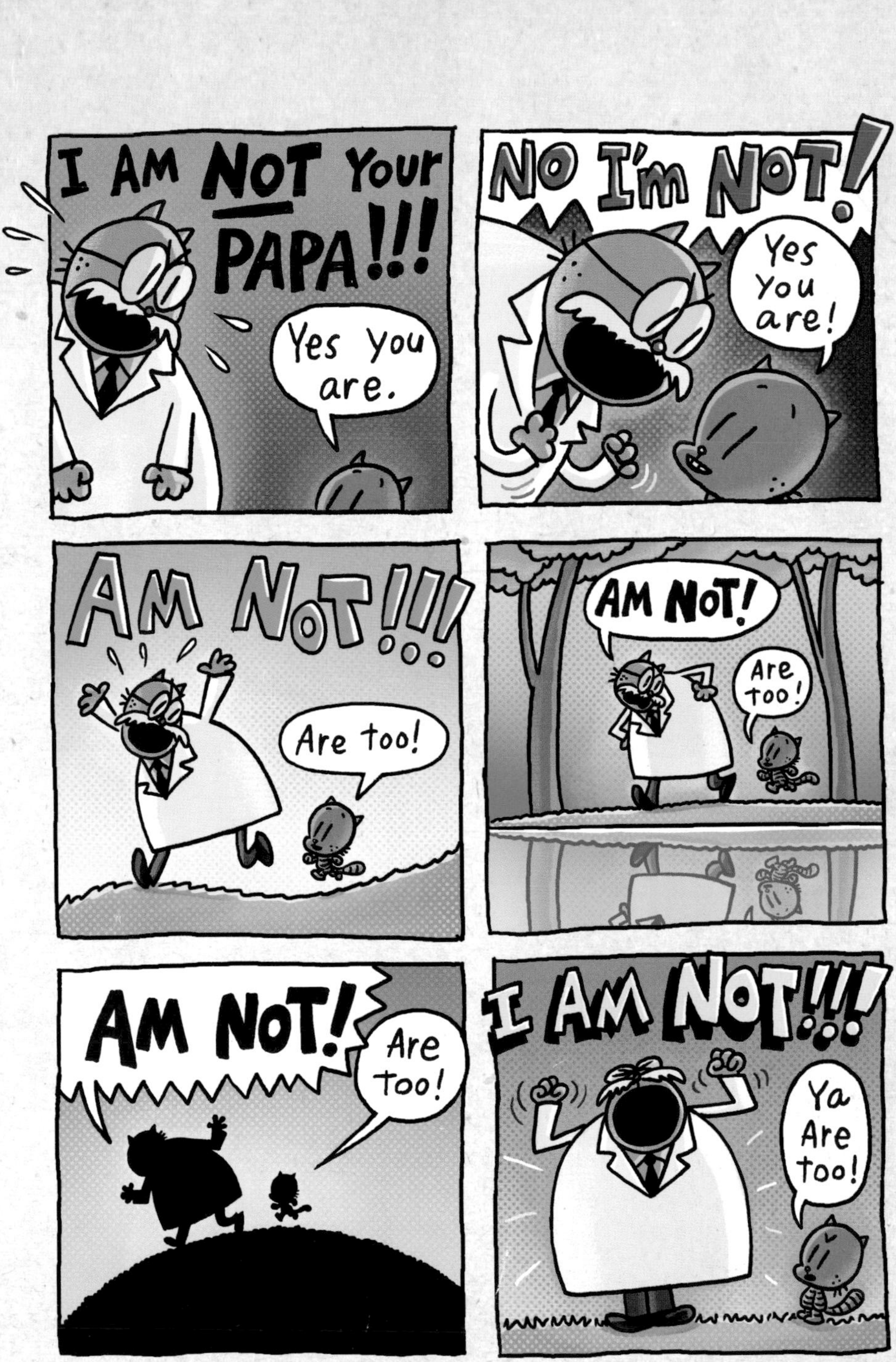
I AM NOT Your PAPA!!!
Yes you are.
NO I'm NOT!
Yes you are!
AM NOT!!!
Are too!
AM NOT!
Are too!
AM NOT!
Are too!
I AM NOT!!!
Ya Are too!

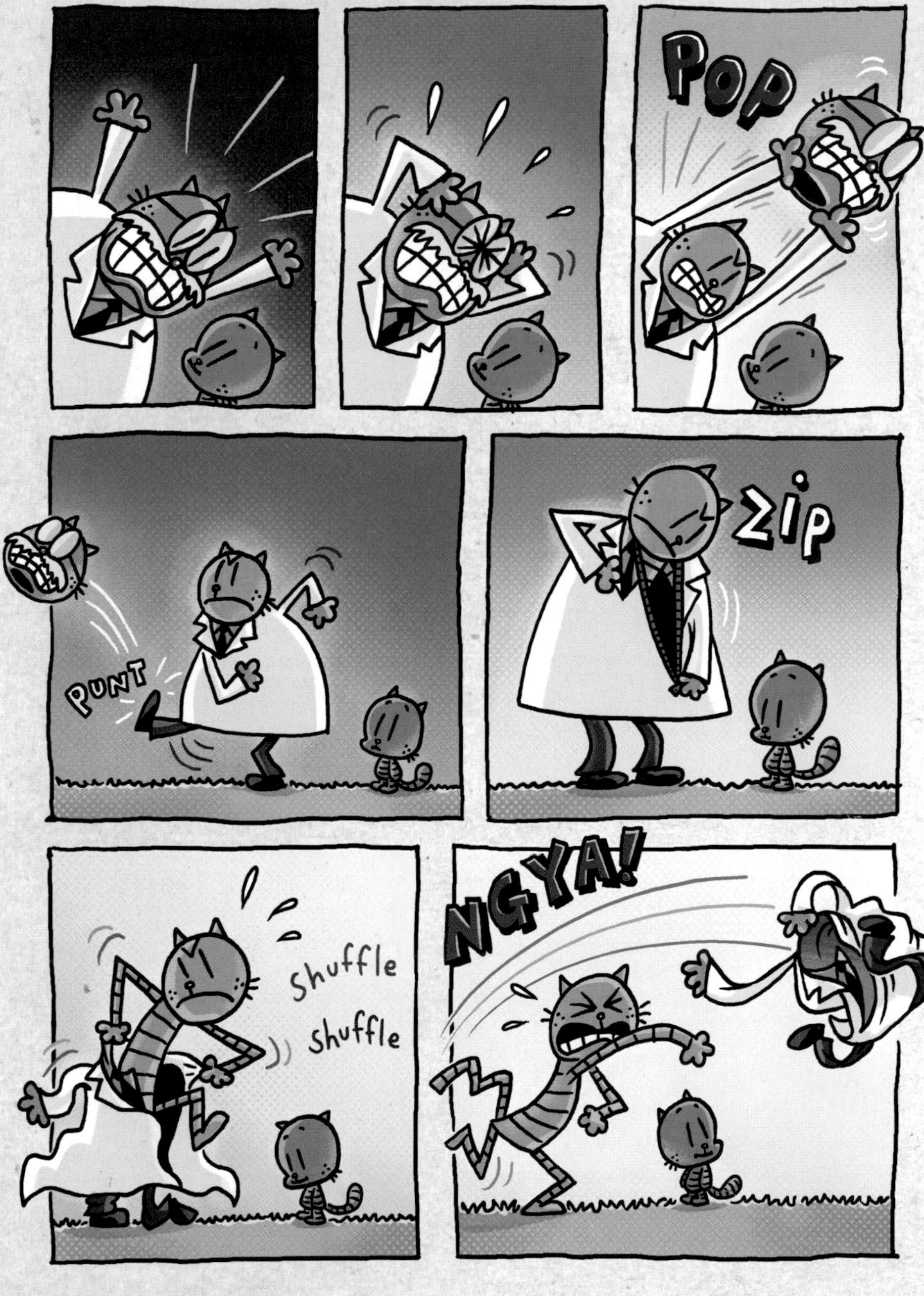
POP
PUNT
ZIP
Shuffle
shuffle
NGYA!

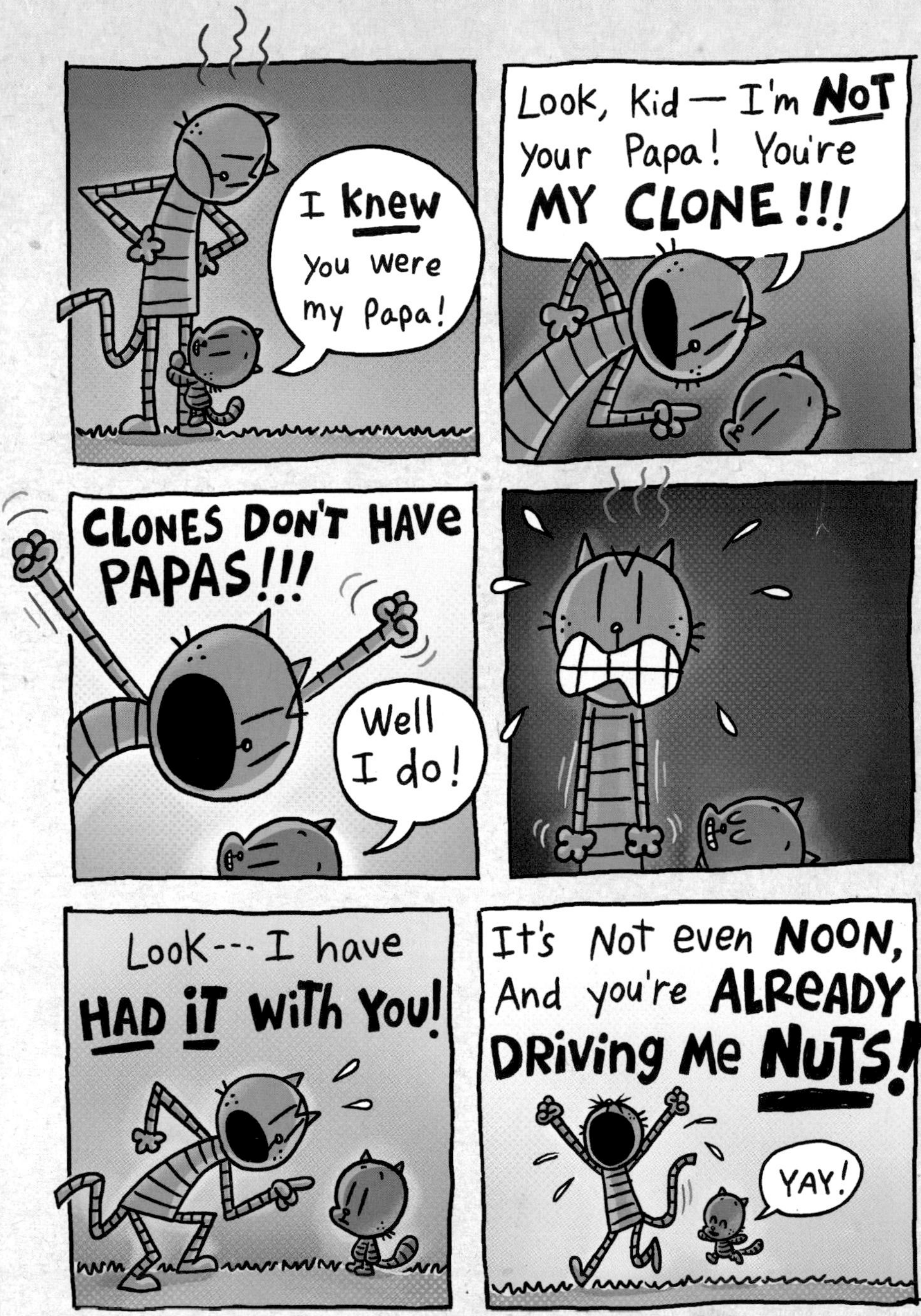
I knew you were my Papa!
Look, Kid — I'm NOT your Papa! You're MY CLONE!!!
CLONES DON'T HAVE PAPAS!!!
Well I do!
Look--- I have HAD iT WiTh YOU!
It's Not even NOON, And you're ALReADY DRiving Me NUTS!
YAY!

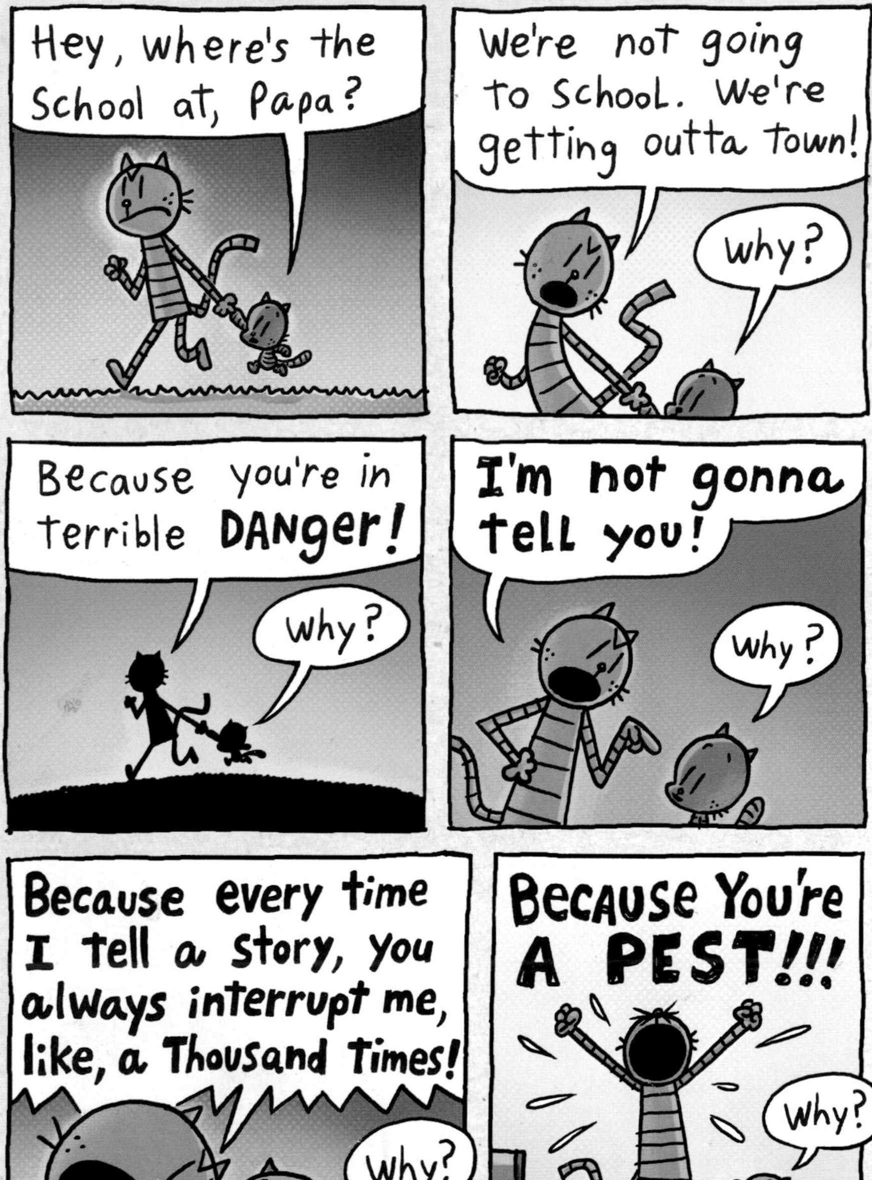
Hey, where's the School at, Papa?
We're not going to School. We're getting outta town!
Why?
Because you're in terrible DANGER!
Why?
I'm not gonna tell you!
Why?
Because every time I tell a Story, you always interrupt me, like, a Thousand Times!
Why?
BECAUSE You're A PEST!!!
Why?

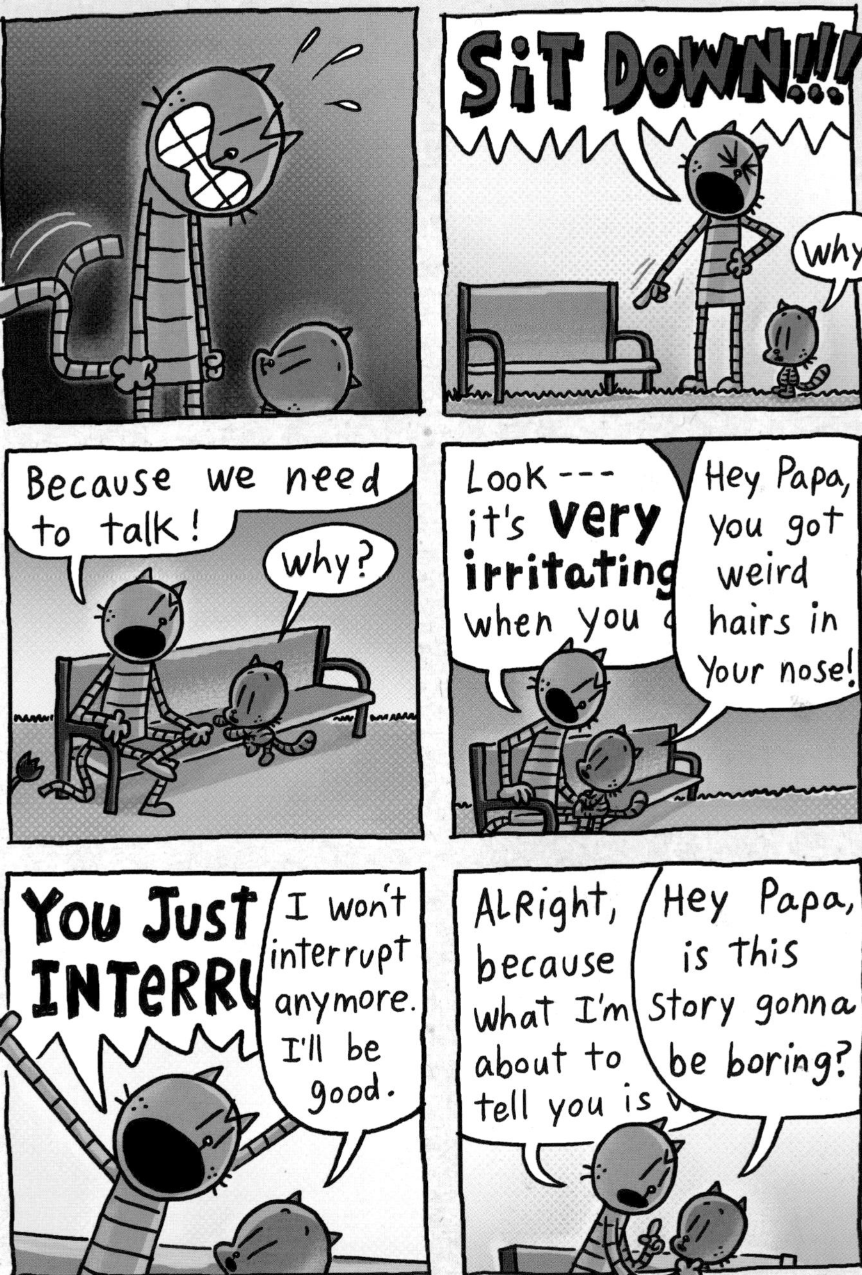
SiT DOWN!!!
why?
Because we need to talk!
why?
Look --- it's **very** **irritating** when you
Hey Papa, you got weird hairs in your nose!
YOU JUST INTERRU
I won't interrupt anymore. I'll be good.
ALRight, because what I'm about to tell you is
Hey Papa, is this story gonna be boring?

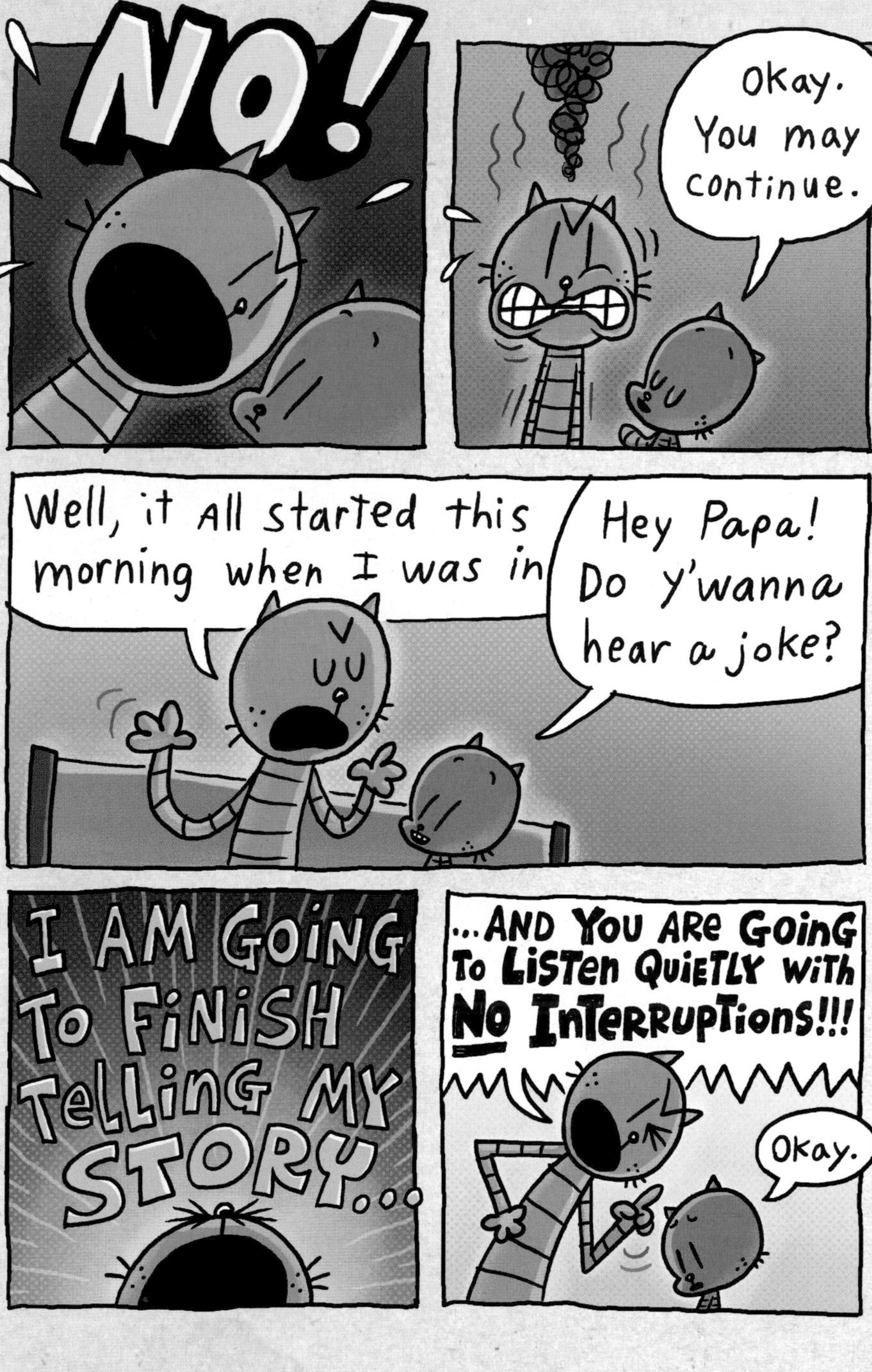
NO!
Okay. You may continue.
Well, it All started this morning when I was in
Hey Papa! Do y'wanna hear a joke?
I AM GOING TO FINISH TELLING MY STORY...
...AND YOU ARE GOING TO LISTEN QUIETLY WITH NO INTERRUPTIONS!!!
Okay.

CHAPTER 2

Petey's Story

(With Many Interruptions)

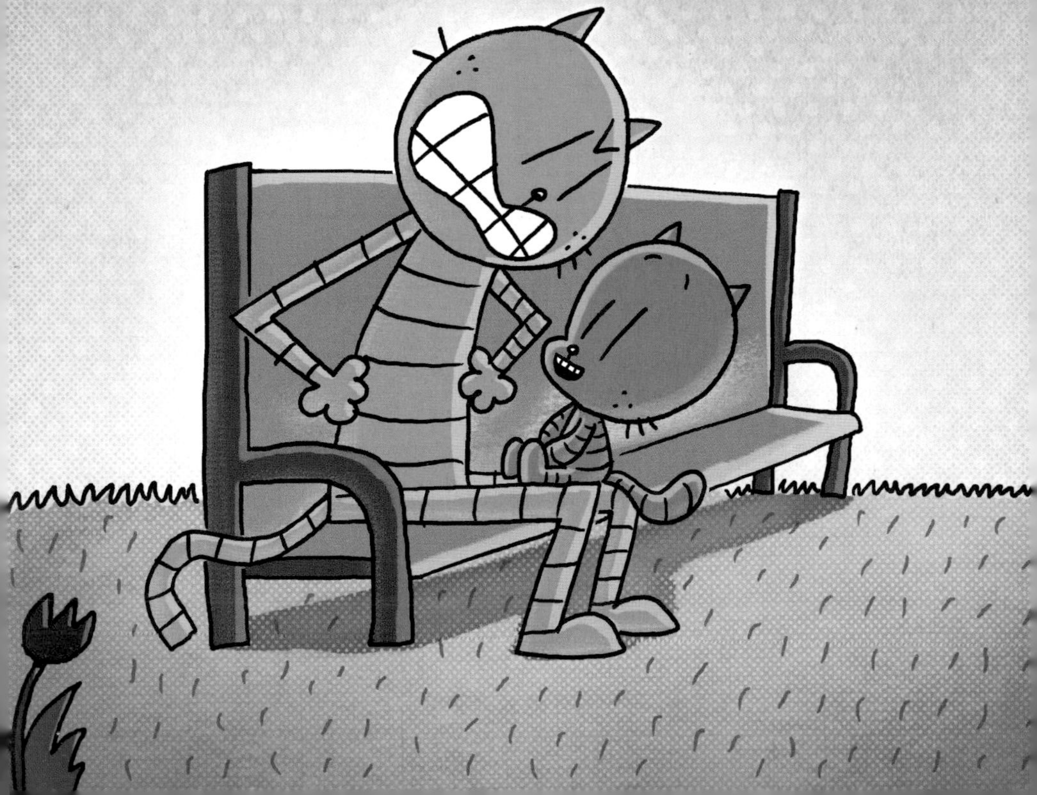

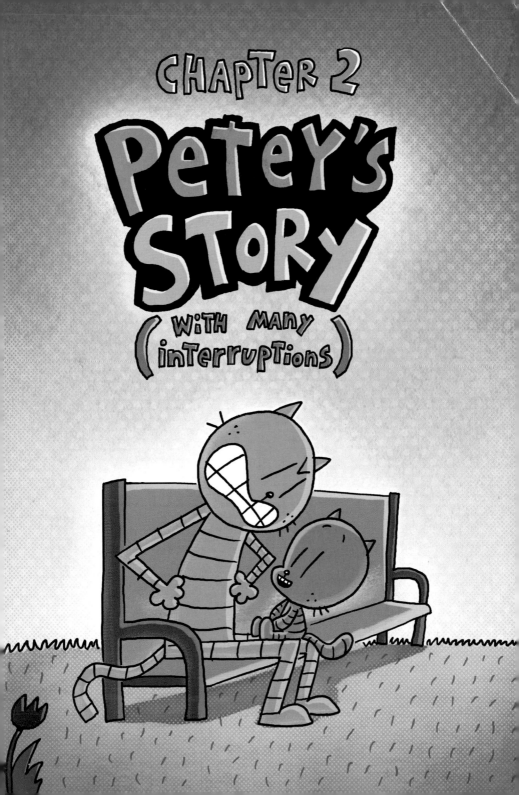

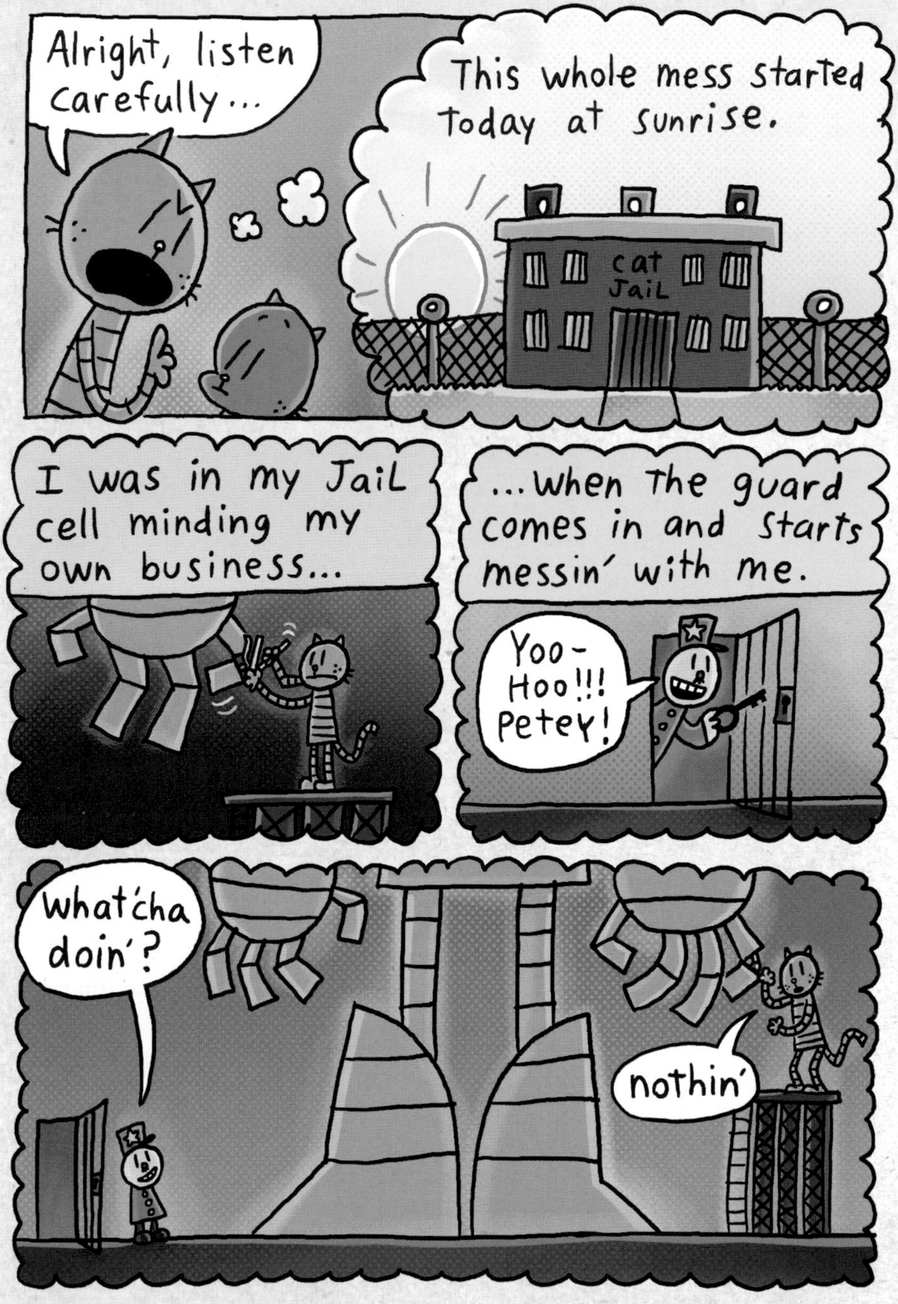
Alright, listen carefully...
This whole mess started Today at sunrise.
cat JaiL
I was in my JaiL cell minding my own business...
...when the guard comes in and starts messin' with me.
Yoo-Hoo!!! Petey!
What'cha doin'?
nothin'

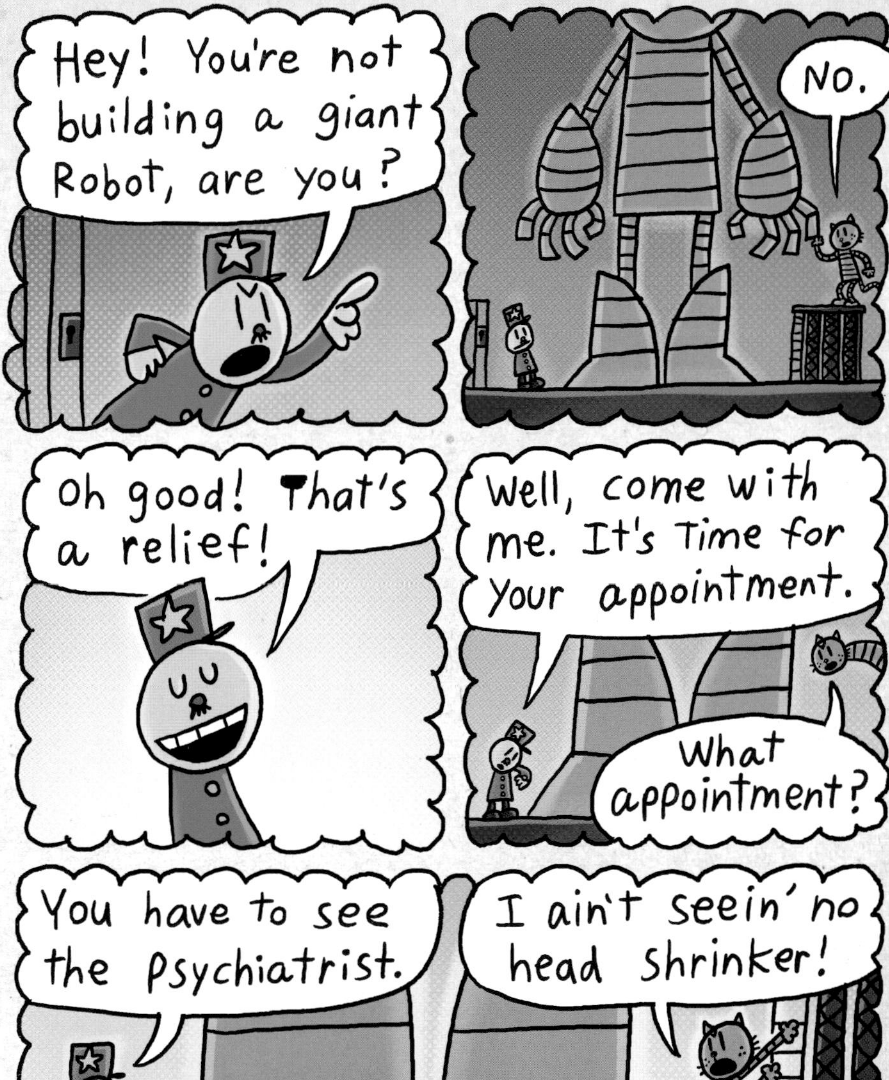
Hey! You're not building a giant Robot, are you?
No.
Oh good! That's a relief!
Well, come with me. It's time for your appointment.
What appointment?
You have to see the Psychiatrist.
I ain't seein' no head shrinker!

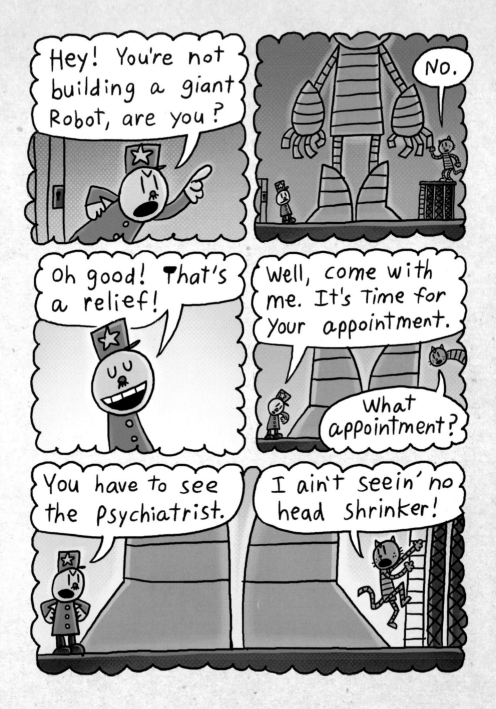

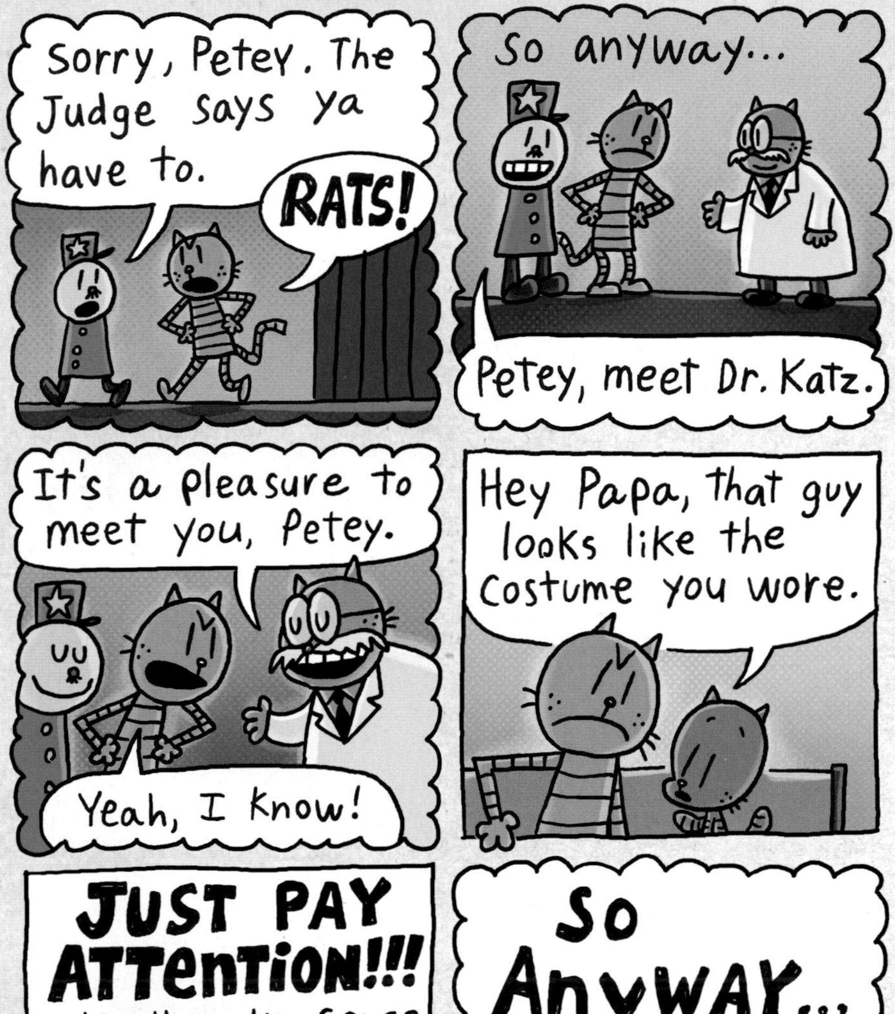
Sorry, Petey. The Judge says ya have to.
RATS!
So anyway...
Petey, meet Dr. Katz.
It's a pleasure to meet you, Petey.
Yeah, I know!
Hey Papa, that guy looks like the costume you wore.
JUST PAY ATTENTION!!! It'll all make sense soon!
OK.
So Anyway...
Dr. Katz

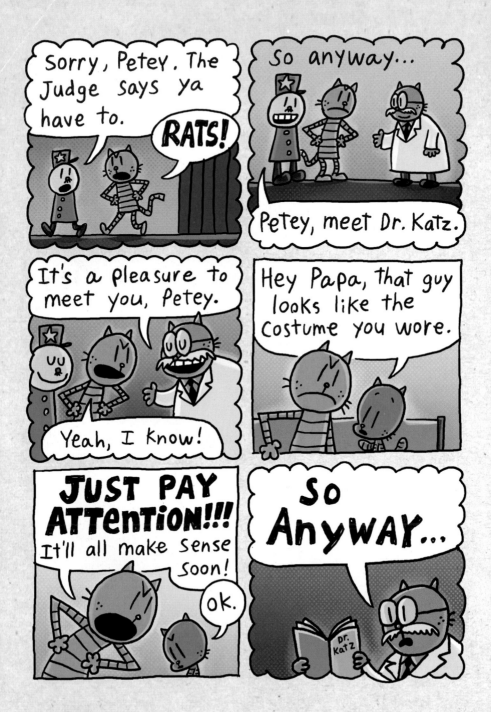

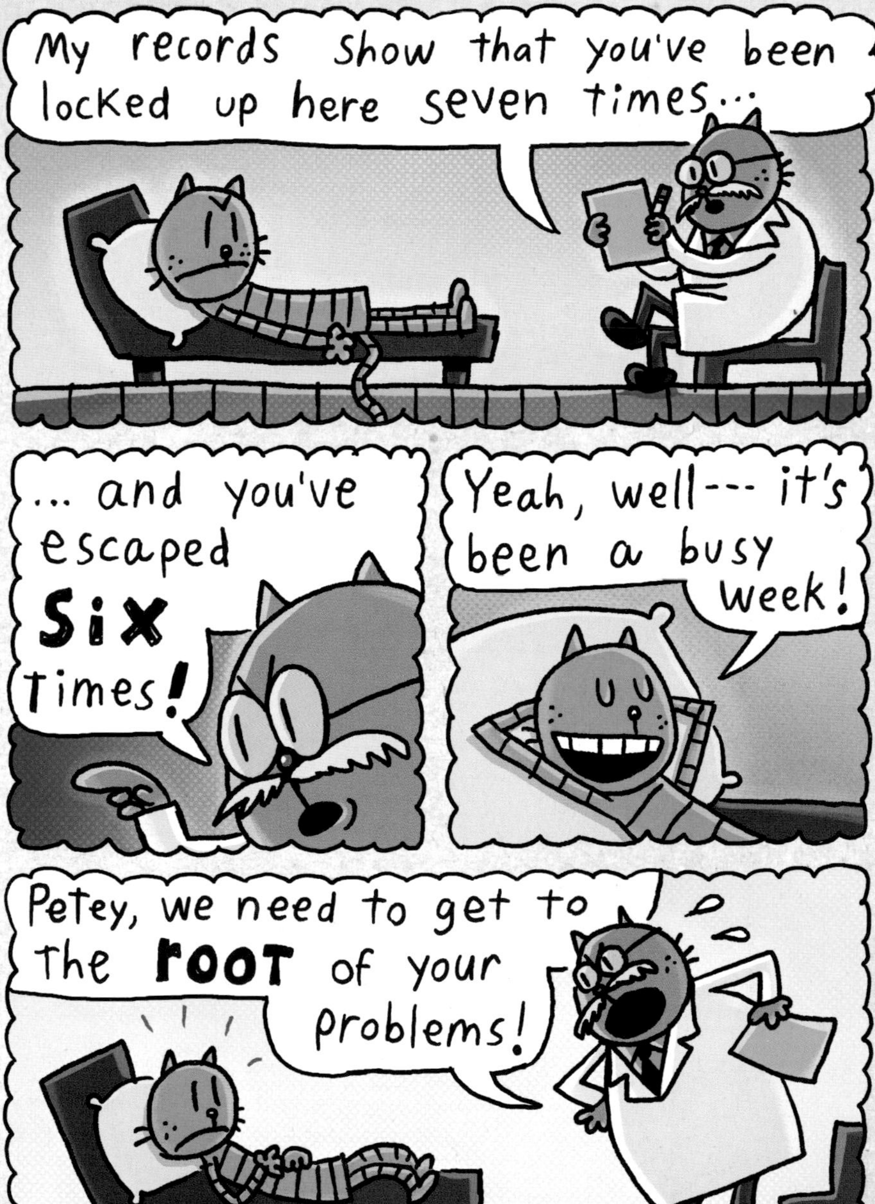
My records show that you've been locked up here seven times...
... and you've escaped SIX times!
Yeah, well--- it's been a busy week!
Petey, we need to get to the ROOT of your problems!

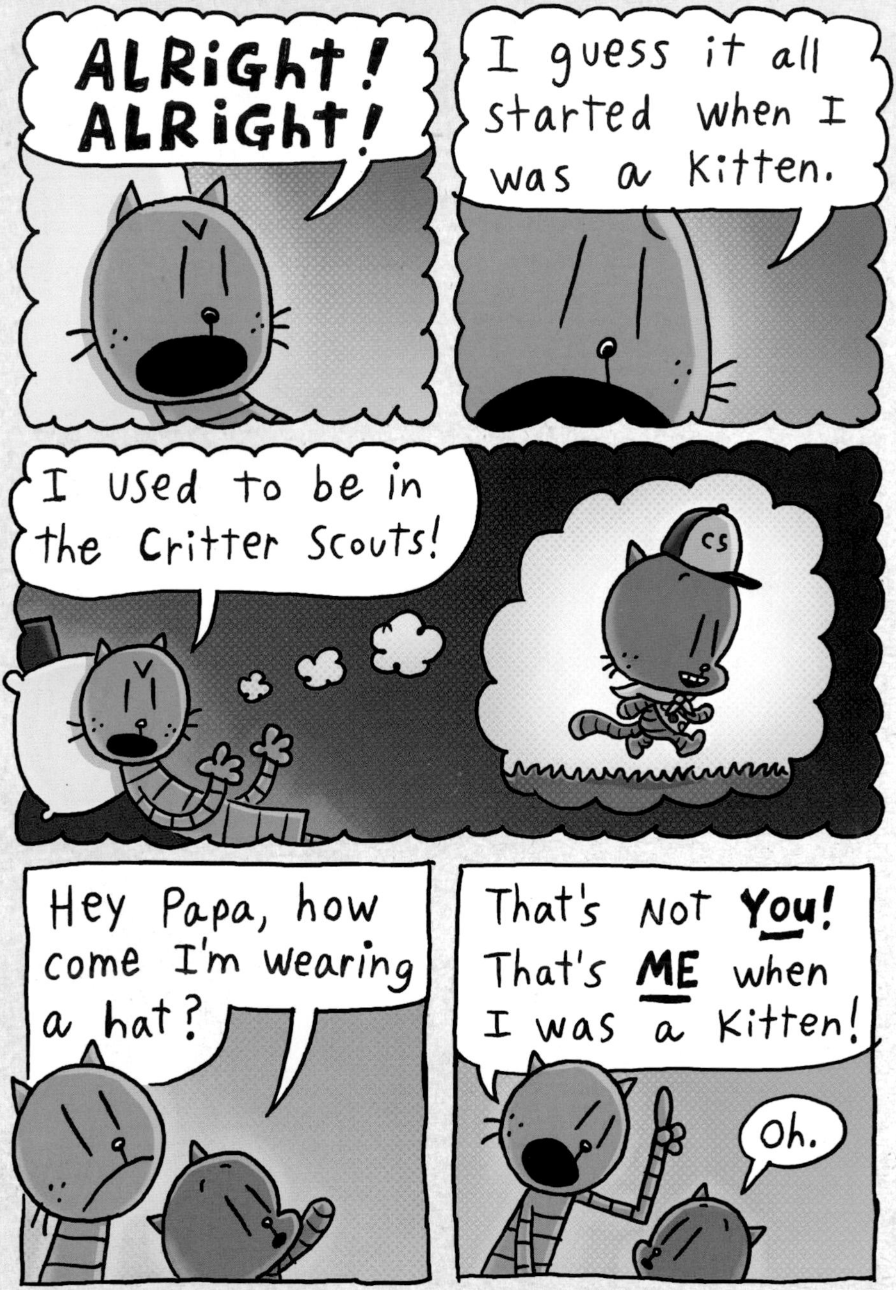

ALRIGHT! ALRIGHT!
I guess it all started when I was a kitten.
I used to be in the Critter Scouts!
CS
Hey Papa, how come I'm wearing a hat?
That's not YOU! That's ME when I was a kitten!
Oh.

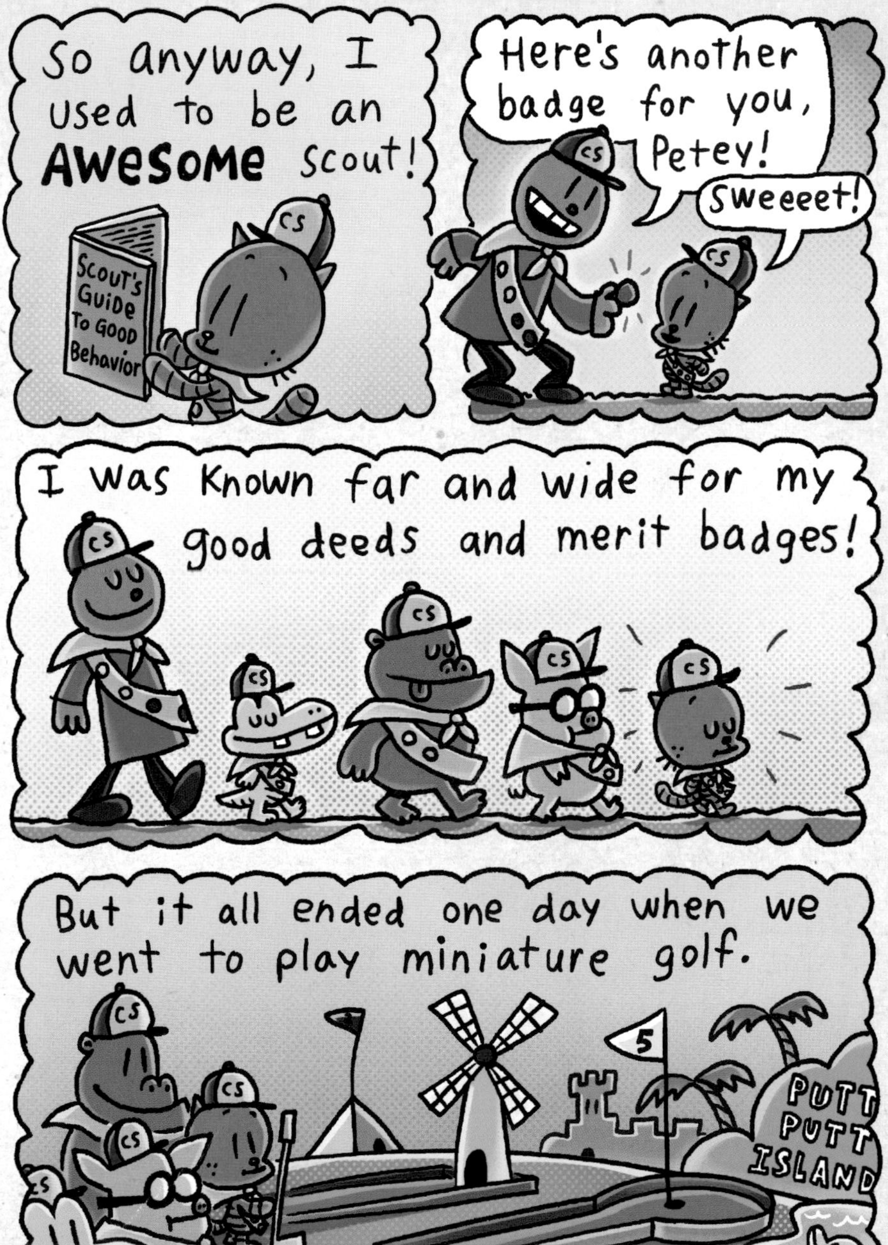
So anyway, I used to be an AWESOME scout!
SCOUT'S GUIDE TO GOOD Behavior
CS
Here's another badge for you, Petey!
Sweeeet!
I was known far and wide for my good deeds and merit badges!
But it all ended one day when we went to play miniature golf.
5
PUTT PUTT ISLAND

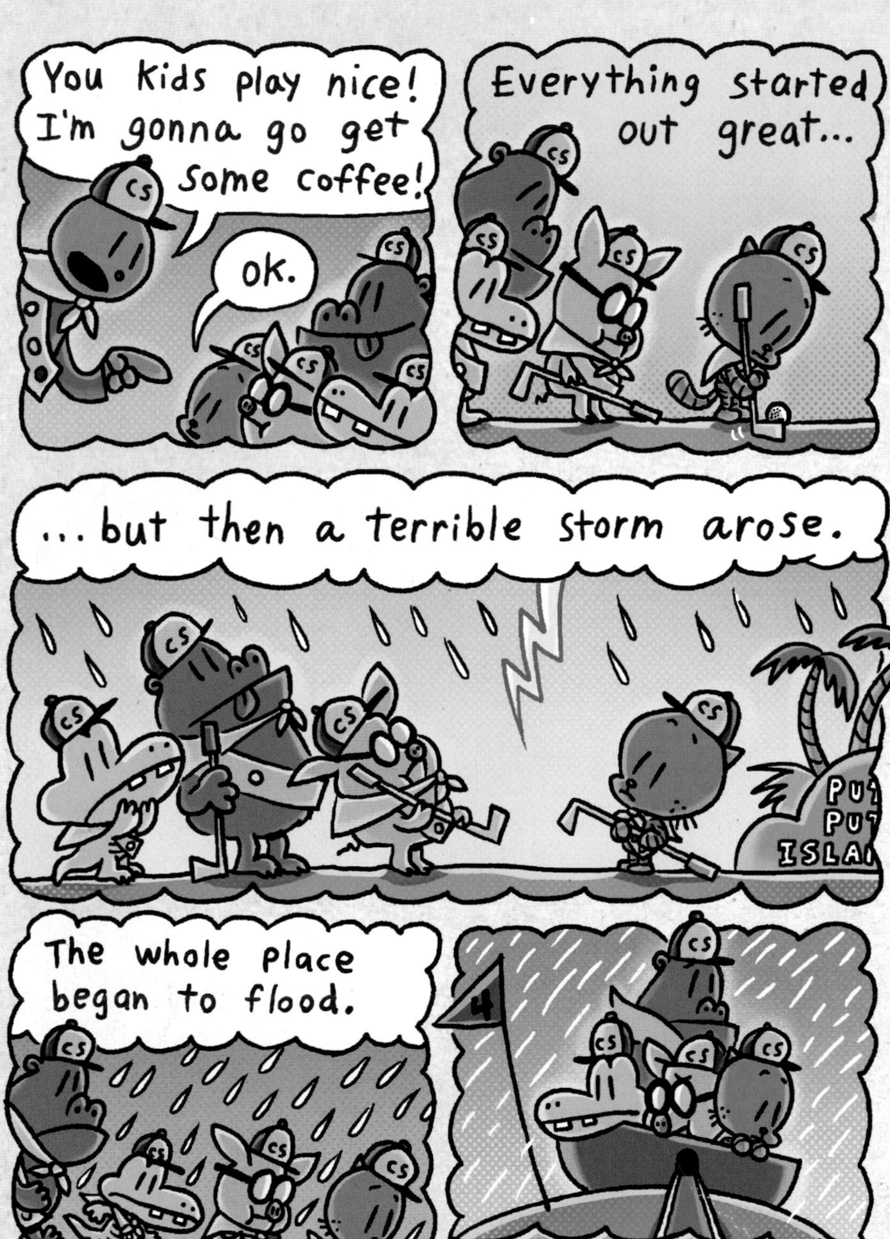
You kids play nice! I'm gonna go get some coffee!
ok.
Everything started out great...
...but then a terrible storm arose.
PUT
PUT
ISLA
The whole place began to flood.
4
We hid on a tiny boat.

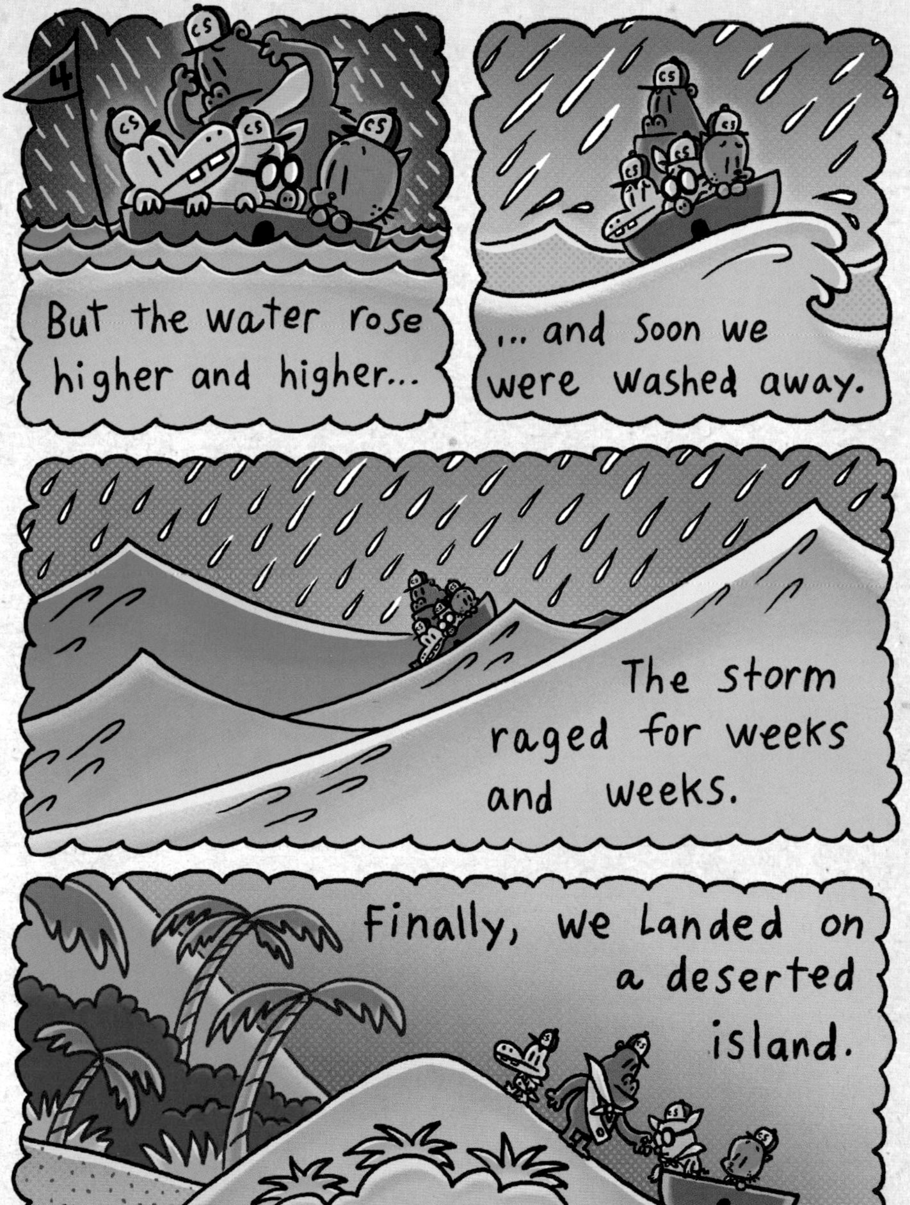
But the water rose higher and higher...
... and soon we were washed away.
The storm raged for weeks and weeks.
Finally, we landed on a deserted island.

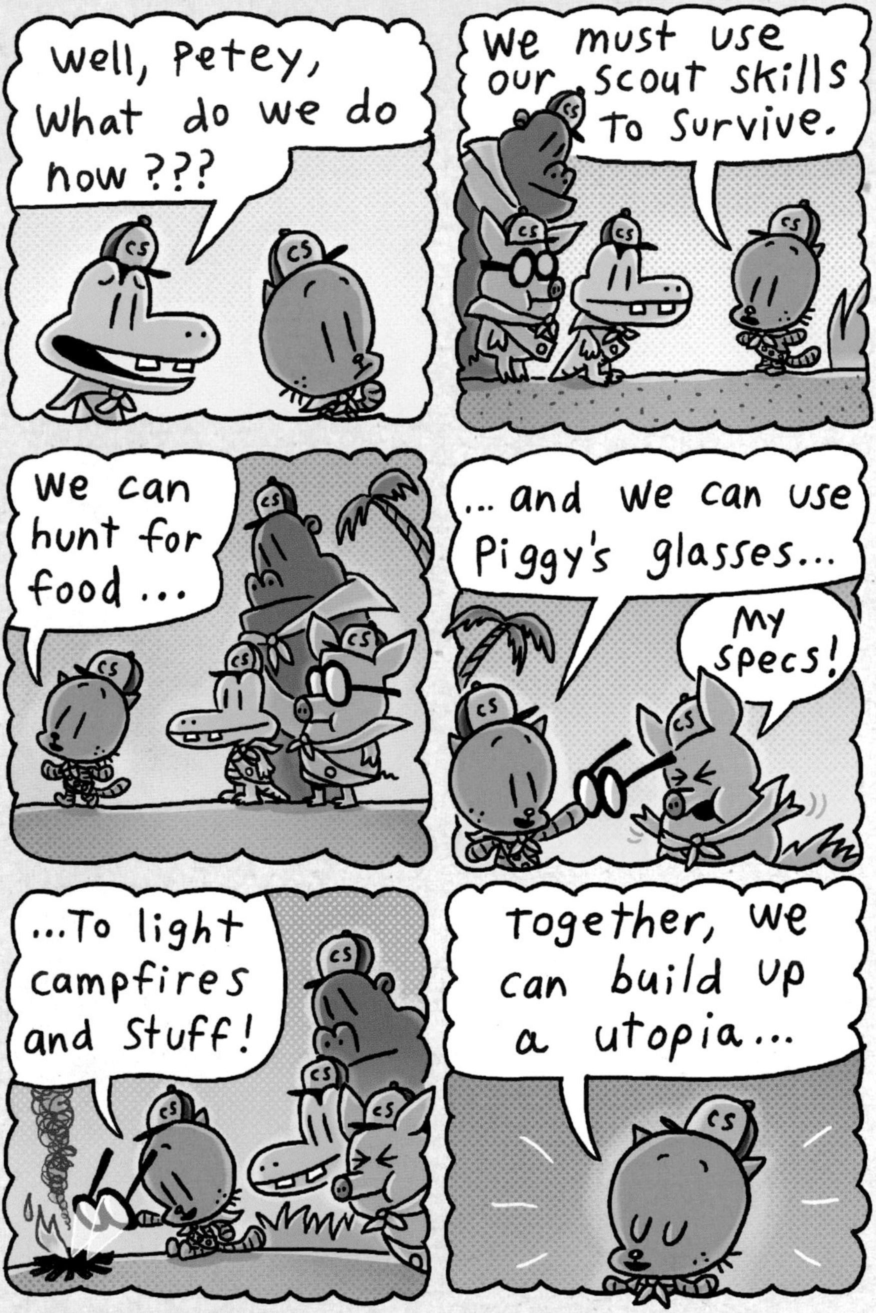
Well, Petey, What do we do now???
We must use our scout skills to survive.
We can hunt for food...
...and we can use Piggy's glasses...
My specs!
...To light campfires and stuff!
Together, we can build up a utopia...

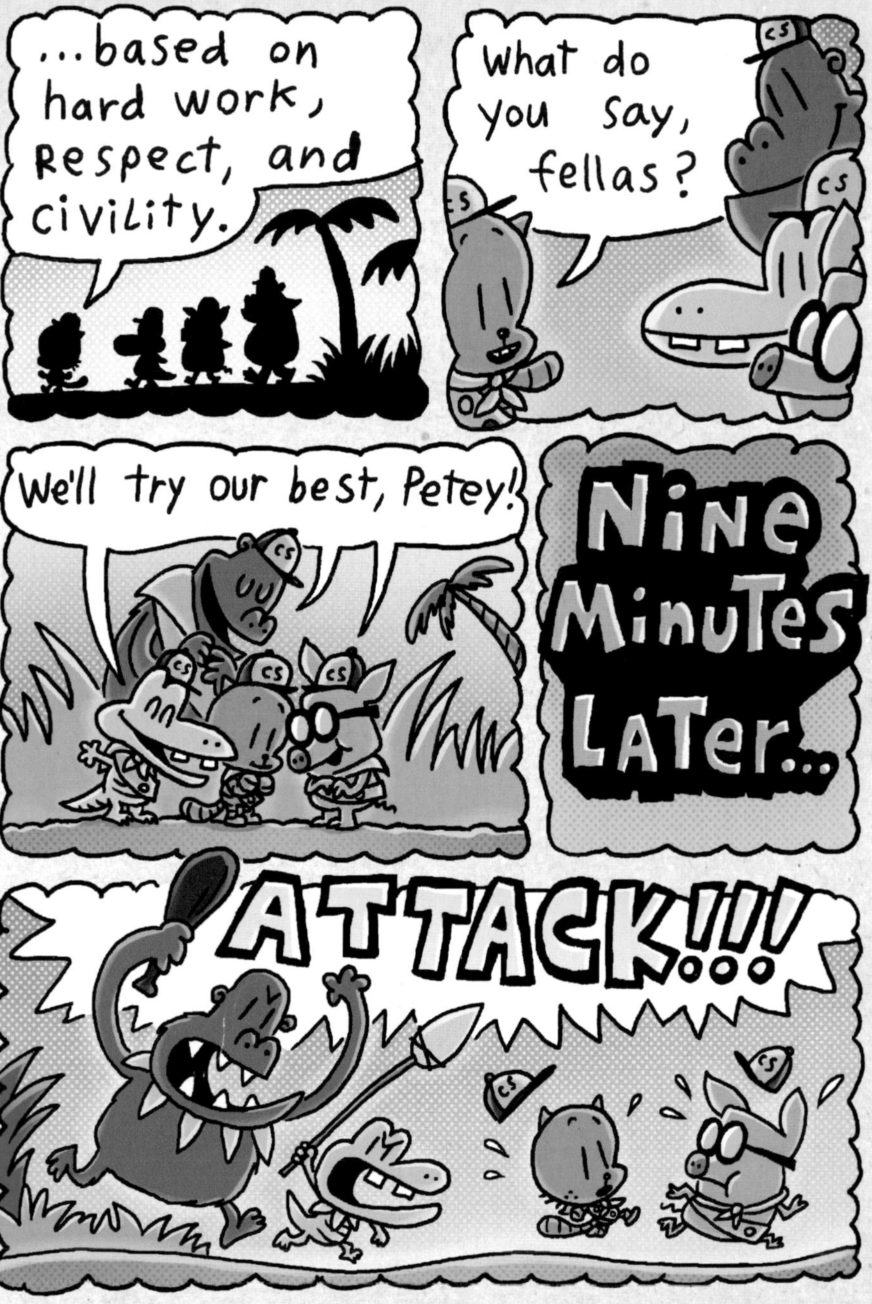
...based on hard work, respect, and civility.
What do you say, fellas?
CS
We'll try our best, Petey!
CS
Nine Minutes Later...
ATTACK!!!
CS

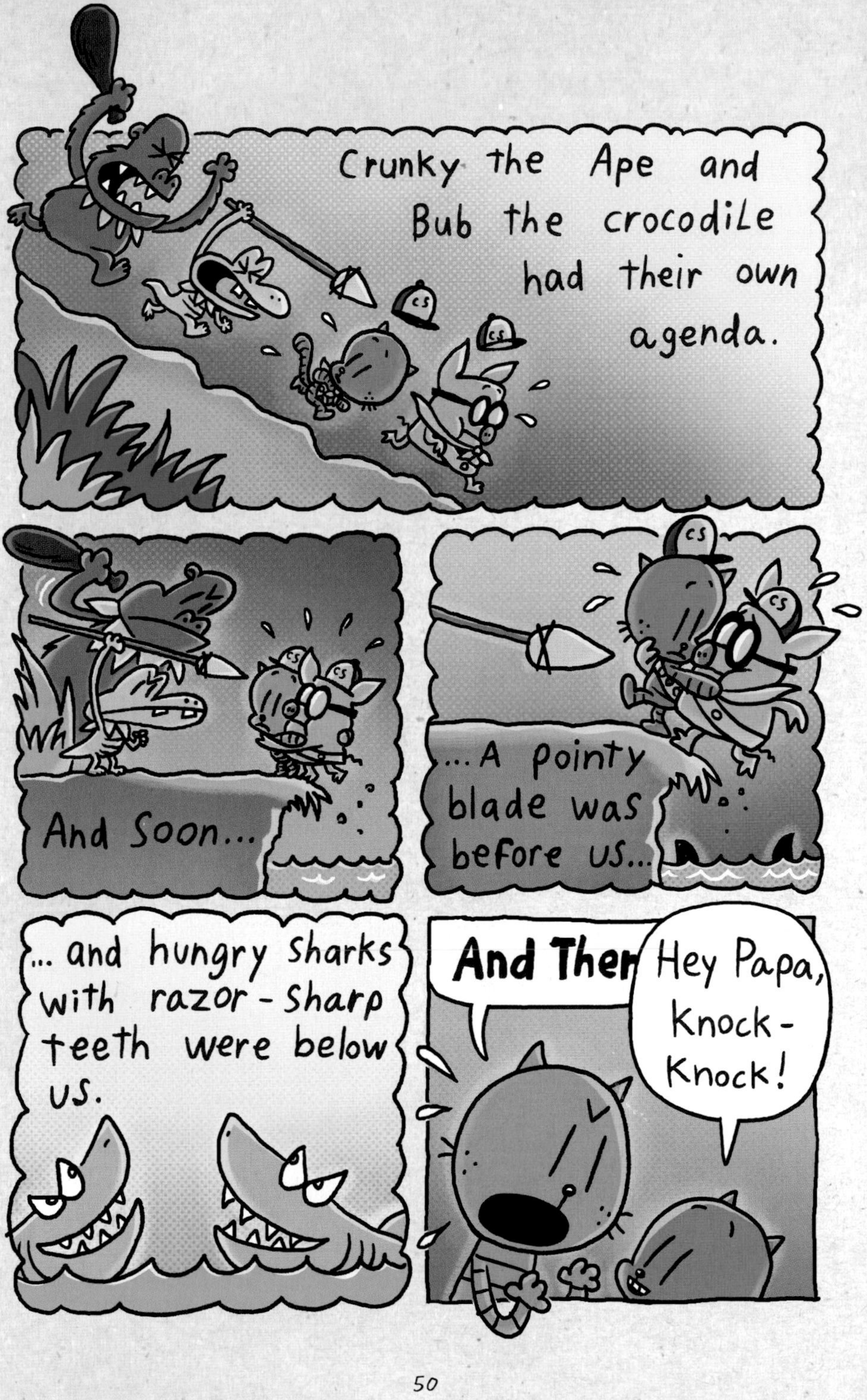
Crunky the Ape and Bub the crocodile had their own agenda.
CS
CS
And Soon...
CS
CS
CS
CS
...A pointy blade was before us...
... and hungry sharks with razor-sharp teeth were below us.
And Then
Hey Papa, Knock-Knock!

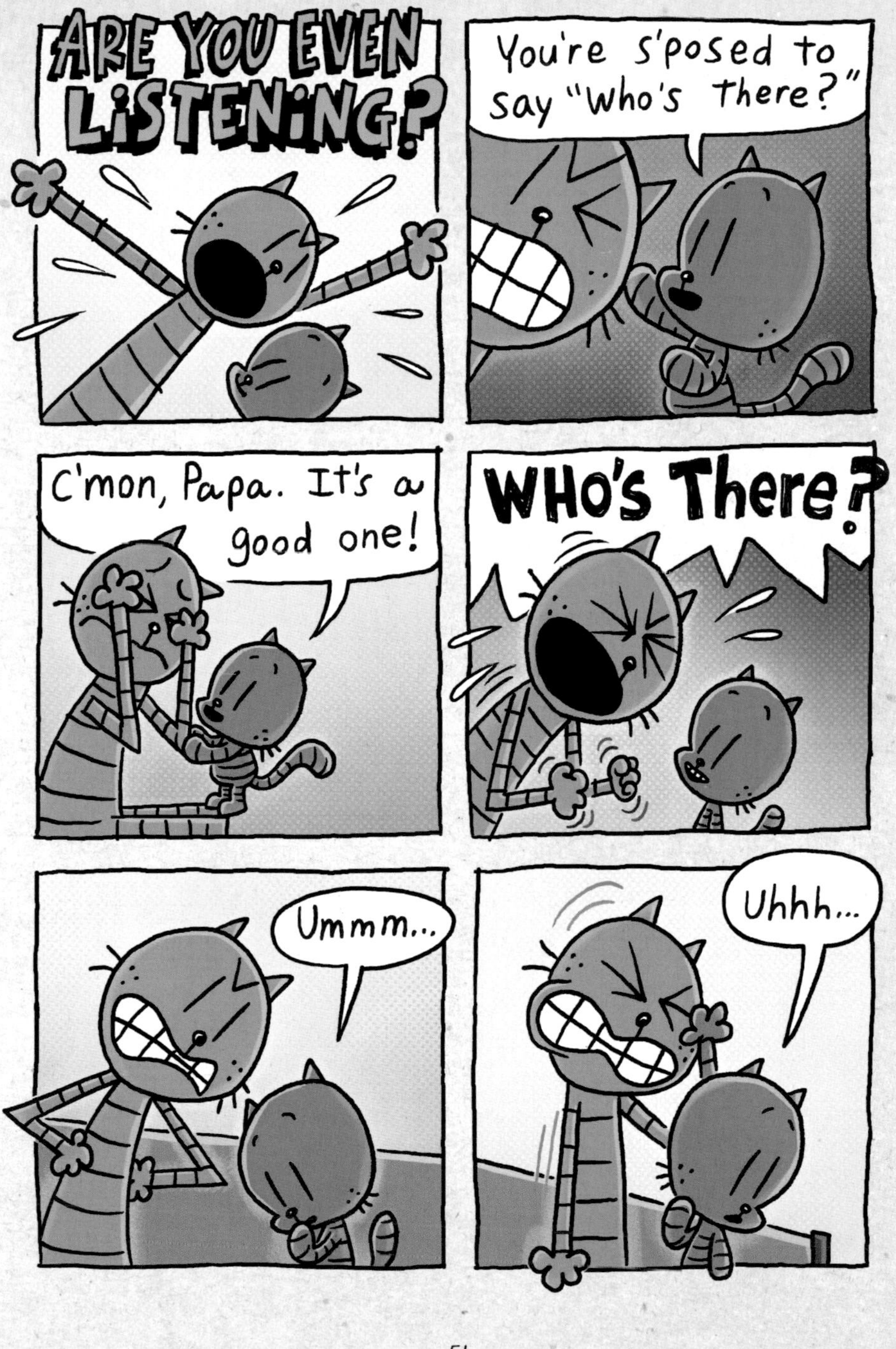
ARE YOU EVEN LISTENING?
You're s'posed to say "who's there?"
C'mon, Papa. It's a good one!
WHO's There?
Ummm...
Uhhh...

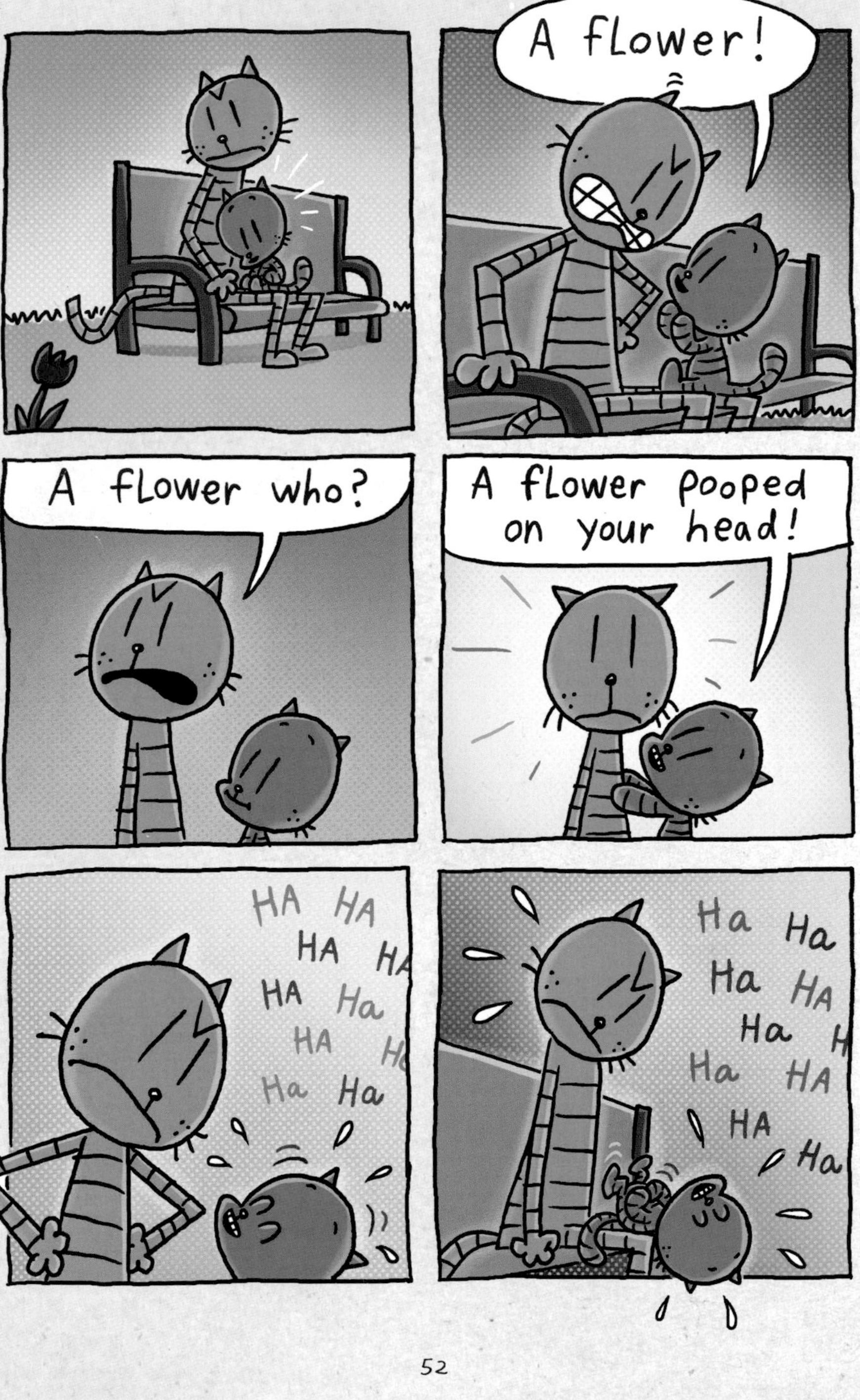
A flower!
A flower who?
A flower pooped on your head!
HA HA HA HA HA Ha HA Ha Ha
Ha Ha Ha HA Ha Ha HA HA Ha

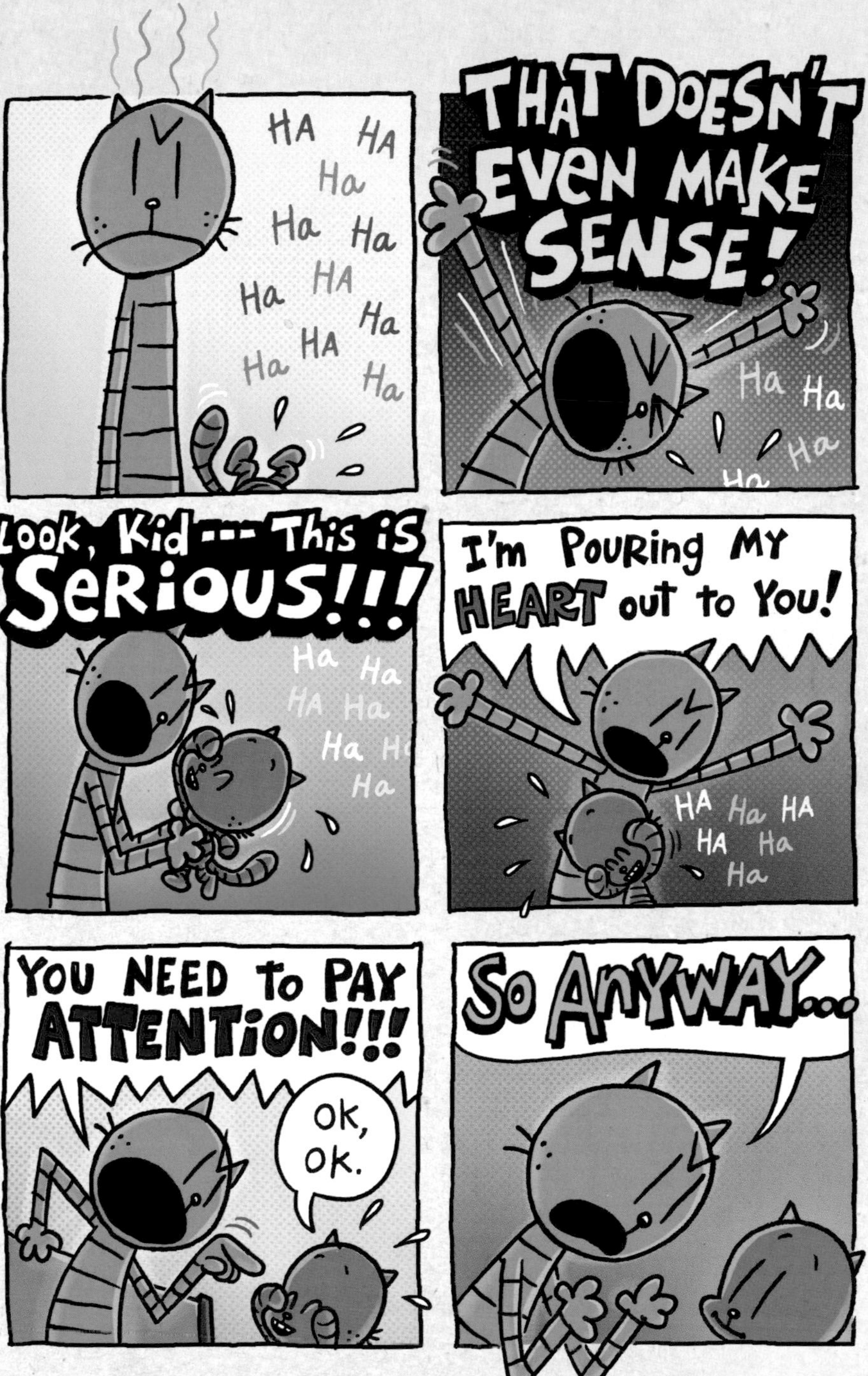
HA HA
Ha
Ha Ha
Ha HA
Ha
Ha HA
Ha
THAT DOESN'T EVEN MAKE SENSE!
Ha Ha
Ha
LOOK, KID --- THIS IS SERIOUS!!!
Ha Ha
HA Ha
Ha
Ha
I'M POURING MY HEART OUT TO YOU!
HA Ha HA
HA Ha
Ha
YOU NEED TO PAY ATTENTION!!!
OK, OK.
SO ANYWAY...

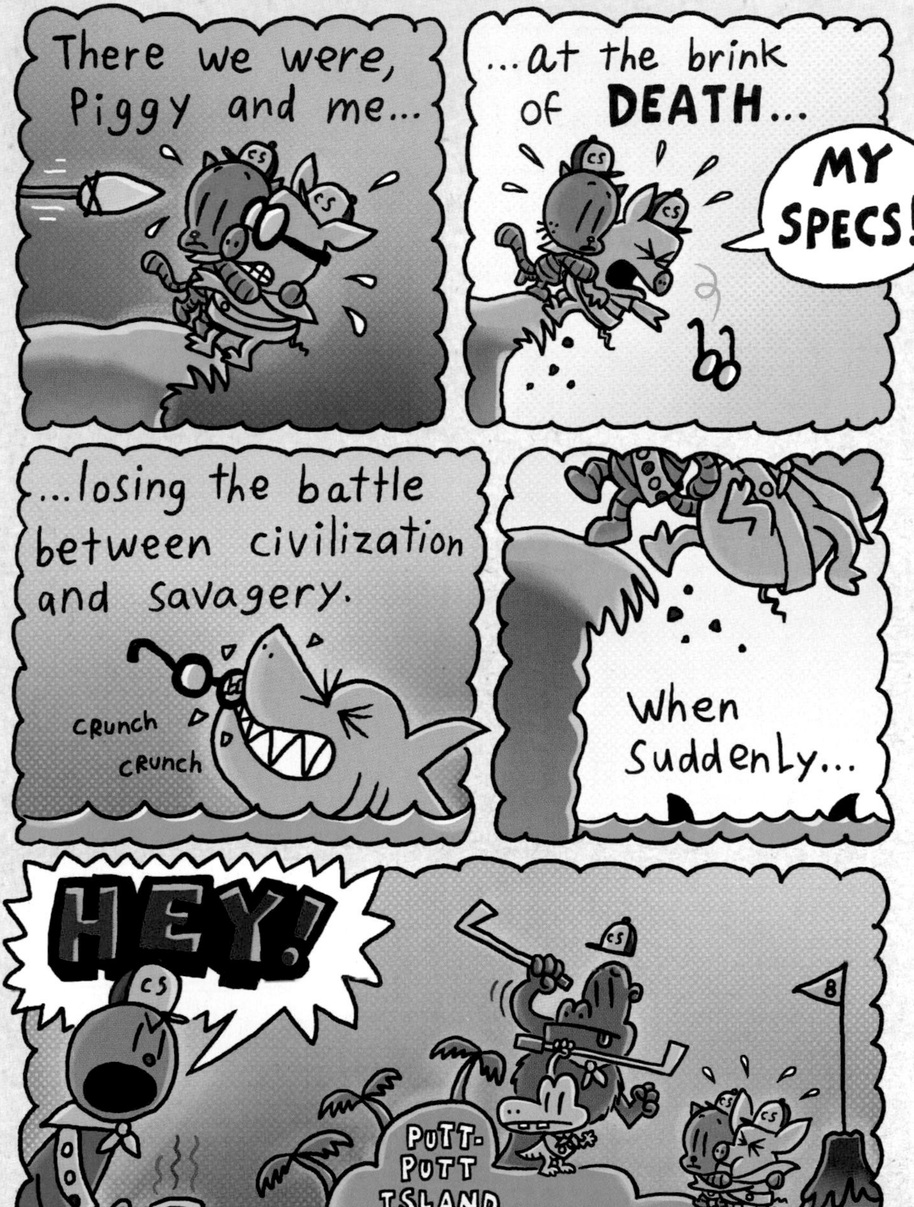

There we were, Piggy and me...
...at the brink of DEATH...
MY SPECS!
...losing the battle between civilization and savagery.
CRUNCH
CRUNCH
When suddenly...
HEY!
PUTT-PUTT ISLAND
8

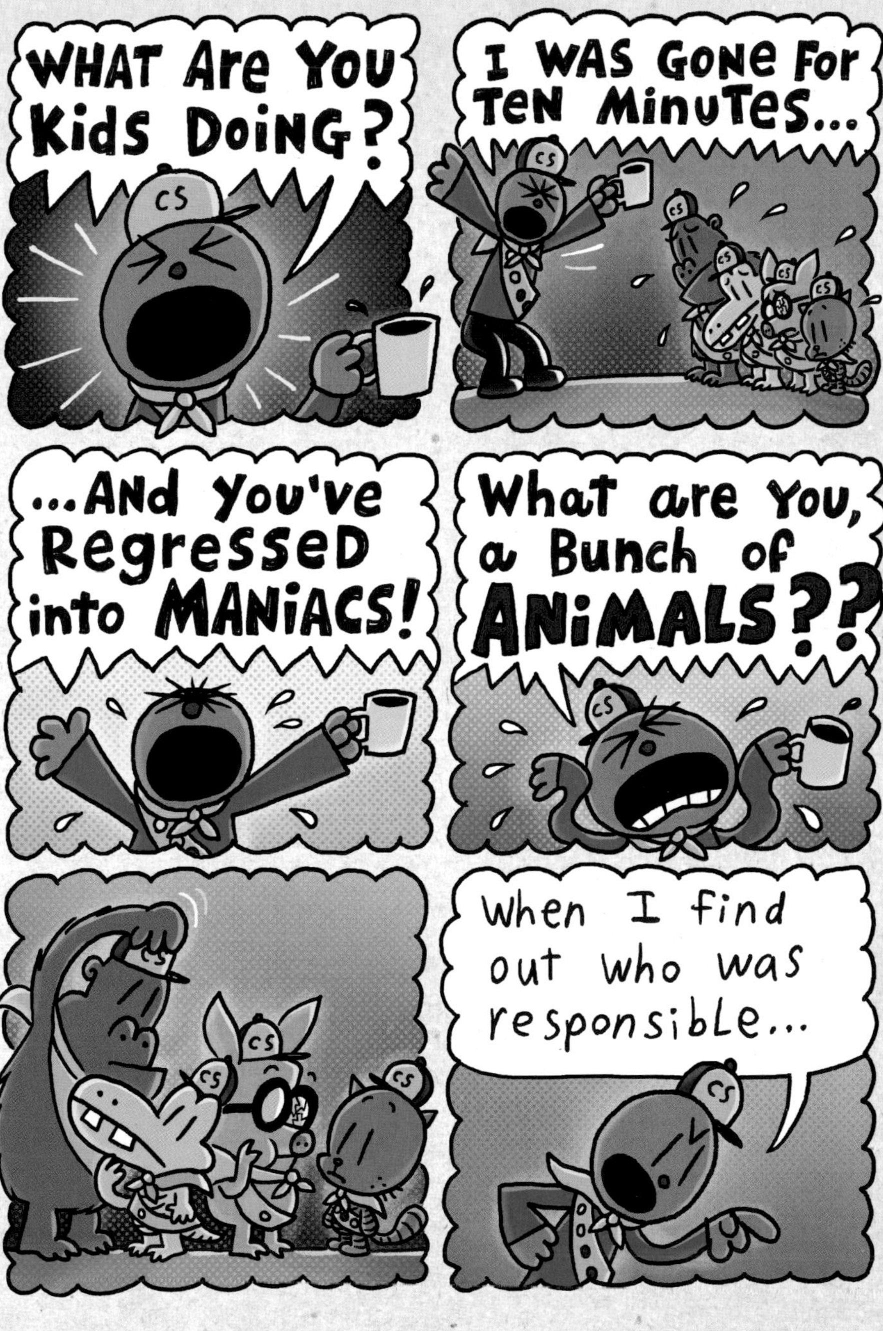
WHAT Are You Kids DoinG?
I WAS Gone For TEN MinuTES...
...AND You've Regressed into MANIACS!
What are You, a Bunch of ANIMALS??
When I find out who was responsible...

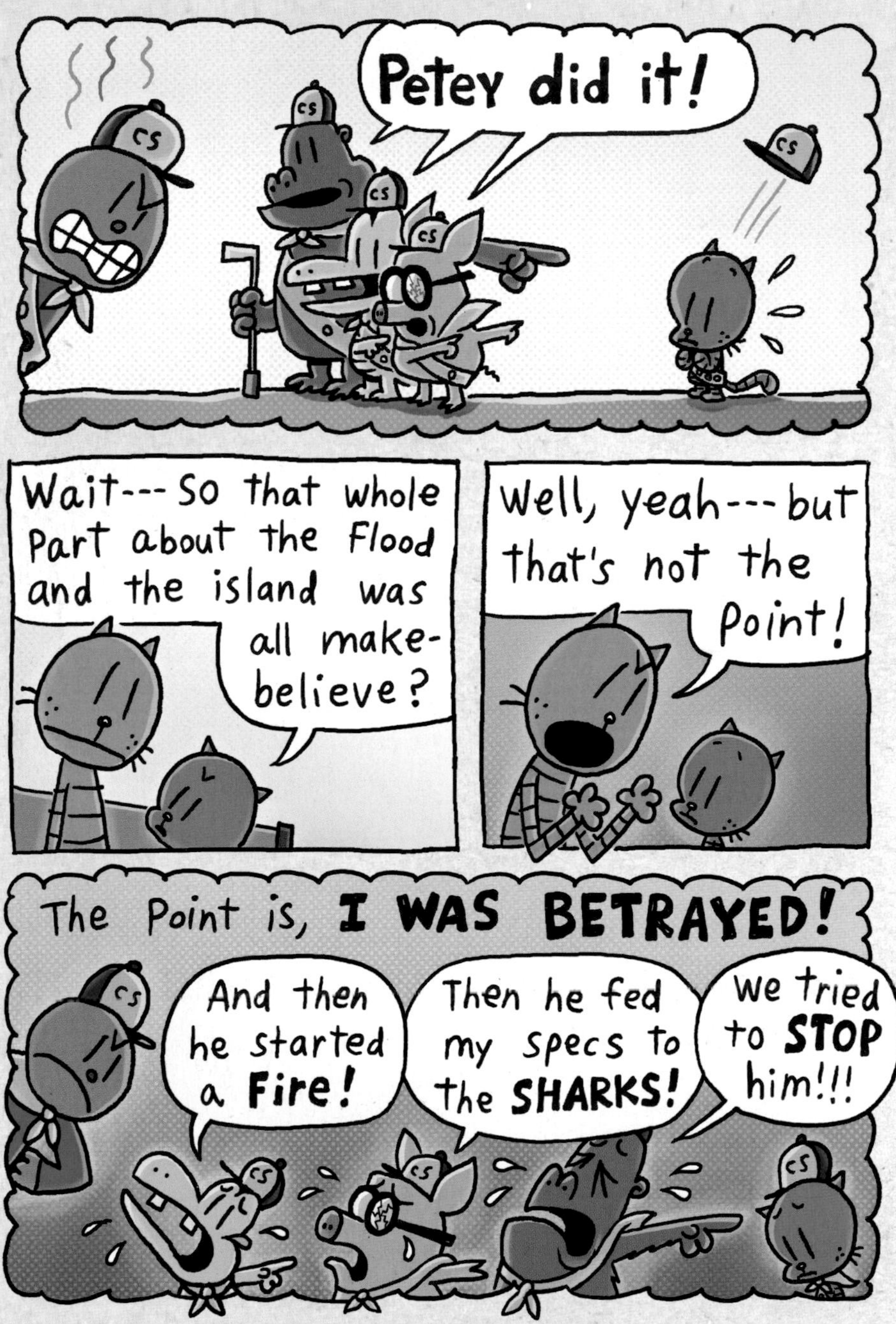
Petey did it!
Wait--- So that whole Part about the Flood and the island was all make-believe?
Well, yeah---but that's not the Point!
The Point is, I WAS BETRAYED!
And then he started a Fire!
Then he fed my specs to the SHARKS!
We tried to STOP him!!!

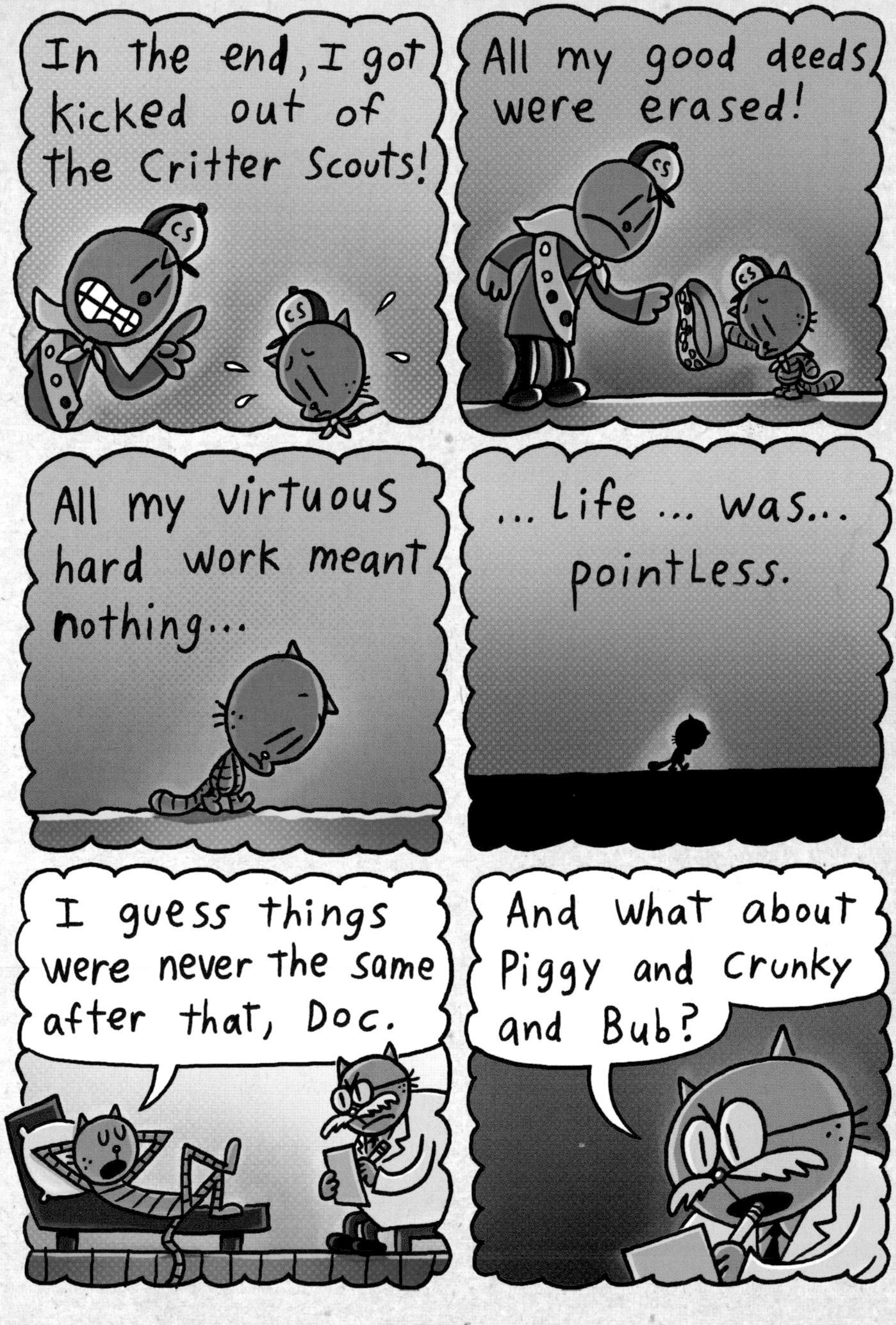
In the end, I got kicked out of the Critter Scouts!
All my good deeds were erased!
All my virtuous hard work meant nothing...
... Life ... was... pointless.
I guess things were never the same after that, Doc.
And what about Piggy and Crunky and Bub?

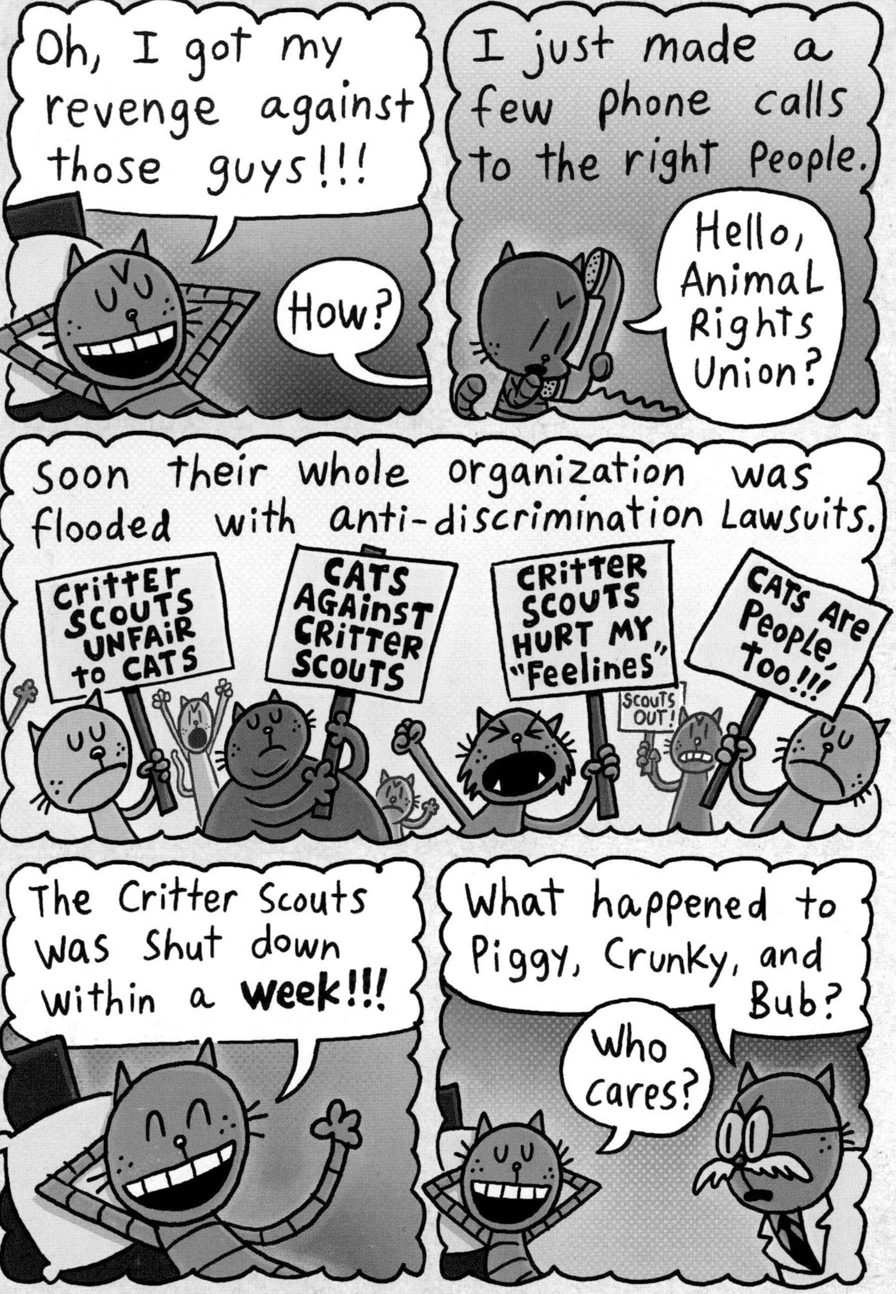
Oh, I got my revenge against those guys!!!
How?
I just made a few phone calls to the right people.
Hello, Animal Rights Union?
Soon their whole organization was flooded with anti-discrimination lawsuits.
CRITTER SCOUTS UNFAIR to CATS
CATS AGAINST CRITTER SCOUTS
CRITTER SCOUTS HURT MY "Feelines"
SCOUTS OUT!
CATS Are People, Too!!!
The Critter Scouts was shut down within a **week!!!**
What happened to Piggy, Crunky, and Bub?
Who cares?

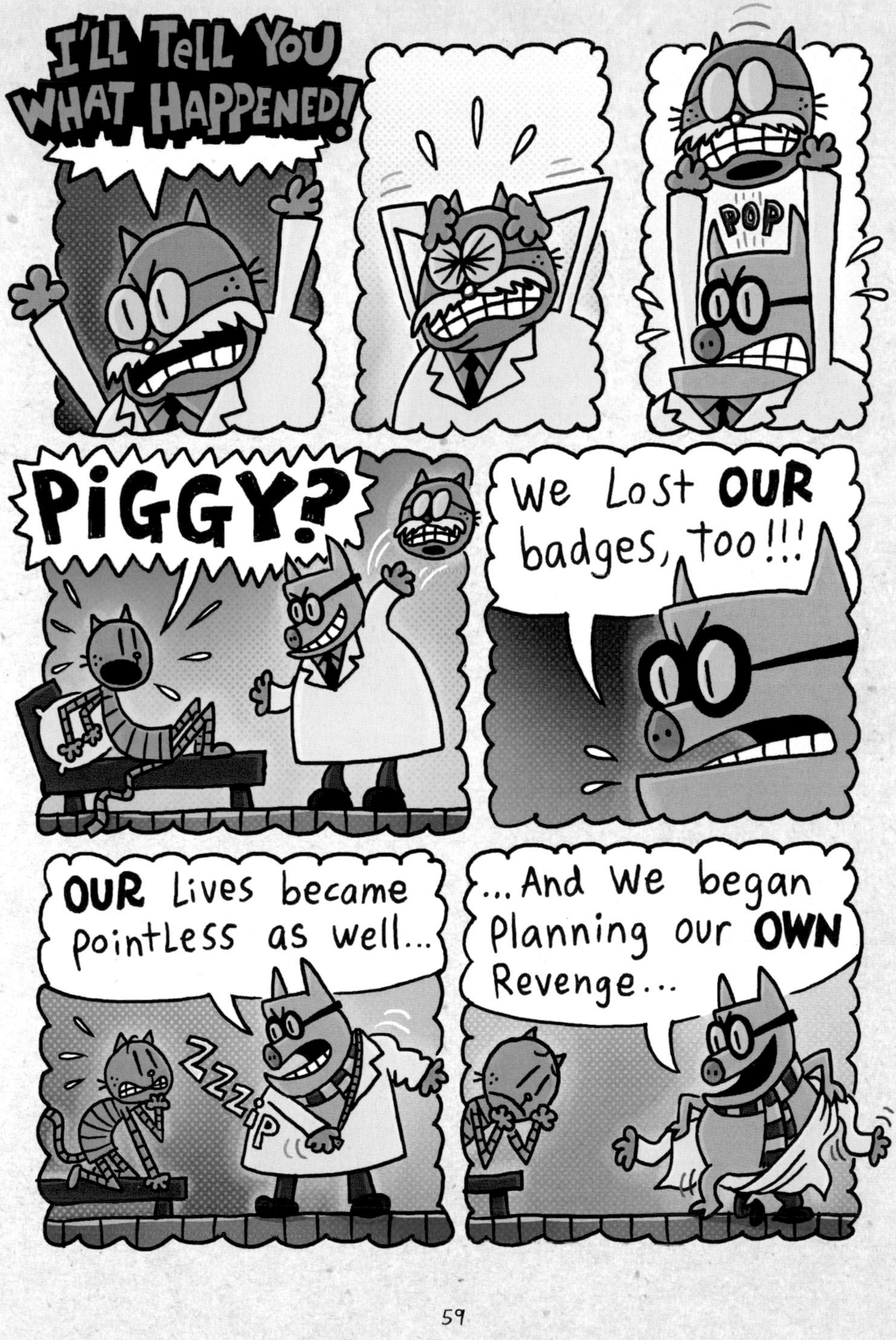
I'LL TeLL YOU WHAT HAPPENED!
POP
PiGGY?
We Lost OUR badges, too!!!
OUR Lives became pointLess as well...
ZZZiP
...And We began Planning our OWN Revenge...

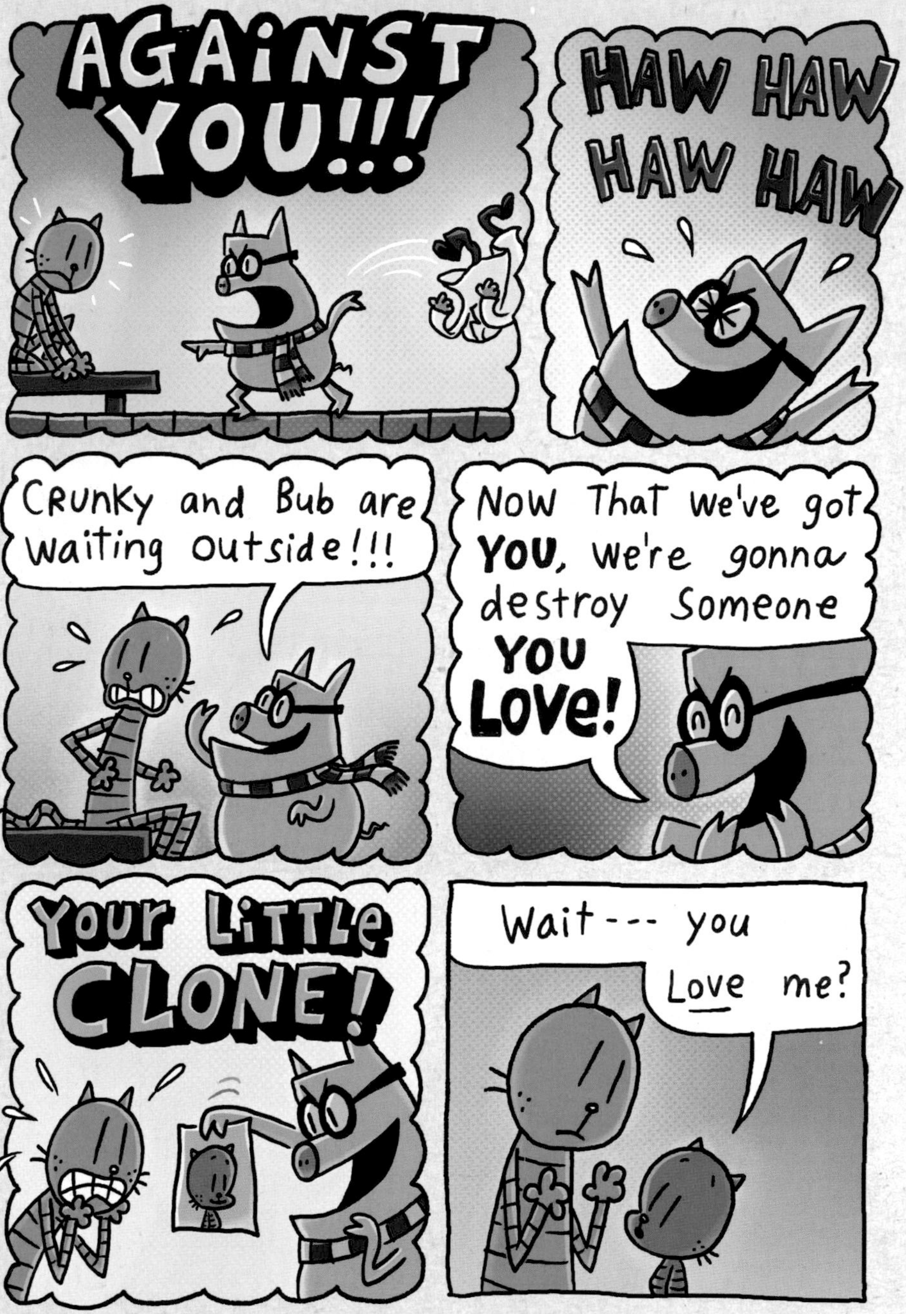
AGAINST YOU!!!
HAW HAW HAW HAW
CRUNKY and Bub are waiting outside!!!
Now That we've got YOU, we're gonna destroy Someone YOU LOVE!
YOUR LITTLE CLONE!
Wait--- you Love me?

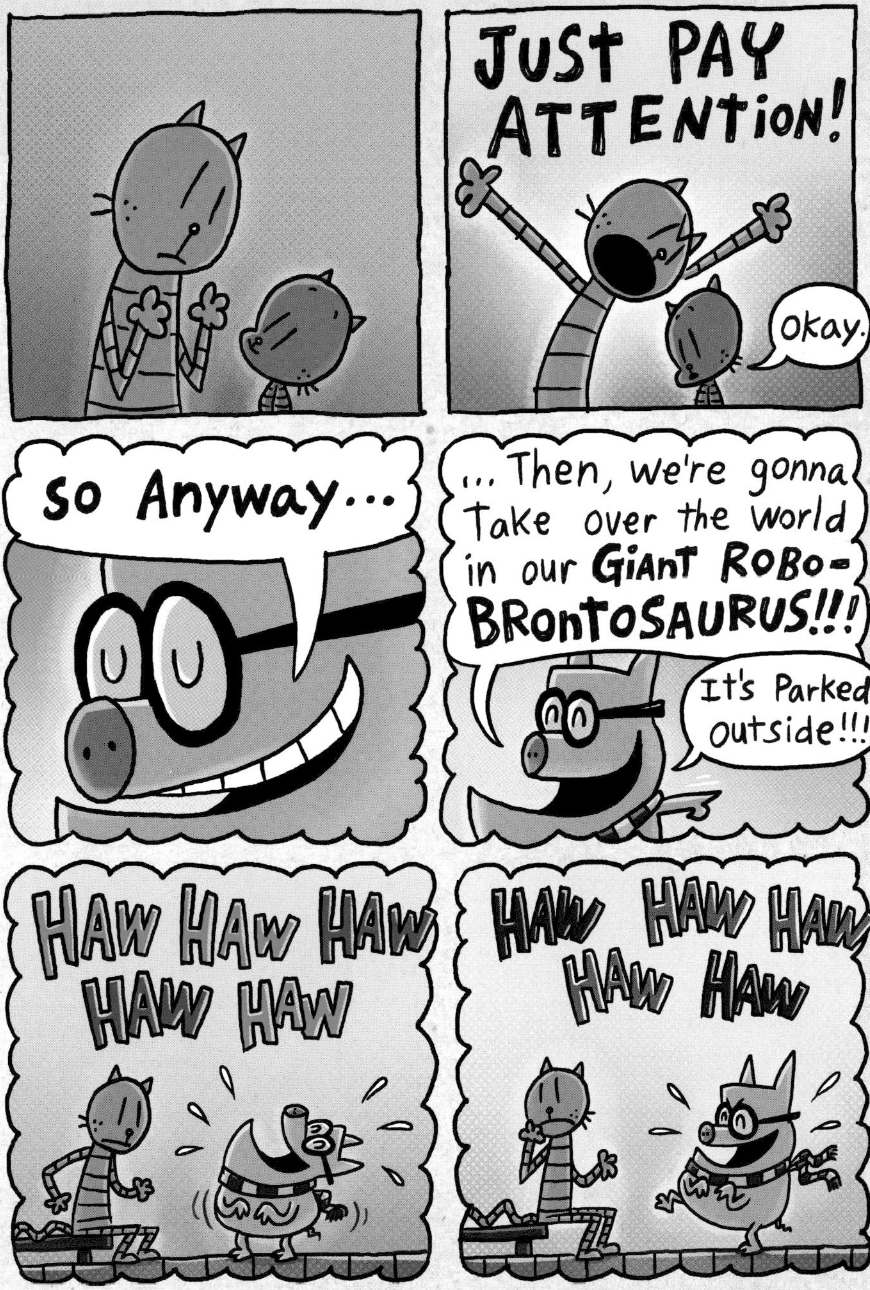
JUST PAY ATTENTion!
Okay.
so Anyway...
... Then, we're gonna Take over the world in our GIANT ROBO-BRONTOSAURUS!!!
It's Parked outside!!!
HAW HAW HAW HAW HAW
HAW HAW HAW HAW HAW

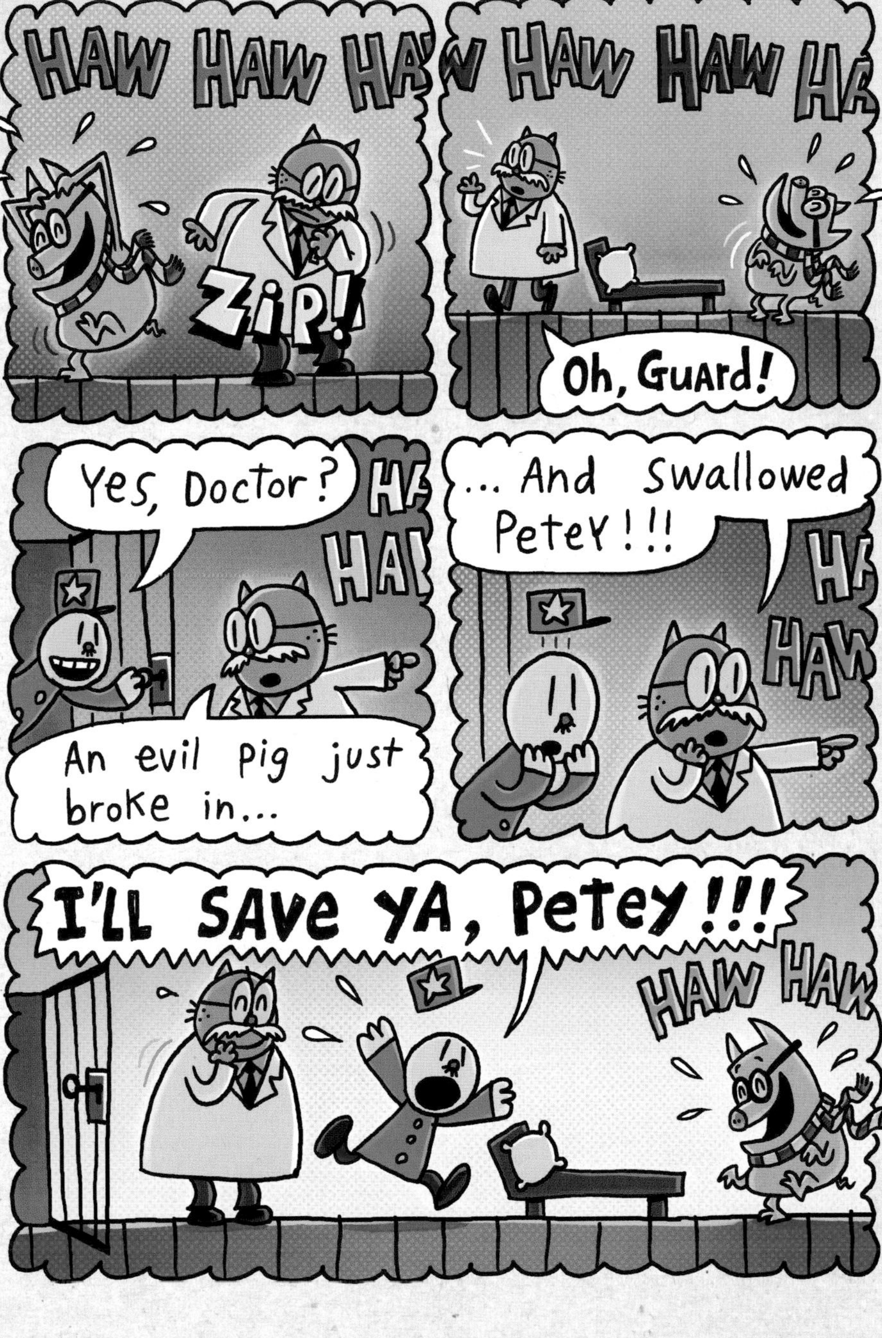
HAW HAW HAW
ZIP!
HAW HAW HA
Oh, Guard!
Yes, Doctor?
An evil pig just broke in...
... And swallowed Petey!!!
I'LL SAVE YA, Petey!!!
HAW HAW

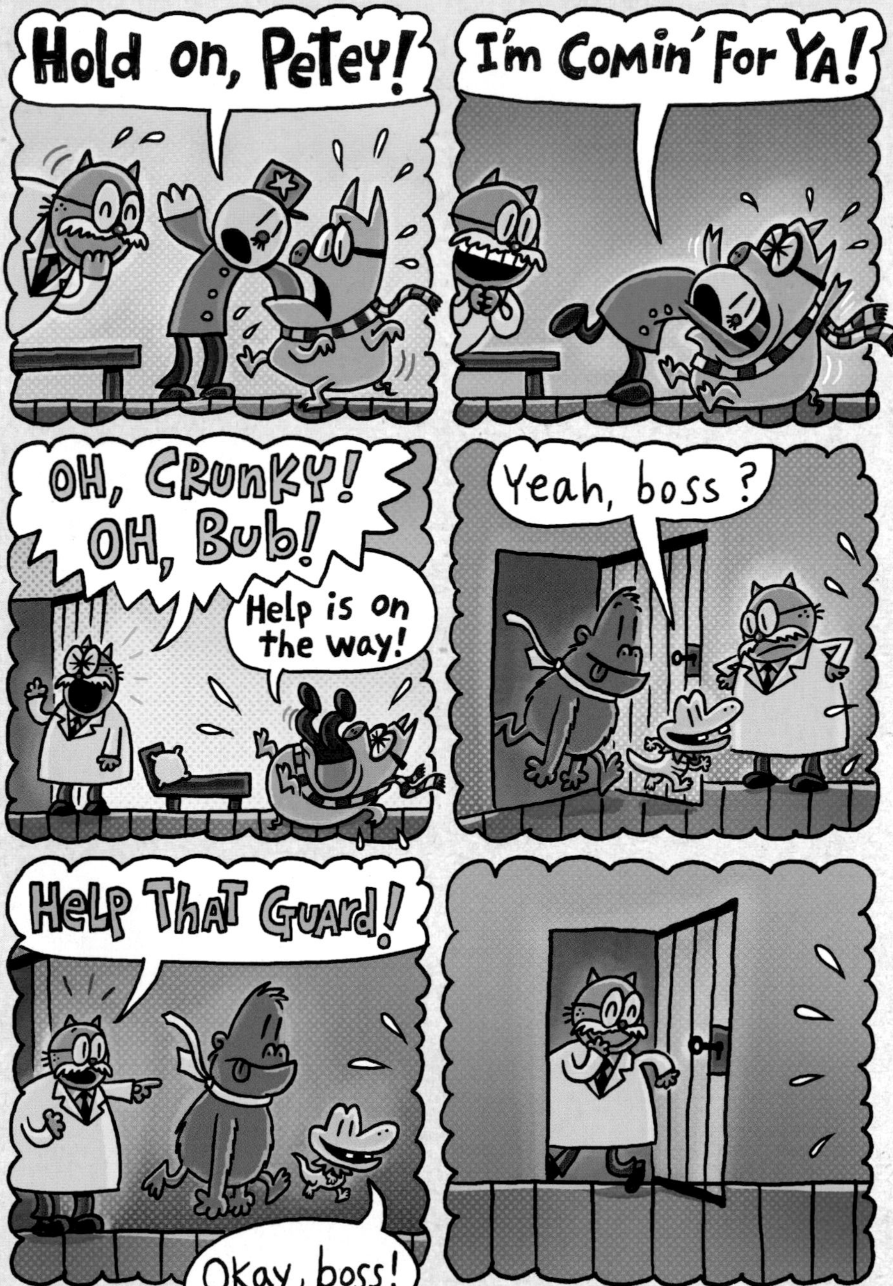
Hold on, Petey!
I'm Comin' For YA!
OH, CRUNKY! OH, Bub!
Help is on the way!
Yeah, boss?
HELP THAT GUARD!
Okay, boss!

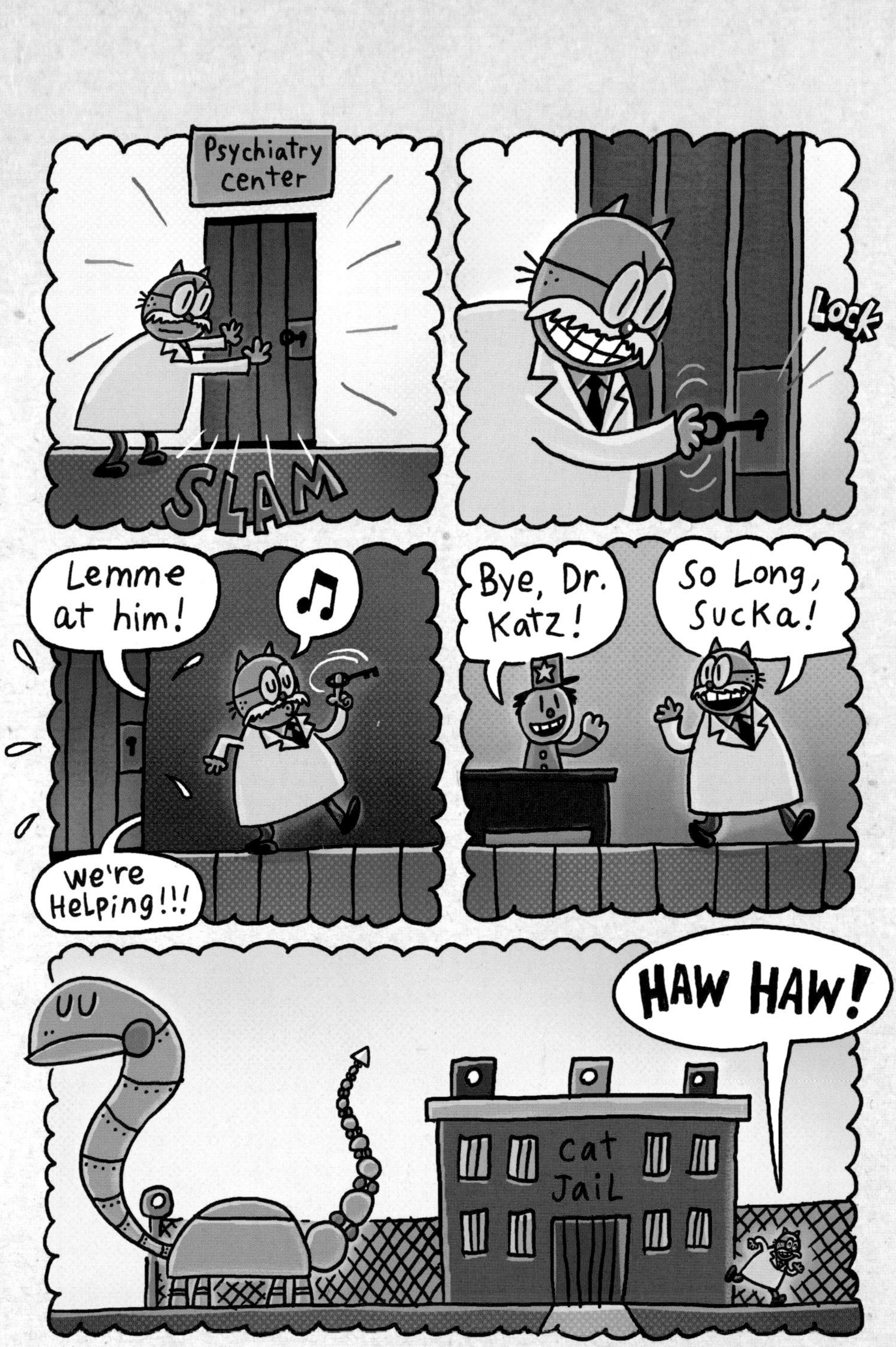
Psychiatry center
SLAM
LOCK
Lemme at him!
We're Helping!!!
Bye, Dr. Katz!
So Long, Sucka!
HAW HAW!
Cat Jail

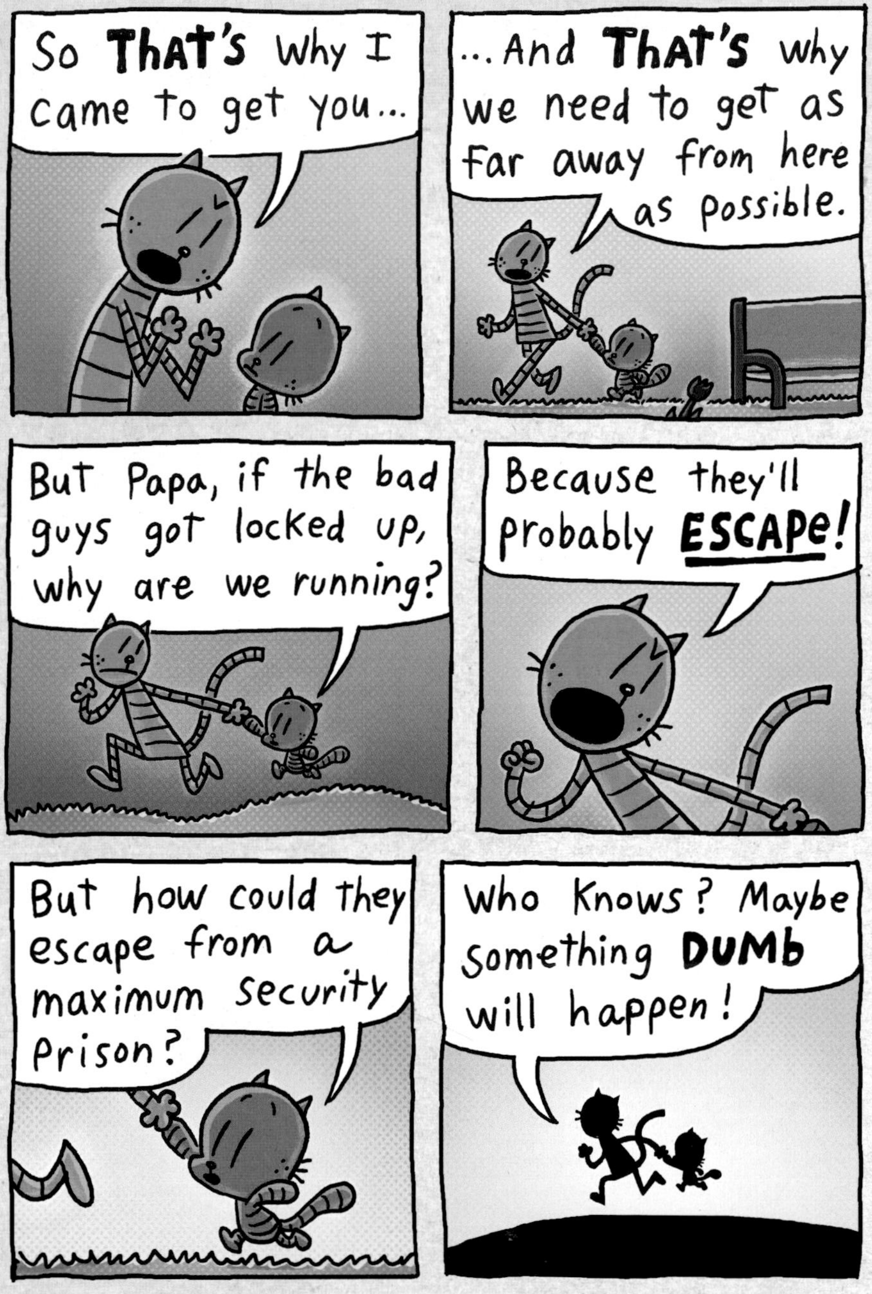
So THAT'S why I came to get you...
...And THAT'S why we need to get as far away from here as possible.
But Papa, if the bad guys got locked up, why are we running?
Because they'll probably ESCAPE!
But how could they escape from a maximum security prison?
Who knows? Maybe something DUMB will happen!

Tree-House Comix Proudly Presents

Chapter 3

Something Dumb Happens!

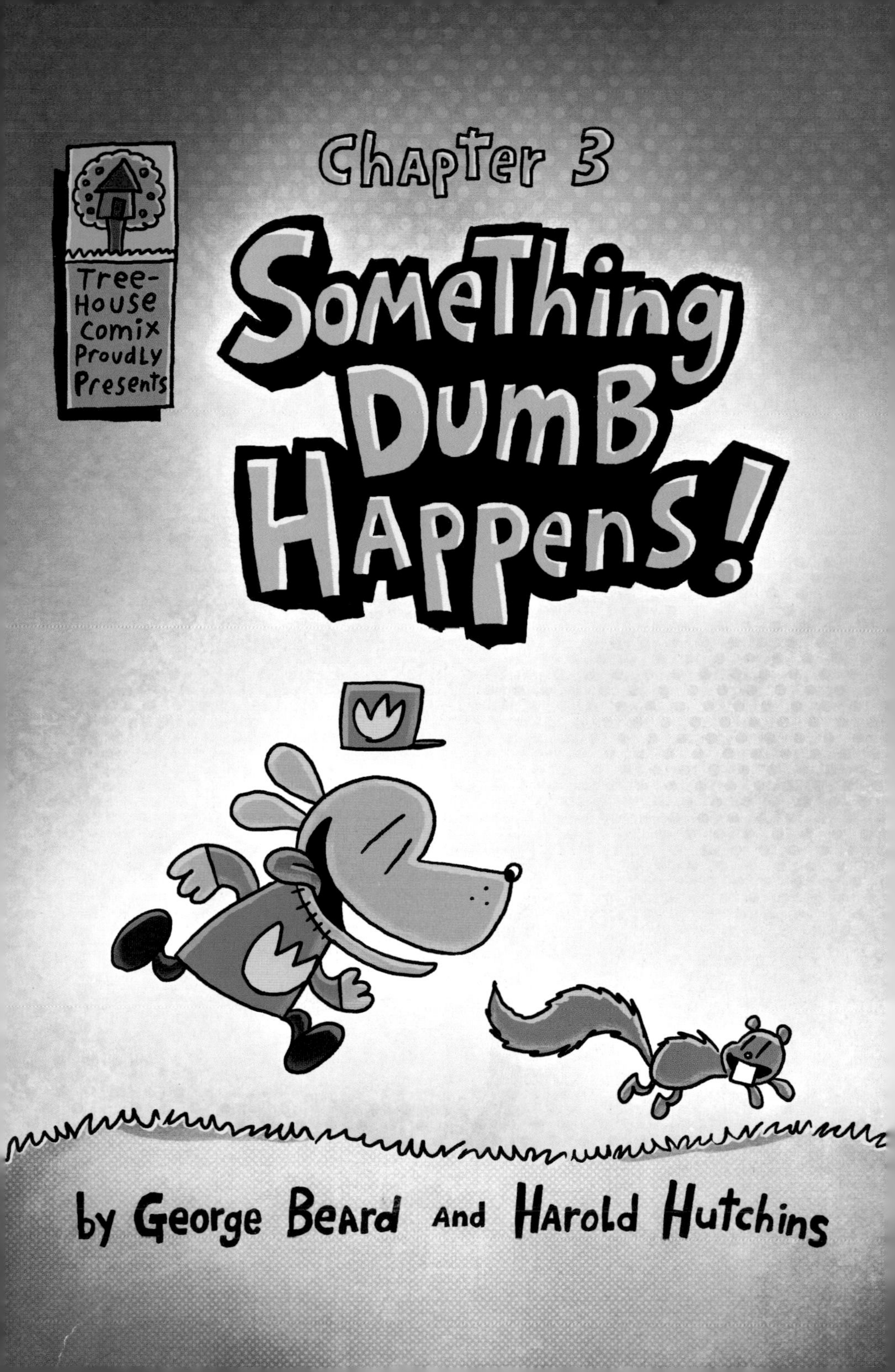

by George Beard and Harold Hutchins

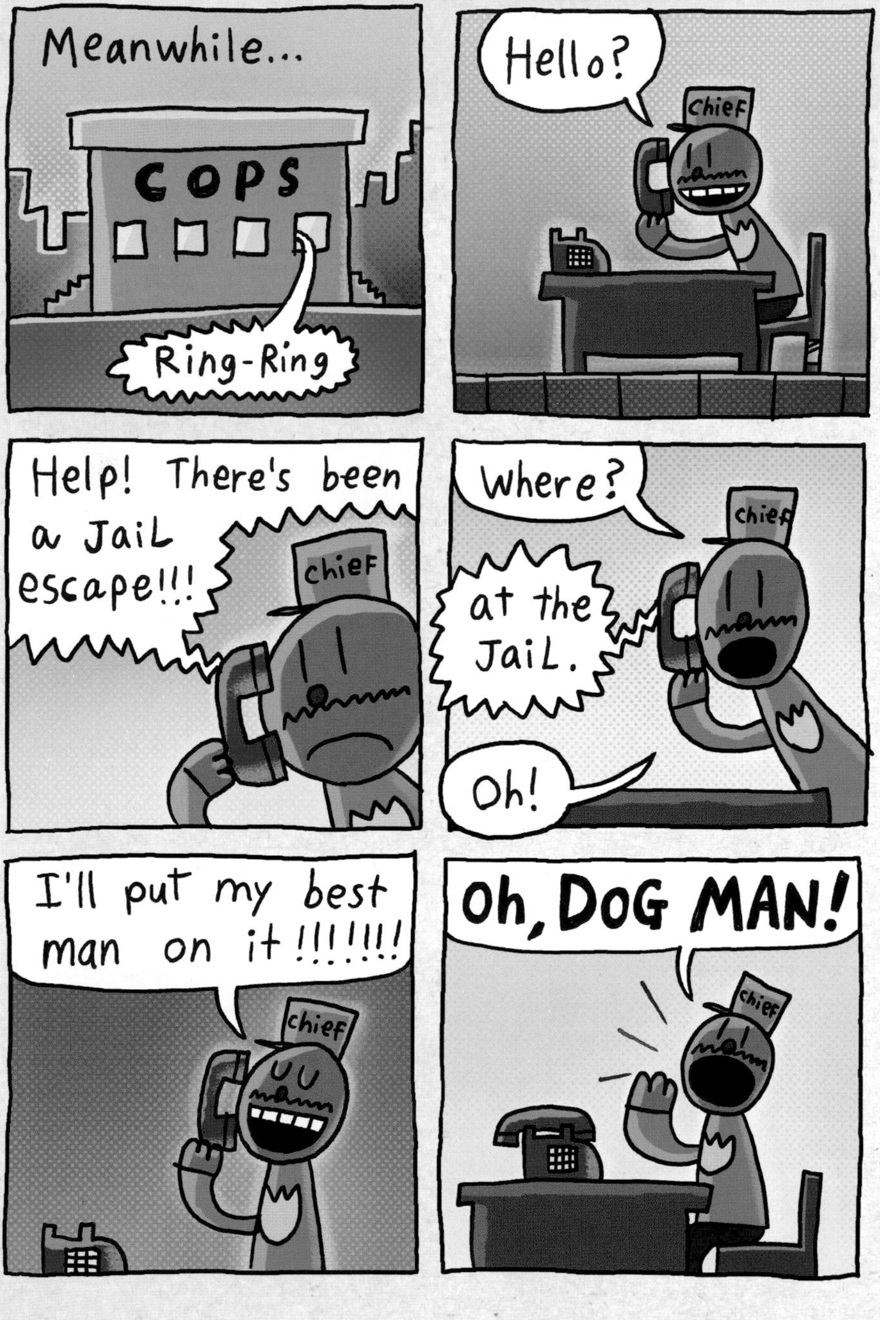
Meanwhile...
COPS
Ring-Ring
Hello?
Chief
Help! There's been a JaiL escape!!!
chieF
Where?
at the JaiL.
Oh!
I'll put my best man on it !!!!!!!
Oh, DOG MAN!

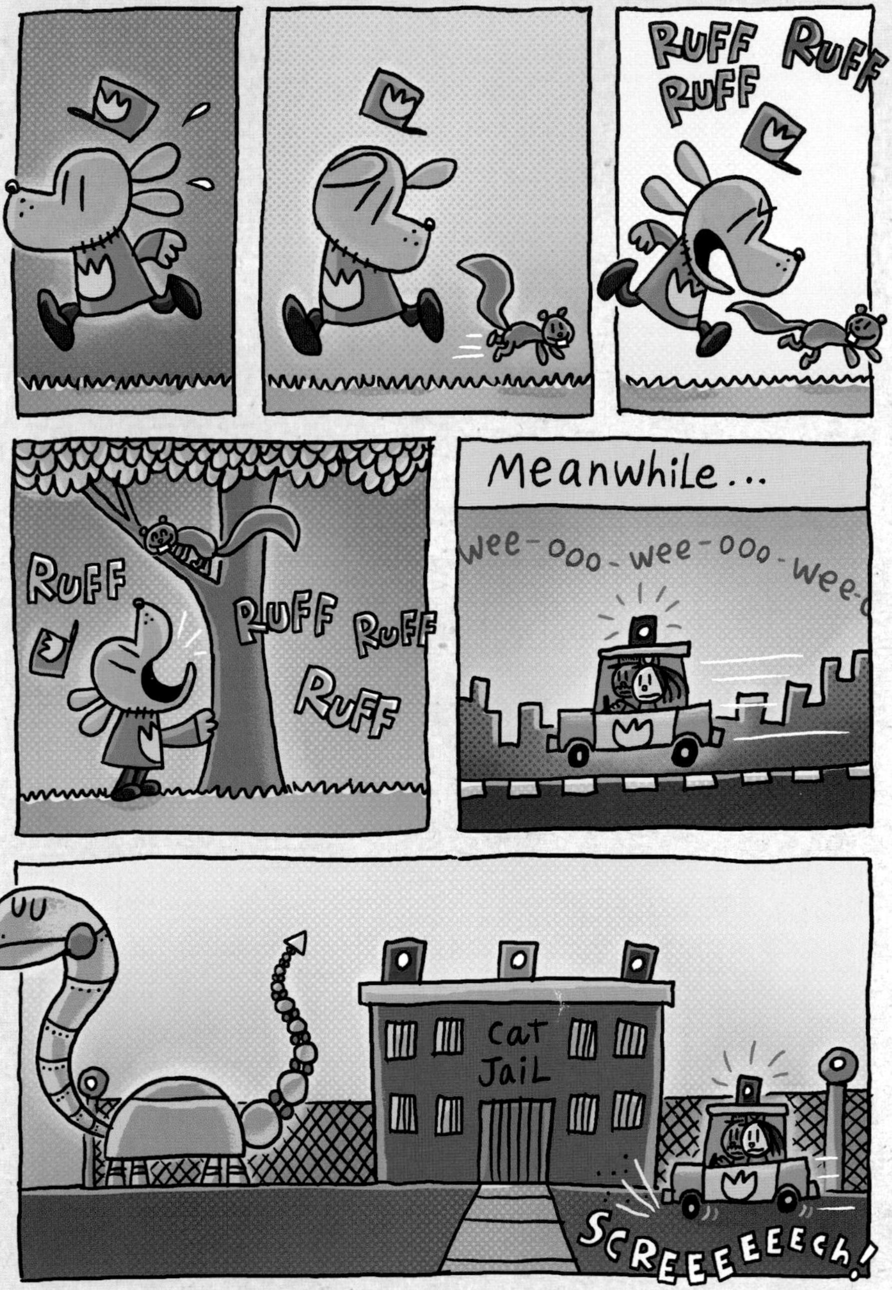
RUFF RUFF
RUFF
RUFF
RUFF RUFF
RUFF
Meanwhile...
wee-ooo-wee-ooo-wee-
Cat
JaiL
SCREEEEEECh!

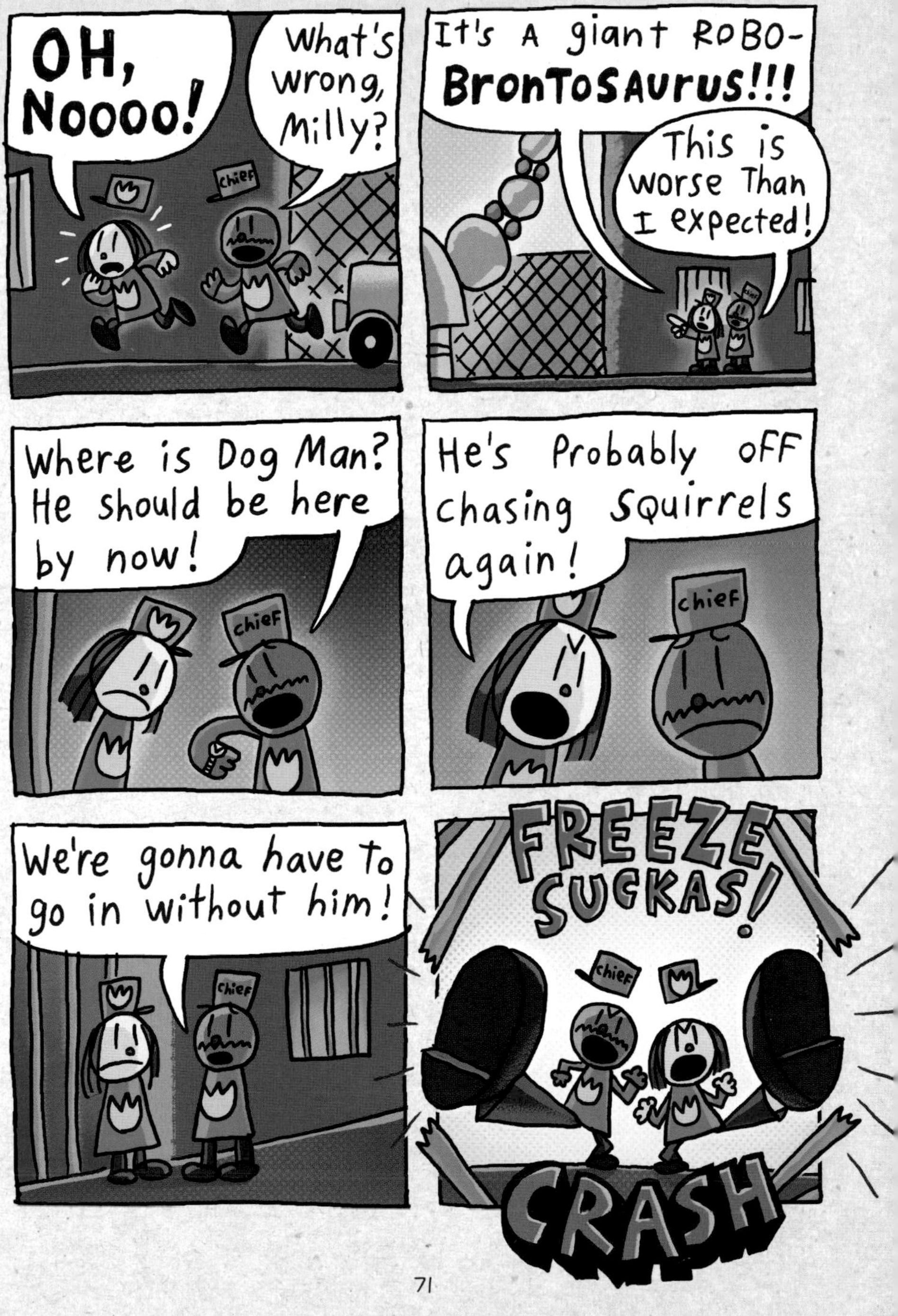
OH, NOOOO!
What's wrong, Milly?
It's A giant ROBO-BRONTOSAURUS!!!
This is worse Than I expected!
Where is Dog Man? He should be here by now!
He's Probably off chasing Squirrels again!
We're gonna have to go in without him!
FREEZE SUCKAS!
CRASH

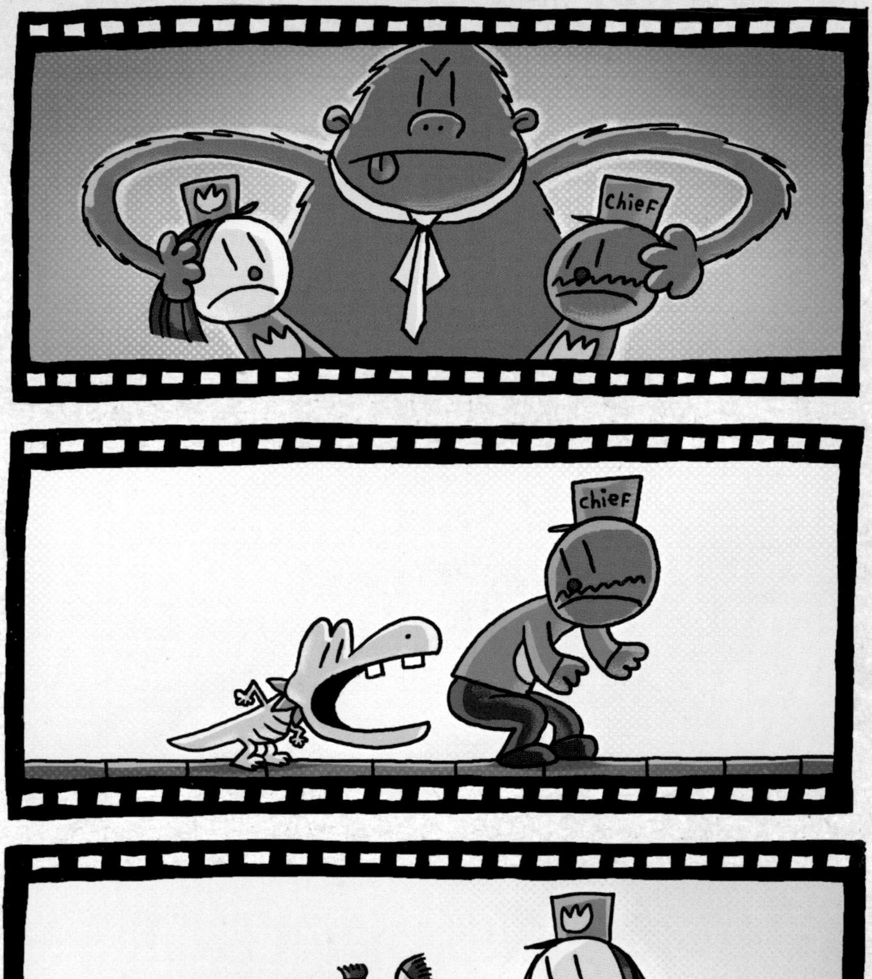
chief
chief

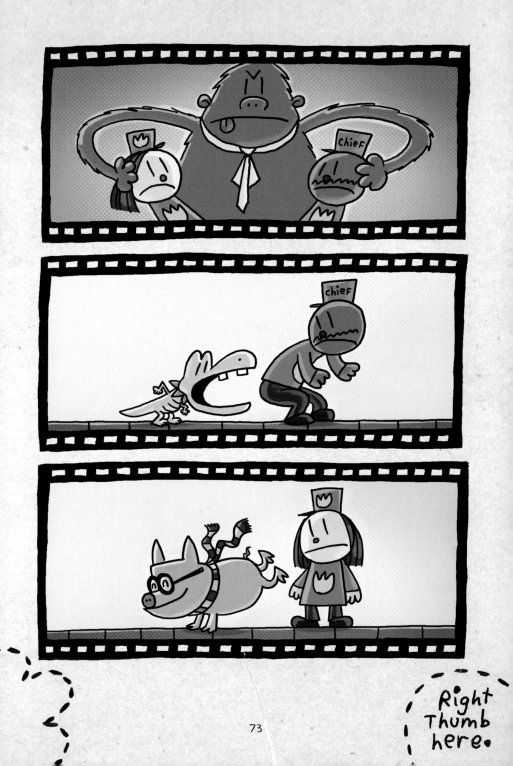

Right Thumb here.

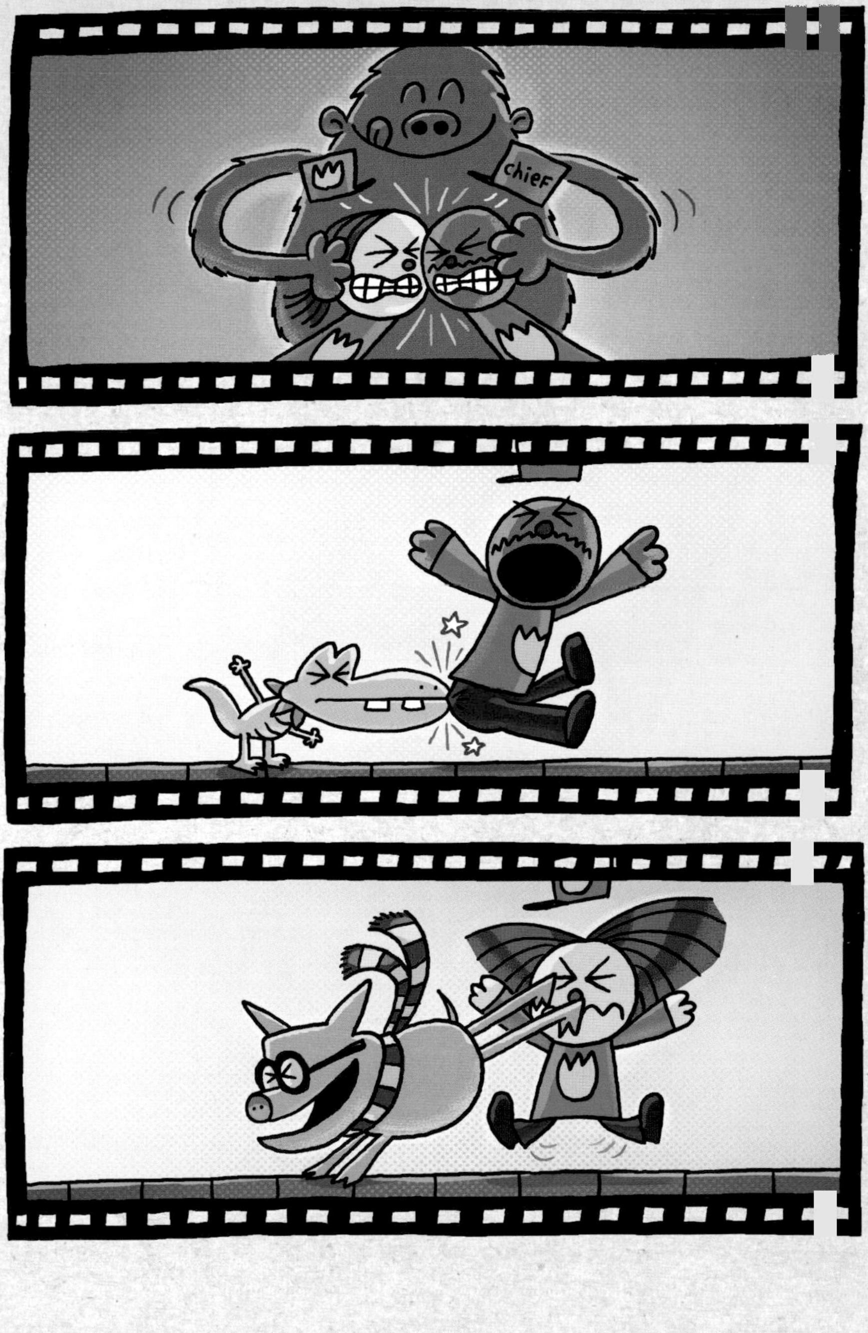
chieF

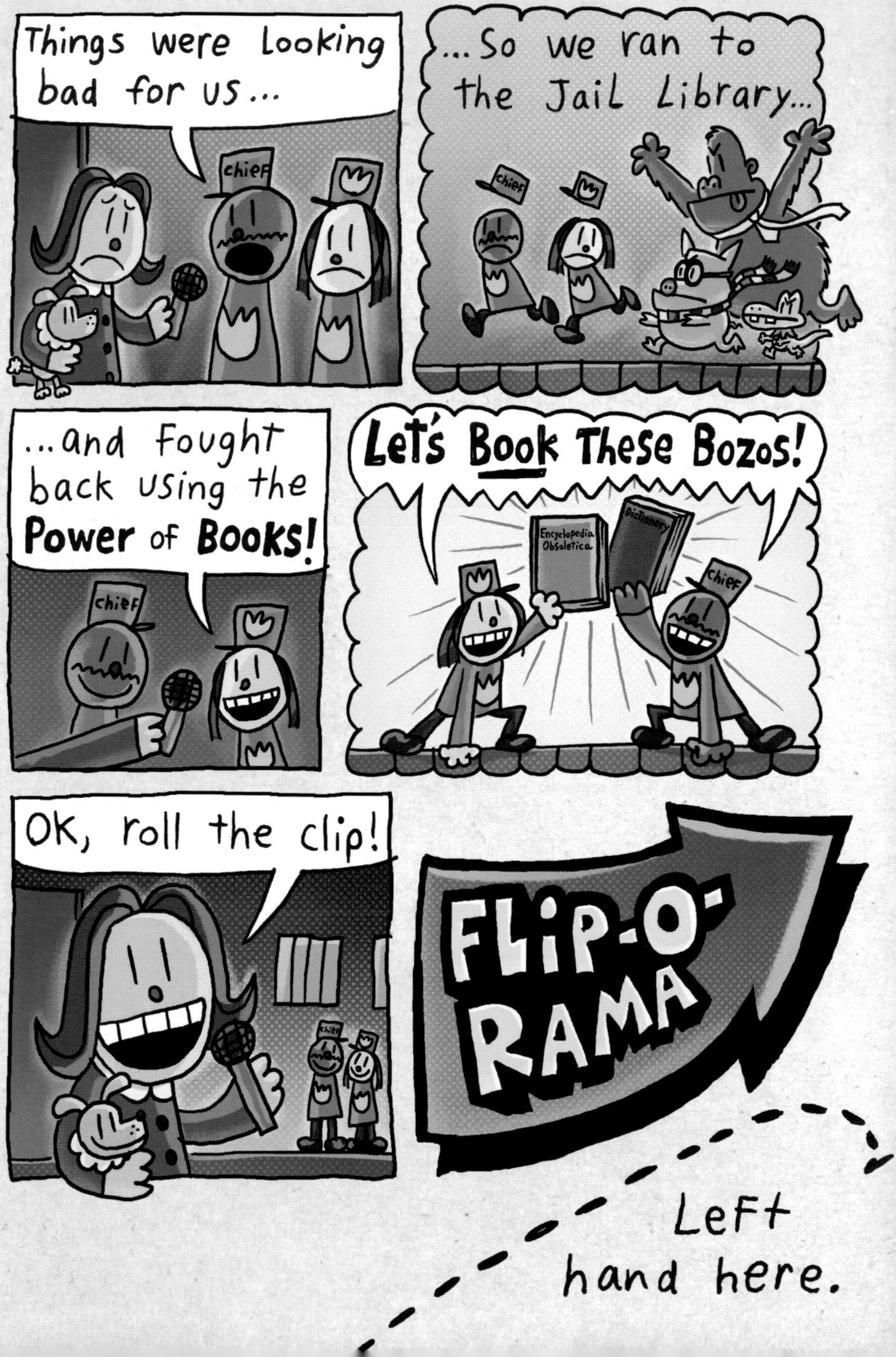

Things were looking bad for us...
...So we ran to the Jail Library...
...and Fought back using the Power of BOOKS!
Let's Book These Bozos!
Encyclopedia Obsoletica
Dictionary
OK, roll the clip!
FLIP-O-RAMA
Left hand here.

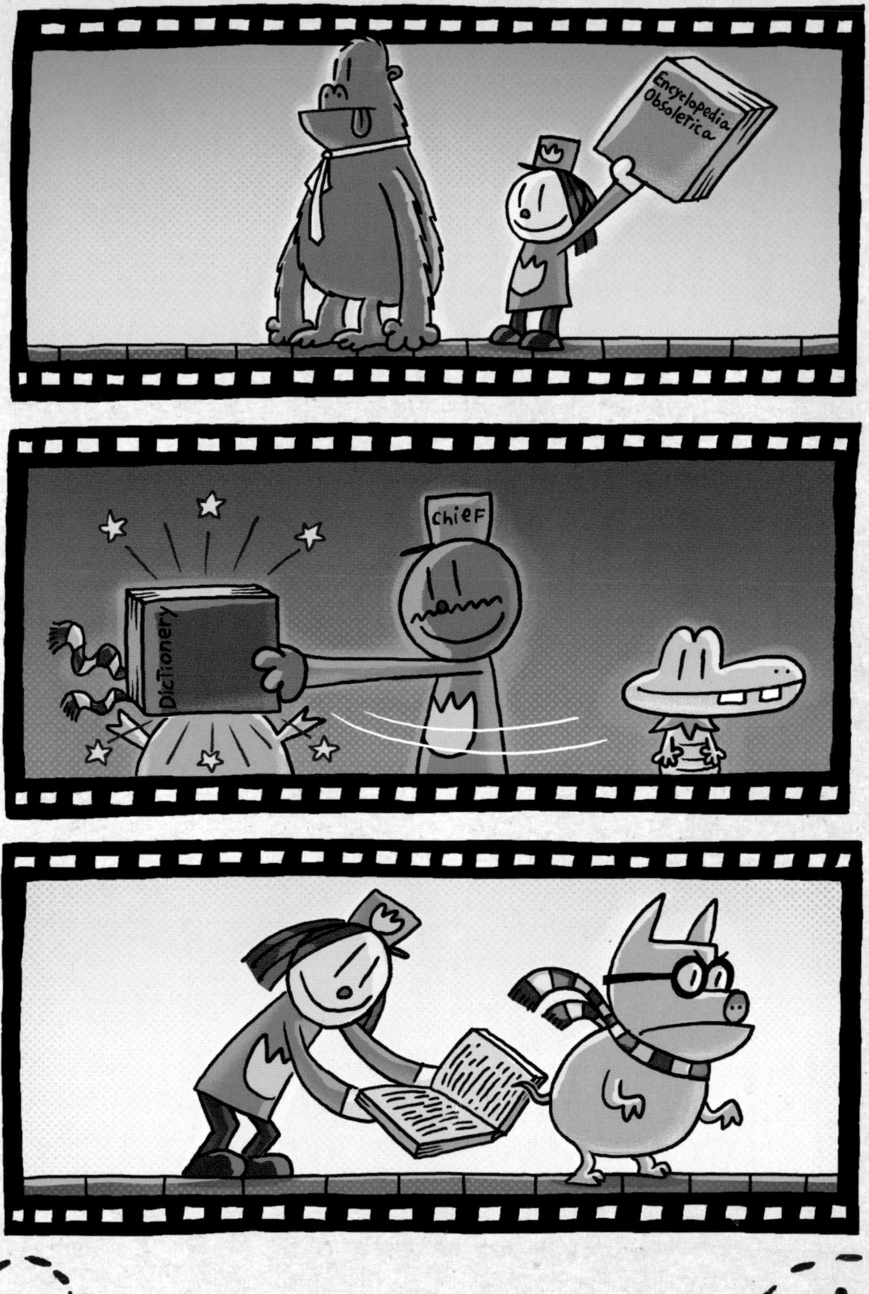
Encyclopedia Obsolerica
Chief
DicTionery

Right Thumb here.

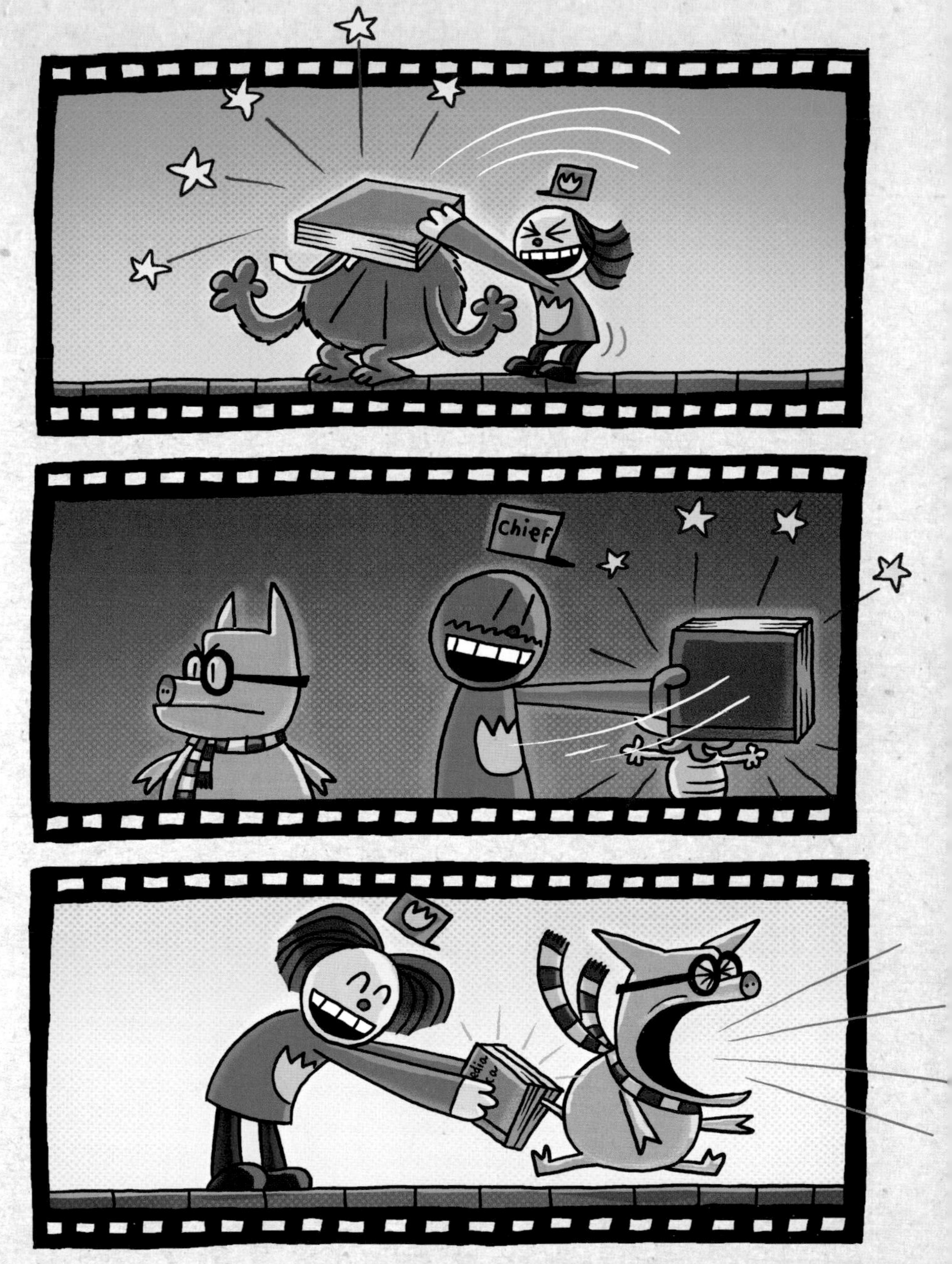
chief

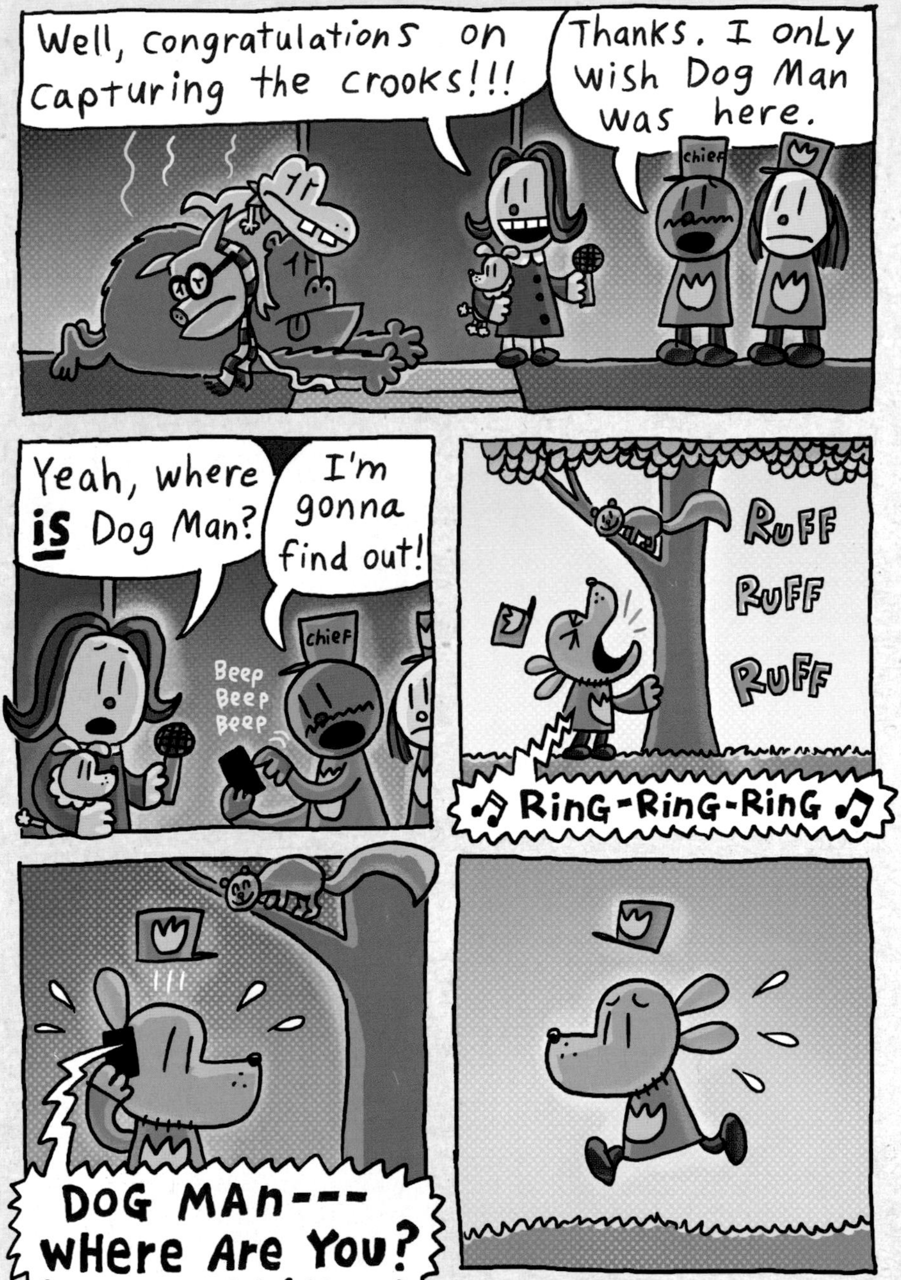
Well, congratulations on capturing the crooks!!!
Thanks. I only wish Dog Man was here.
chief
Yeah, where **is** Dog Man?
I'm gonna find out!
chief
Beep Beep Beep
RUFF
RUFF
RUFF
RING-RING-RING
DOG MAN---
WHERE ARE YOU?

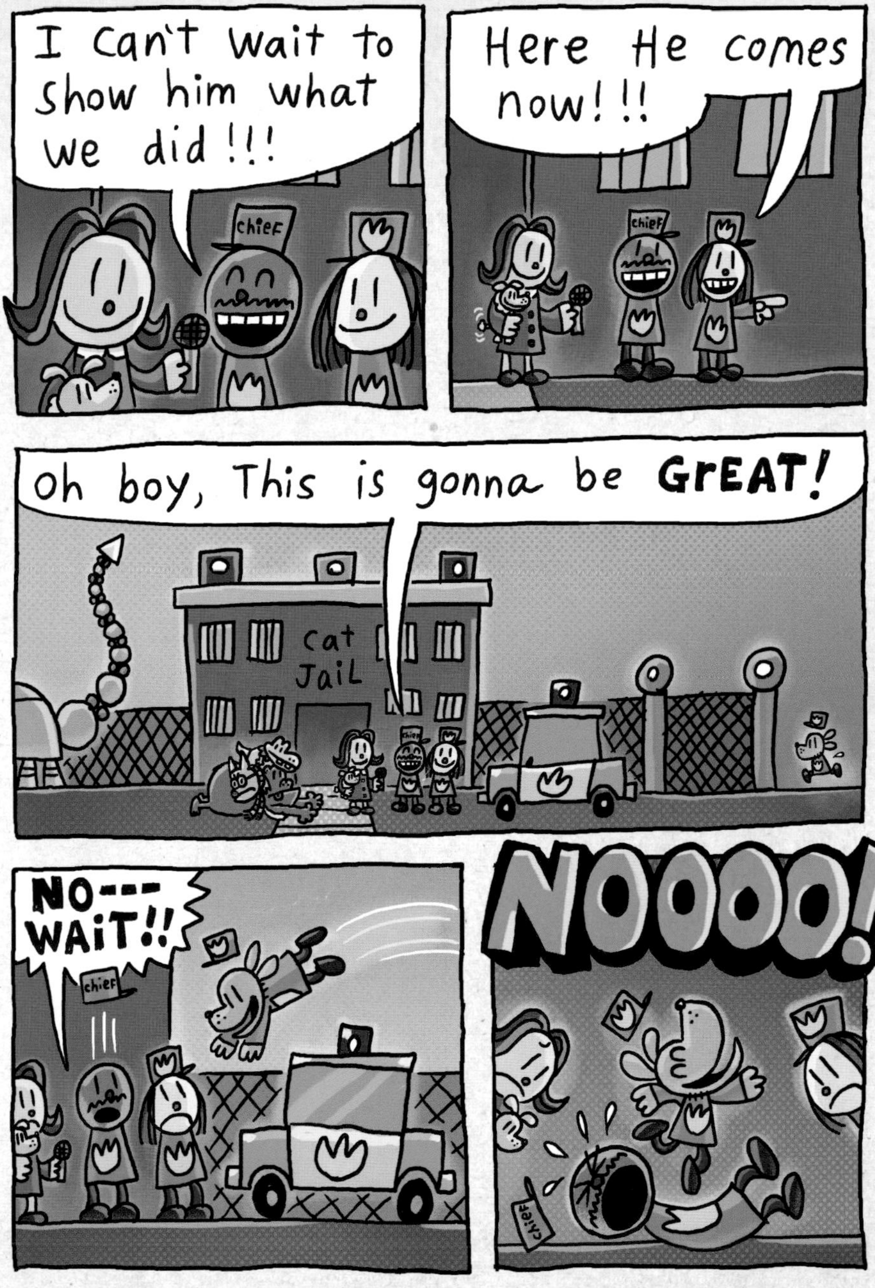
I can't wait to show him what we did!!!
chief
Here He comes now!!!
chief
Oh boy, This is gonna be GREAT!
cat JaiL
chief
NO--- WAIT!!
chief
NOOOO!
chief

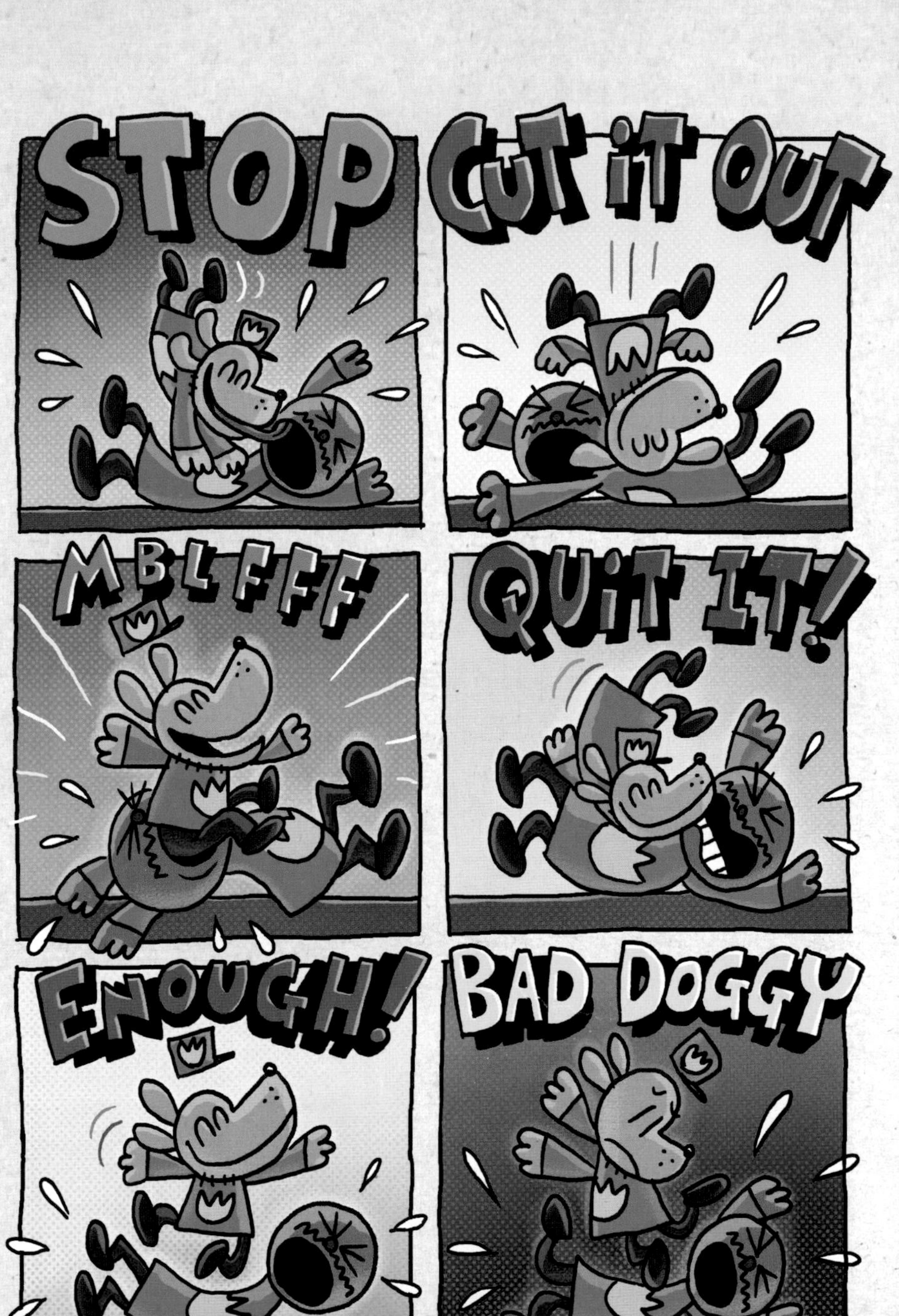
STOP
CUT IT OUT
MBLFFF
QUIT IT!
ENOUGH!
BAD DOGGY

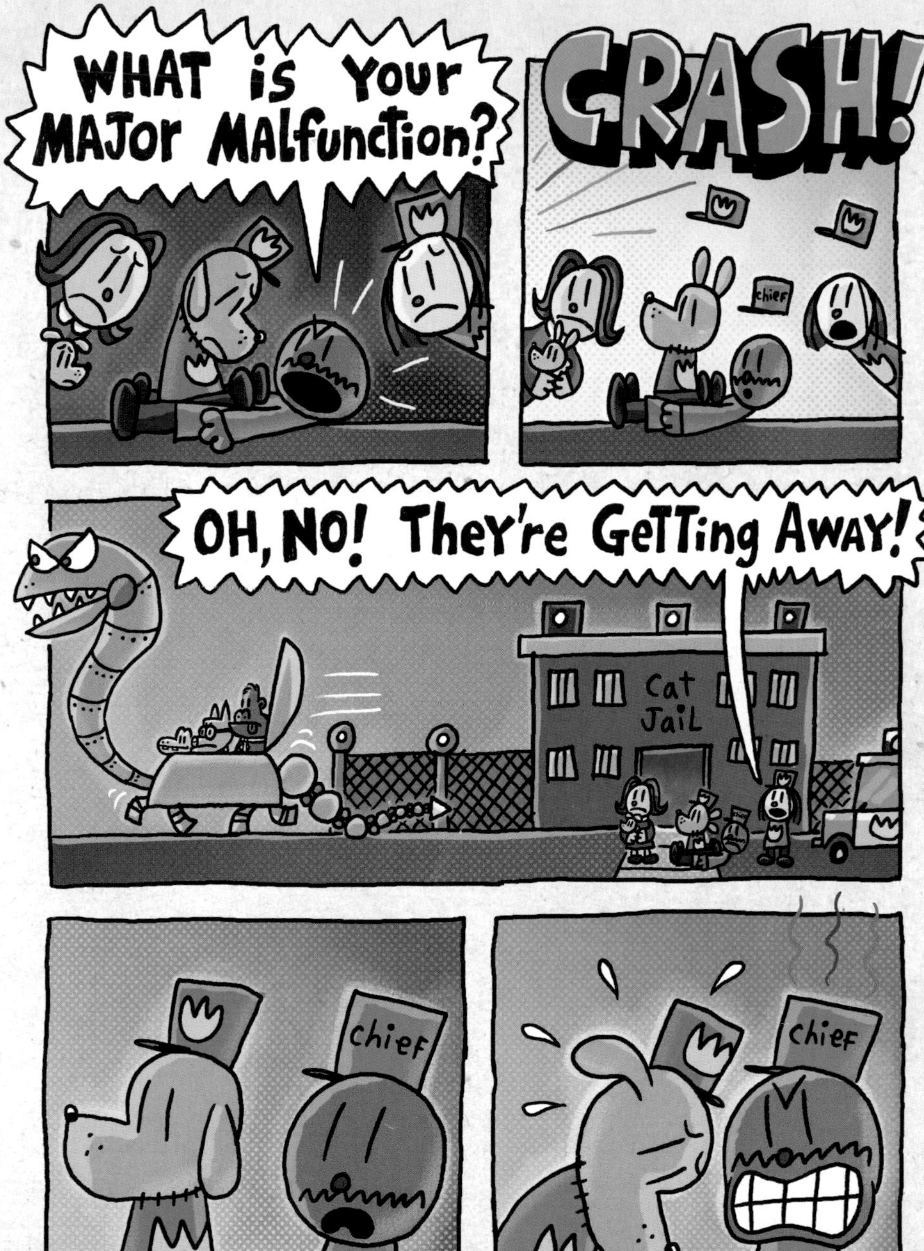
WHAT is Your MAJOr MALfunction?
CRASH!
chief
OH, NO! They're GetTing AWAY!
Cat JaiL
chief
chief

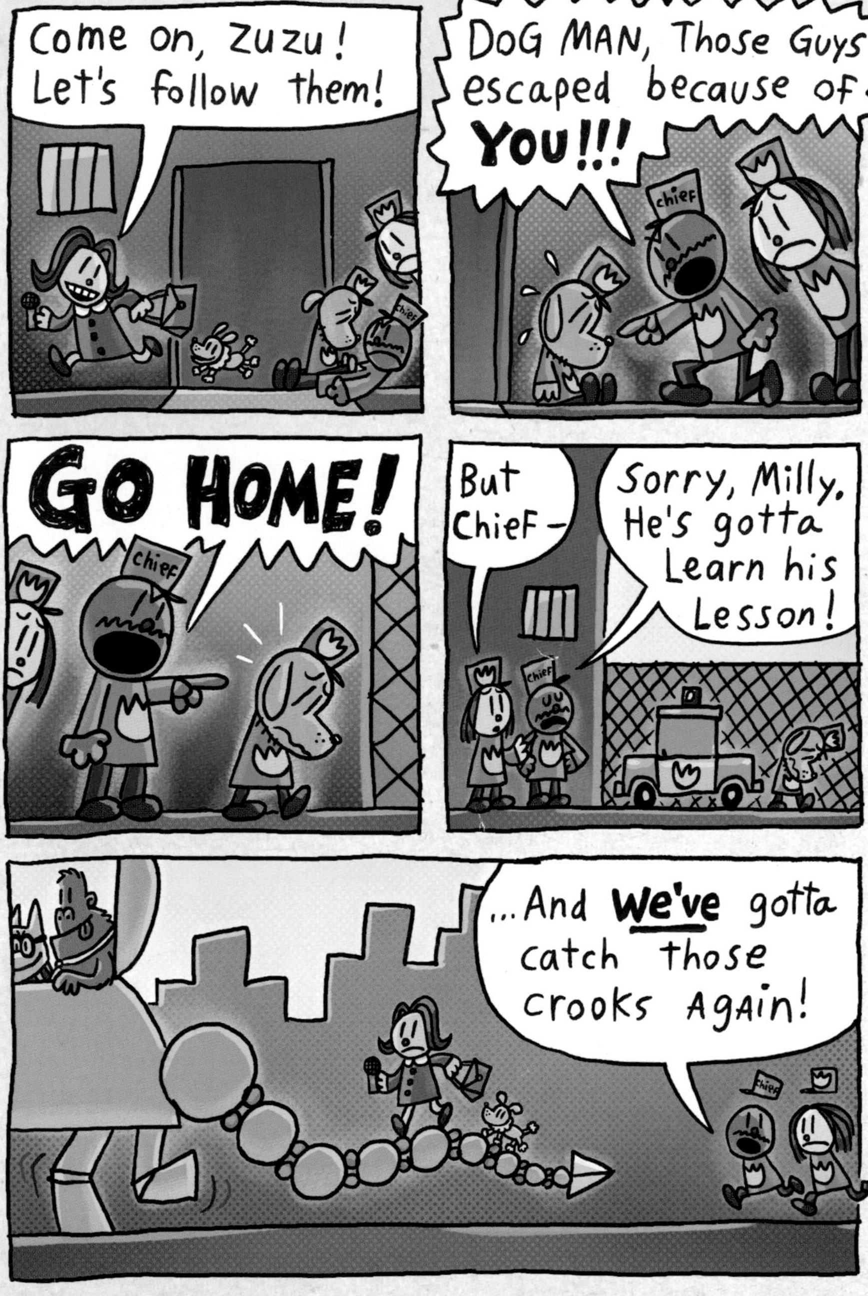
Come on, Zuzu! Let's follow them!
DOG MAN, Those Guys escaped because of YOU!!!
chief
GO HOME!
chief
But Chief—
Sorry, Milly. He's gotta Learn his Lesson!
...And We've gotta catch those crooks Again!

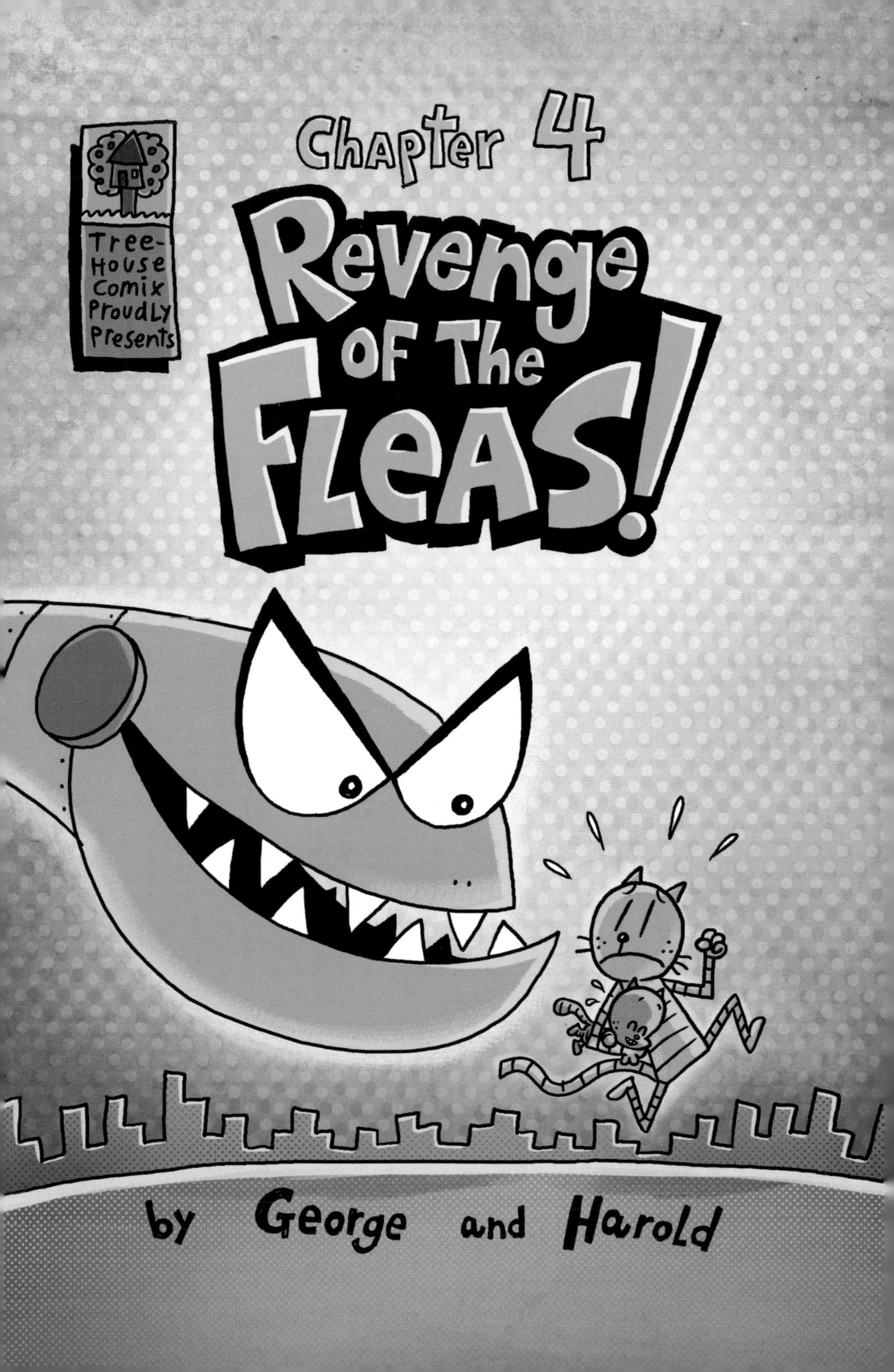
Chapter 4
Tree-House Comix Proudly Presents
Revenge of the Fleas!
by George and Harold

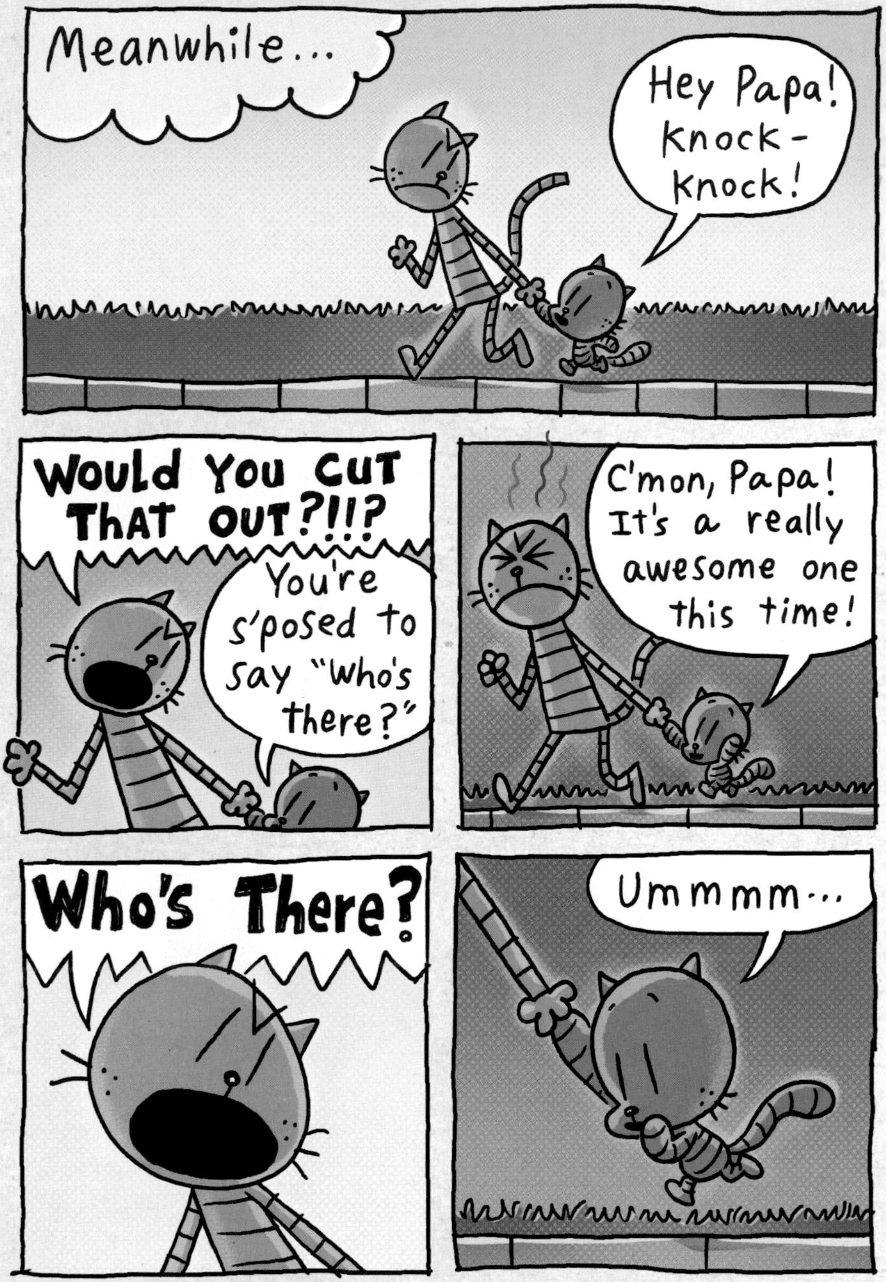
Meanwhile...
Hey Papa! Knock-Knock!
WOULD YOU CUT THAT OUT?!!?
You're s'posed to say "Who's there?"
C'mon, Papa! It's a really awesome one this time!
Who's There?
Ummmm...

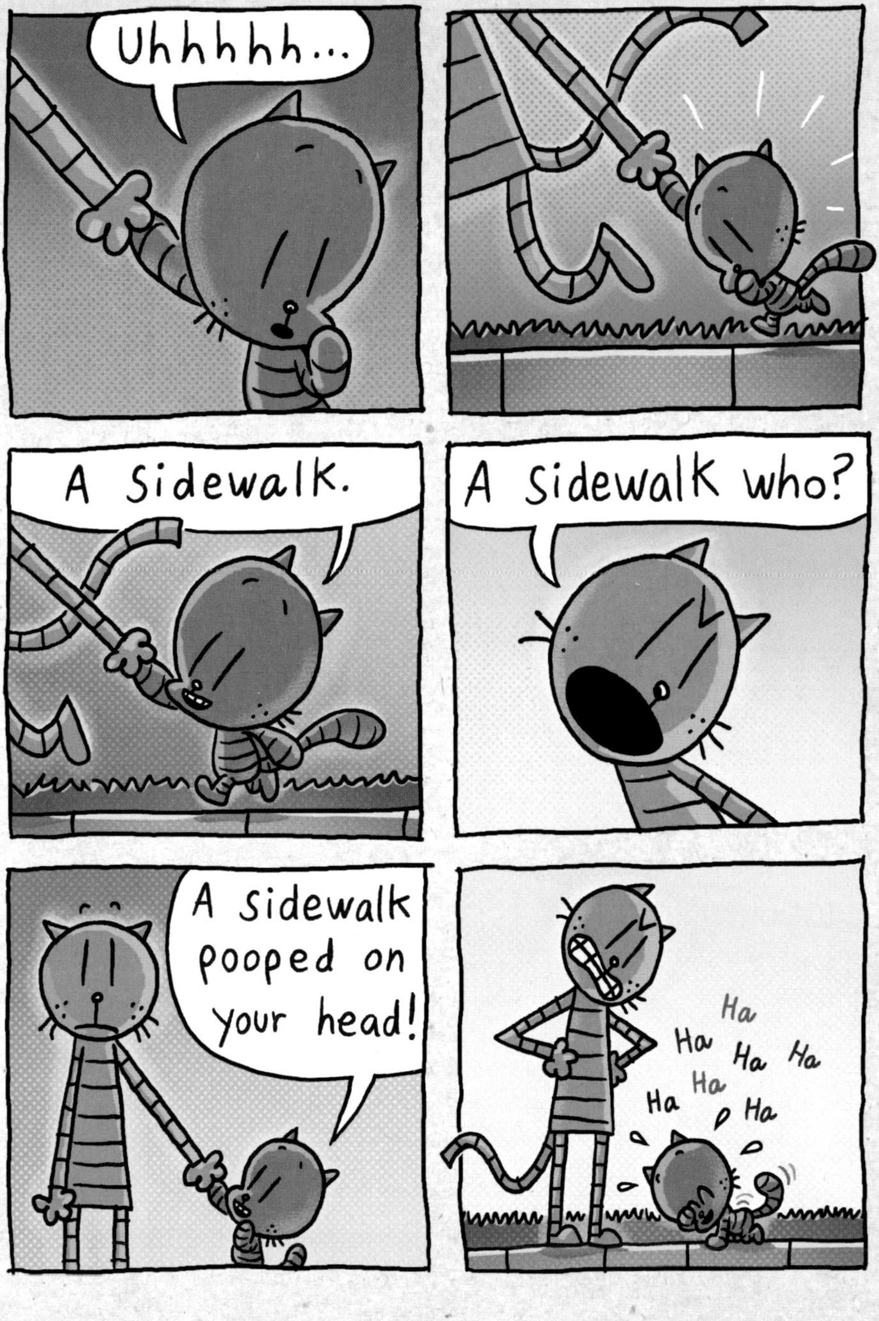
Uhhhhh...
A Sidewalk.
A Sidewalk who?
A Sidewalk pooped on your head!
Ha
Ha Ha Ha
Ha Ha
Ha Ha

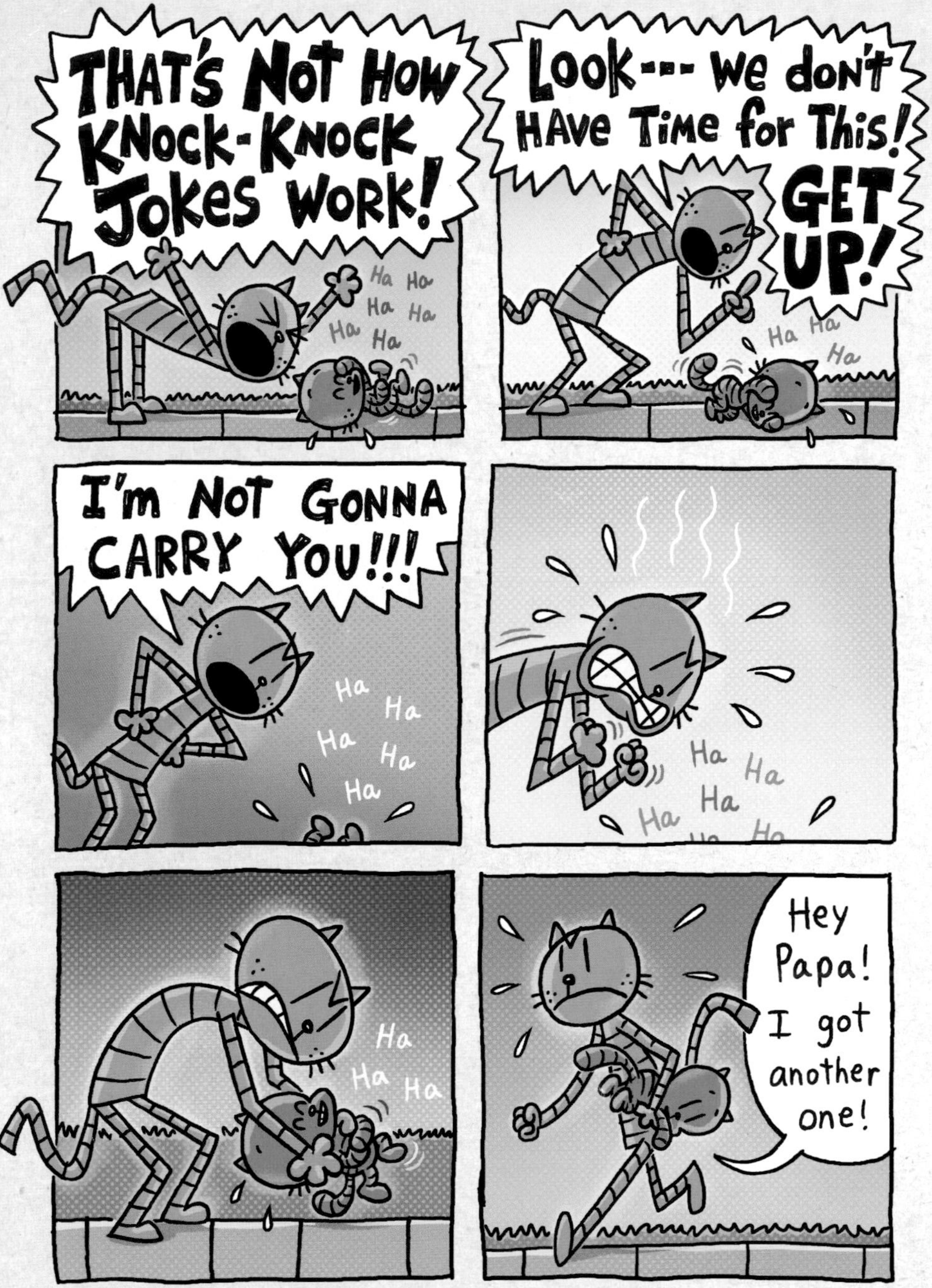
THAT'S NOT HOW KNOCK-KNOCK JOKES WORK!
Ha Ha Ha Ha Ha Ha
LOOK--- WE DON'T HAVE TIME FOR THIS!
GET UP!
Ha Ha Ha
I'M NOT GONNA CARRY YOU!!!
Ha Ha Ha Ha Ha
Ha Ha Ha Ha
Ha Ha Ha
Hey Papa! I got another one!

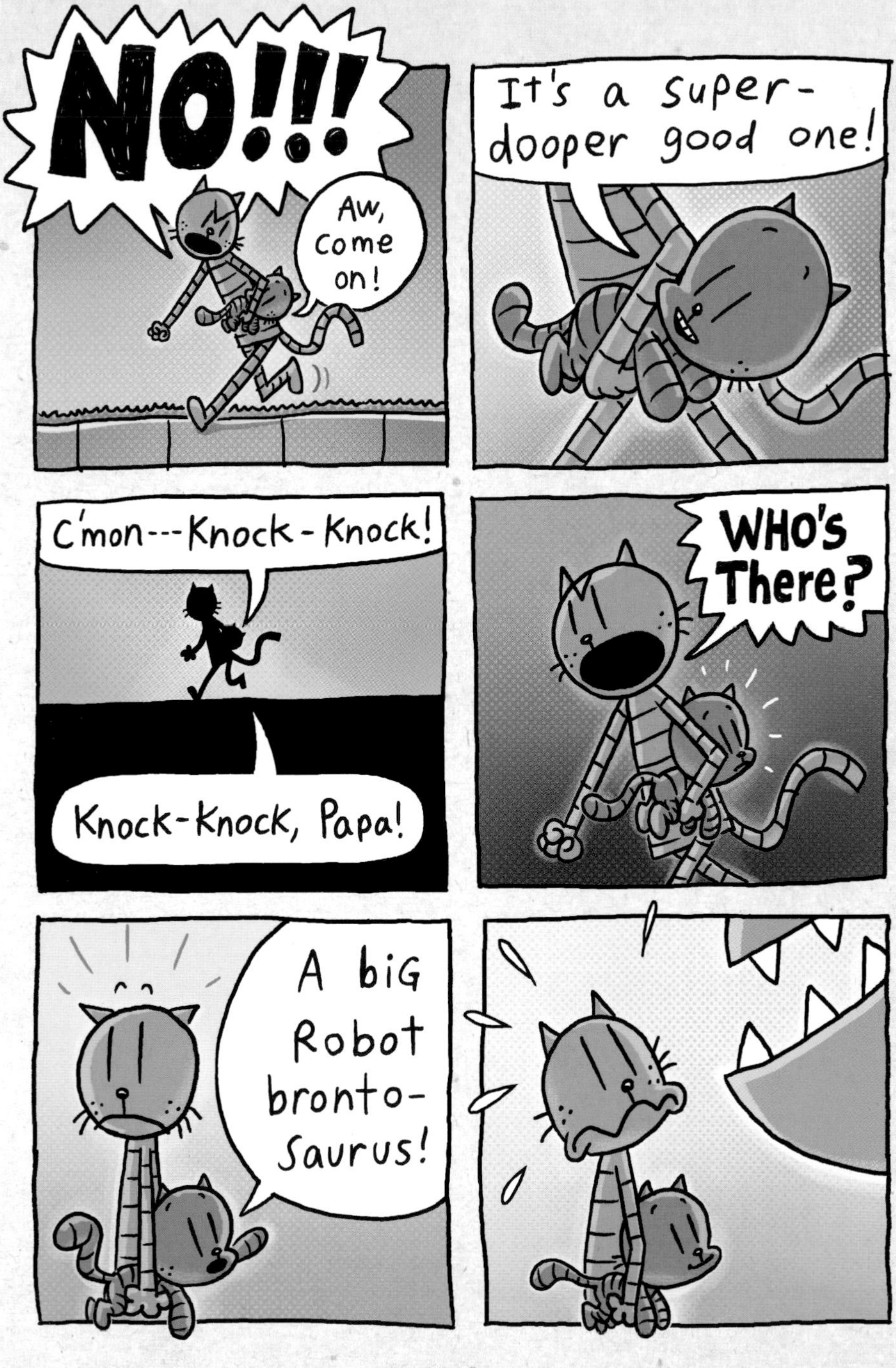
NO!!!
Aw, come on!
It's a super-dooper good one!
C'mon---Knock-Knock!
Knock-Knock, Papa!
WHO'S There?
A biG Robot bronto-Saurus!

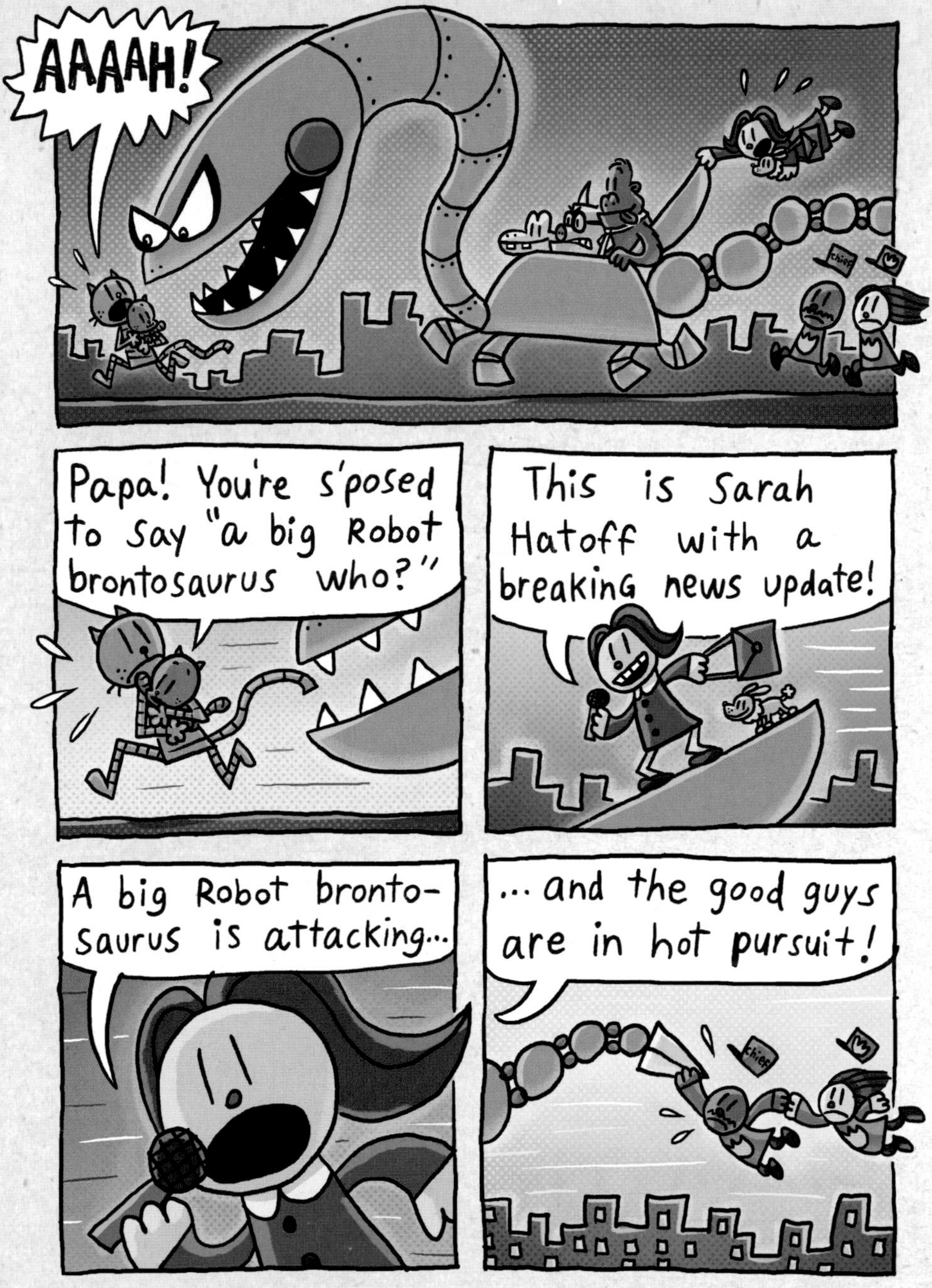
AAAAH!
chief
Papa! You're s'posed to say "a big Robot brontosaurus who?"
This is Sarah Hatoff with a breaking news update!
A big Robot bronto-saurus is attacking...
... and the good guys are in hot pursuit!
chief

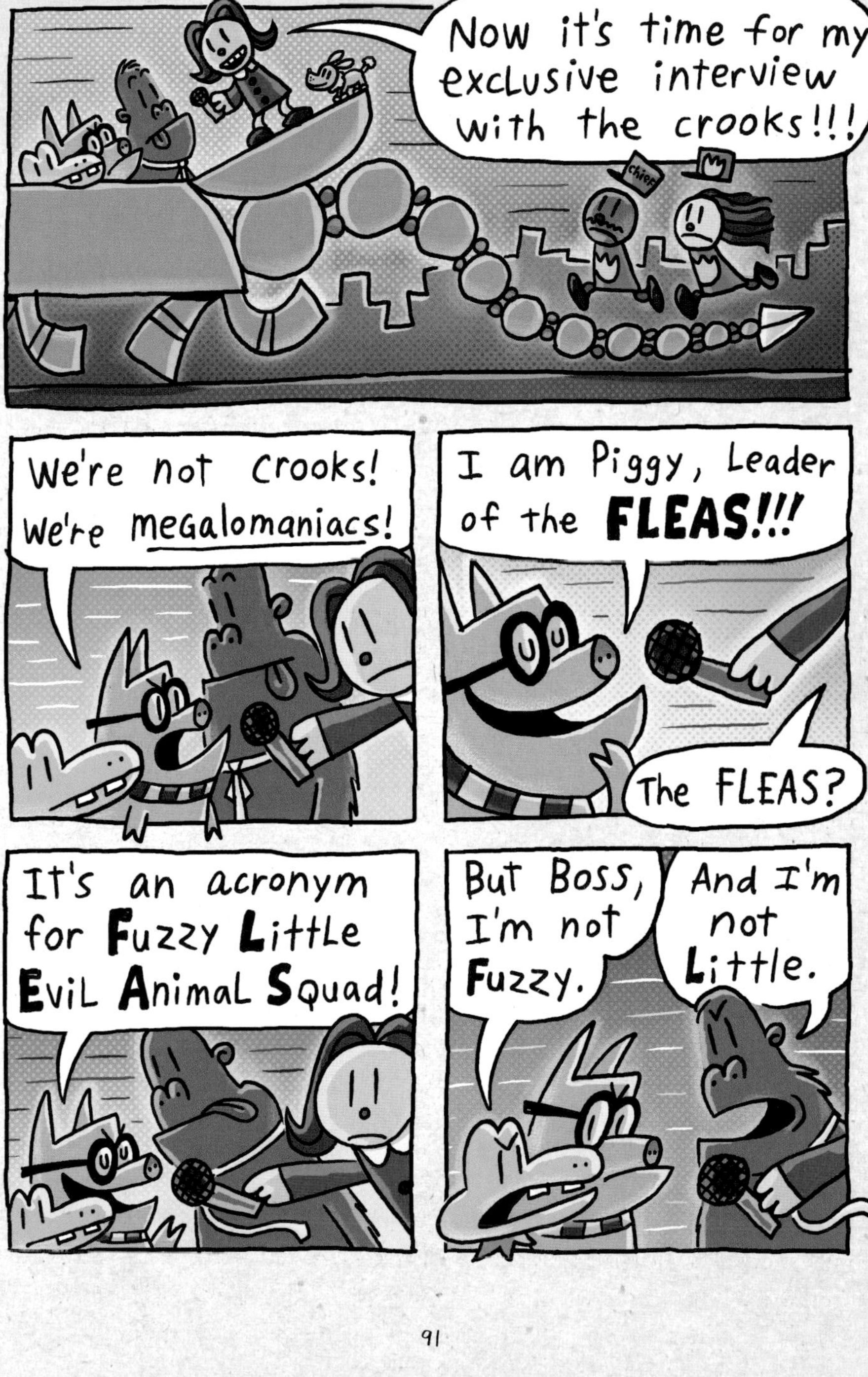

Now it's time for my exclusive interview with the crooks!!!
Chief
We're not crooks! We're megalomaniacs!
I am Piggy, Leader of the FLEAS!!!
The FLEAS?
It's an acronym for Fuzzy Little Evil Animal Squad!
But Boss, I'm not Fuzzy.
And I'm not Little.

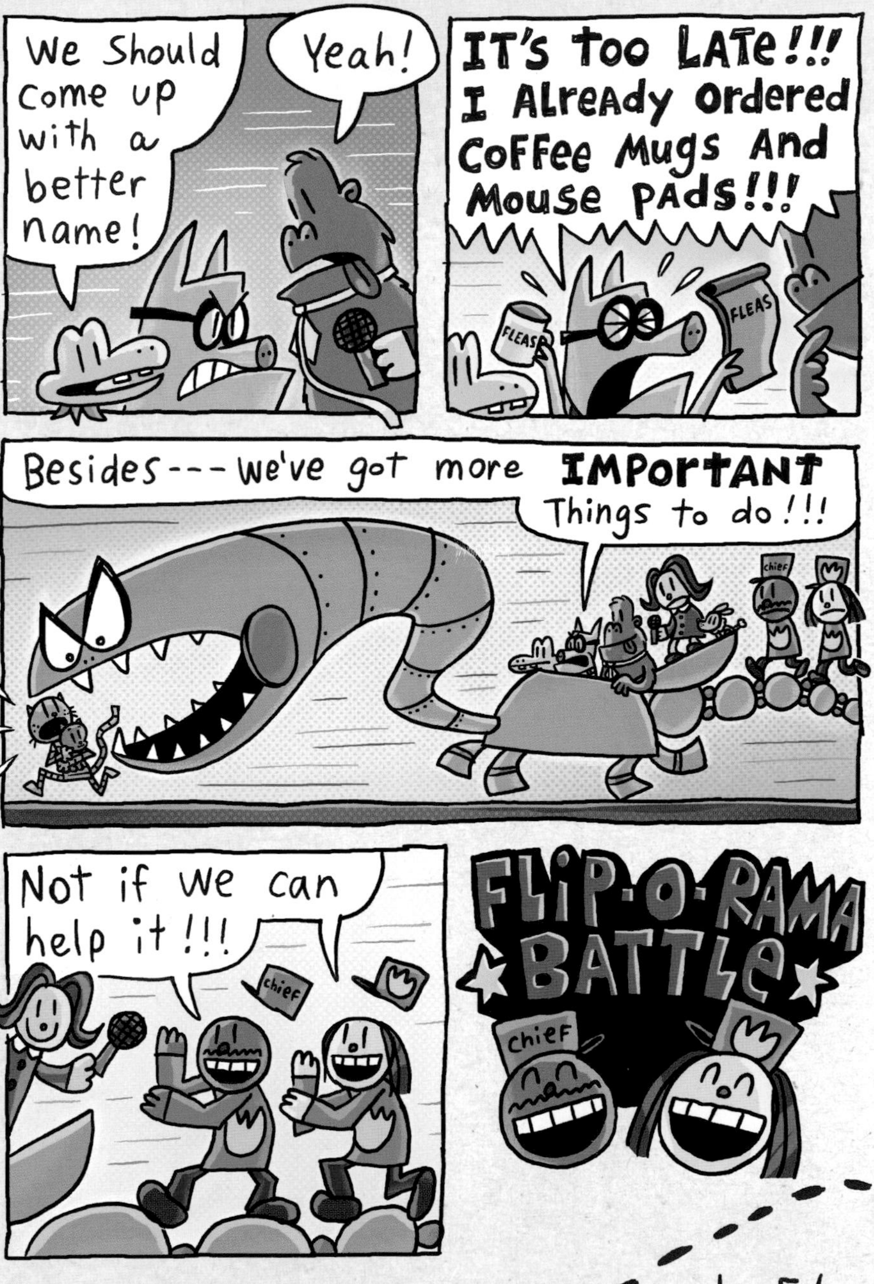
We Should come up with a better name!
Yeah!
IT'S TOO LATE!!! I ALREADY ORDERED COFFEE MUGS AND MOUSE PADS!!!
FLEAS
FLEAS
Besides---we've got more IMPORTANT Things to do!!!
chief
Not if we can help it!!!
chief
FLIP-O-RAMA BATTLE
chief

Left hand here.

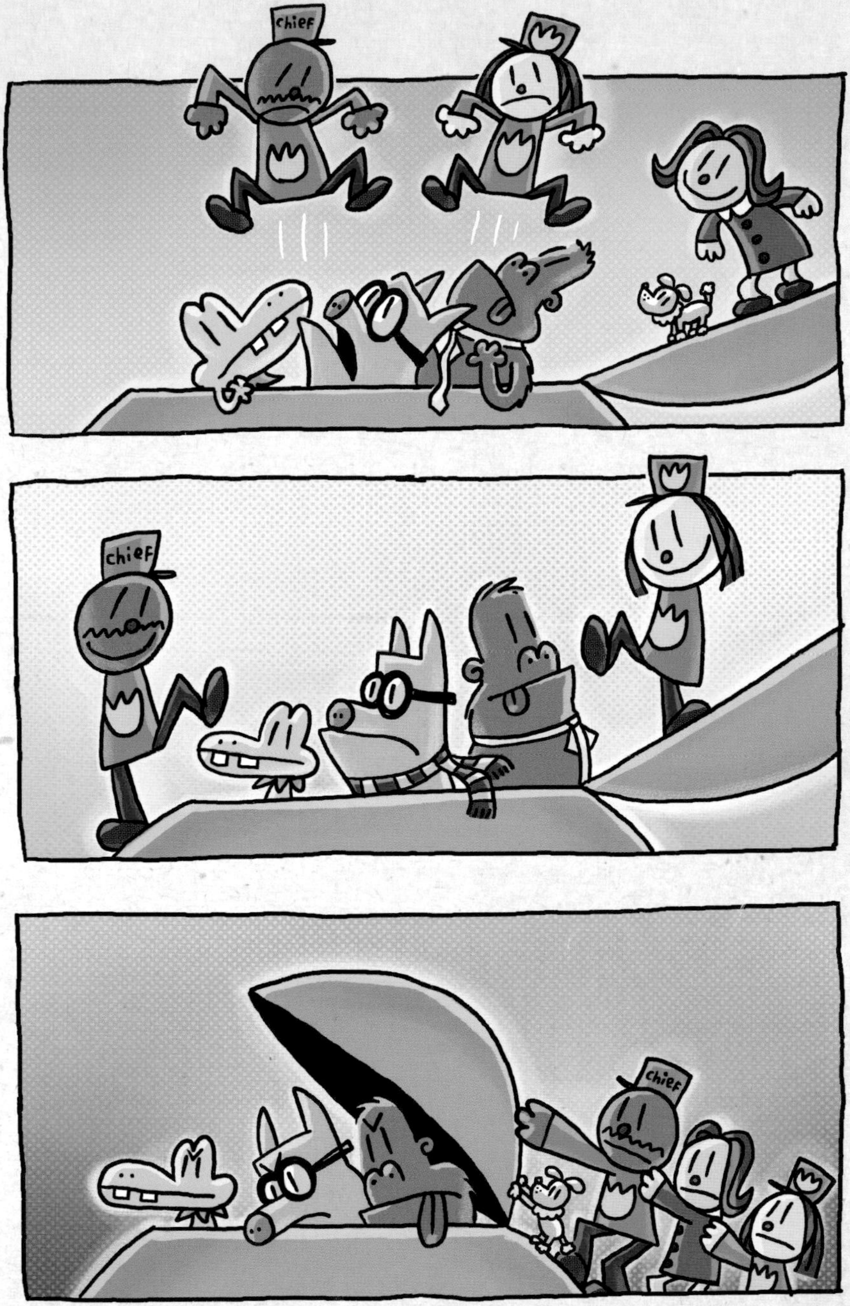
chief
chief
chief

Right
Thumb
here.

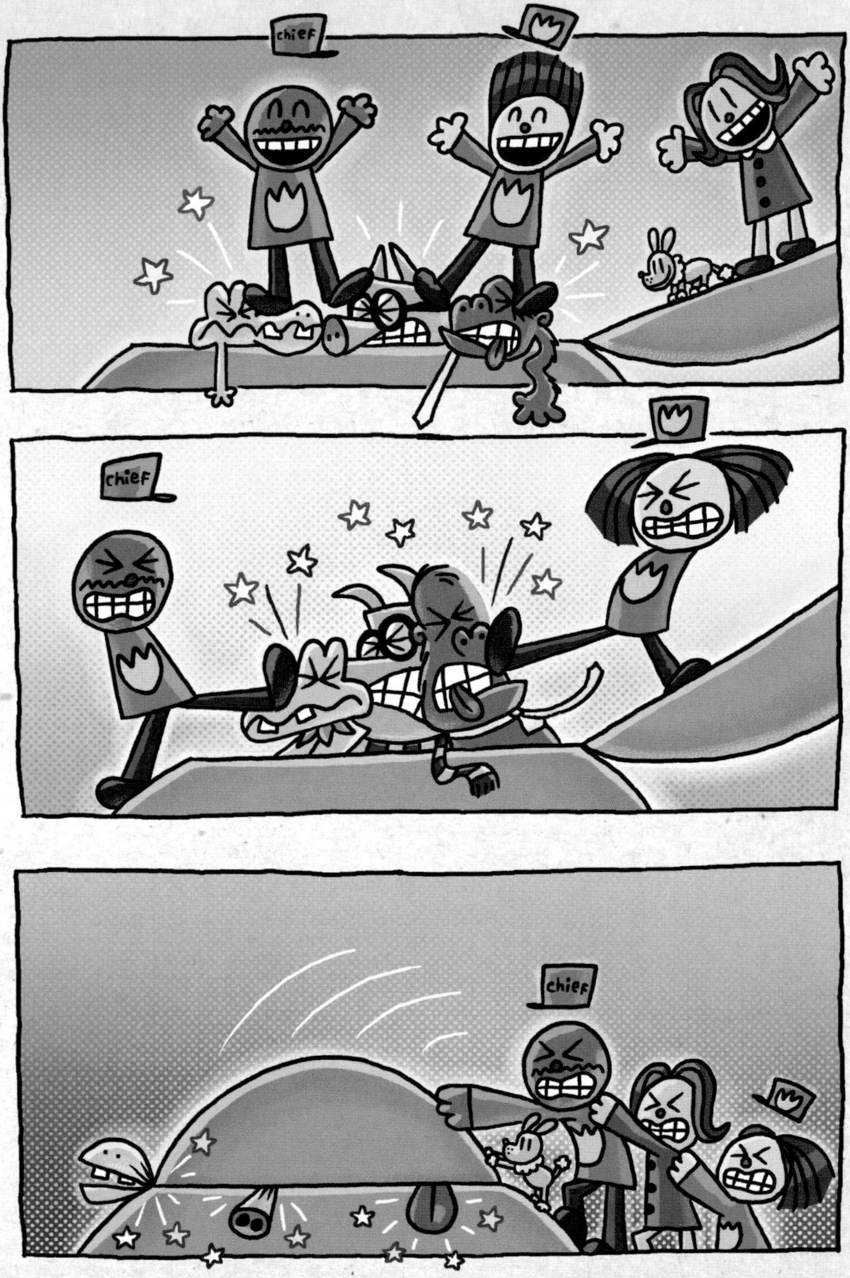
chief
chief
chief

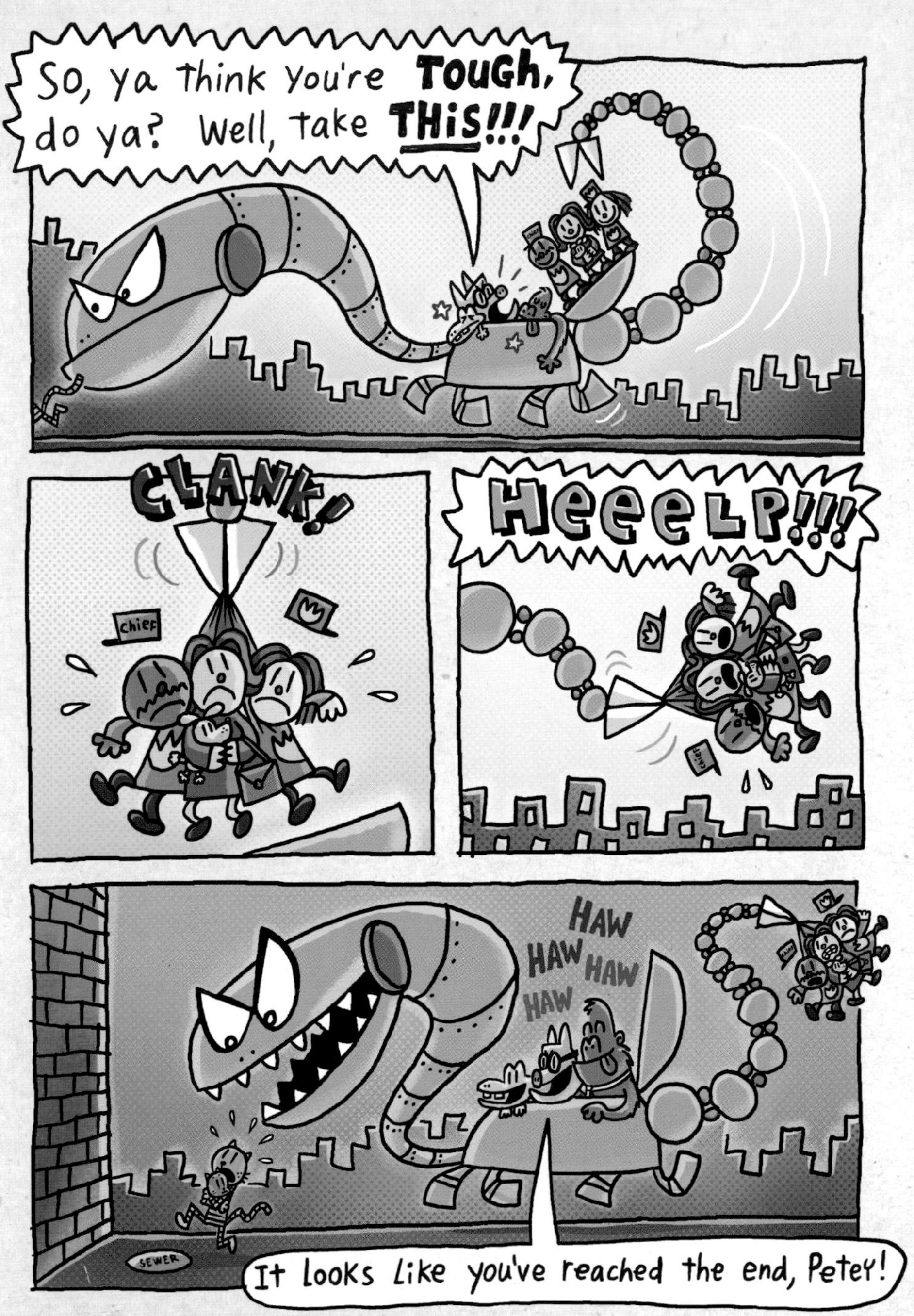
So, ya think you're TOUGH, do ya? Well, take THIS!!!
CLANK!
HEEELP!!!
chief
HAW HAW HAW HAW
SEWER
It looks like you've reached the end, Petey!

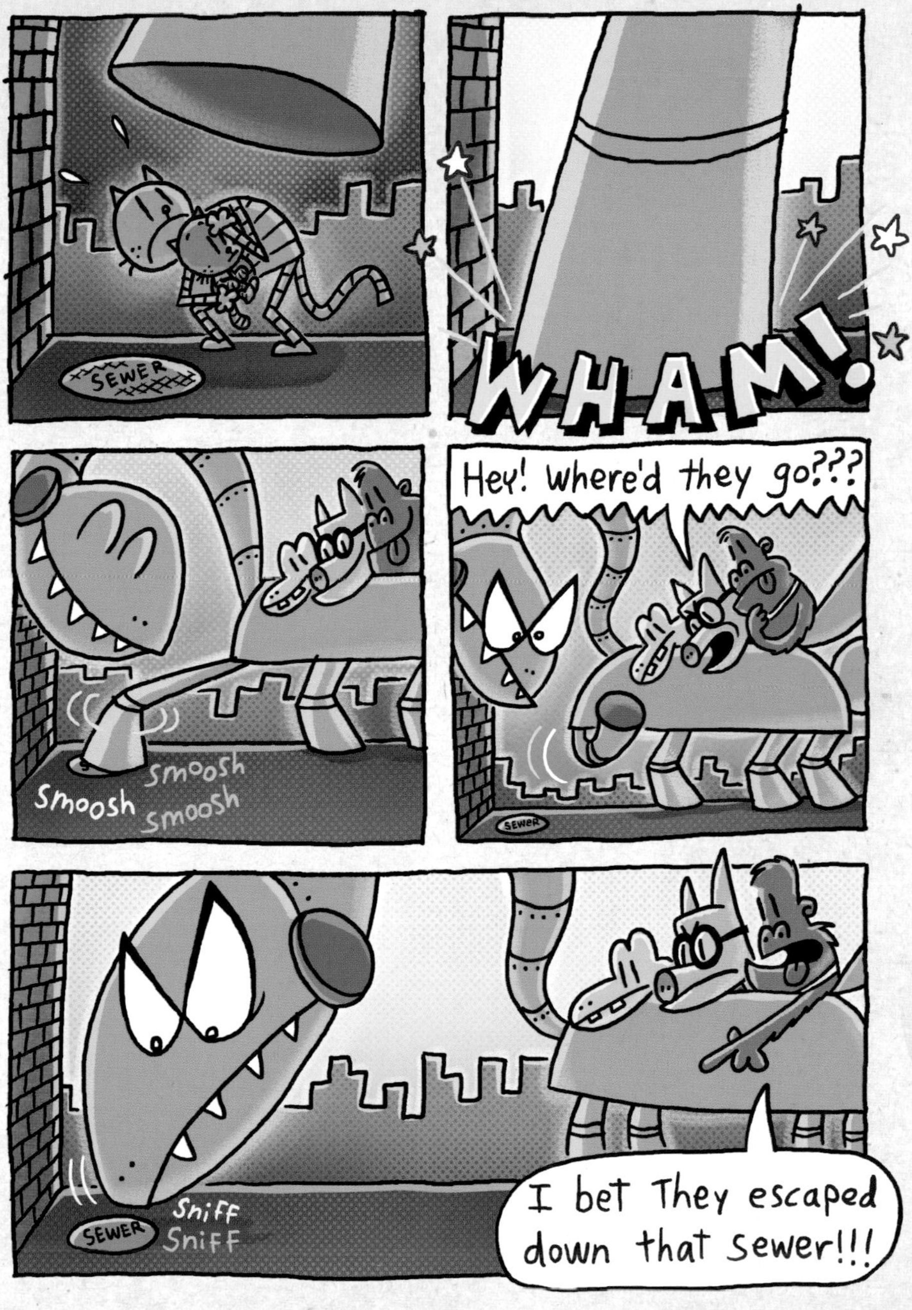
SEWER
WHAM!
Smoosh
smoosh
smoosh
Hey! where'd they go???
SEWER
SEWER
Sniff
Sniff
I bet They escaped down that sewer!!!

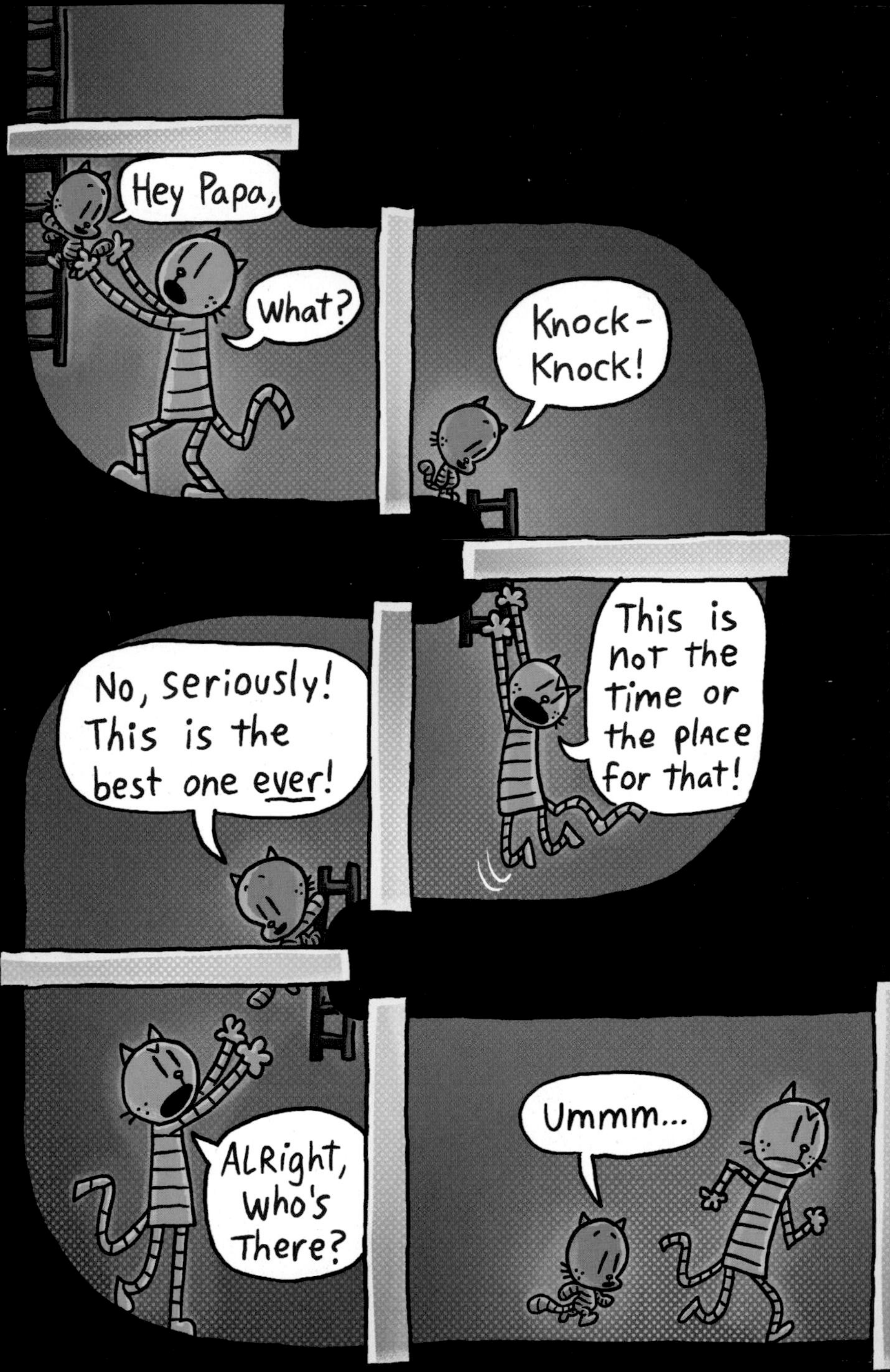
Hey Papa,
What?
Knock-Knock!
This is not the time or the place for that!
No, seriously! This is the best one ever!
ALRight, Who's There?
Ummm...

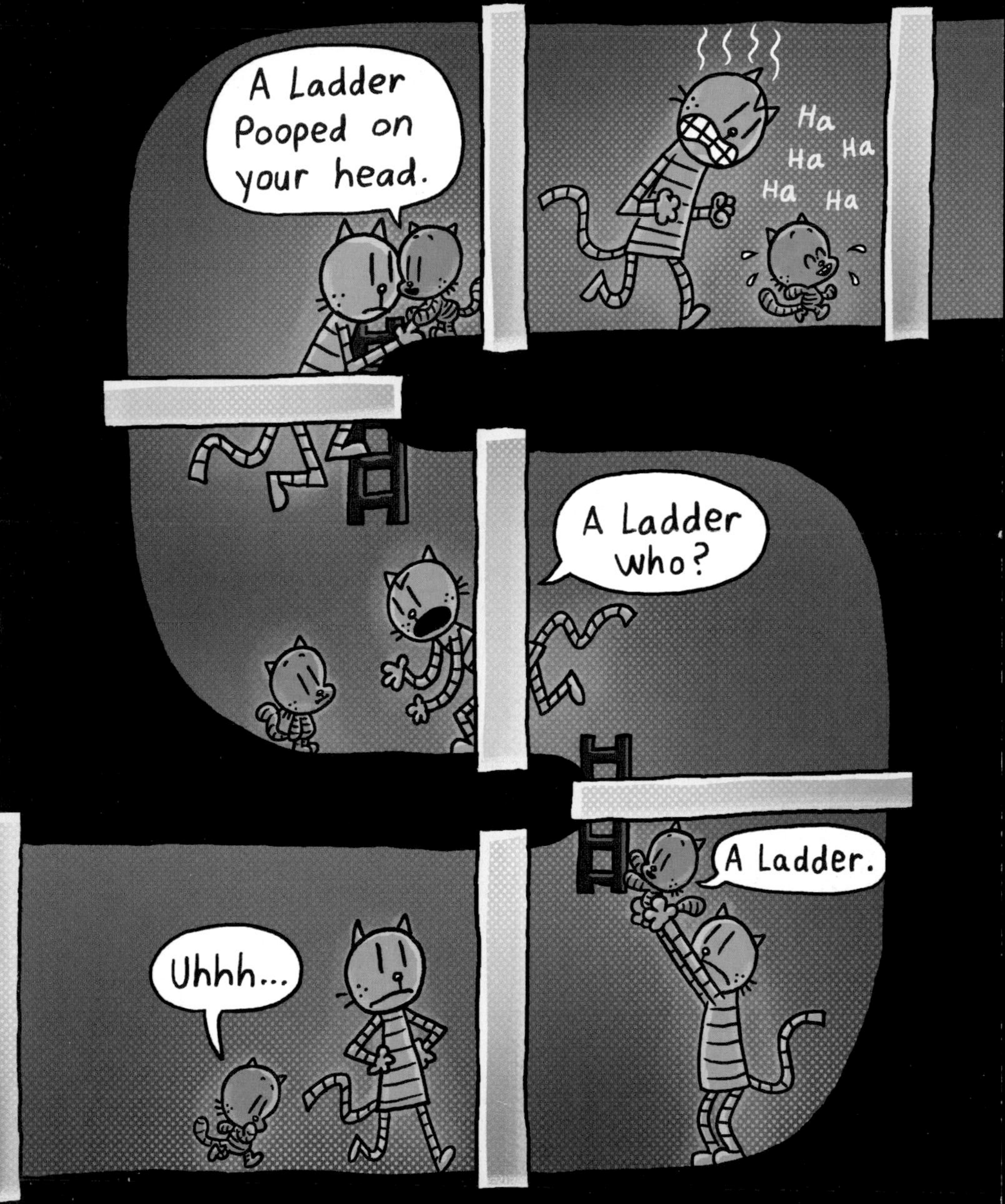
A Ladder Pooped on your head.
Ha Ha Ha Ha Ha
A Ladder who?
A Ladder.
Uhhh...

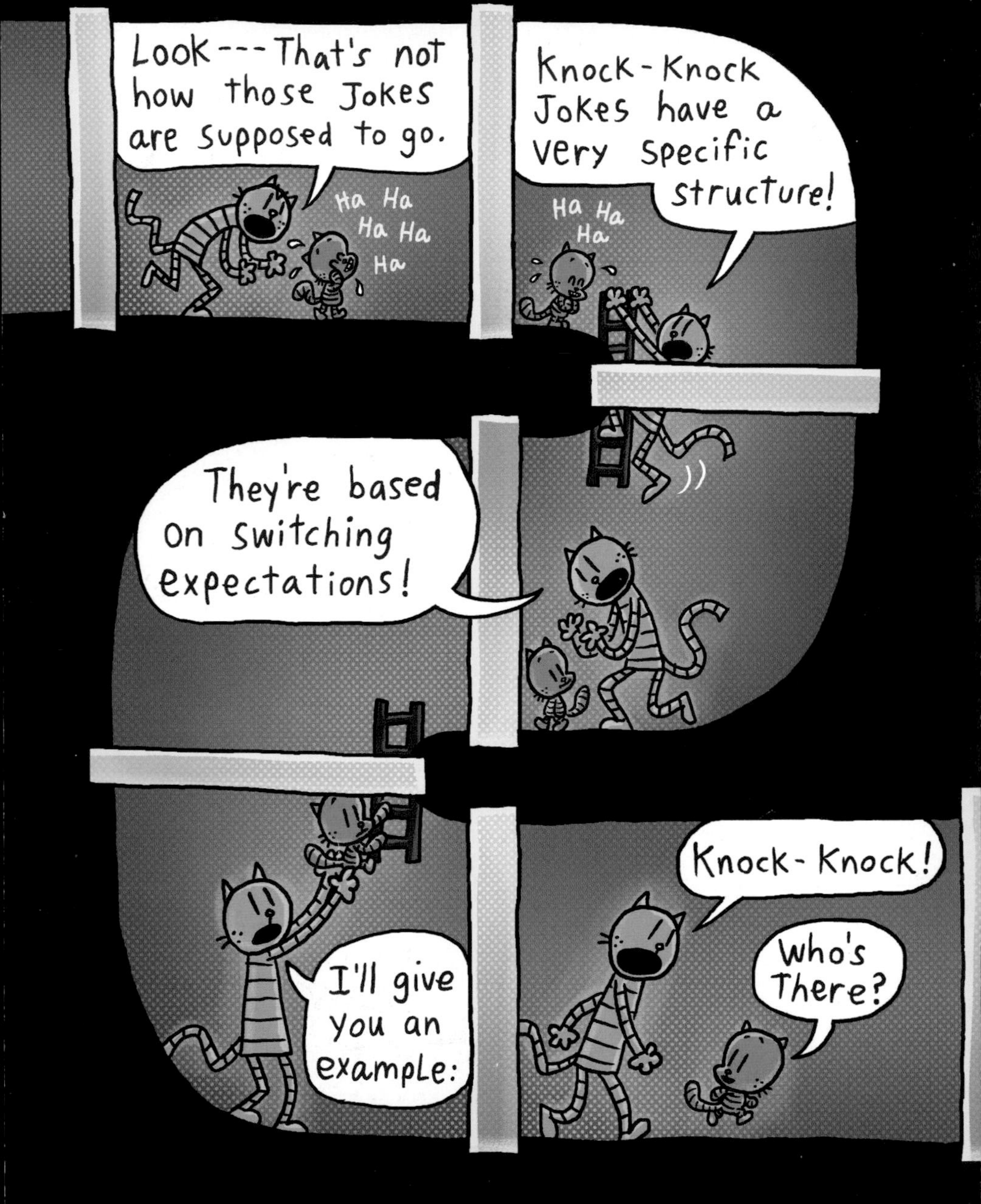
Look---That's not how those Jokes are supposed to go.
Ha Ha Ha Ha Ha
Knock-Knock Jokes have a very specific structure!
Ha Ha Ha
They're based on switching expectations!
I'll give you an example:
Knock-Knock!
Who's There?

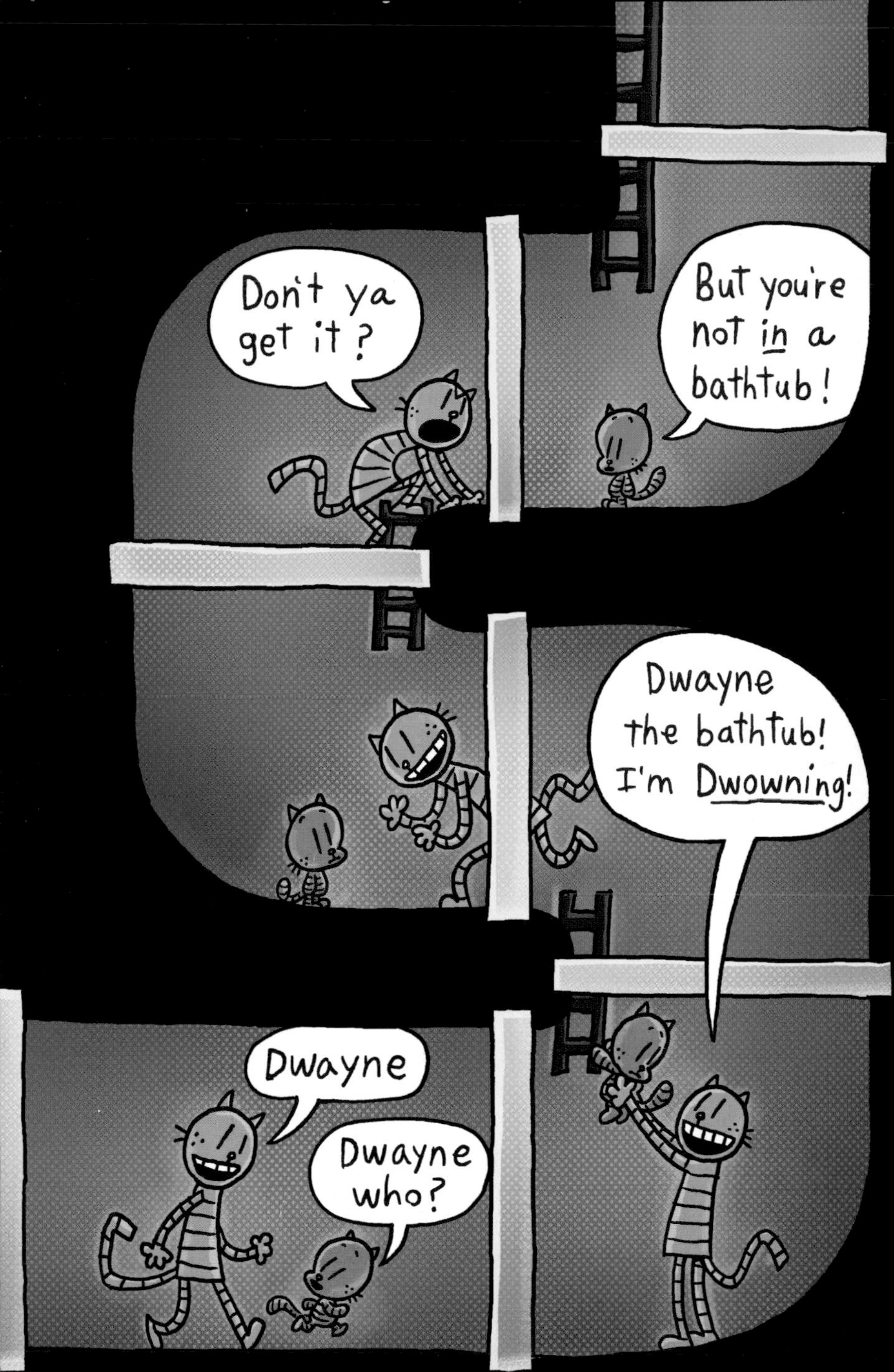

Don't ya get it?
But you're not in a bathtub!
Dwayne the bathtub! I'm Dwowning!
Dwayne
Dwayne who?

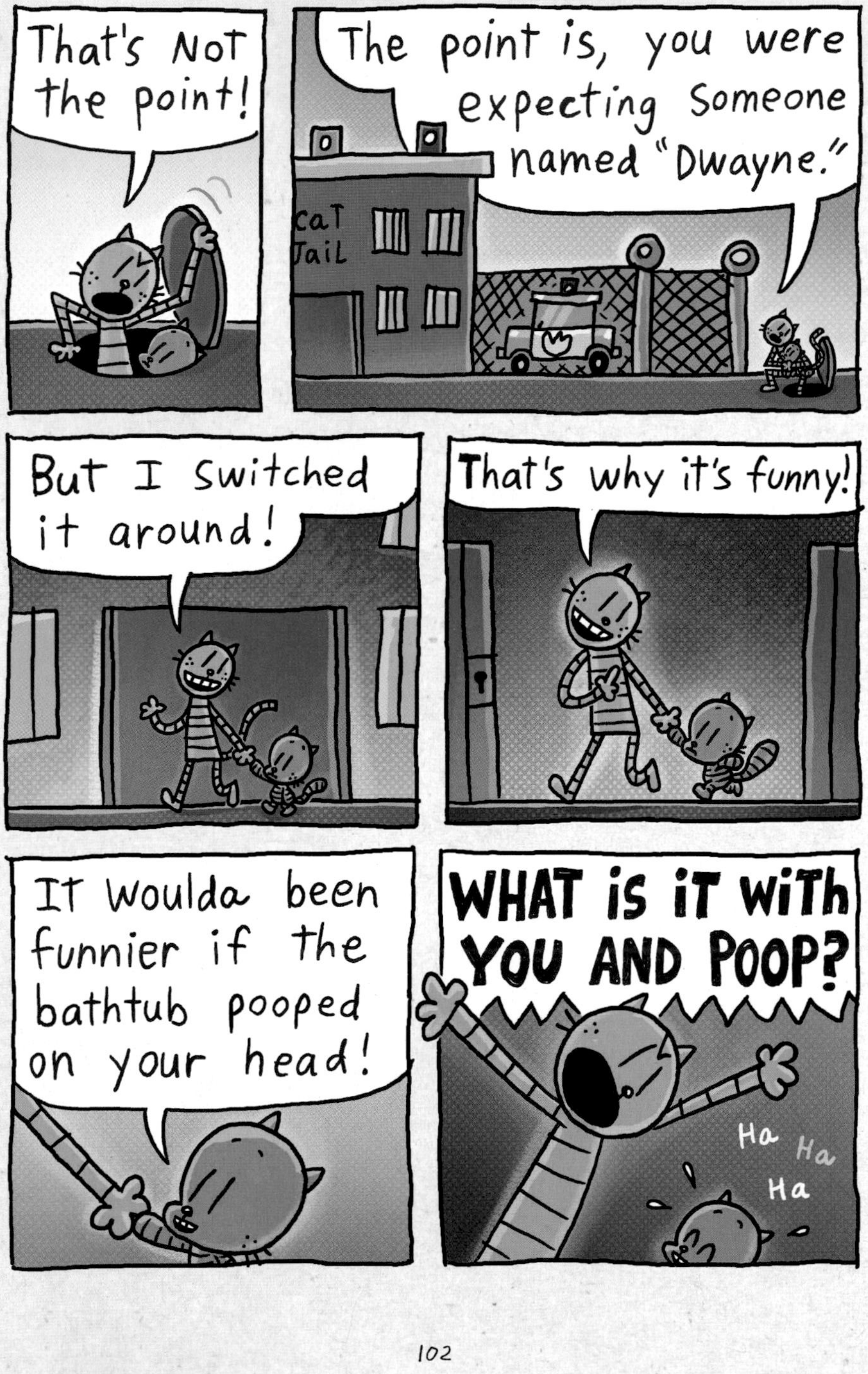
That's NOT the point!
The point is, you were expecting Someone named "Dwayne."
CaT JaiL
But I switched it around!
That's why it's funny!
IT woulda been funnier if the bathtub pooped on your head!
WHAT IS IT WITH YOU AND POOP?
Ha Ha Ha

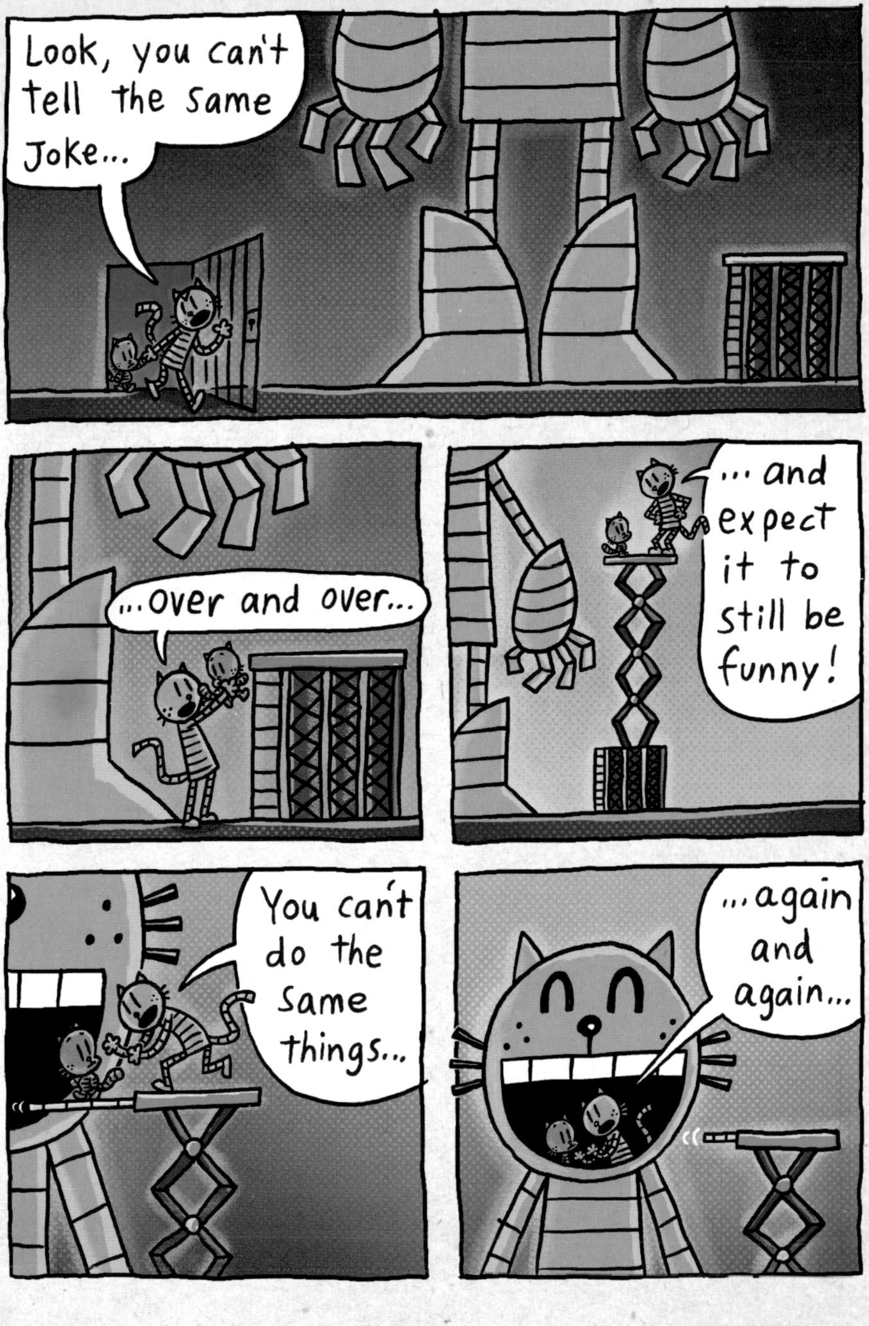
Look, you can't tell the same Joke...
...over and over...
...and expect it to still be funny!
You can't do the same things...
...again and again...

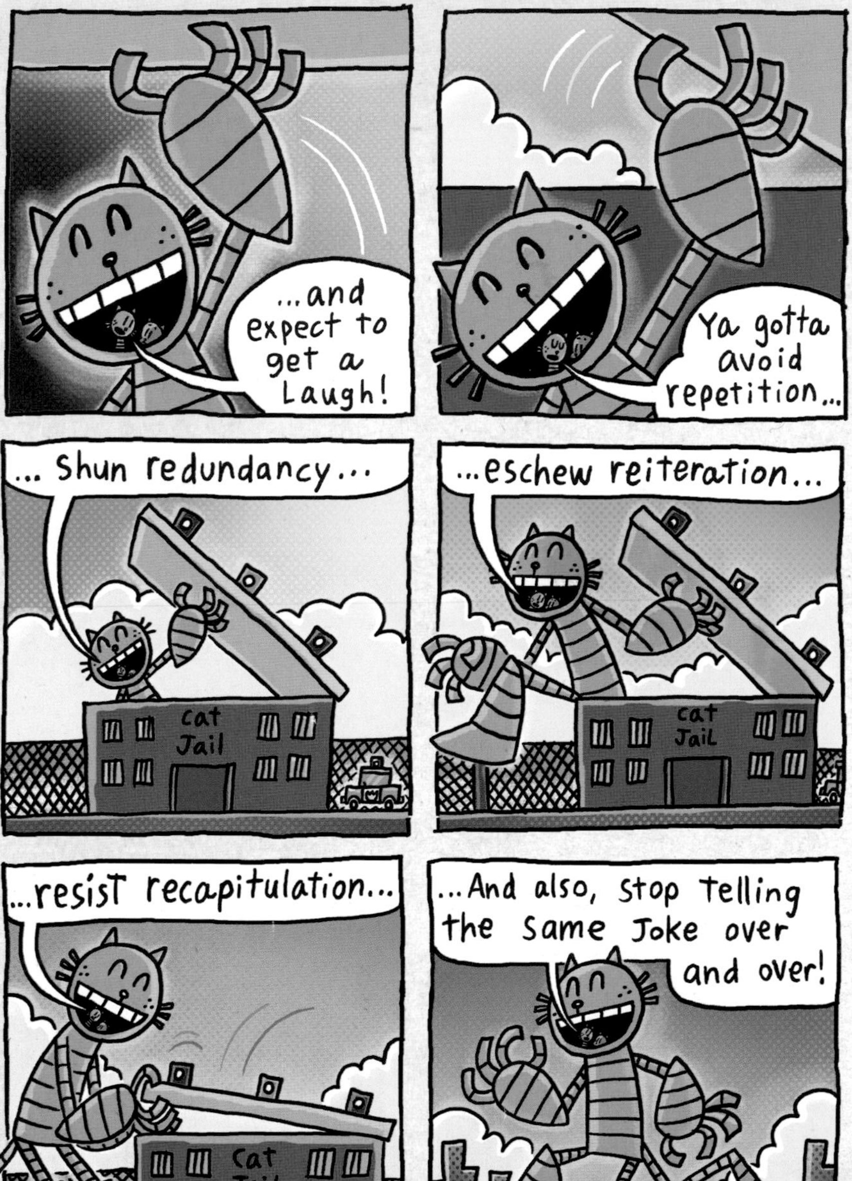
...and expect to get a Laugh!
Ya gotta avoid repetition...
... Shun redundancy...
...eschew reiteration...
Cat Jail
...resist recapitulation...
Cat Jail
...And also, stop telling the same Joke over and over!

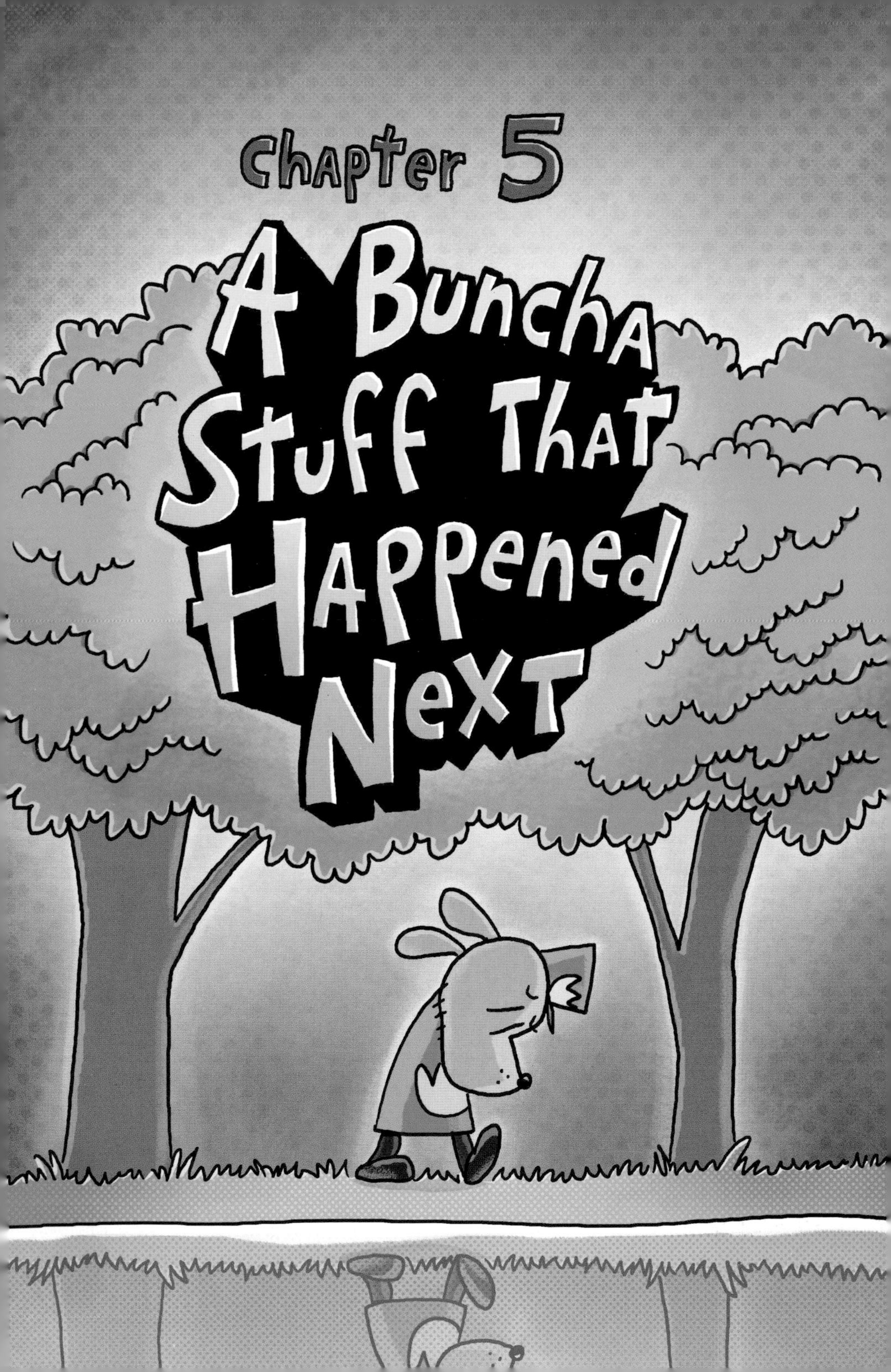
Chapter 5
A Buncha Stuff That Happened Next

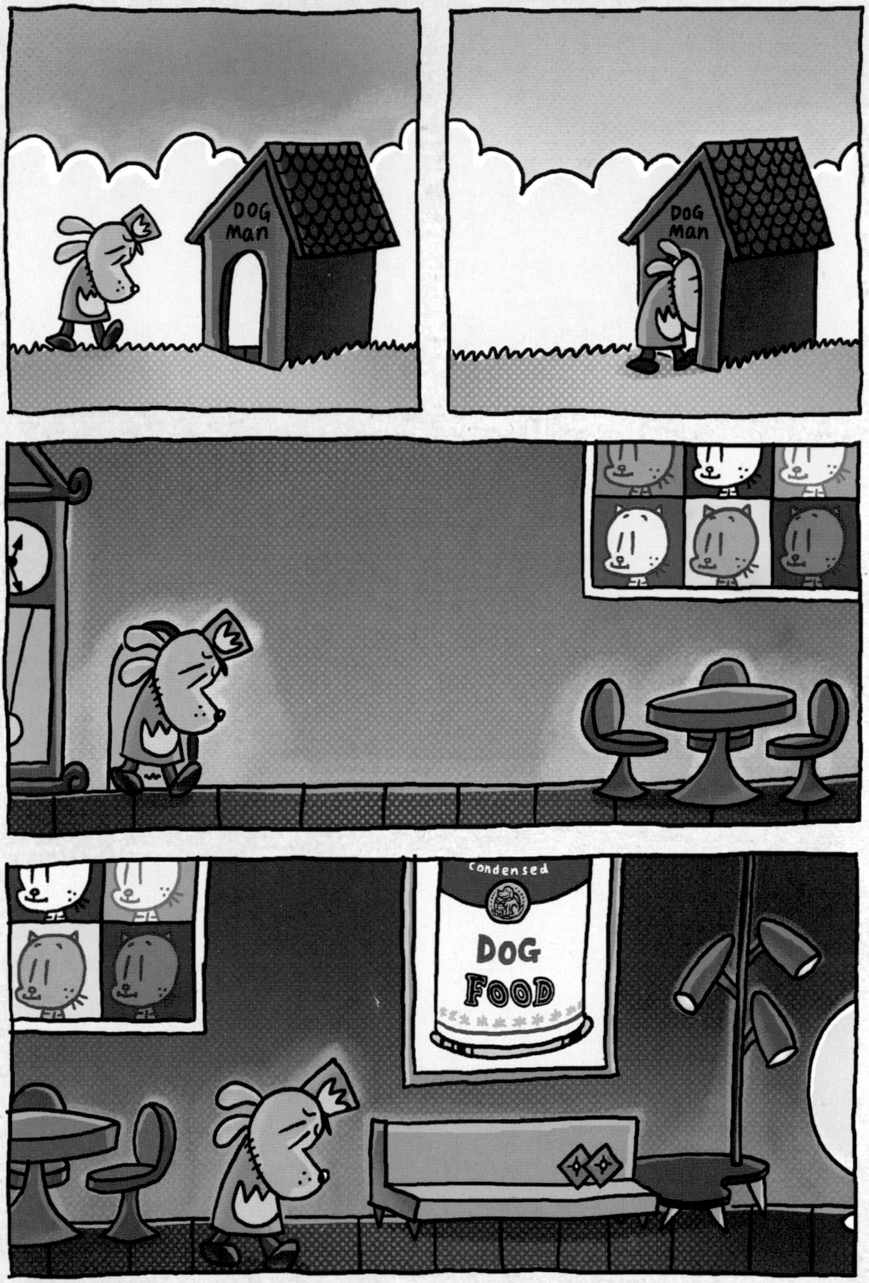
DOG Man
DOG Man
Condensed
DOG FOOD

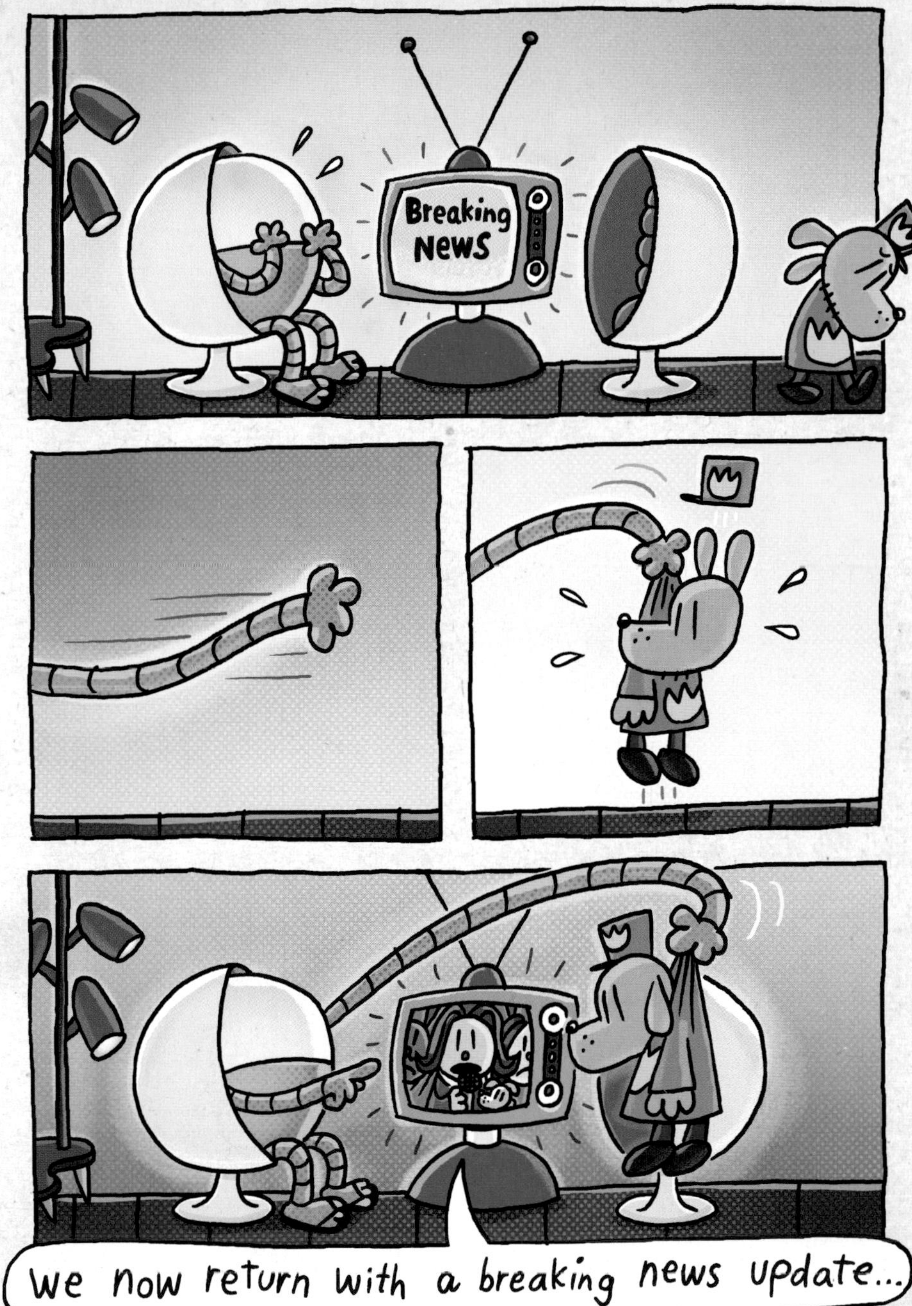
Breaking
News
We now return with a breaking news update...

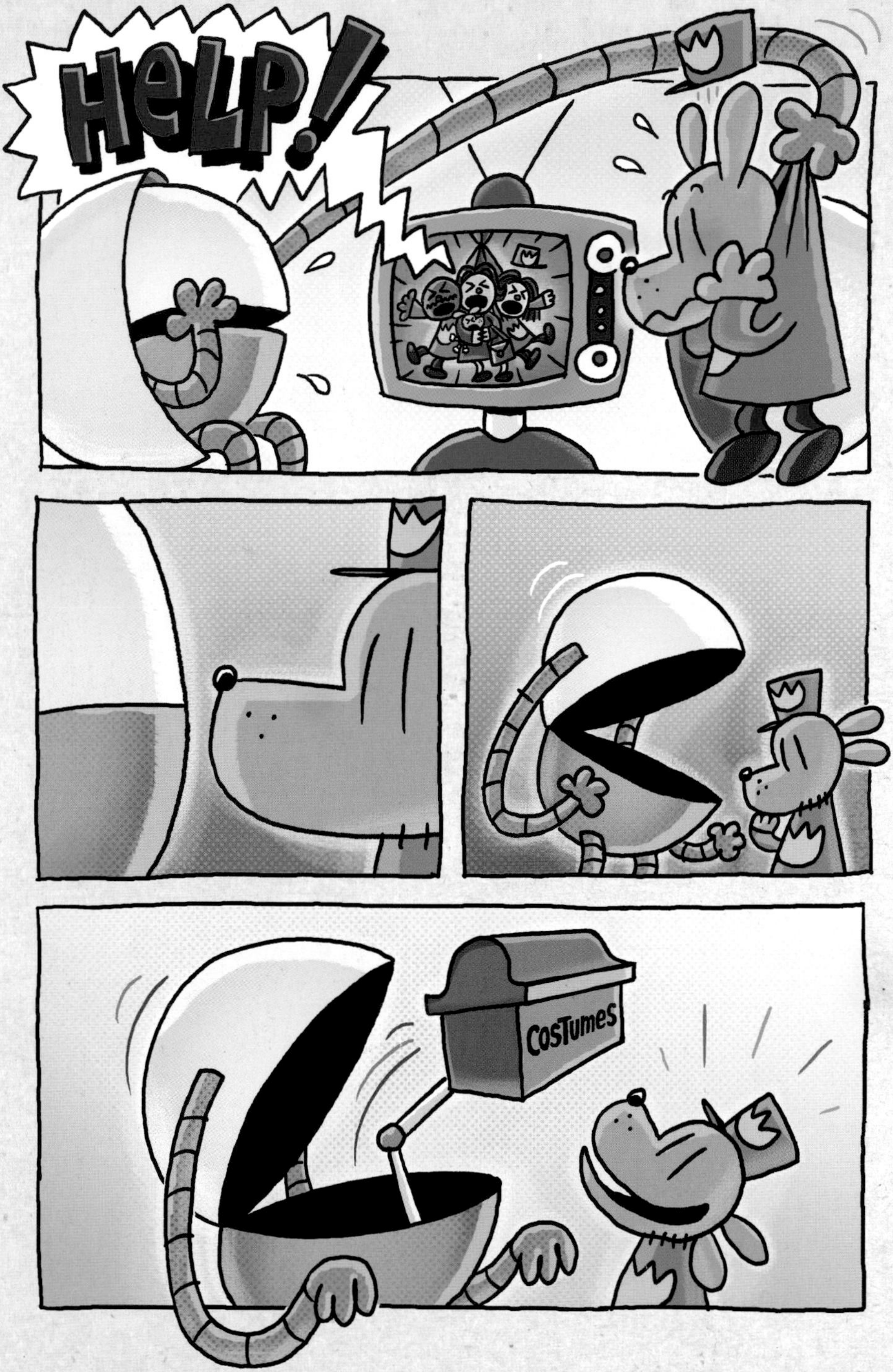
HELP!
COSTUMES

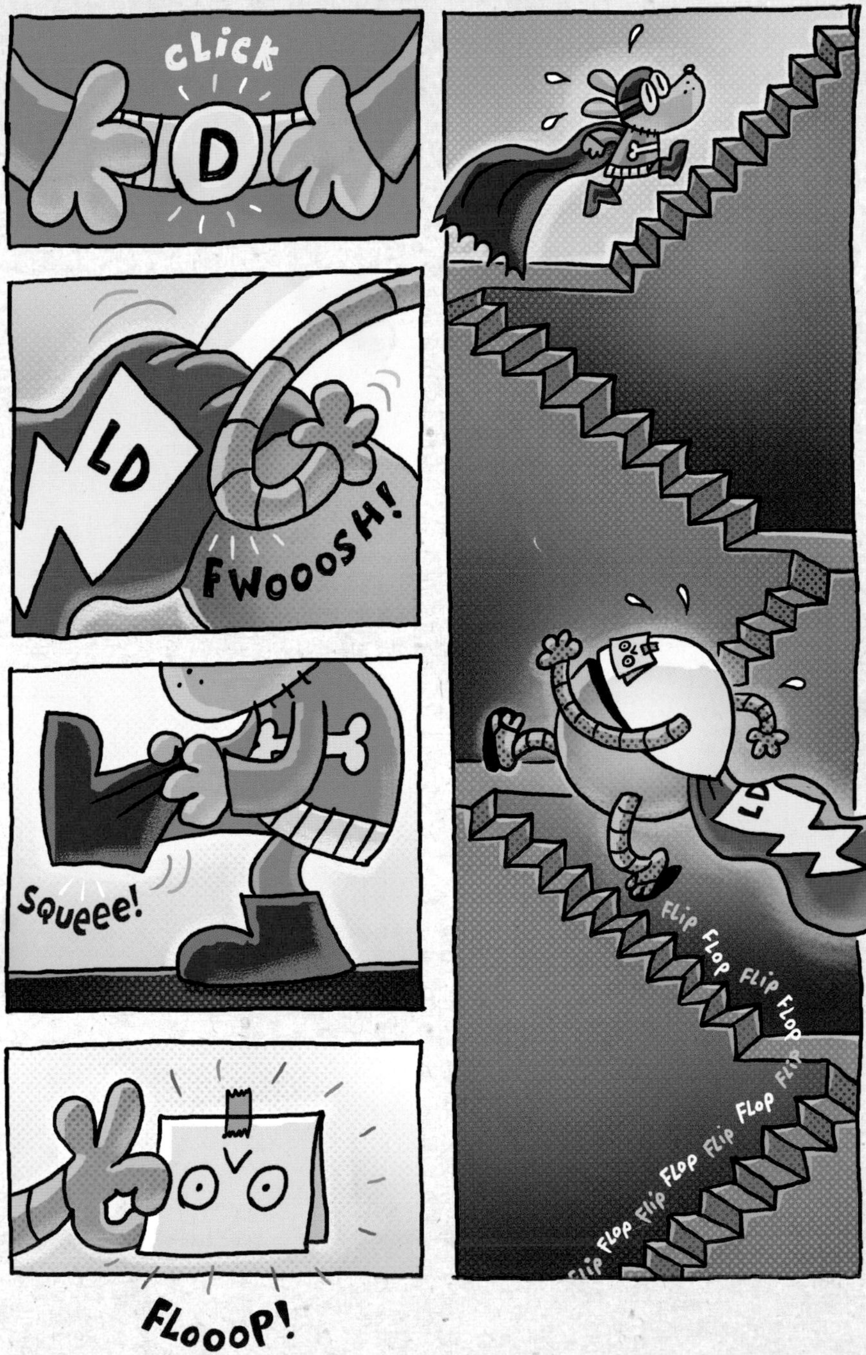
CLICK
D
LD
FWOOOSH!
SQUEEE!
FLOOOP!
LD
FLIP FLOP FLIP FLOP FLIP FLOP FLIP FLOP FLIP FLOP FLIP FLOP FLIP

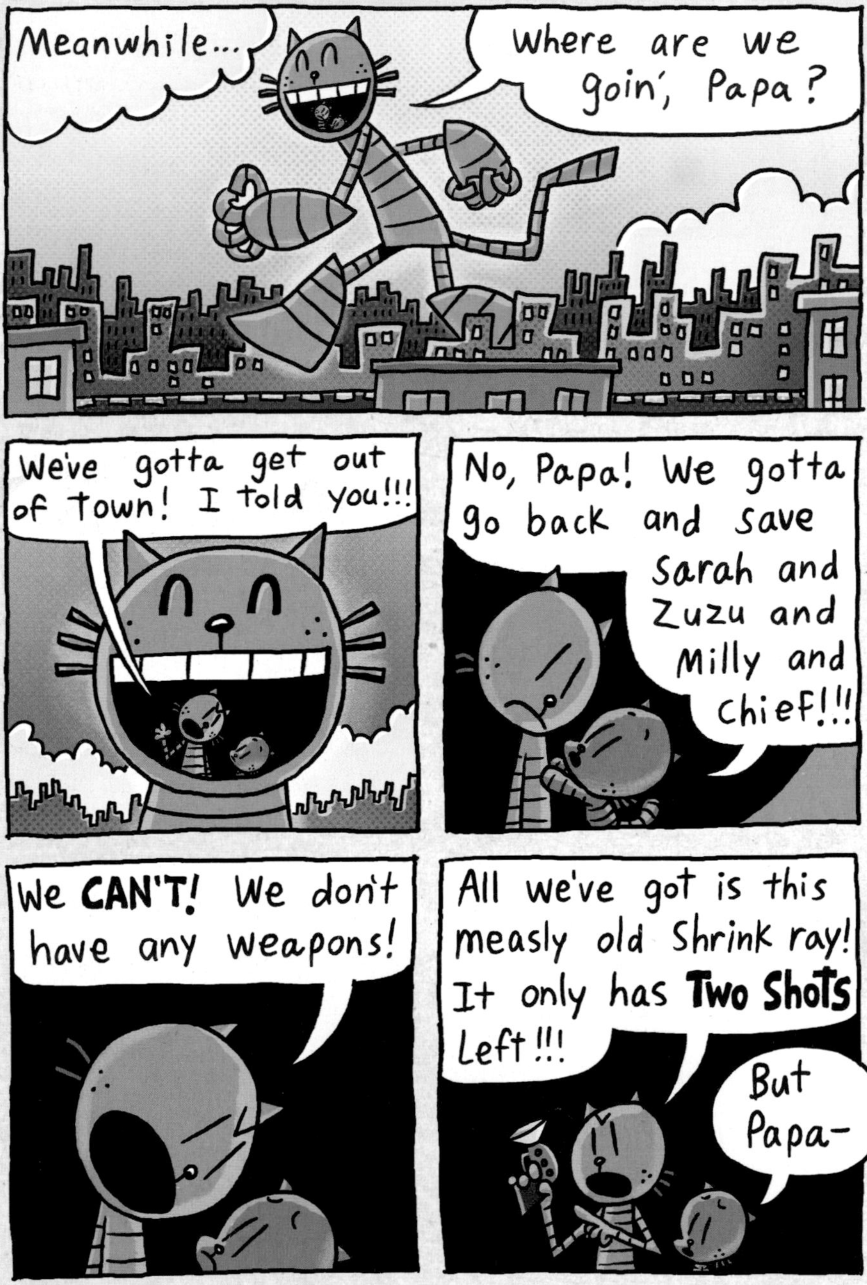
Meanwhile...
Where are we goin', Papa?
We've gotta get out of town! I told you!!!
No, Papa! We gotta go back and save Sarah and Zuzu and Milly and Chief!!!
We **CAN'T!** We don't have any weapons!
All we've got is this measly old Shrink ray! It only has **Two Shots** Left!!!
But Papa-

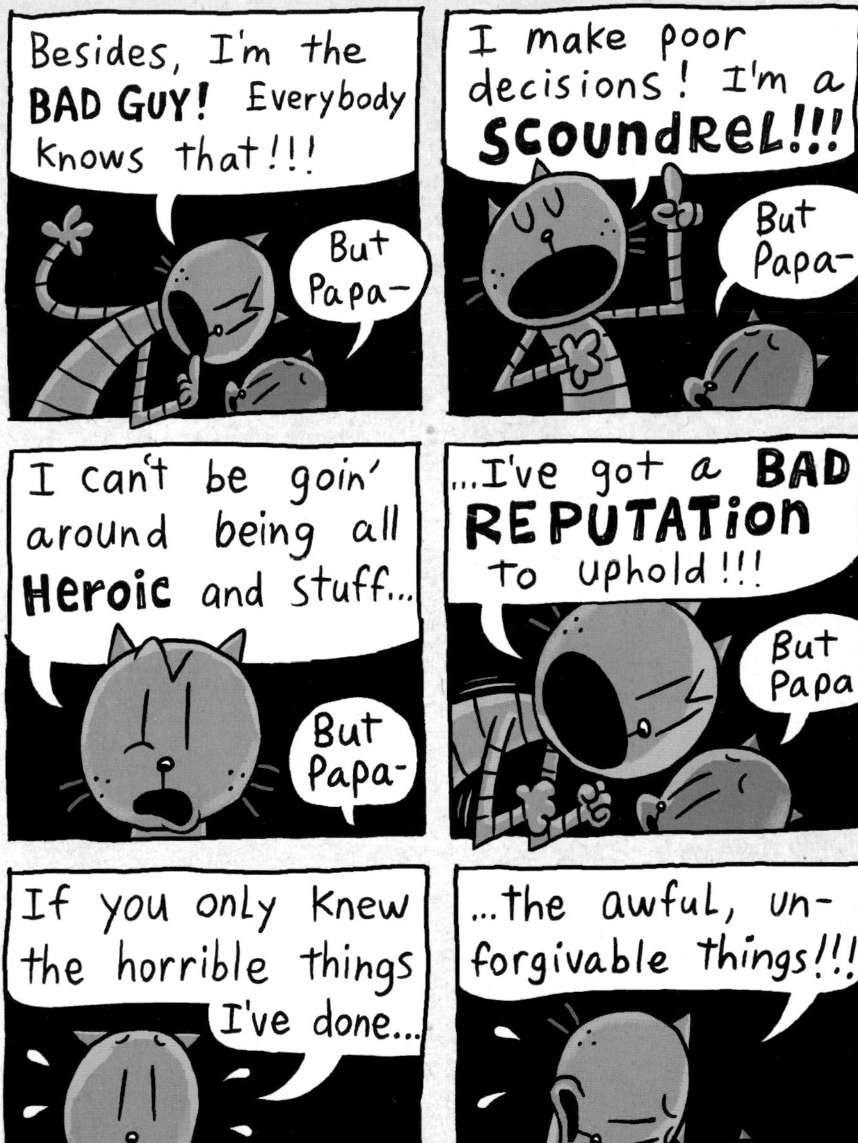
Besides, I'm the BAD GUY! Everybody knows that!!!
But Papa-
I make poor decisions! I'm a SCOUNDREL!!!
But Papa-
I can't be goin' around being all HEROIC and stuff...
But Papa-
...I've got a BAD REPUTATION to uphold!!!
But Papa-
If you only knew the horrible things I've done...
...the awful, unforgivable things!!!

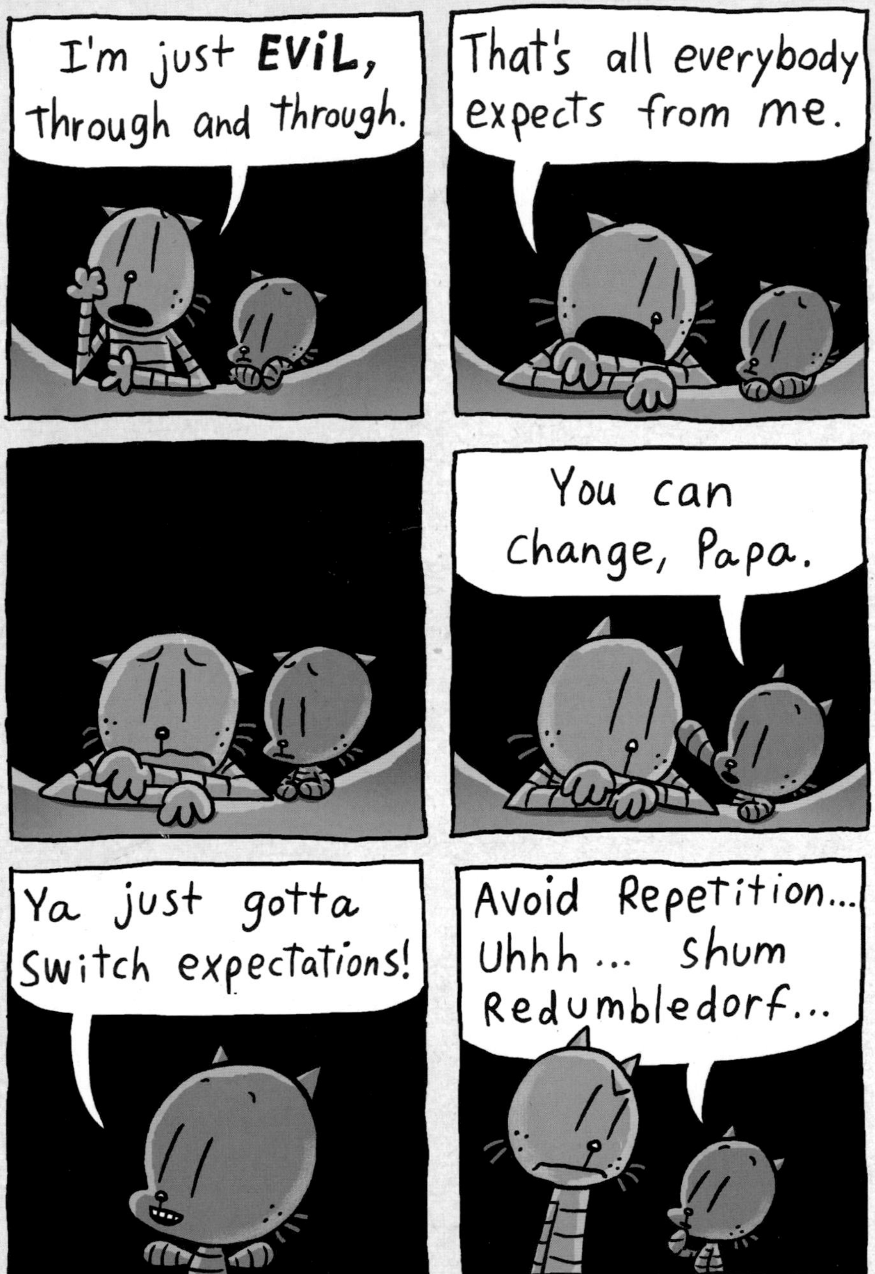
I'm just **EVIL**, through and through.
That's all everybody expects from me.
You can change, Papa.
Ya just gotta switch expectations!
Avoid Repetition... Uhhh... Shum Redumbledorf...

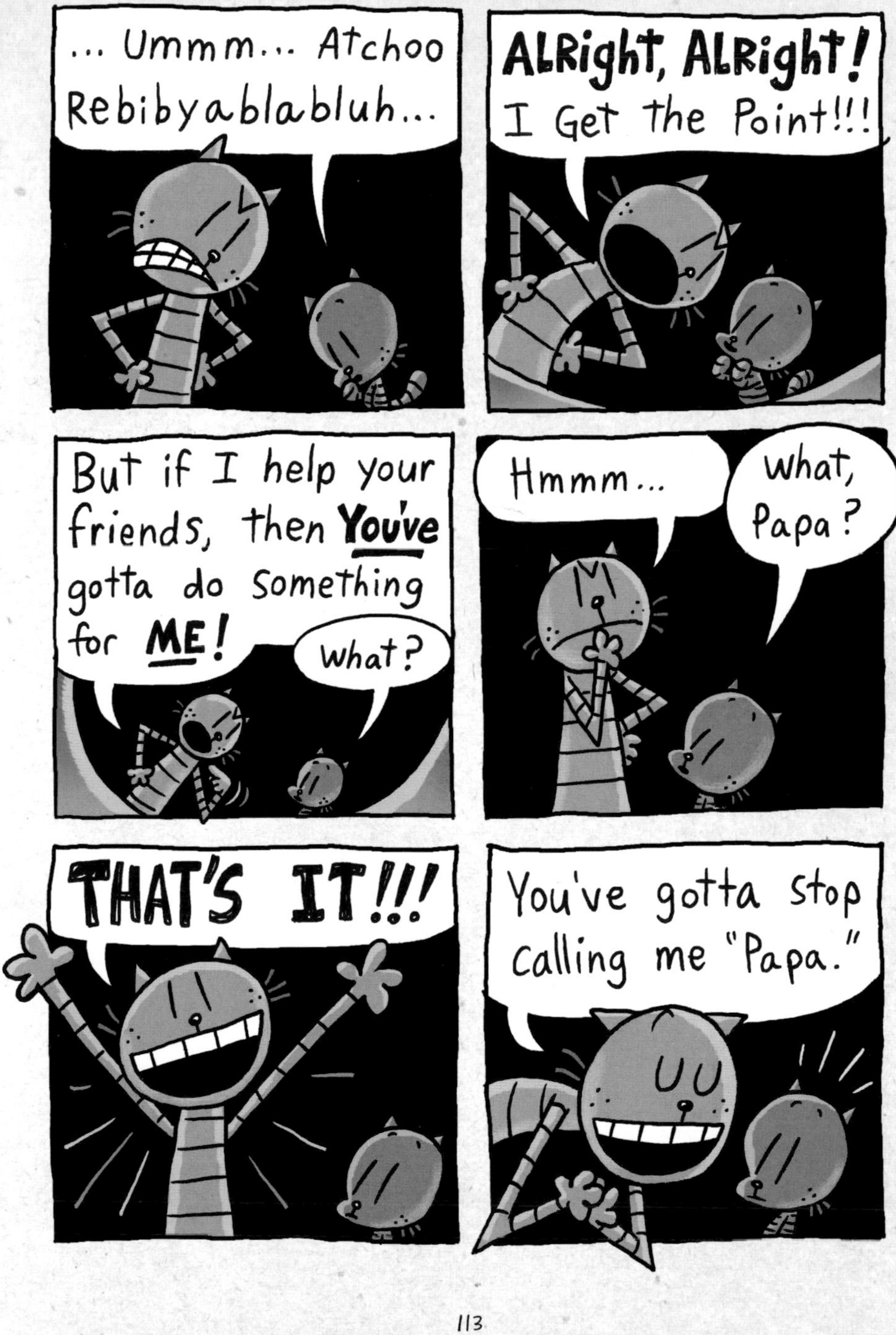
... Ummm... Atchoo Rebibyablabluh...
ALRight, ALRight! I Get the Point!!!
But if I help your friends, then You've gotta do Something for ME!
What?
Hmmm...
What, Papa?
THAT'S IT!!!
You've gotta stop calling me "Papa."

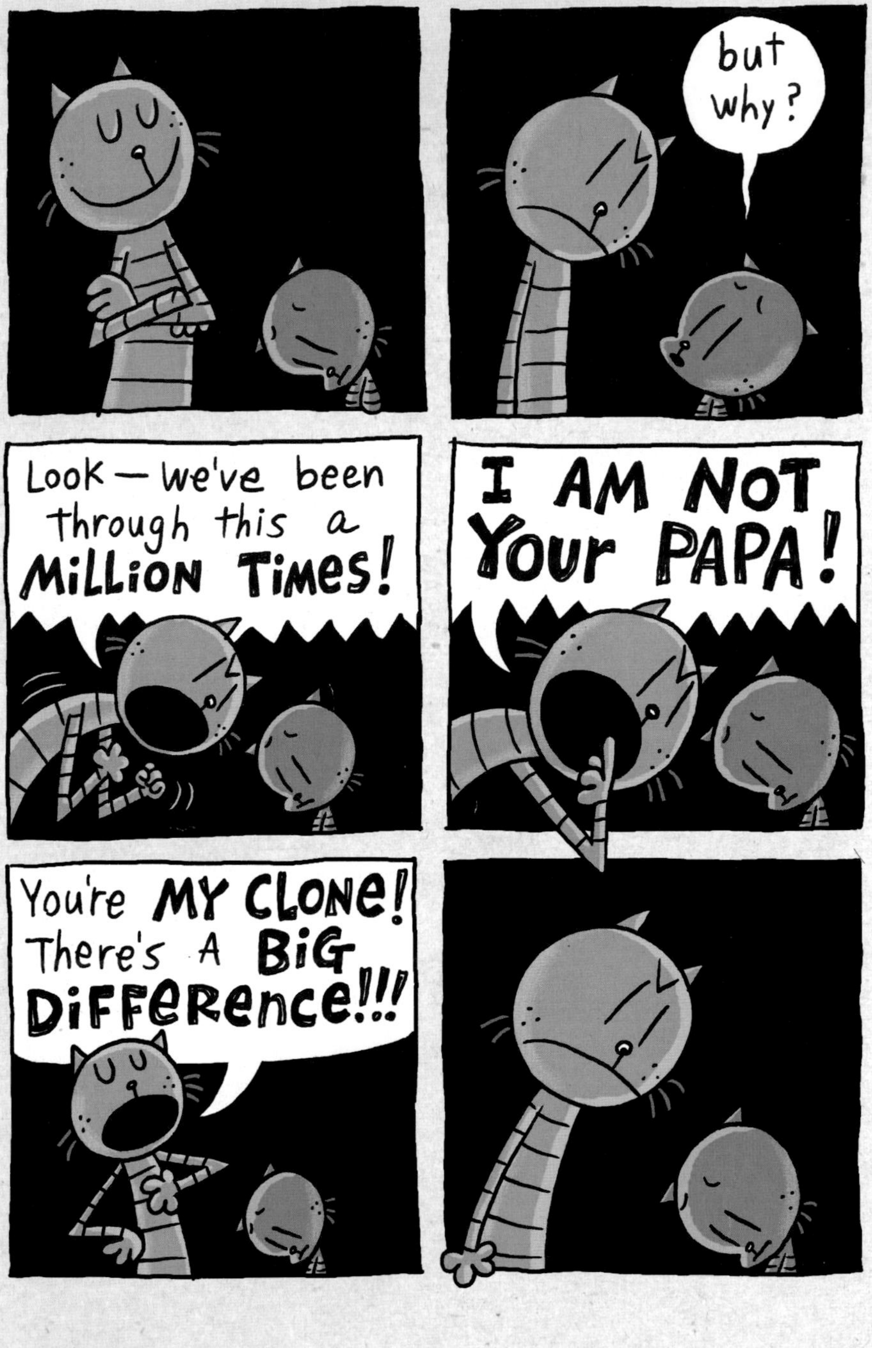

but why?
Look — we've been through this a MILLION TIMES!
I AM NOT YOUR PAPA!
You're MY CLONE! There's A BIG DIFFERENCE!!!

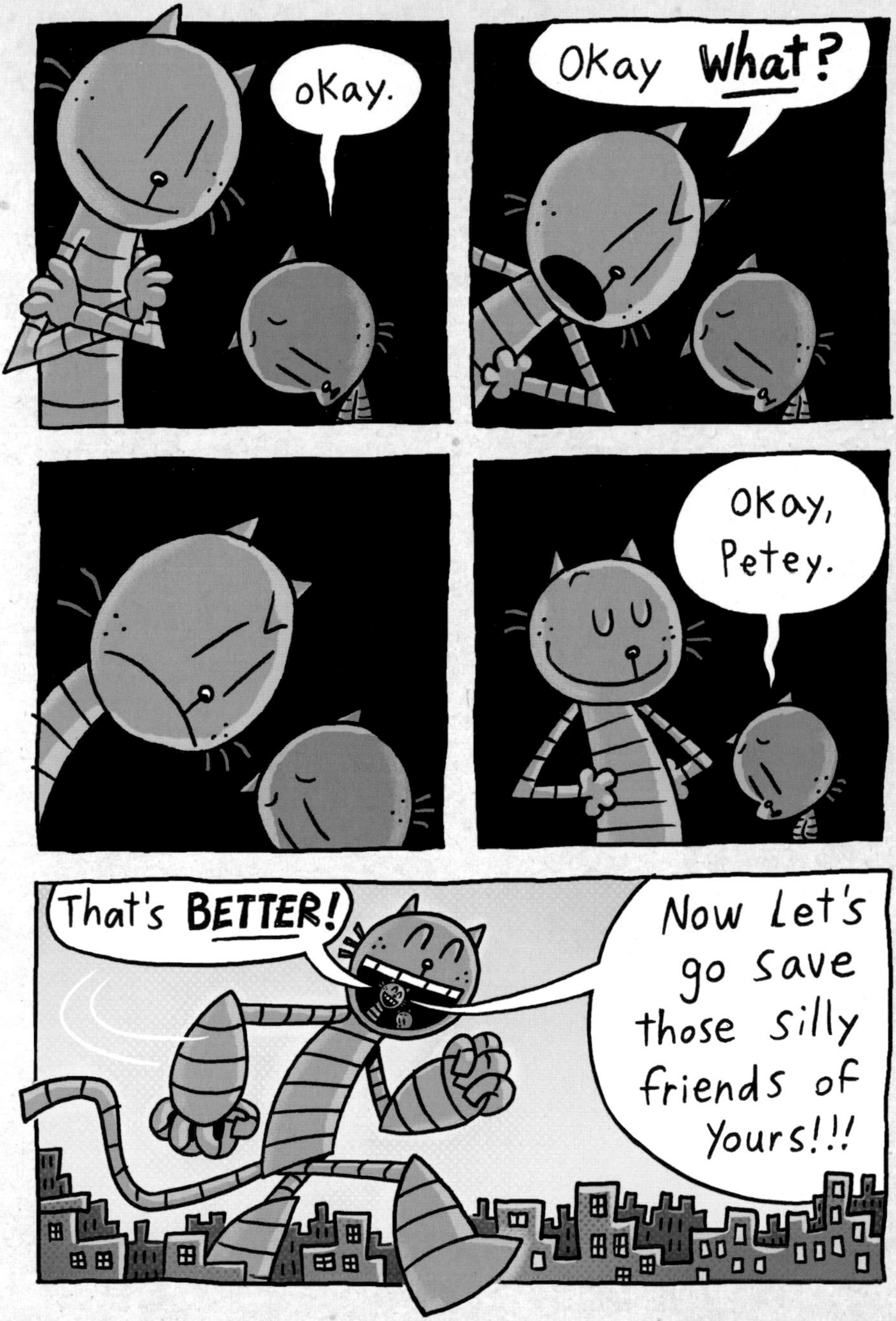
oKay.
OKay What?
OKay,
Petey.
That's BETTER!
Now Let's go Save those Silly friends of Yours!!!

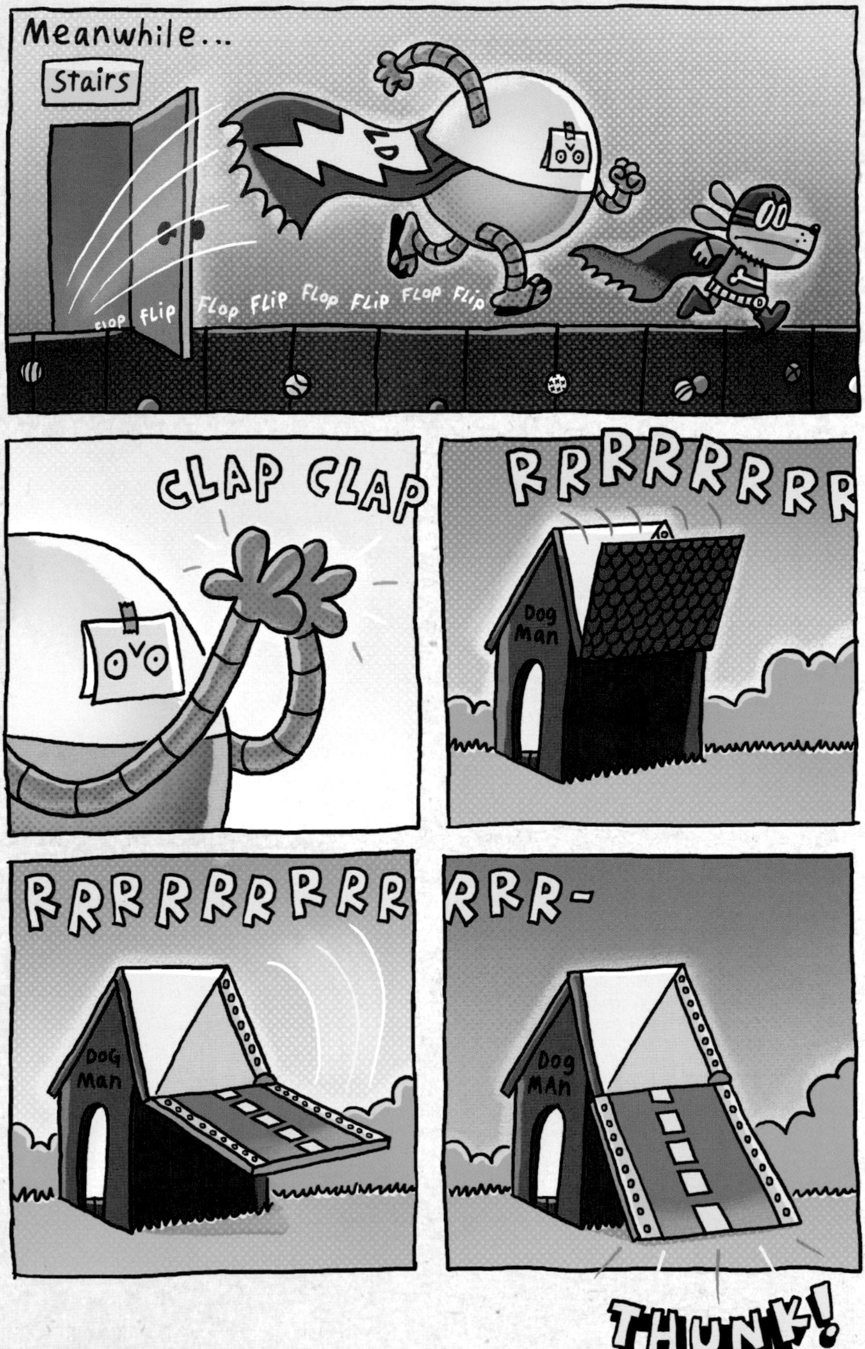
Meanwhile...
Stairs
FLOP FLIP FLOP FLIP FLOP FLIP FLOP FLIP
CLAP CLAP
RRRRRRRRR
Dog Man
RRRRRRRRR
Dog Man
RRR-
Dog Man
THUNK!

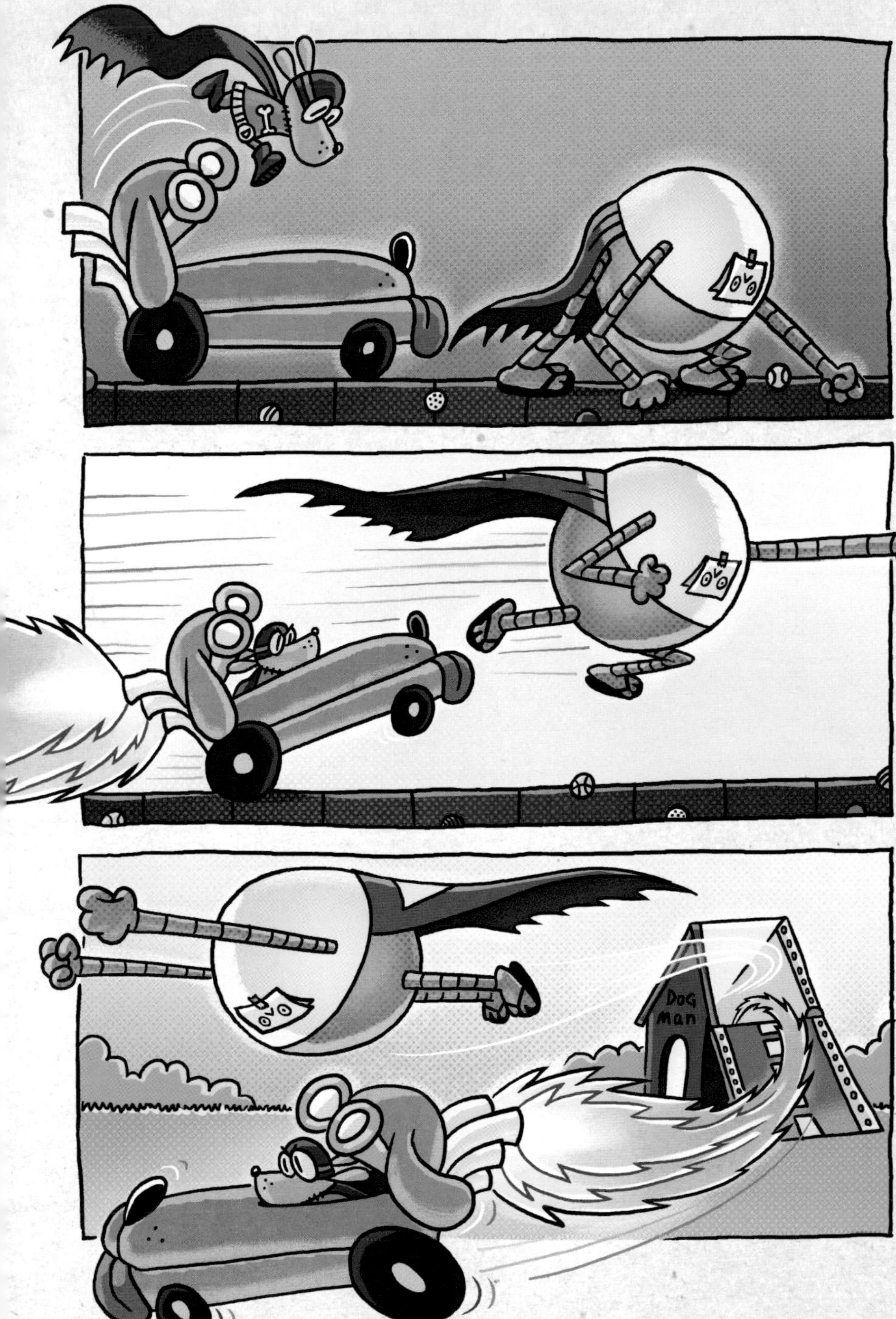
DoG
man

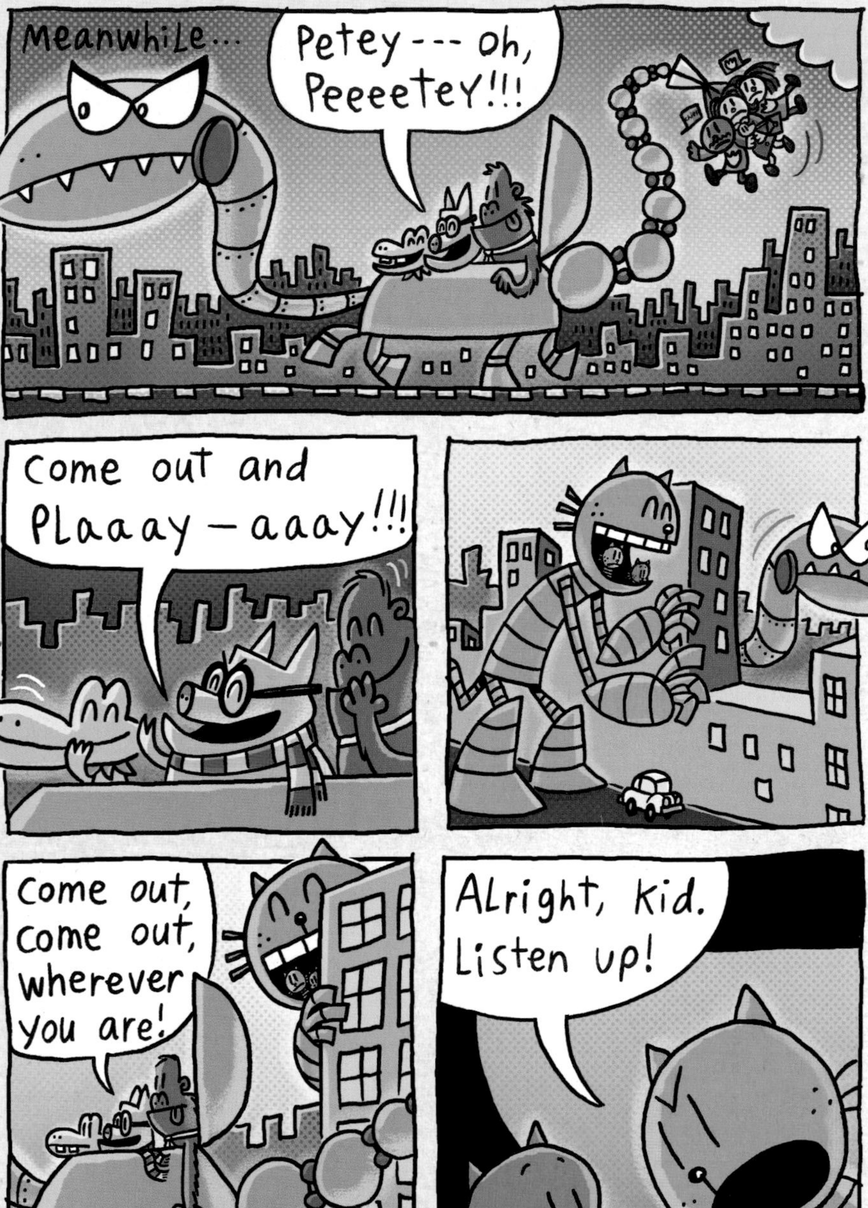
Meanwhile...
Petey--- oh, Peeeetey!!!
Come out and Plaaay-aaay!!!
Come out, come out, wherever you are!
Alright, kid. Listen up!

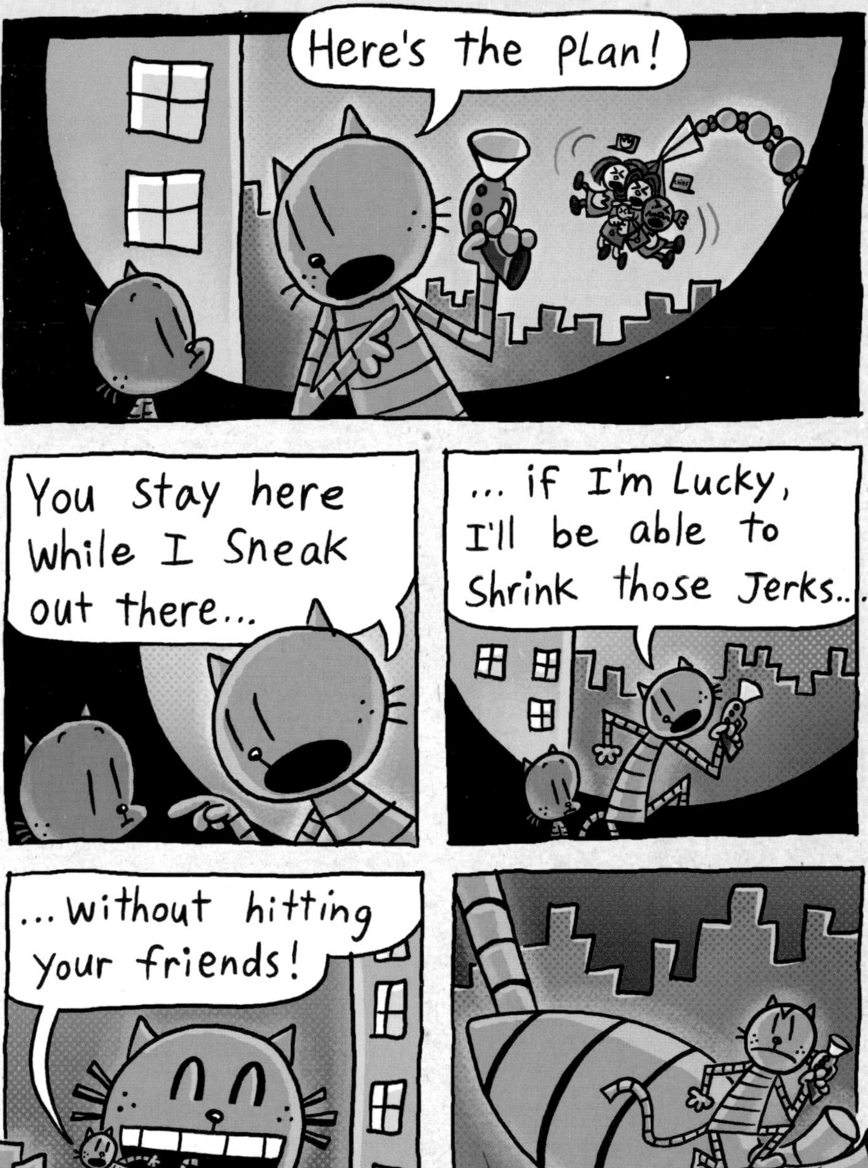
Here's the plan!
You stay here while I sneak out there...
... if I'm lucky, I'll be able to shrink those jerks...
... without hitting your friends!

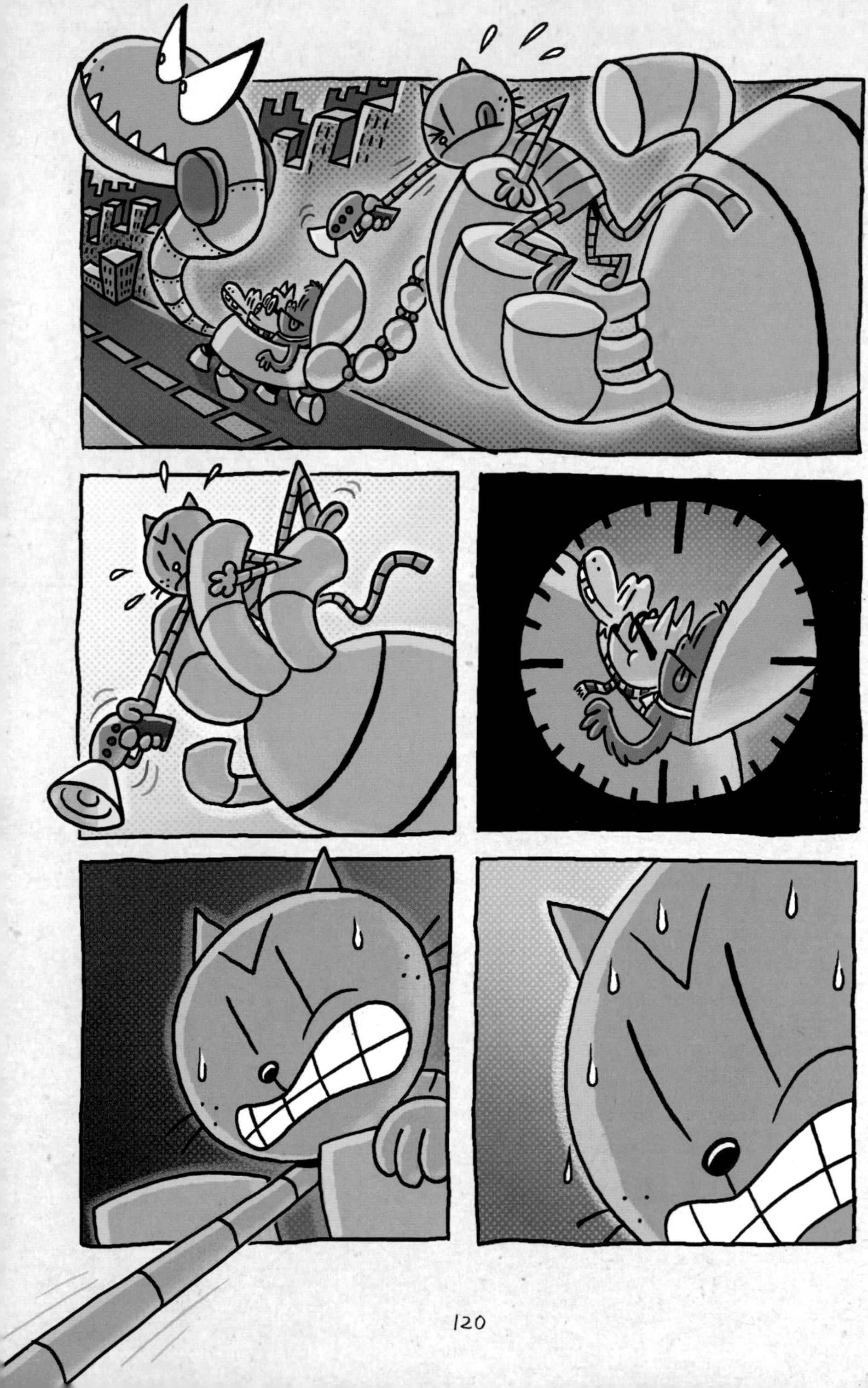

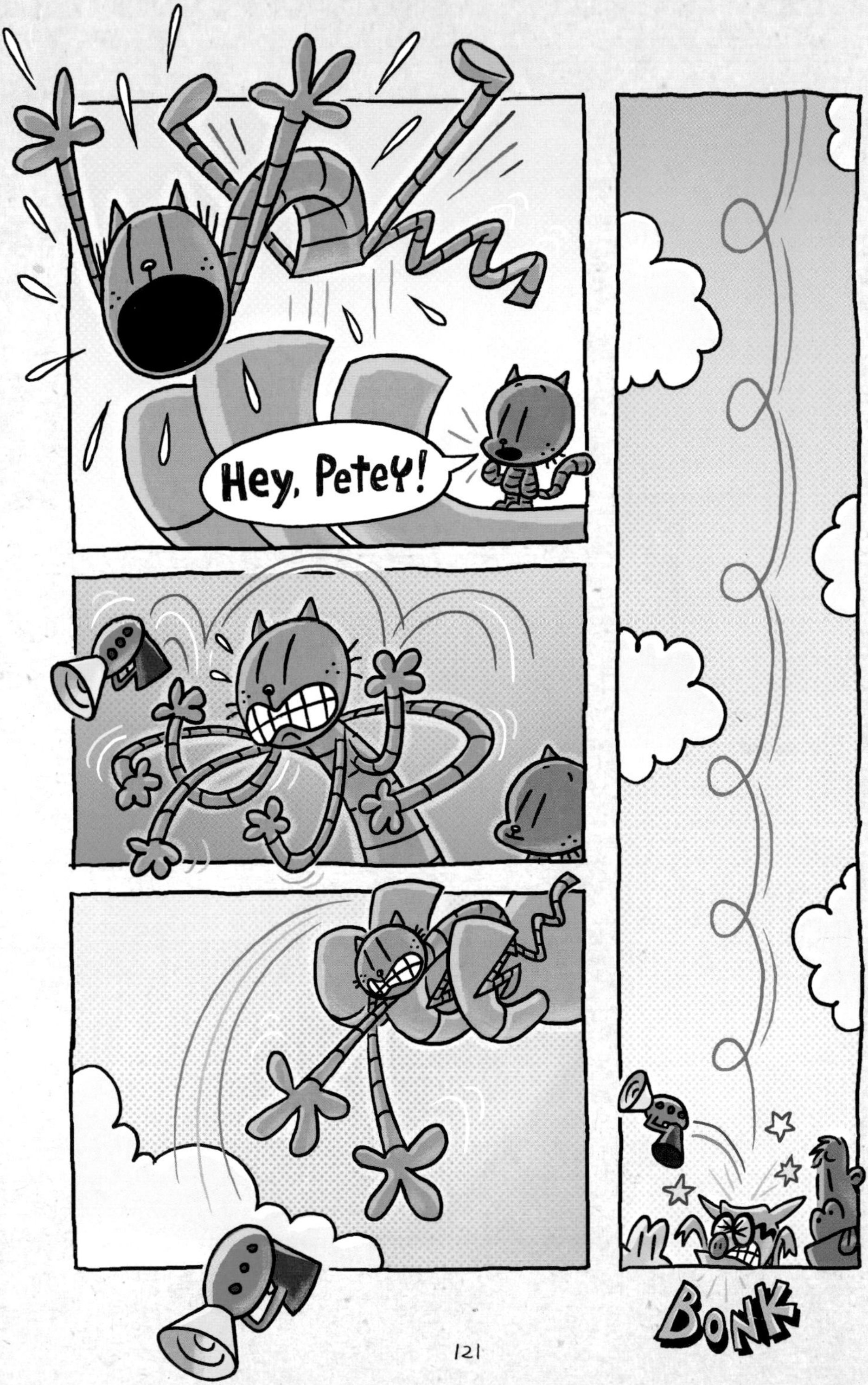
Hey, Petey!
BONK

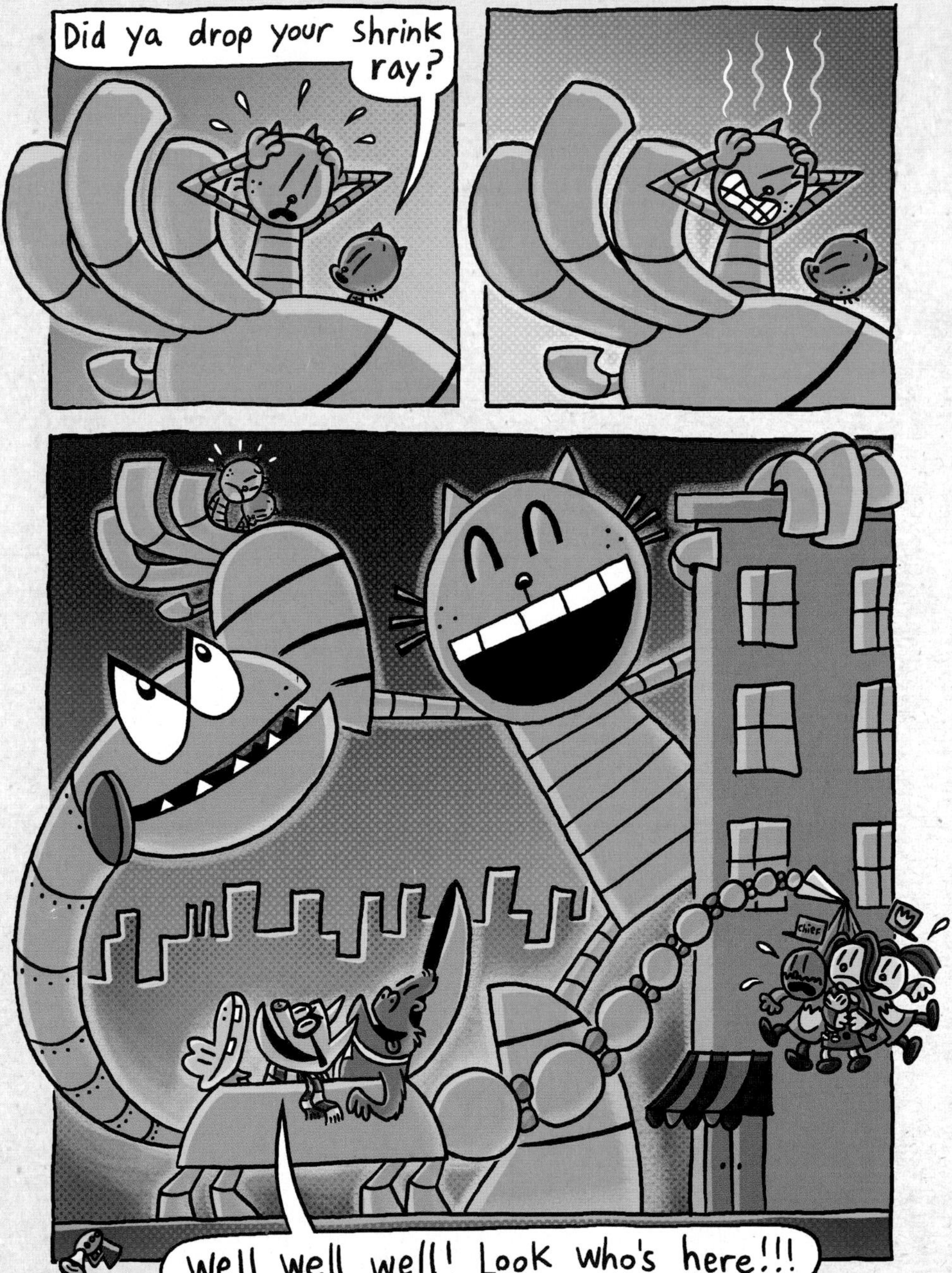
Did ya drop your shrink ray?
Chief
Well, well, well! Look who's here!!!

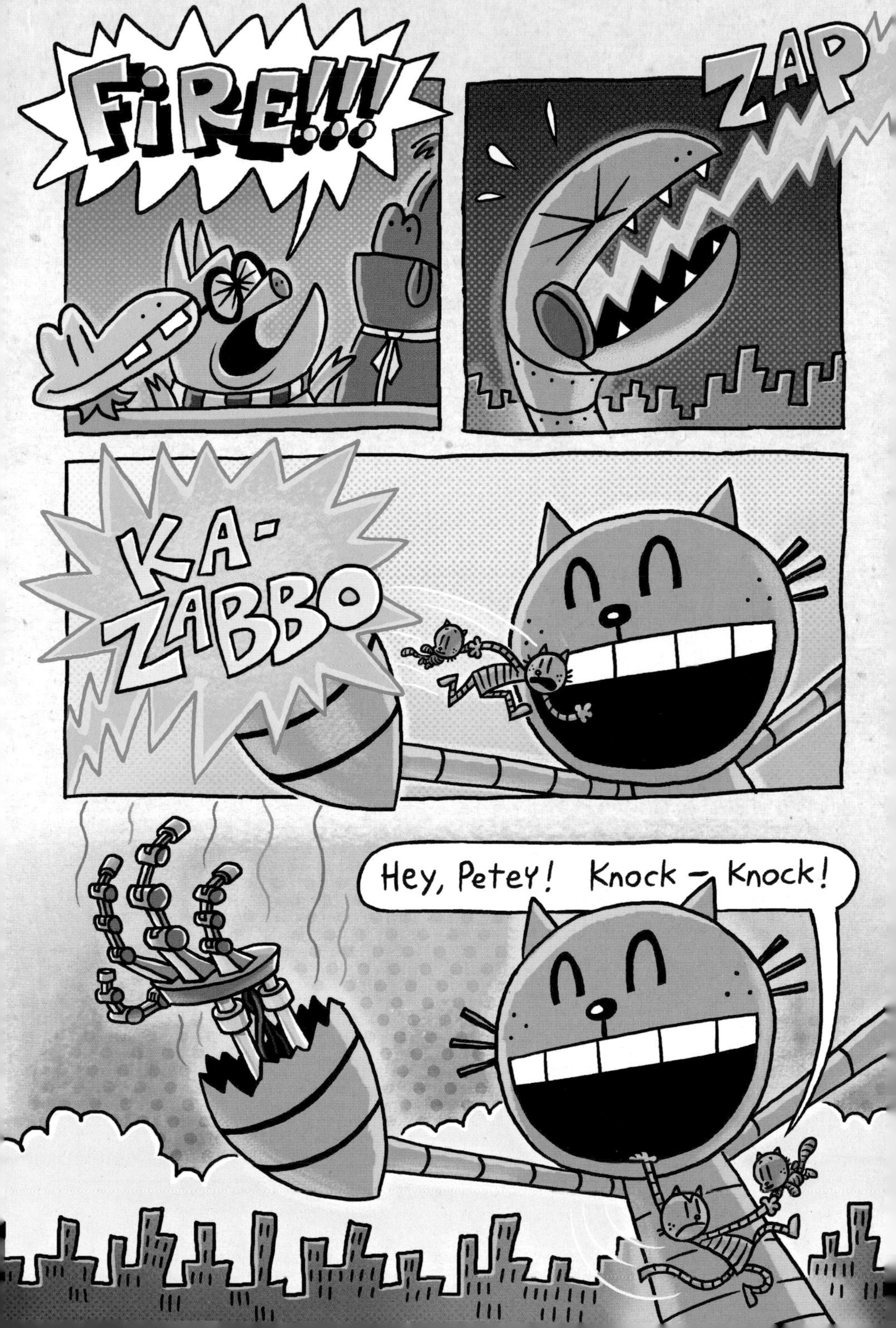
FiRE!!!
ZAP
KA-ZABBO
Hey, Petey! Knock-Knock!

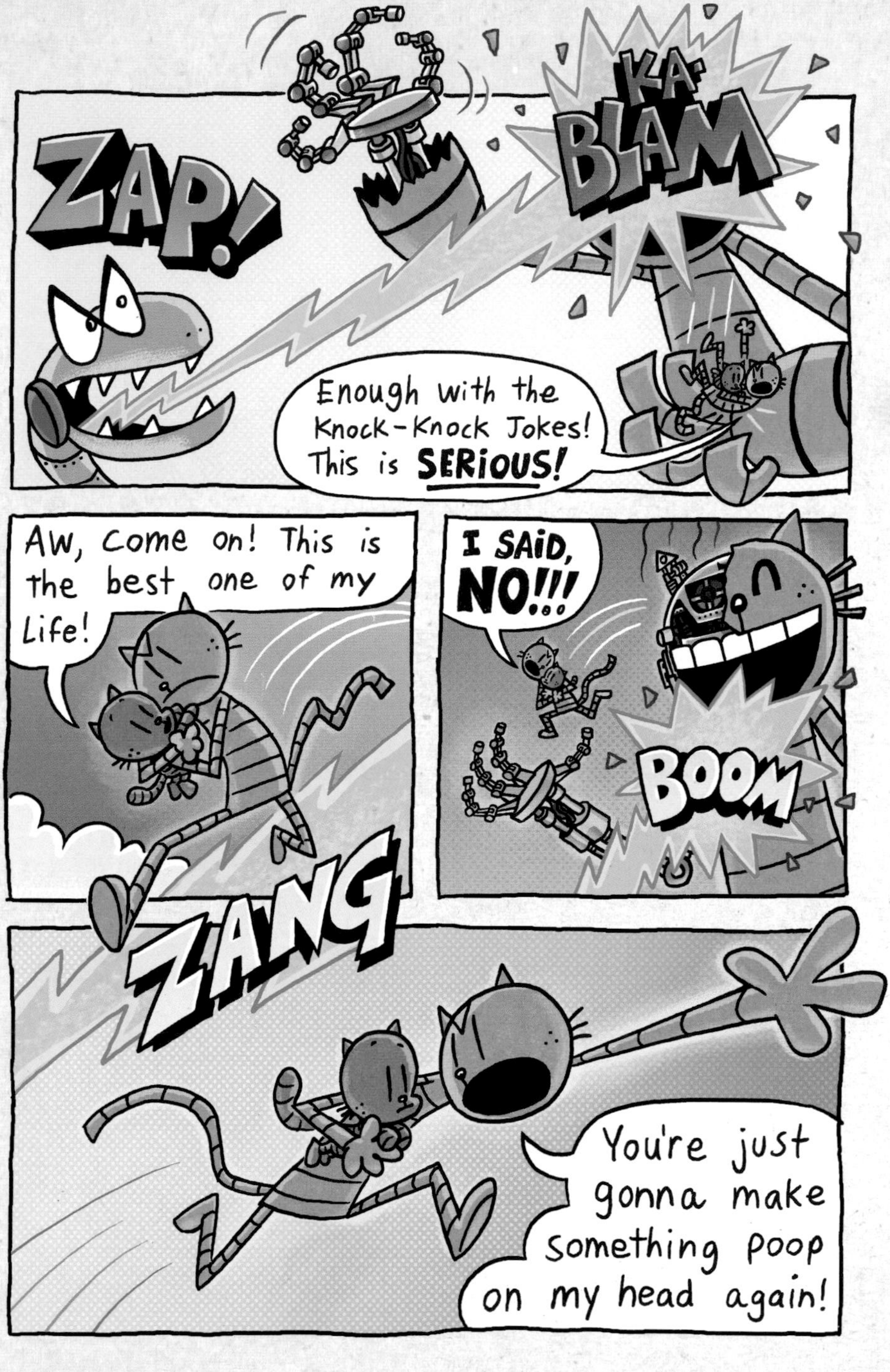
ZAP!
KA-BLAM
Enough with the Knock-Knock Jokes! This is SERIOUS!
Aw, come on! This is the best one of my Life!
I SAID, NO!!!
BOOM
ZANG
You're just gonna make something poop on my head again!

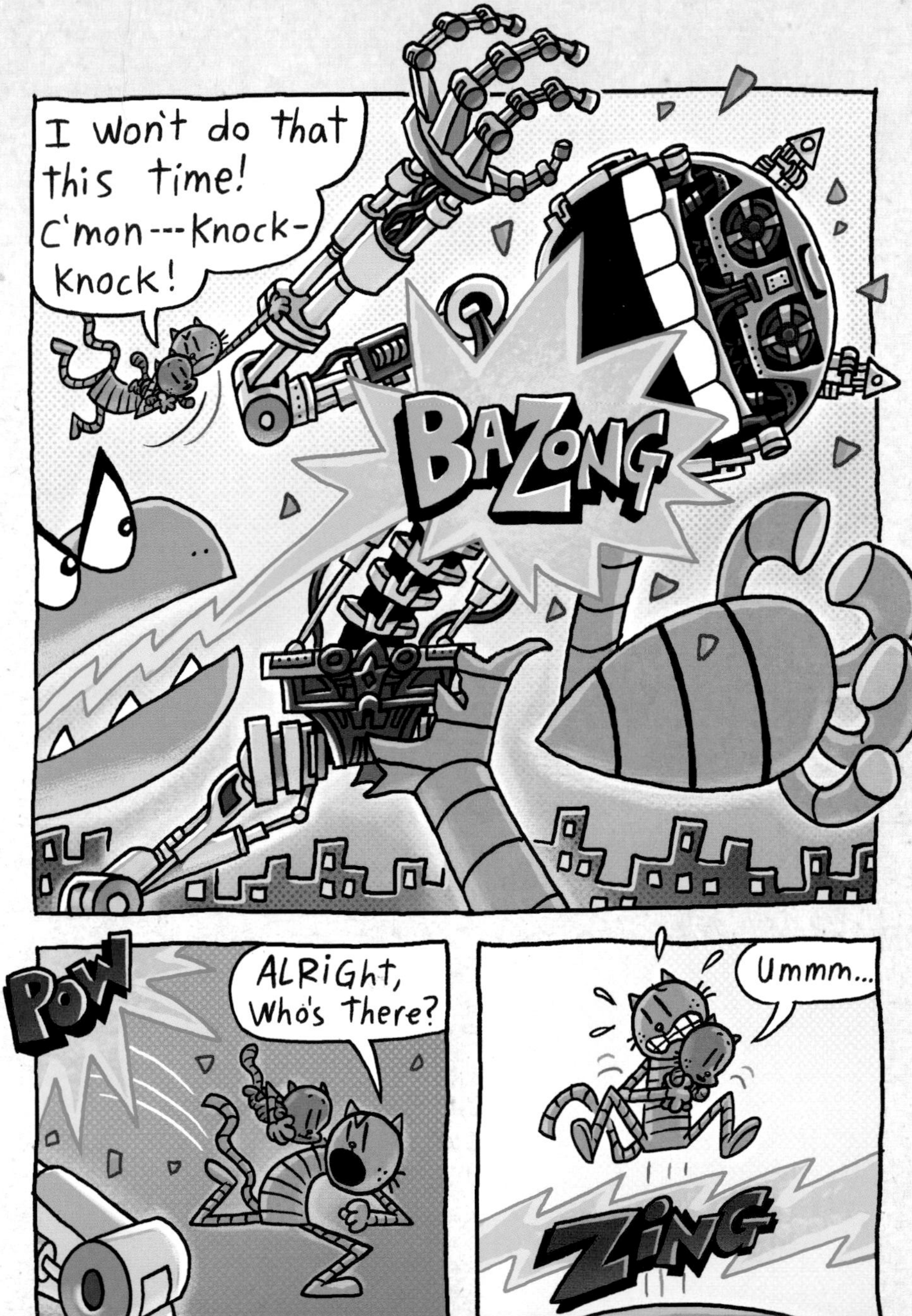
I won't do that this time! C'mon---Knock-knock!
BAZONG
POW
ALRIGHT, Who's there?
Ummm...
ZING

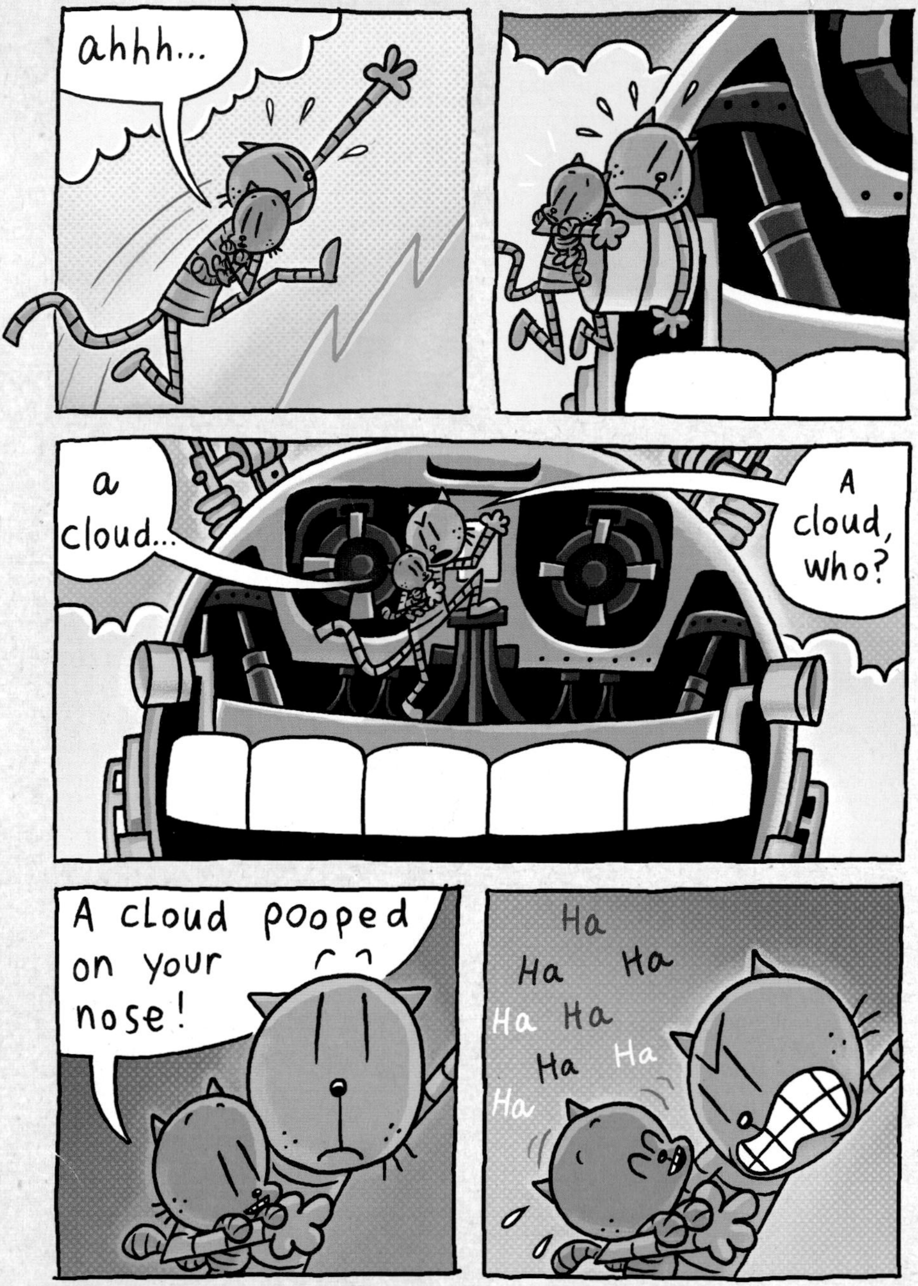
ahhh...
a cloud...
A cloud, who?
A cloud pooped on your nose!
Ha
Ha Ha
Ha Ha
Ha Ha
Ha

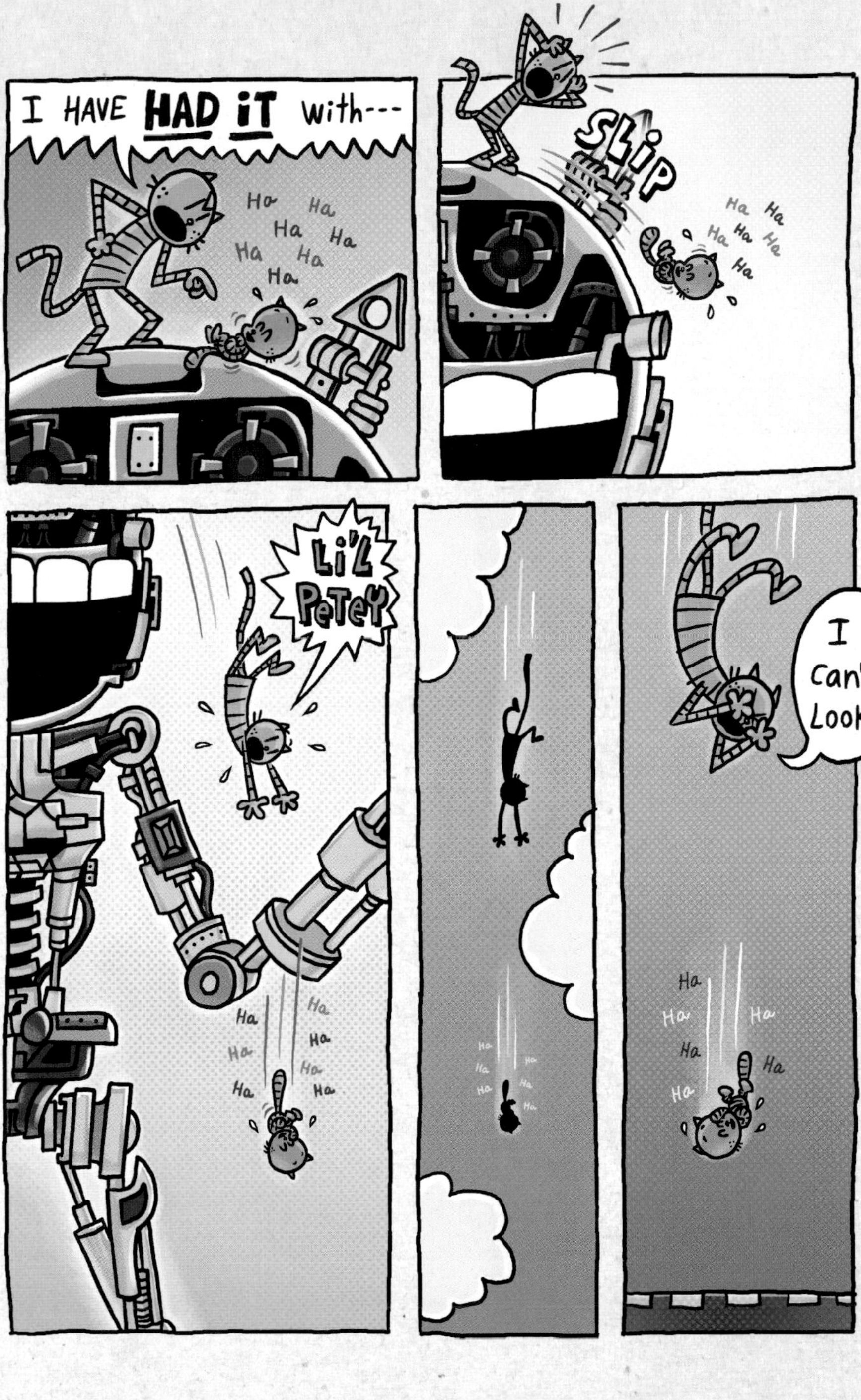
I HAVE HAD iT with---
Ha Ha Ha Ha Ha Ha Ha
SLiP
Ha Ha Ha Ha Ha Ha
Li'L PeTeY
Ha Ha Ha Ha Ha Ha Ha
I can't Look!
Ha Ha Ha Ha Ha Ha

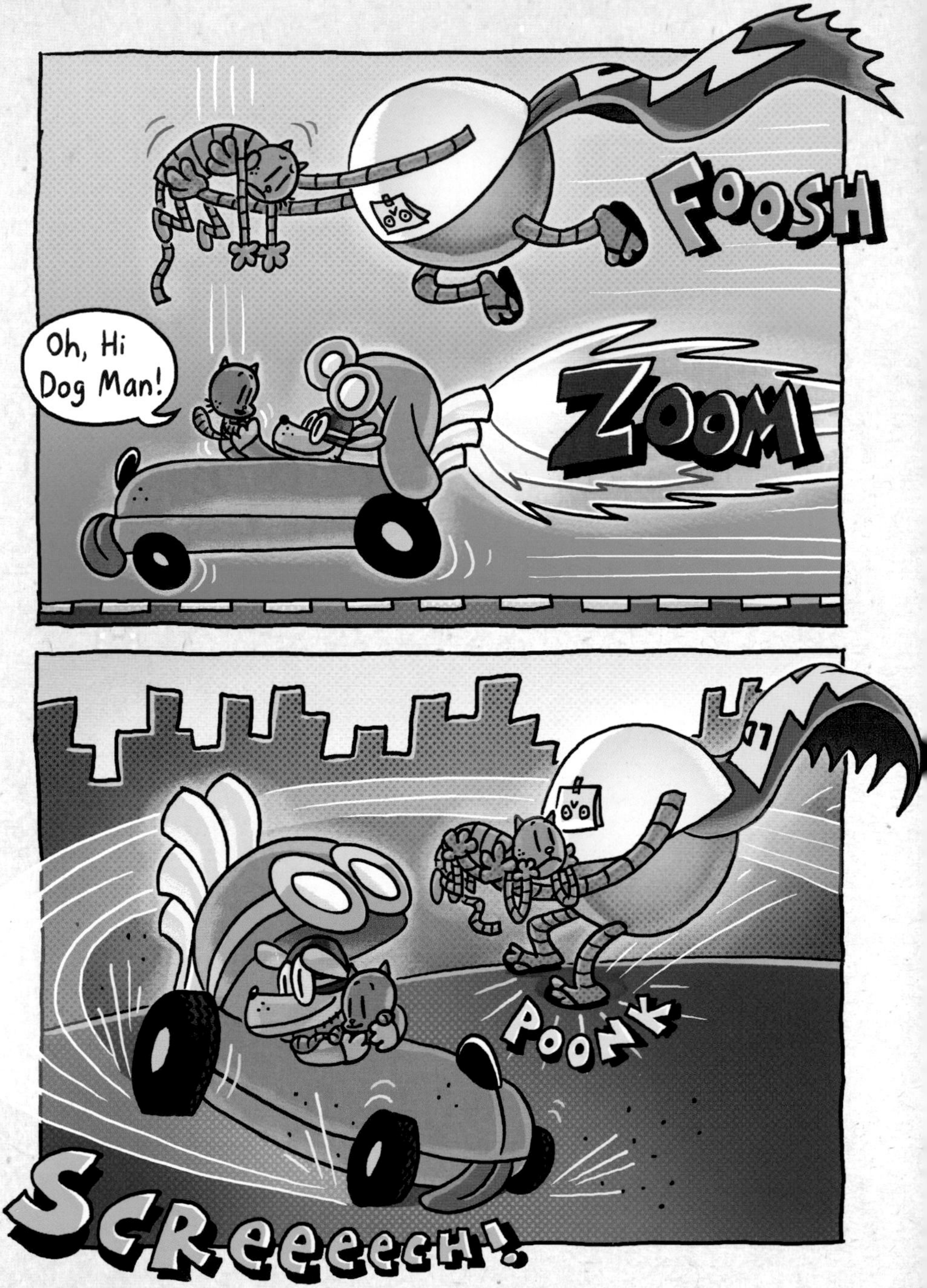
FOOSH
Oh, Hi Dog Man!
ZOOM
POONK
SCREEEECH!

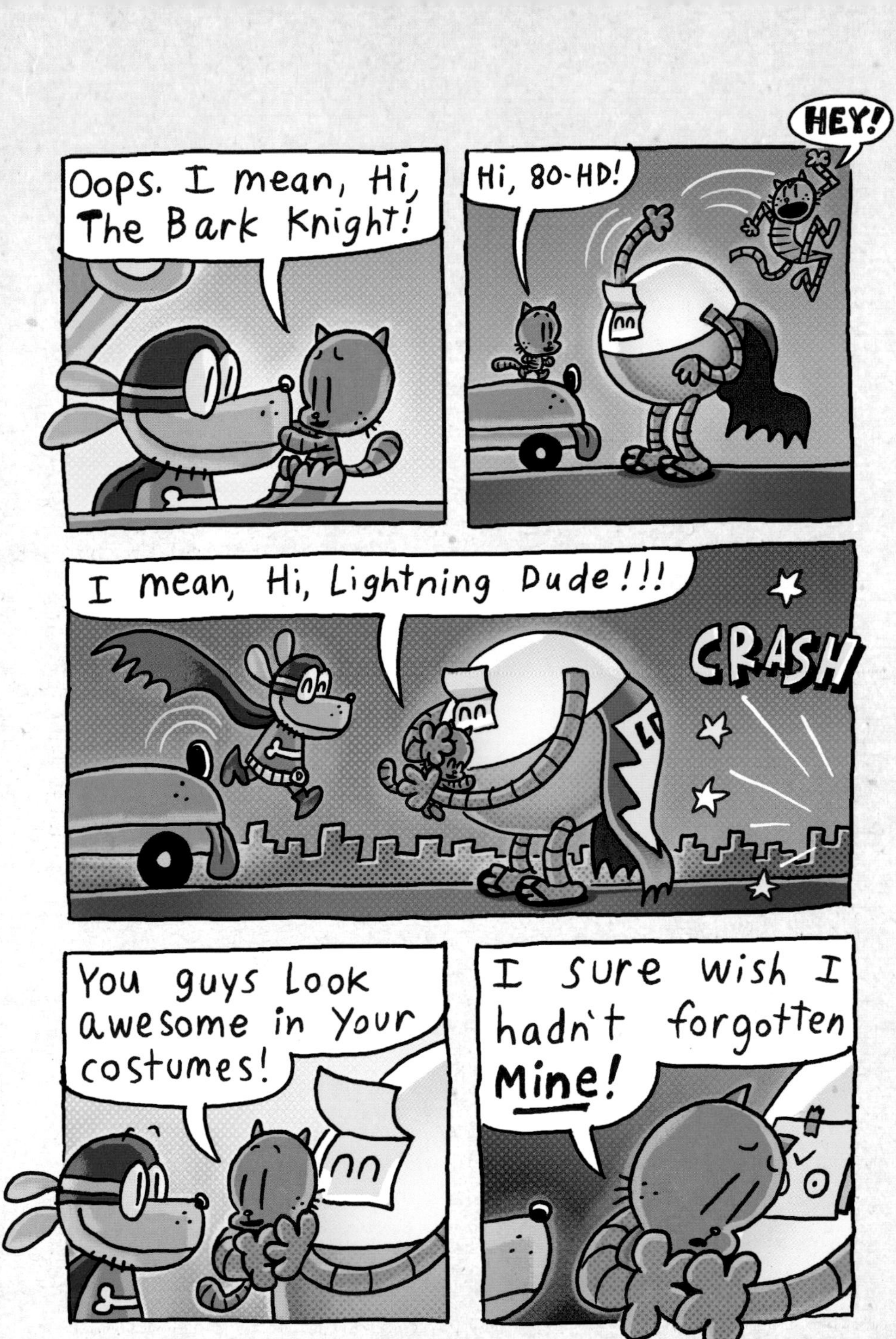
Oops. I mean, Hi, The Bark Knight!
Hi, 80-HD!
HEY!
I mean, Hi, Lightning Dude!!!
CRASH
You guys look awesome in your costumes!
I sure wish I hadn't forgotten Mine!

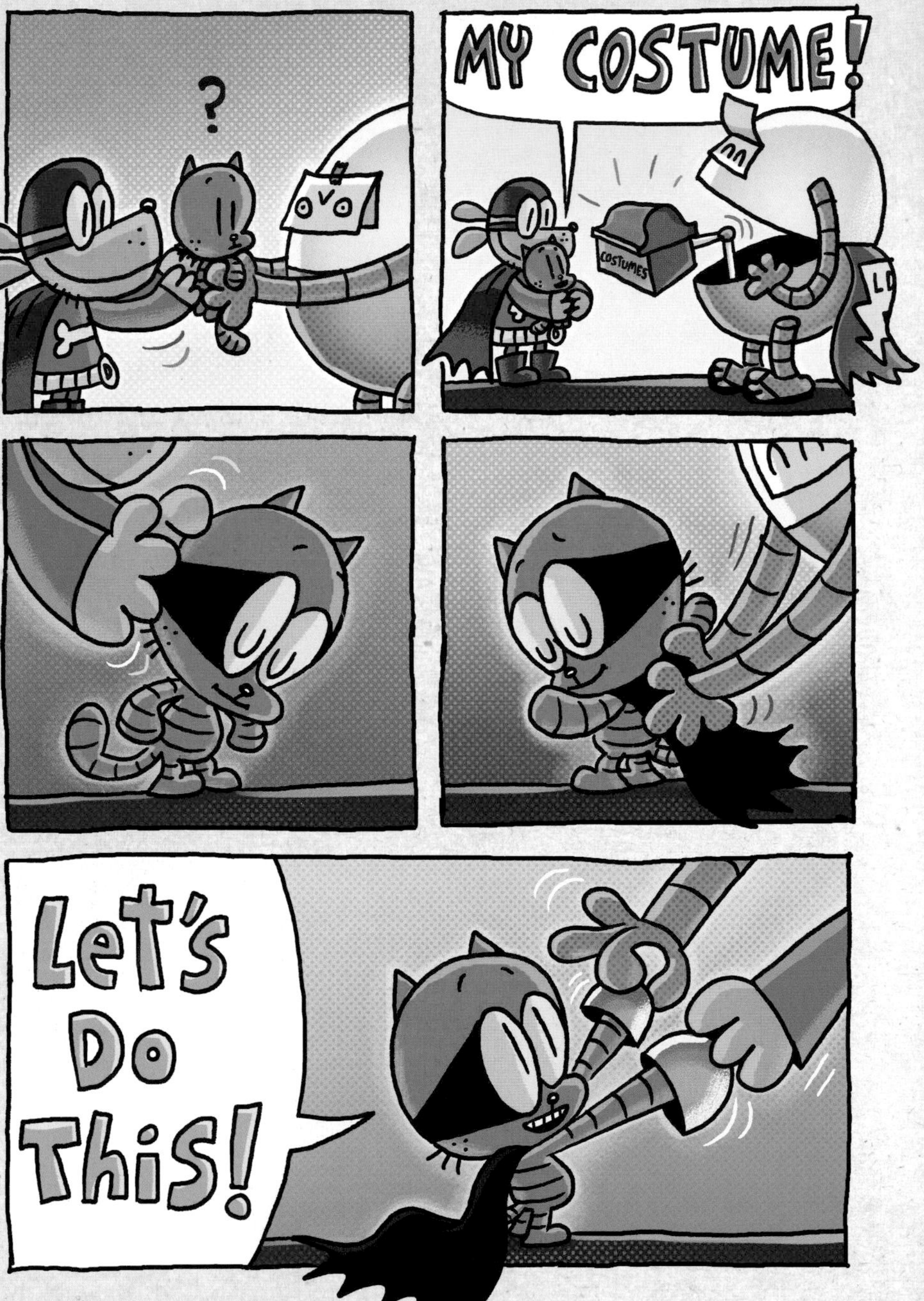
?
MY COSTUME!
COSTUMES
Let's Do This!

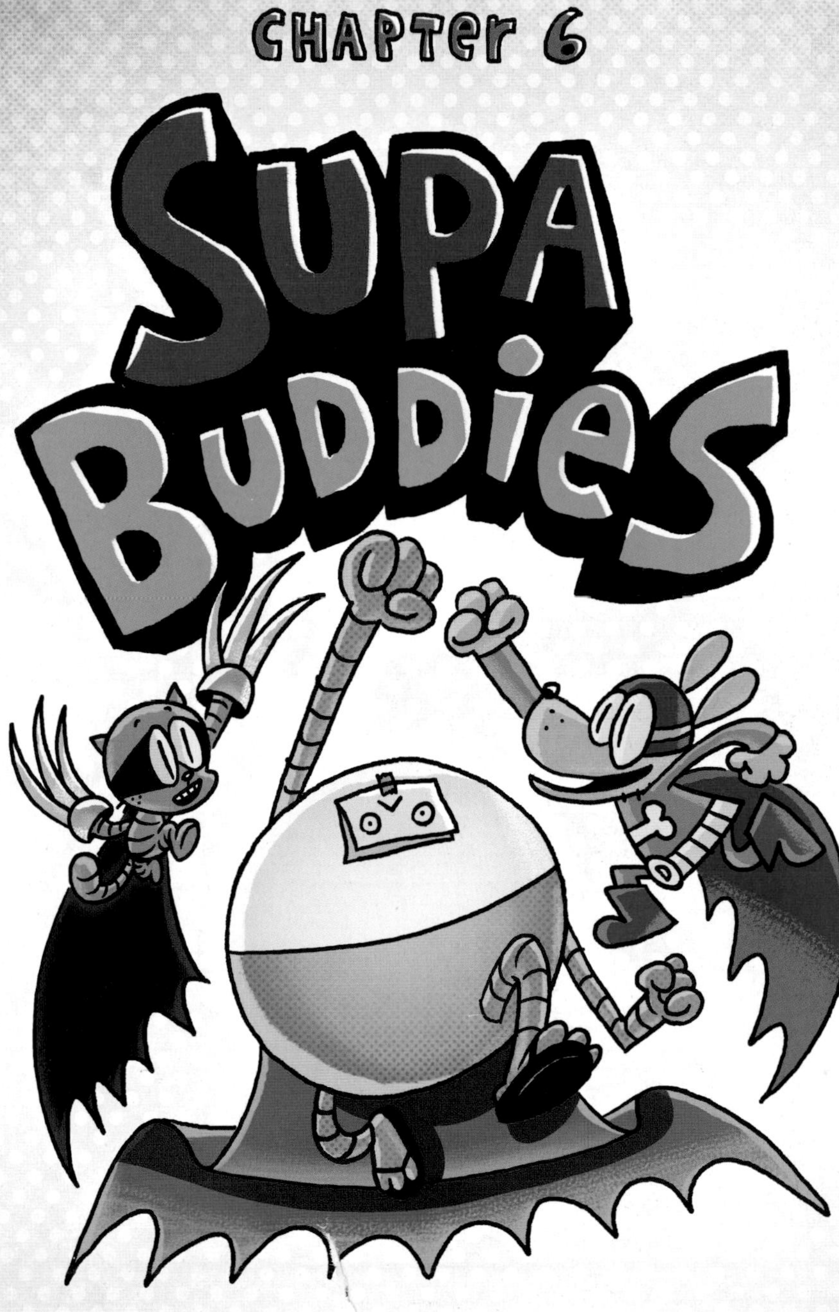
CHAPTER 6
SUPA BUDDIES

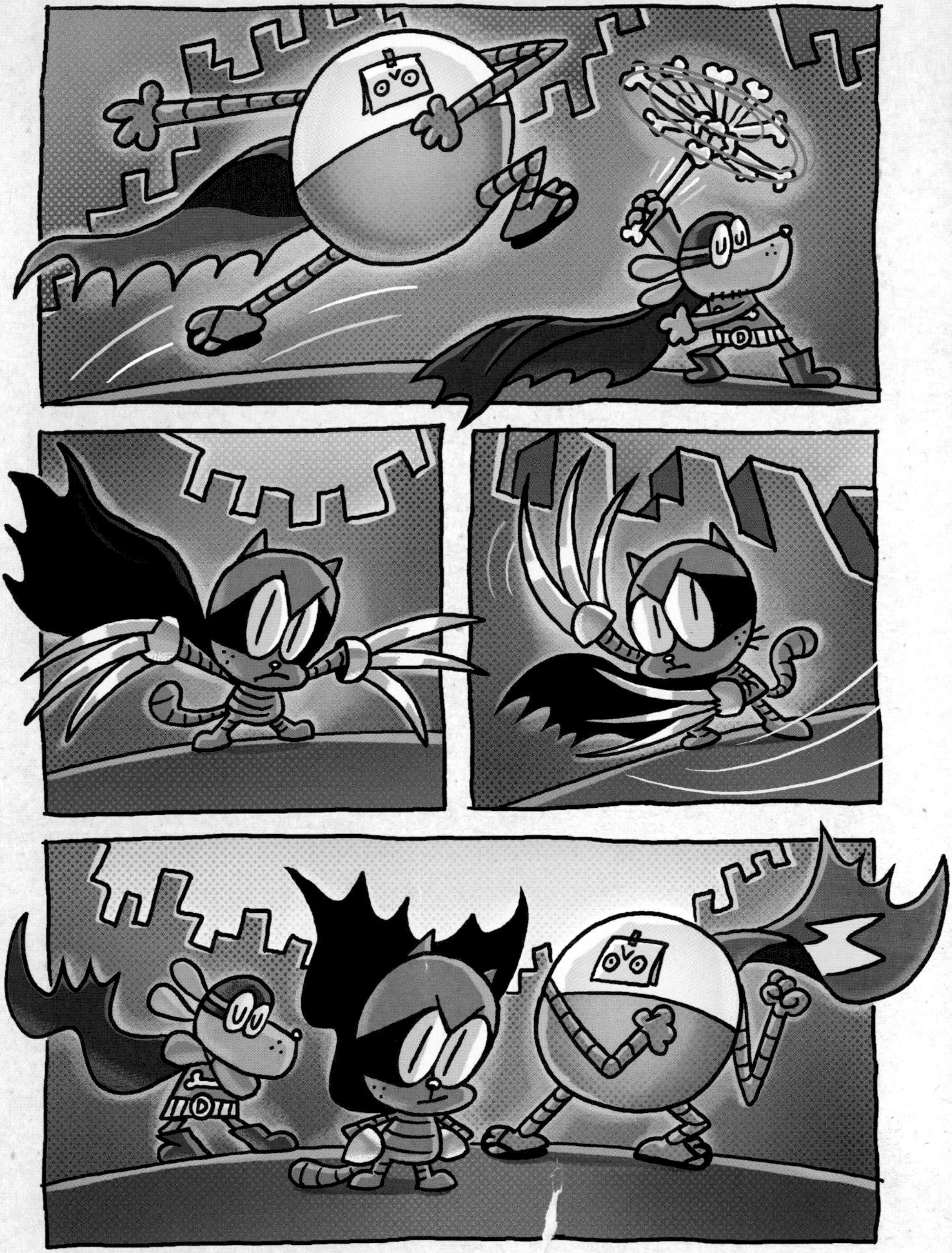
OVO
OVO

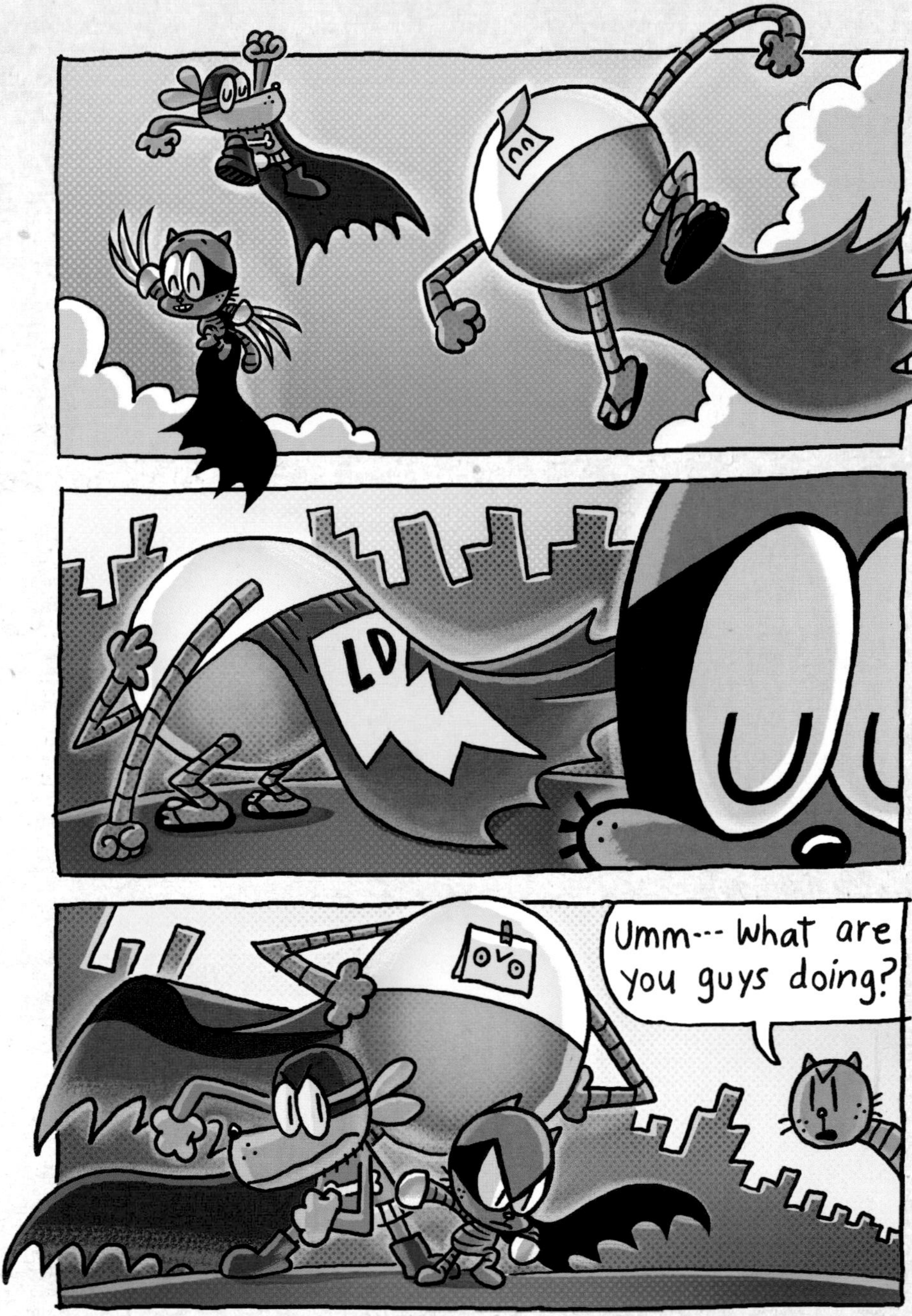
LD
Umm--- What are you guys doing?

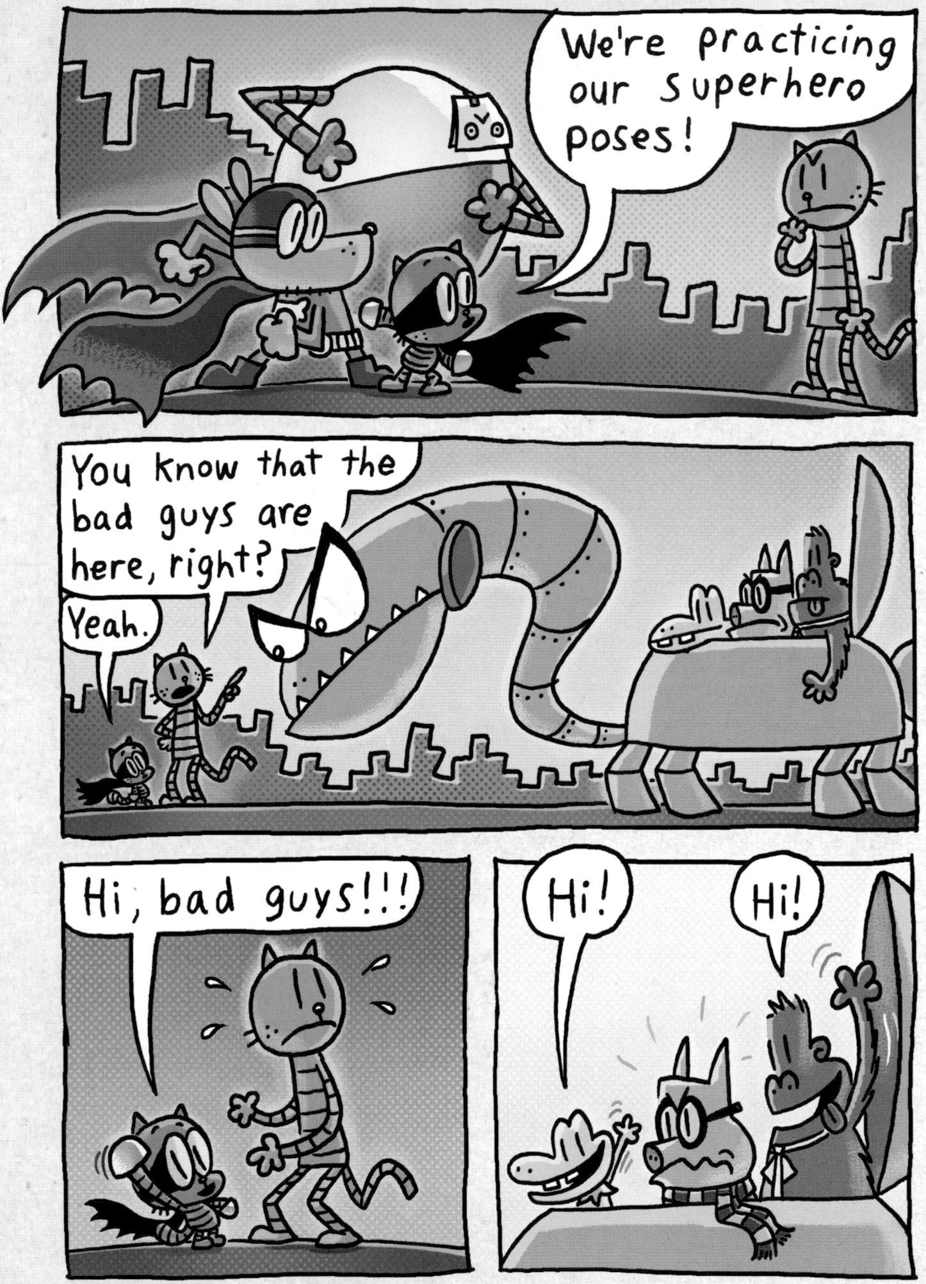
We're practicing our superhero poses!
You know that the bad guys are here, right?
Yeah.
Hi, bad guys!!!
Hi!
Hi!

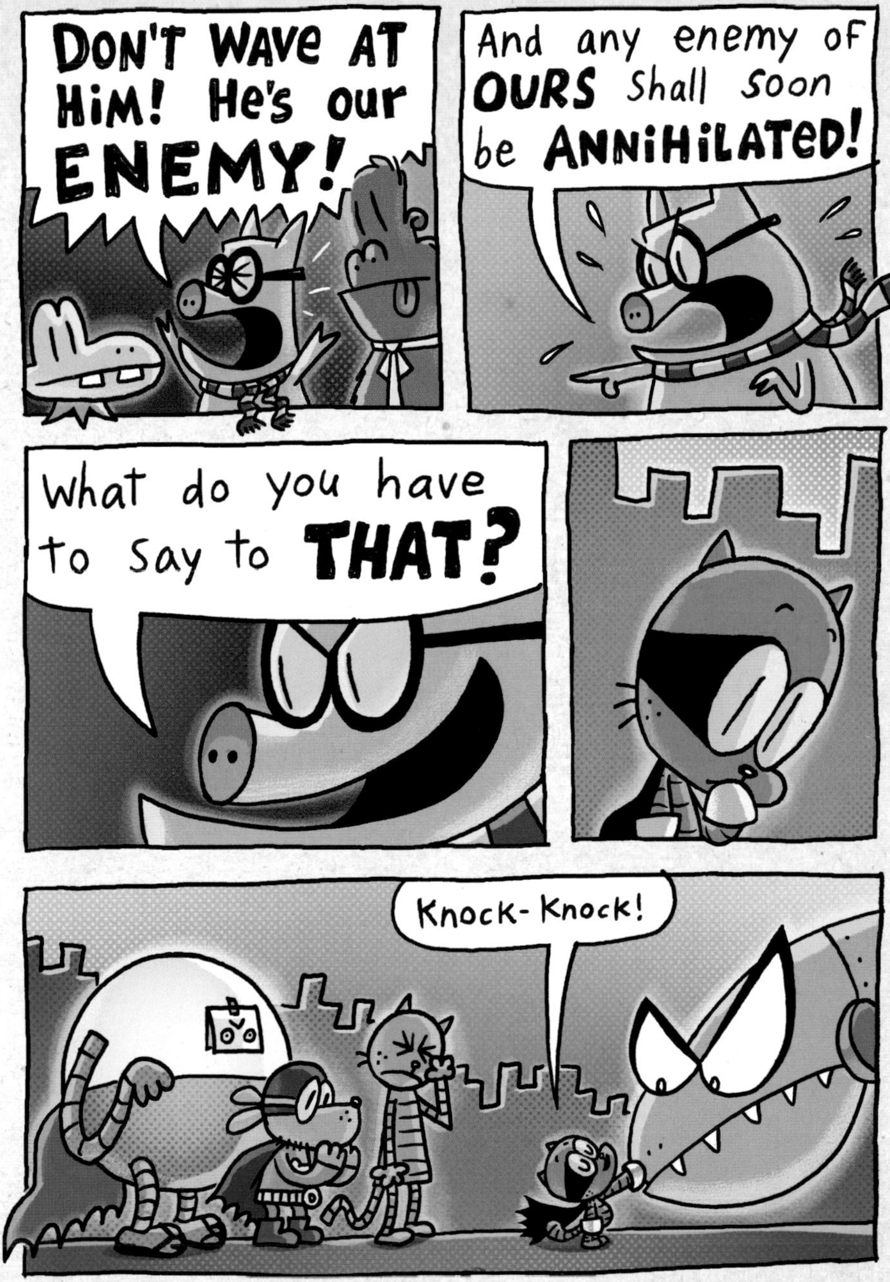
DON'T WAVE AT HIM! He's our ENEMY!
And any enemy of OURS Shall soon be ANNIHILATED!
What do you have to say to THAT?
Knock-Knock!

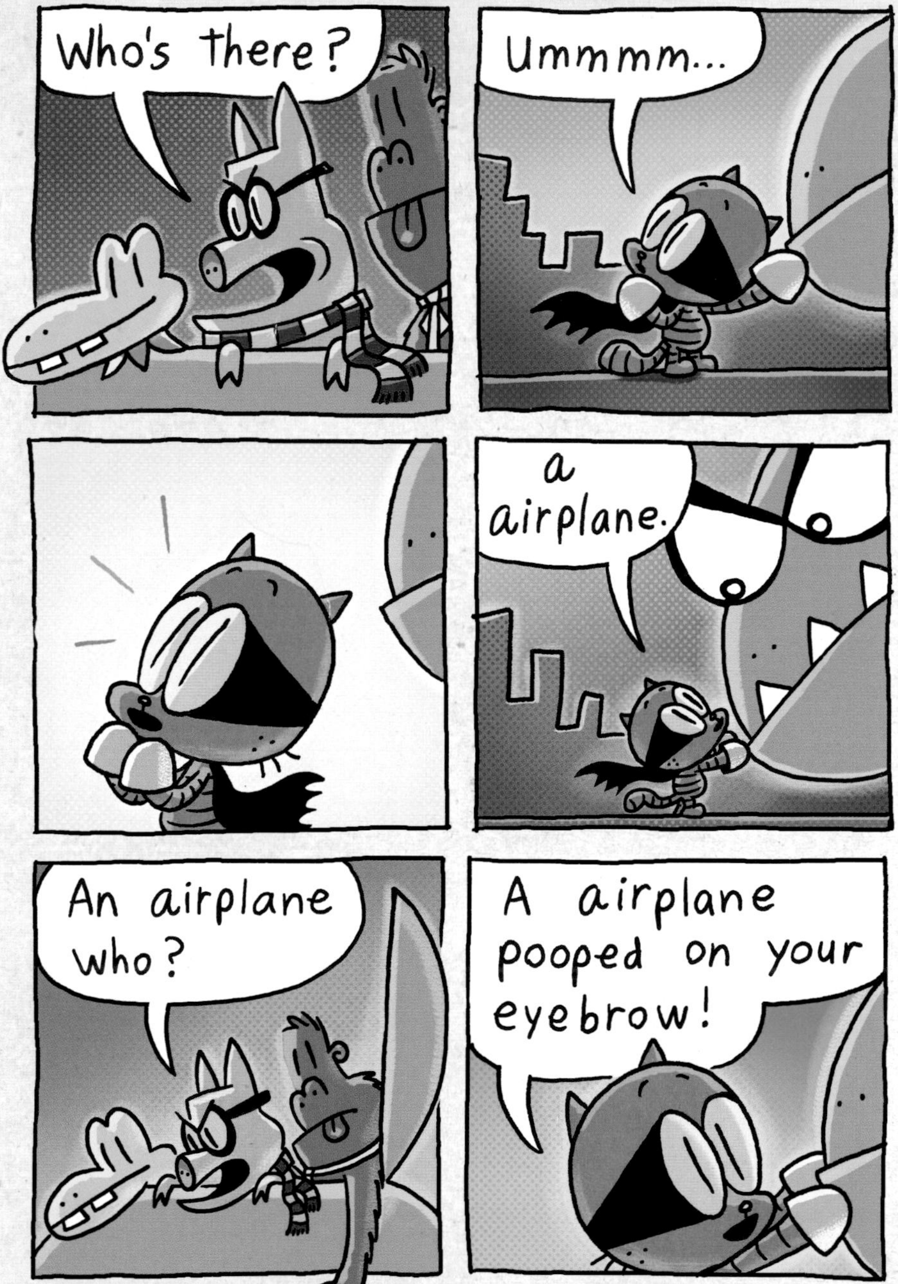
Who's there?
Ummmm...
a
airplane.
An airplane who?
A airplane pooped on your eyebrow!

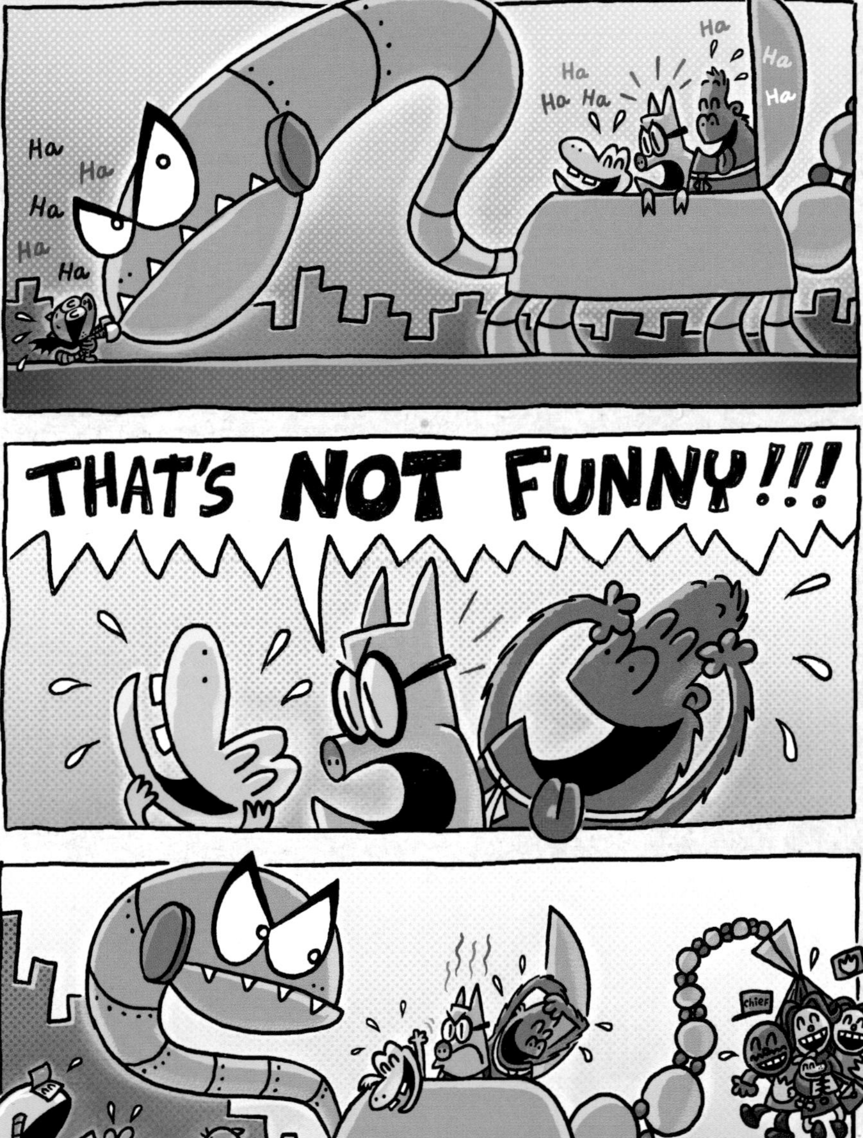
Ha
Ha
Ha
Ha
Ha
Ha
Ha Ha
Ha
Ha
Ha
THAT'S NOT FUNNY!!!
chief

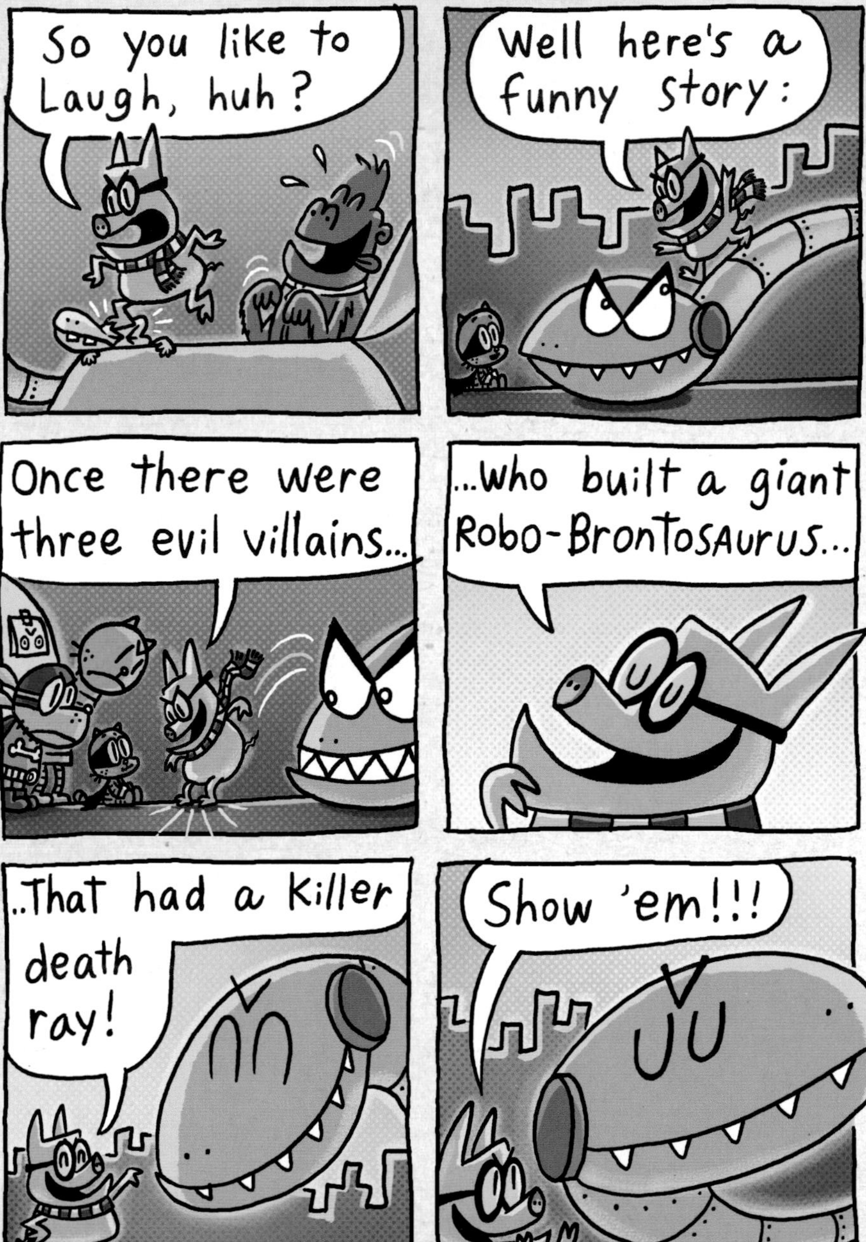
So you like to Laugh, huh?
Well here's a funny story:
Once there were three evil villains...
...who built a giant Robo-Brontosaurus...
...That had a Killer death ray!
Show 'em!!!

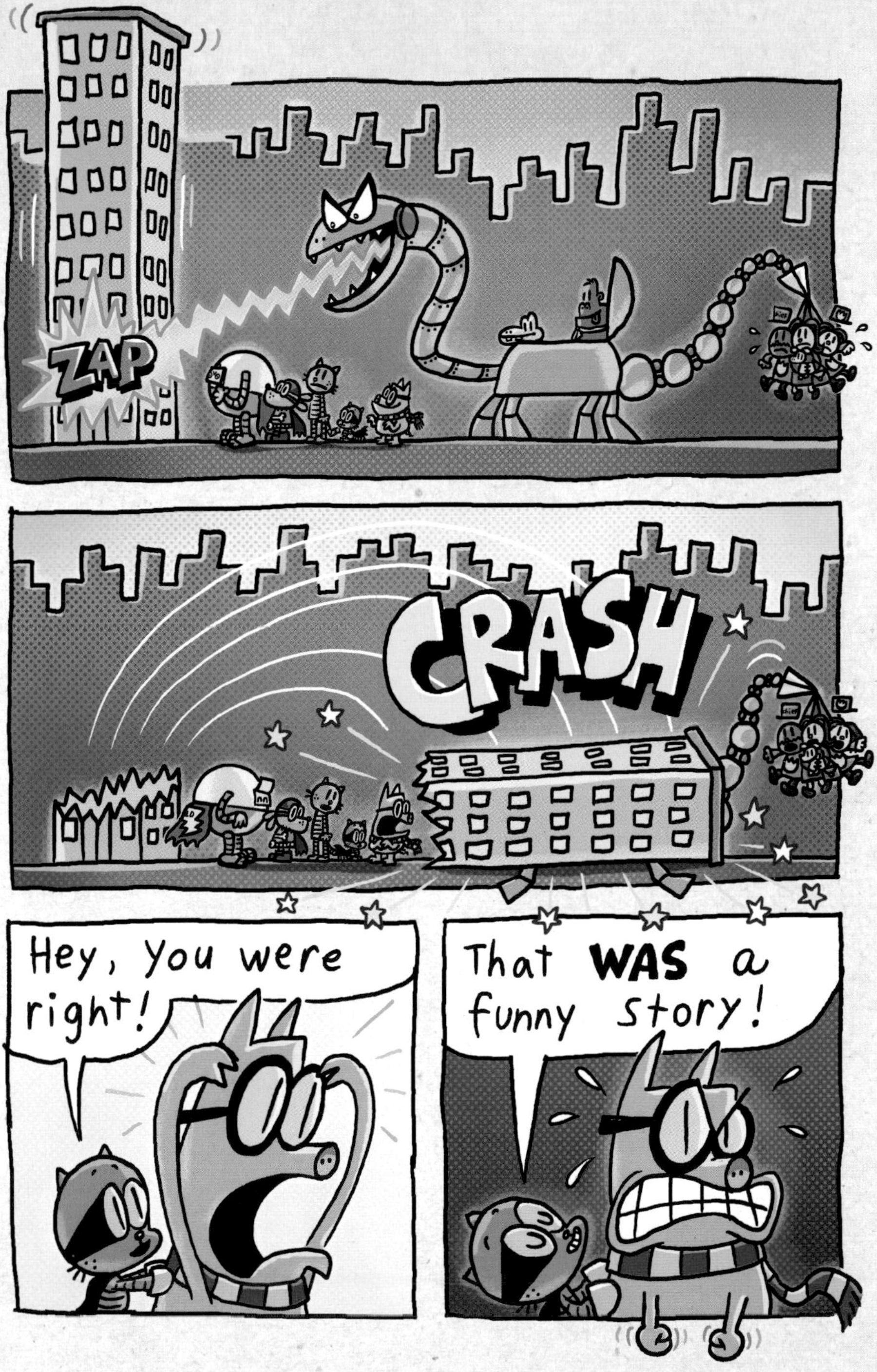
ZAP
CRASH
Hey, you were right!
That WAS a funny story!

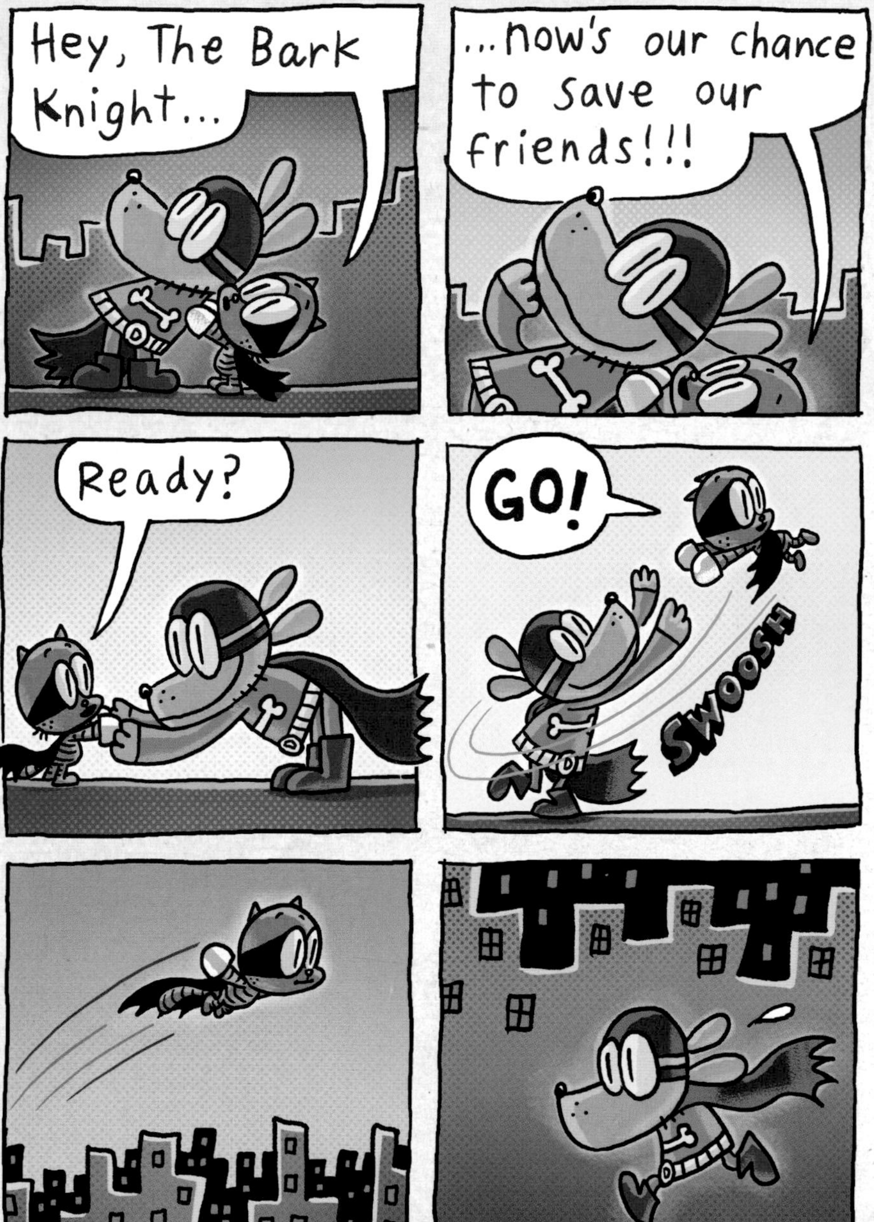
Hey, The Bark Knight...
...now's our chance to save our friends!!!
Ready?
GO!
SWOOSH

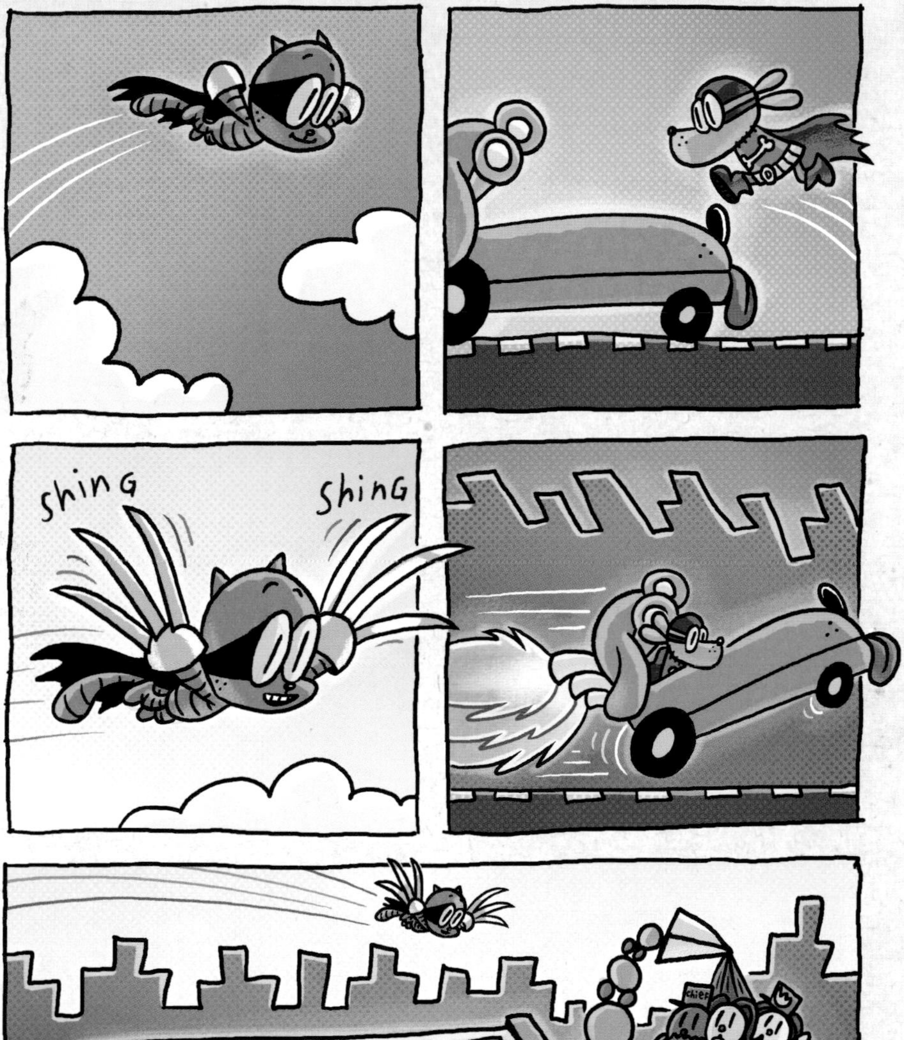
SHING
SHING

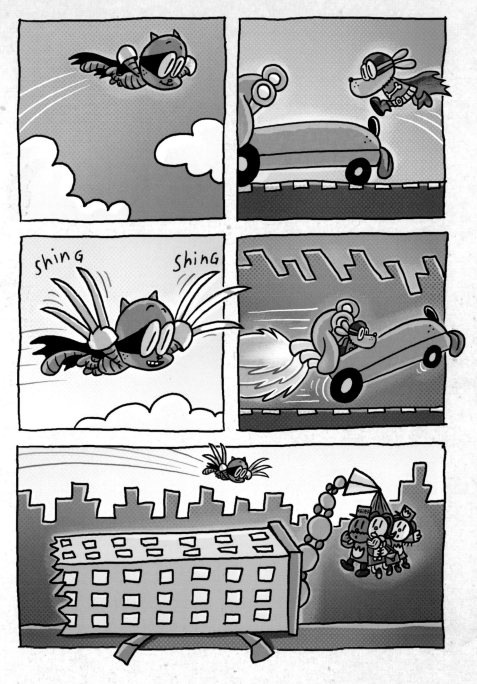

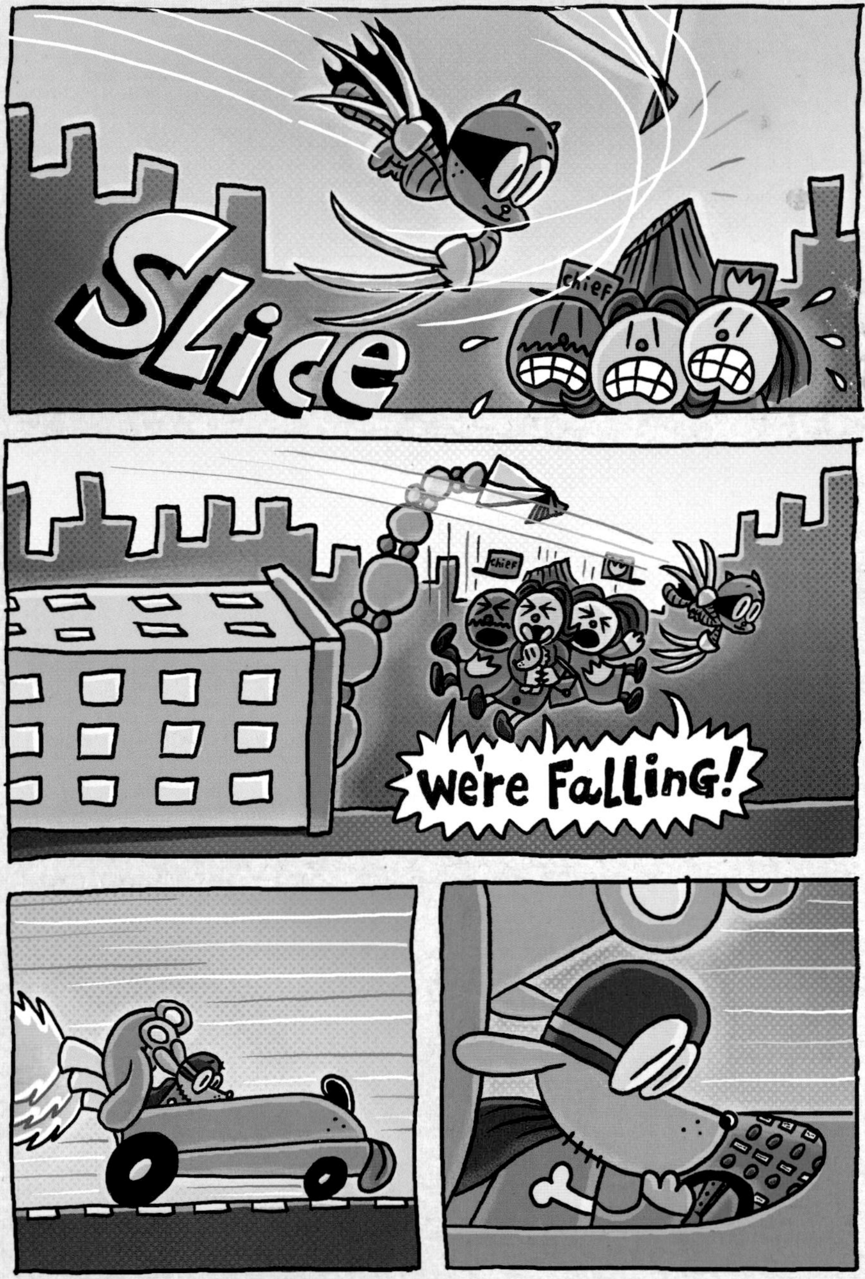
SLice
CHIEF
CHIEF
We're FaLLinG!

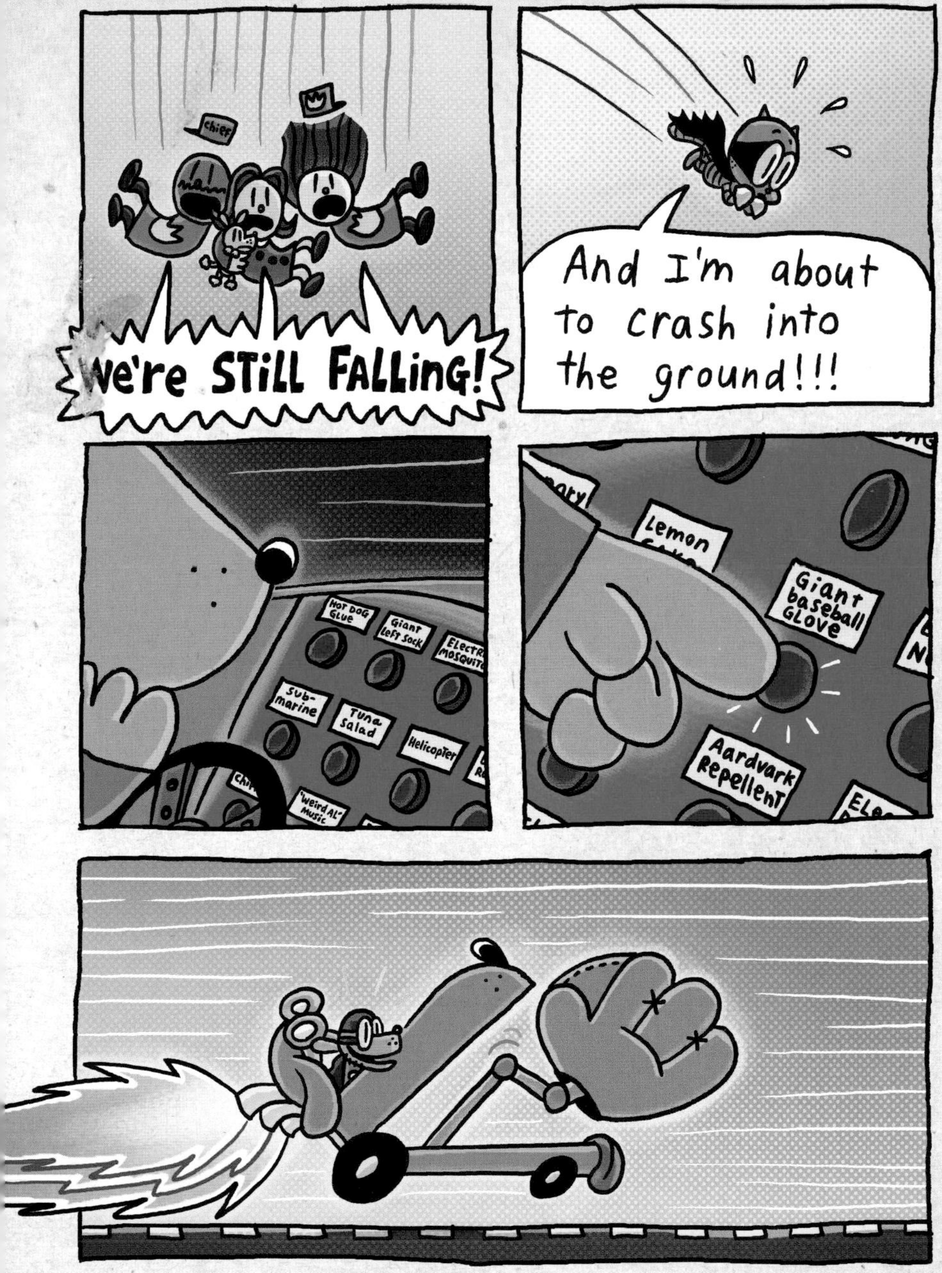
chief
WE'RE STILL FALLING!
And I'm about to crash into the ground!!!
HOT DOG GLUE
Giant Left Sock
Sub-marine
Tuna Salad
Helicopter
"Weird Al" Music
Lemon
Giant baseball GLove
Aardvark Repellent

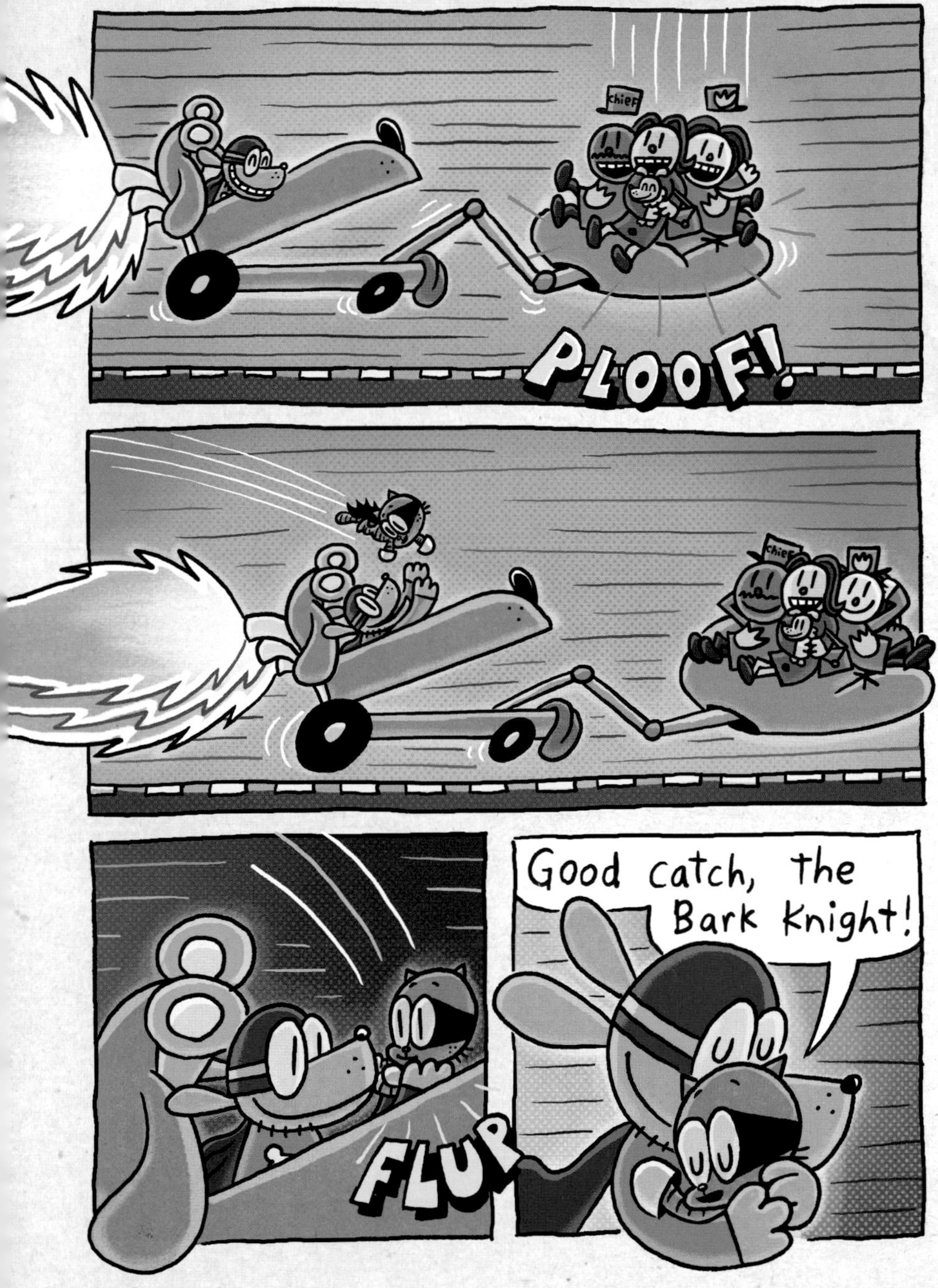
chief
PLOOF!
chief
FLUP
Good catch, the Bark Knight!

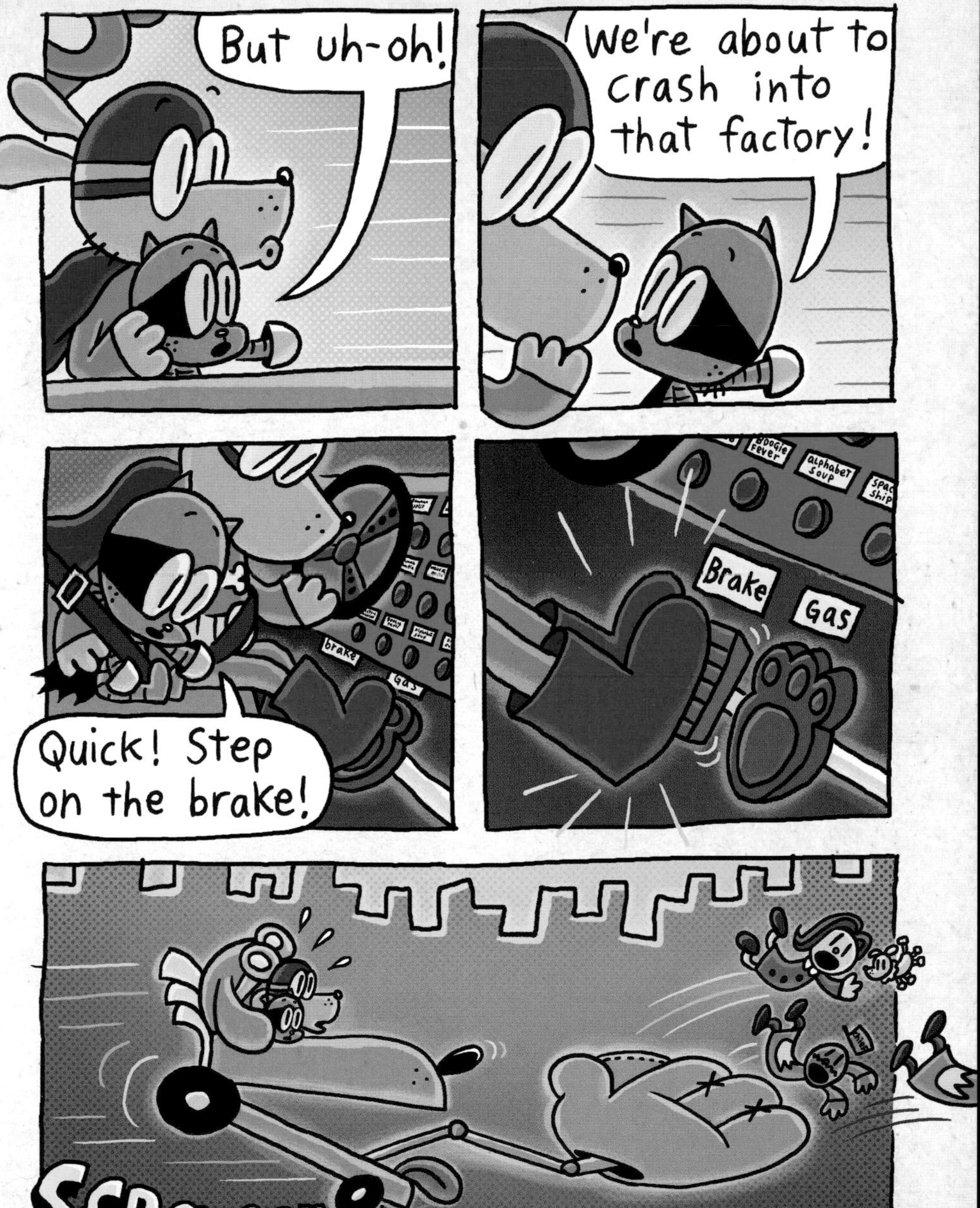
But uh-oh!
We're about to crash into that factory!
Boogie Fever
Alphabet Soup
Quick! Step on the brake!
Brake
Gas
SCREEECH

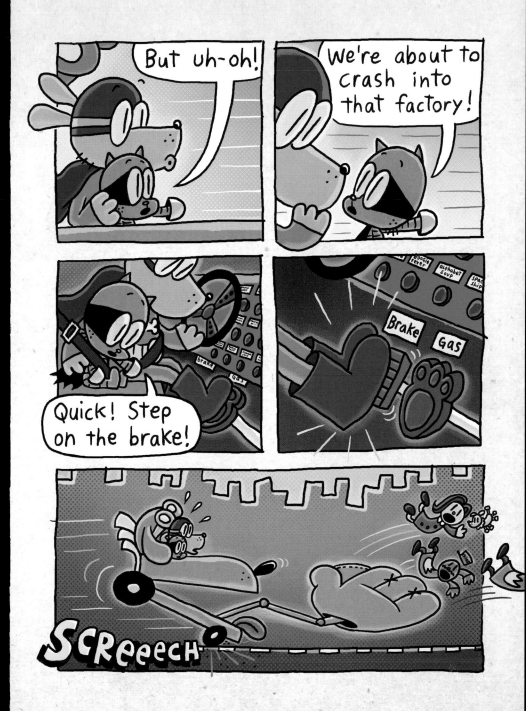

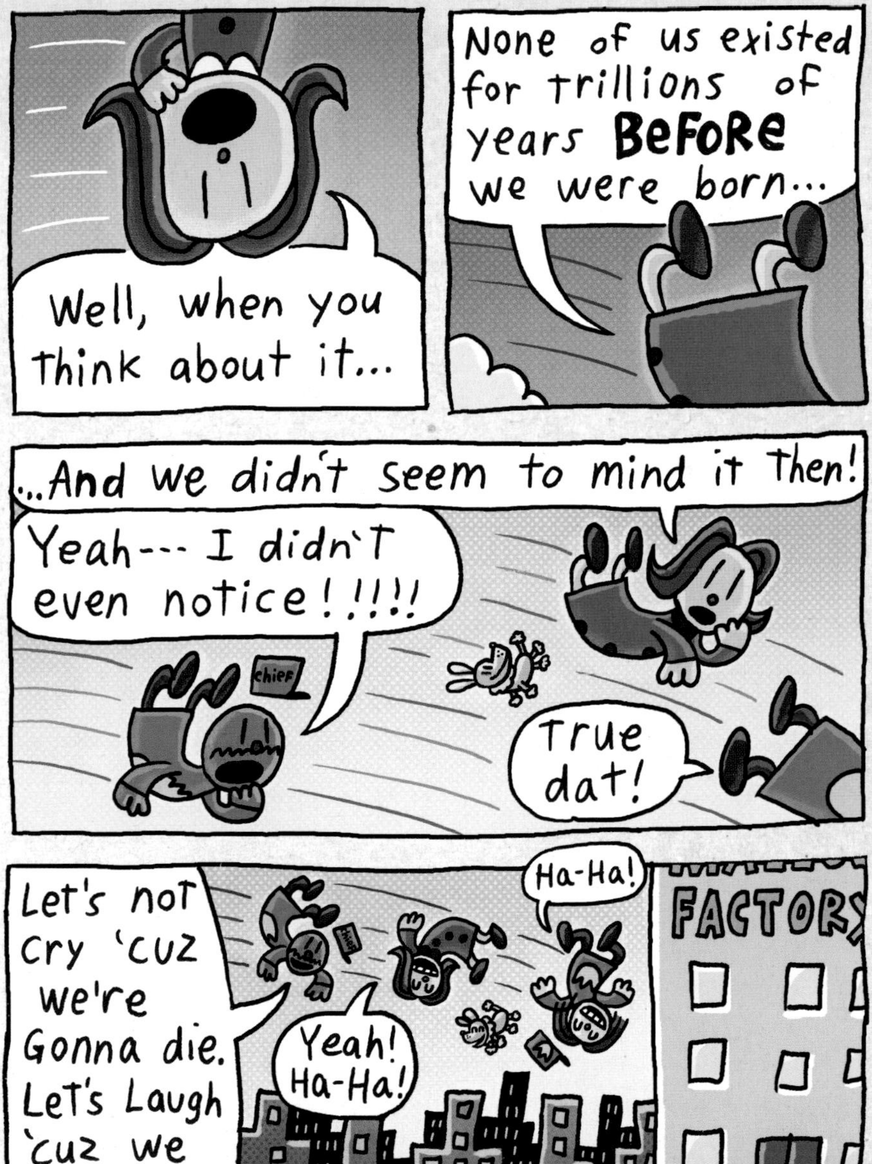

Well, when you think about it...
None of us existed for trillions of years **BEFORE** we were born...
...And we didn't seem to mind it then!
Yeah--- I didn'T even notice!!!!!
chief
True dat!
Let's not cry 'cuz we're Gonna die. Let's Laugh 'cuz we Got to **LIVE!!!**
Ha-Ha!
Yeah! Ha-Ha!
FACTORY

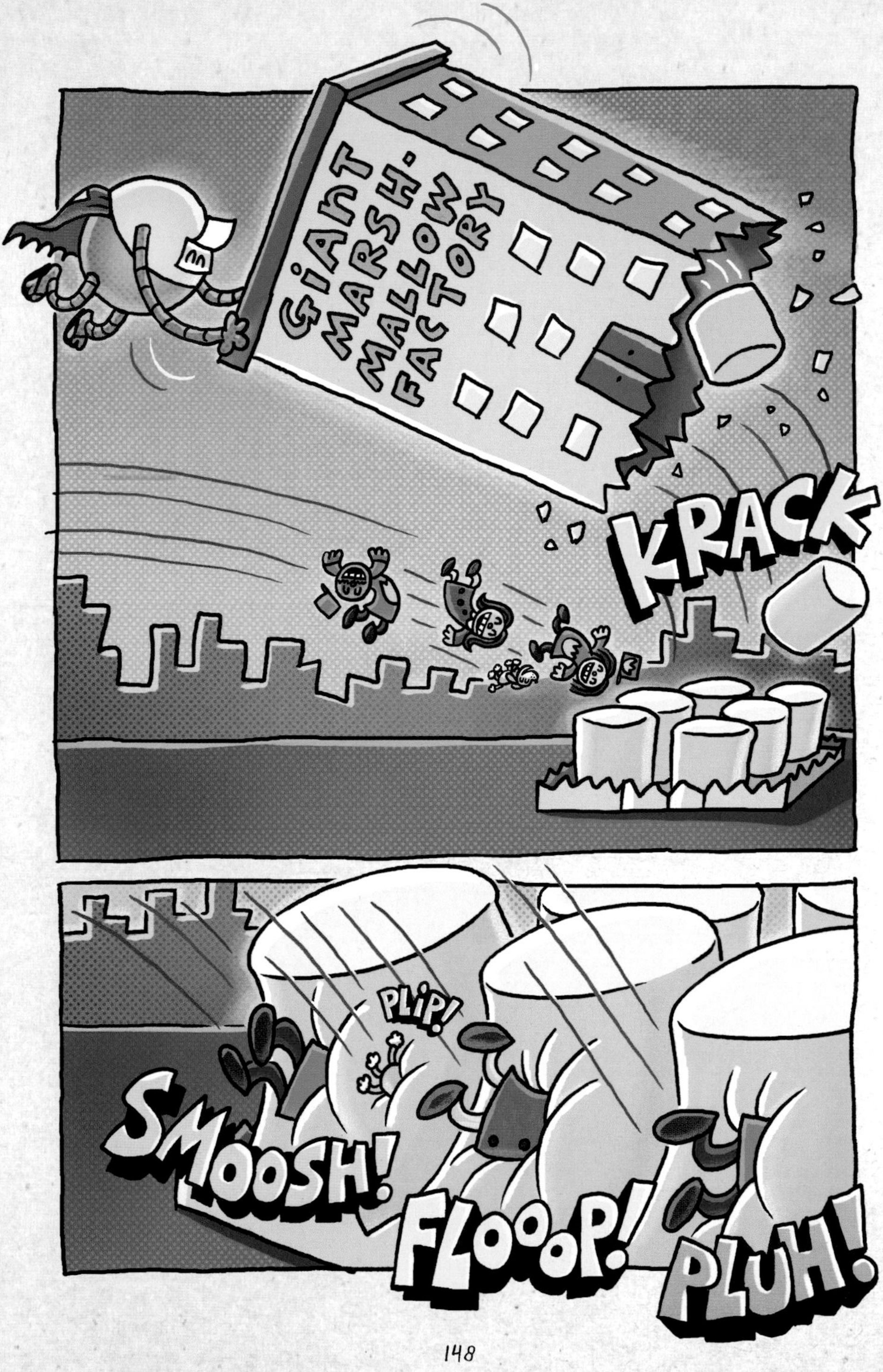
GIANT MARSHMALLOW FACTORY
KRACK
PLIP!
SMOOSH!
FLOOOP!
PLUH!

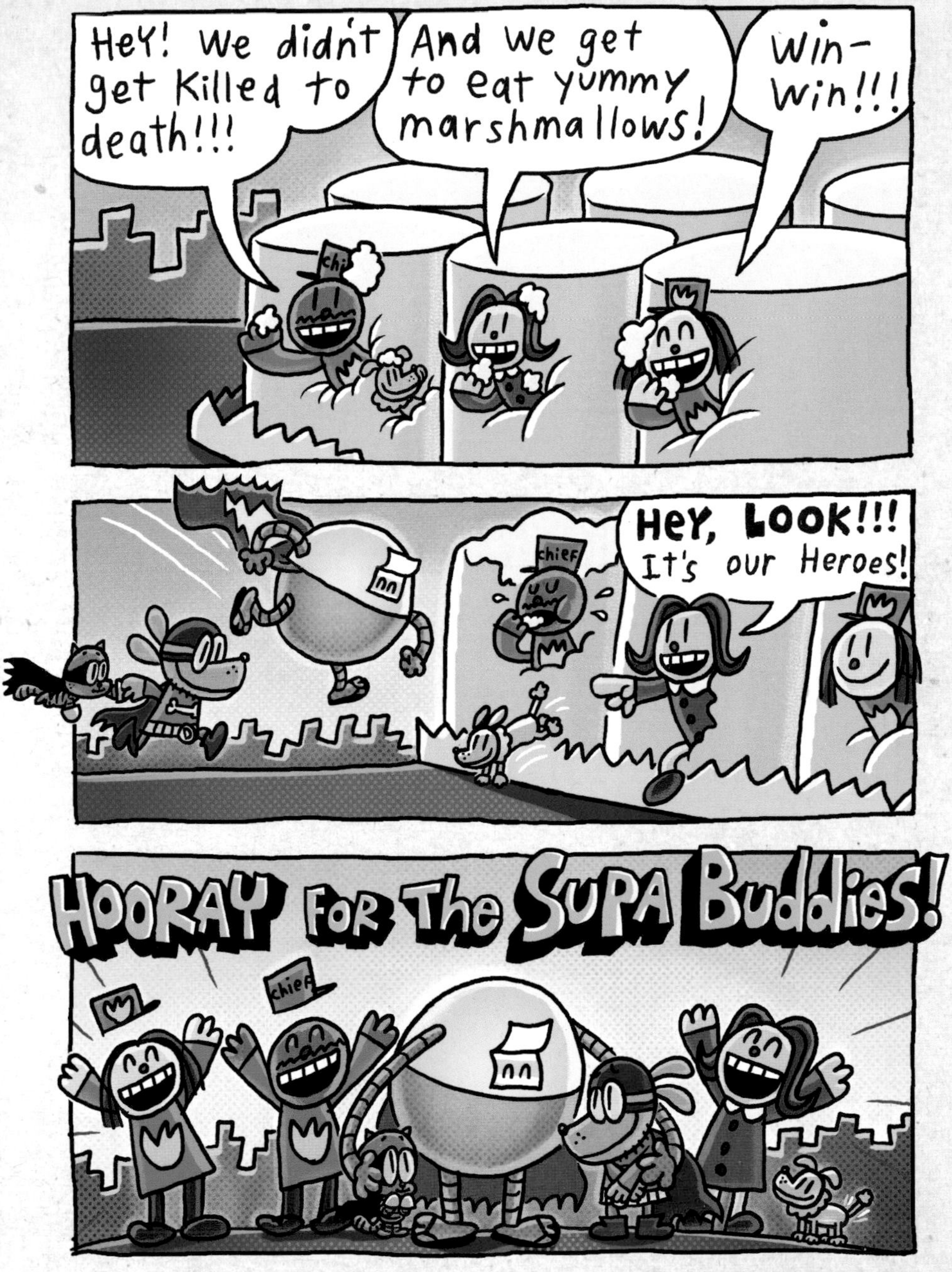
Hey! We didn't get Killed to death!!!
And we get to eat yummy marshmallows!
Win-win!!!
chi
HEY, LOOK!!! It's our Heroes!
chief
HOORAY FOR The SUPA Buddies!
chief

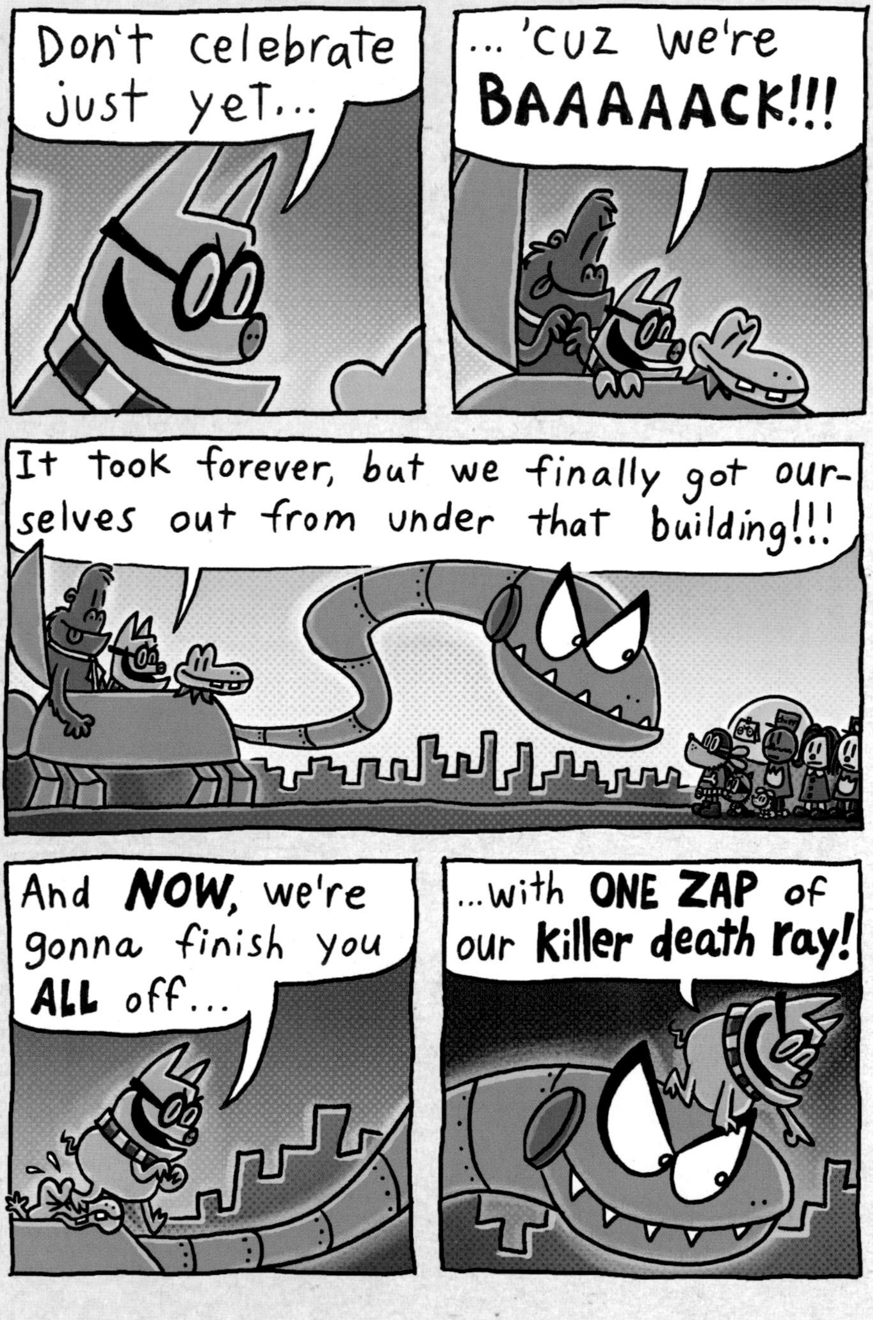
Don't celebrate just yet...
... 'cuz we're BAAAAACK!!!
It took forever, but we finally got our-selves out from under that building!!!
And NOW, we're gonna finish you ALL off...
...with ONE ZAP of our Killer death ray!

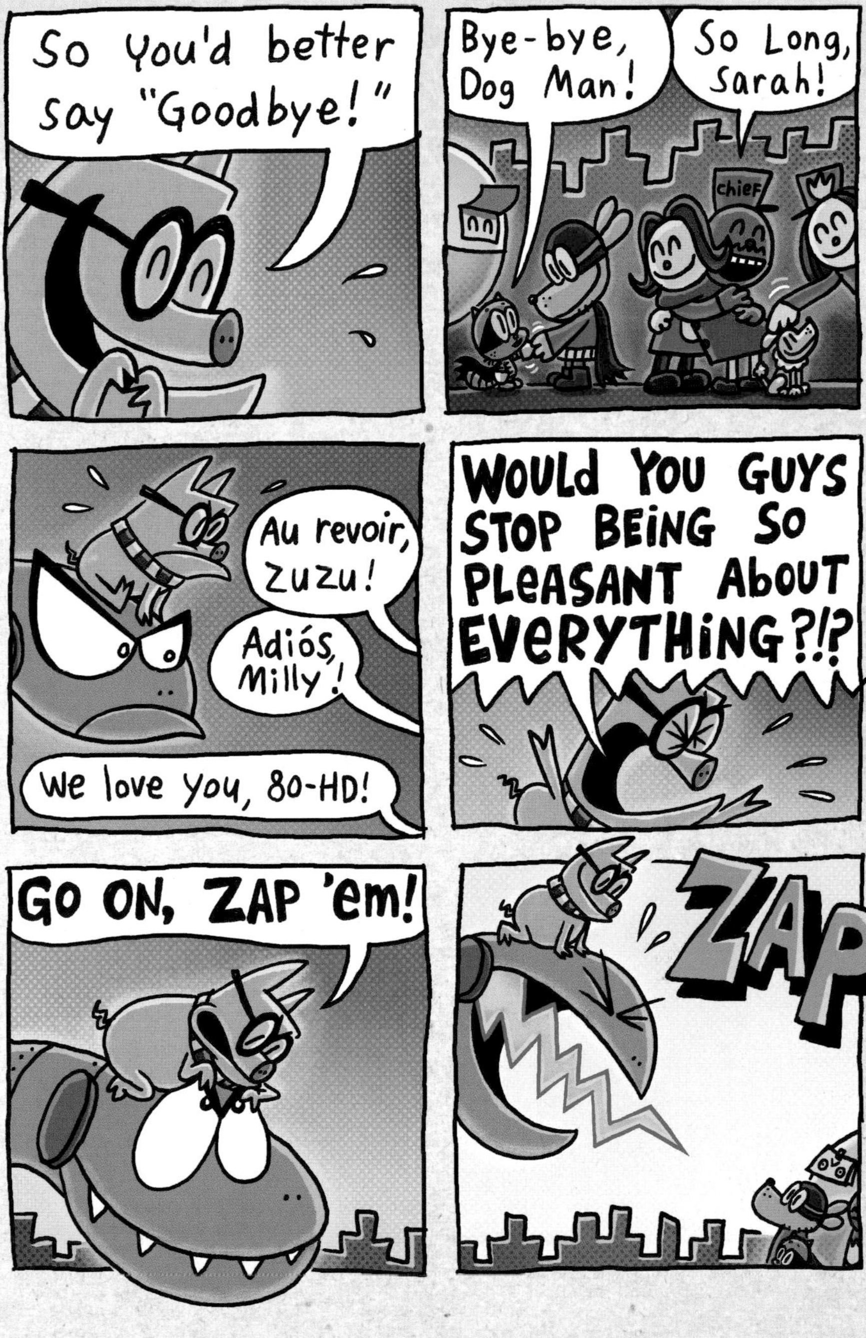
So you'd better say "Goodbye!"
Bye-bye, Dog Man!
So Long, Sarah!
chief
Au revoir, Zuzu!
Adiós, Milly!
We love you, 80-HD!
WOULD YOU GUYS STOP BEING SO PLEASANT ABOUT EVERYTHING?!?
GO ON, ZAP 'em!
ZAP

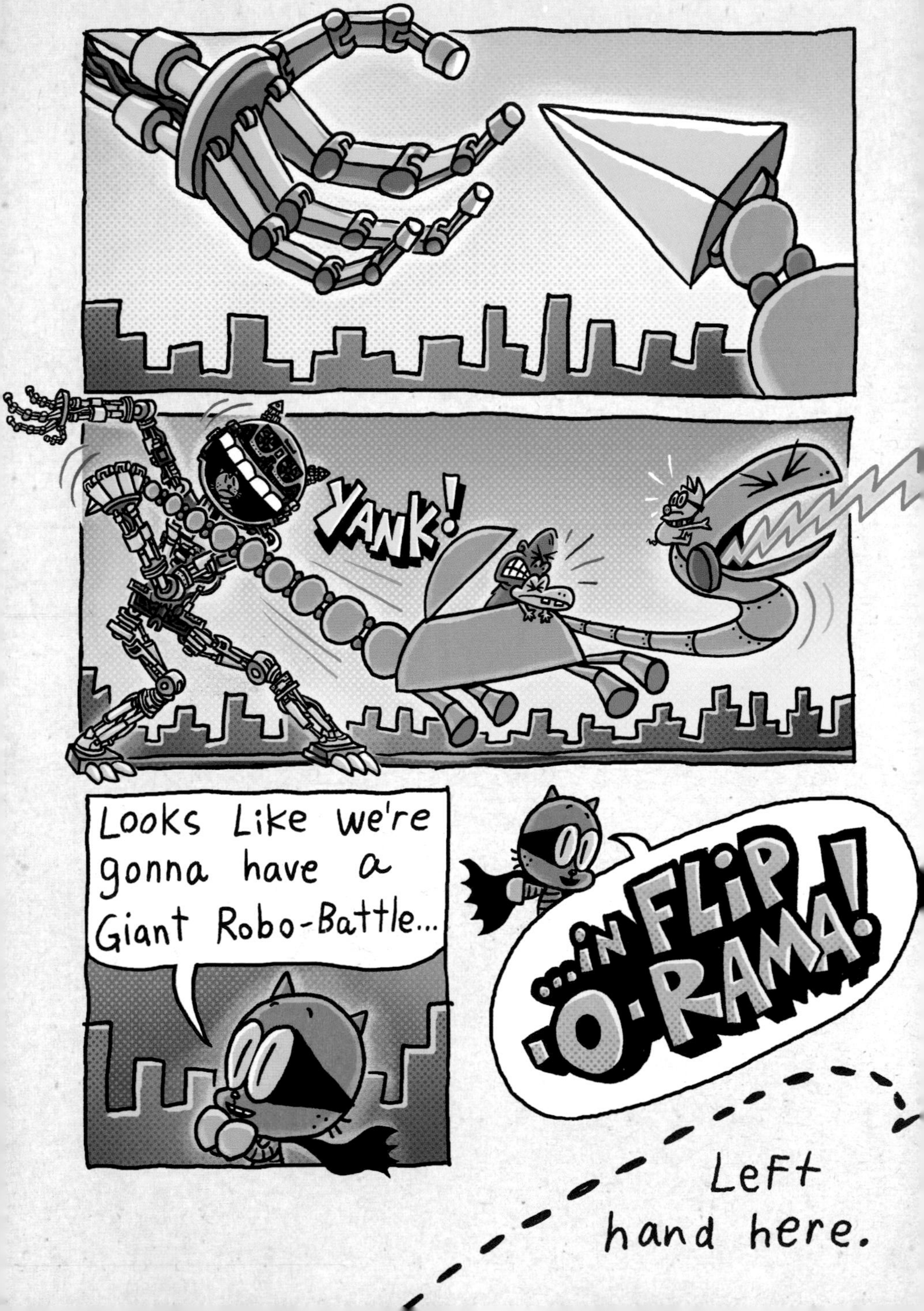
YANK!
Looks Like we're gonna have a Giant Robo-Battle...
...in FLIP-O-RAMA!
Left hand here.

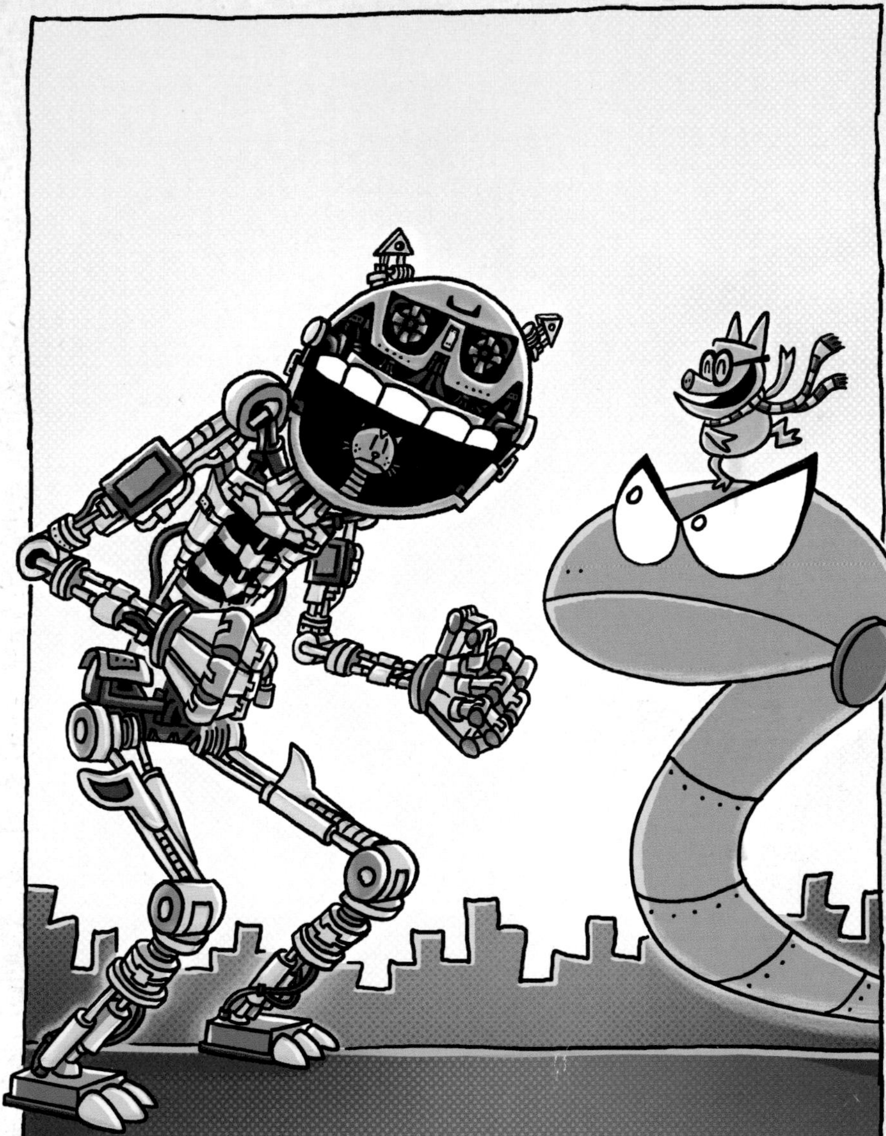

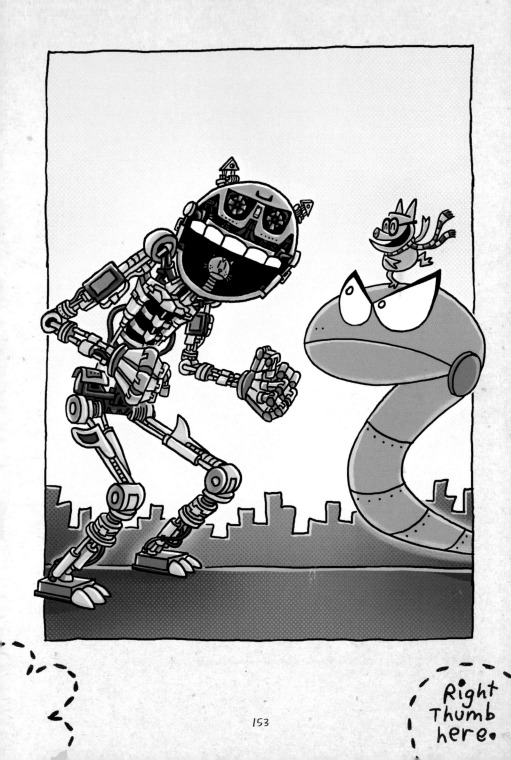

Right Thumb here.

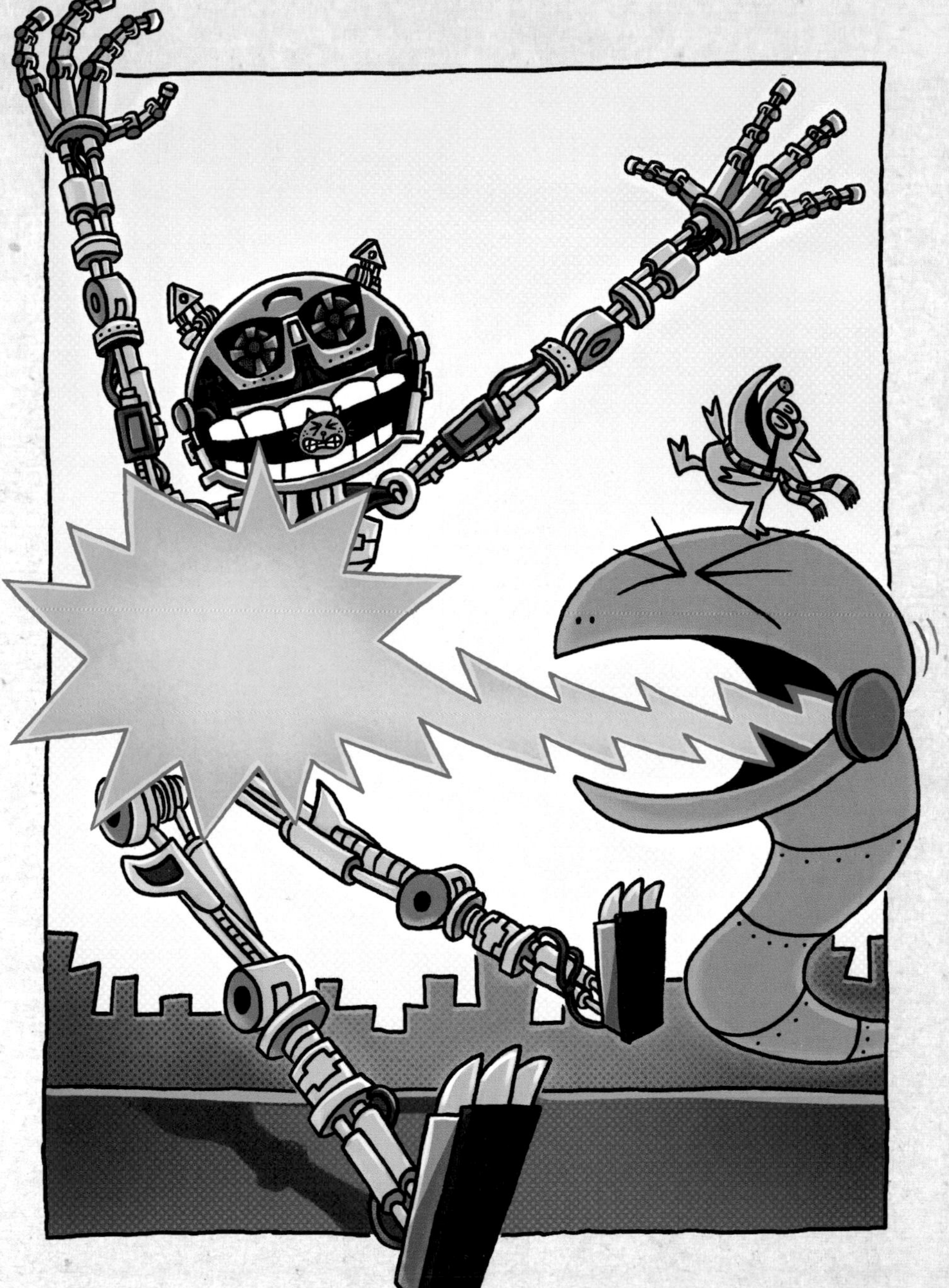

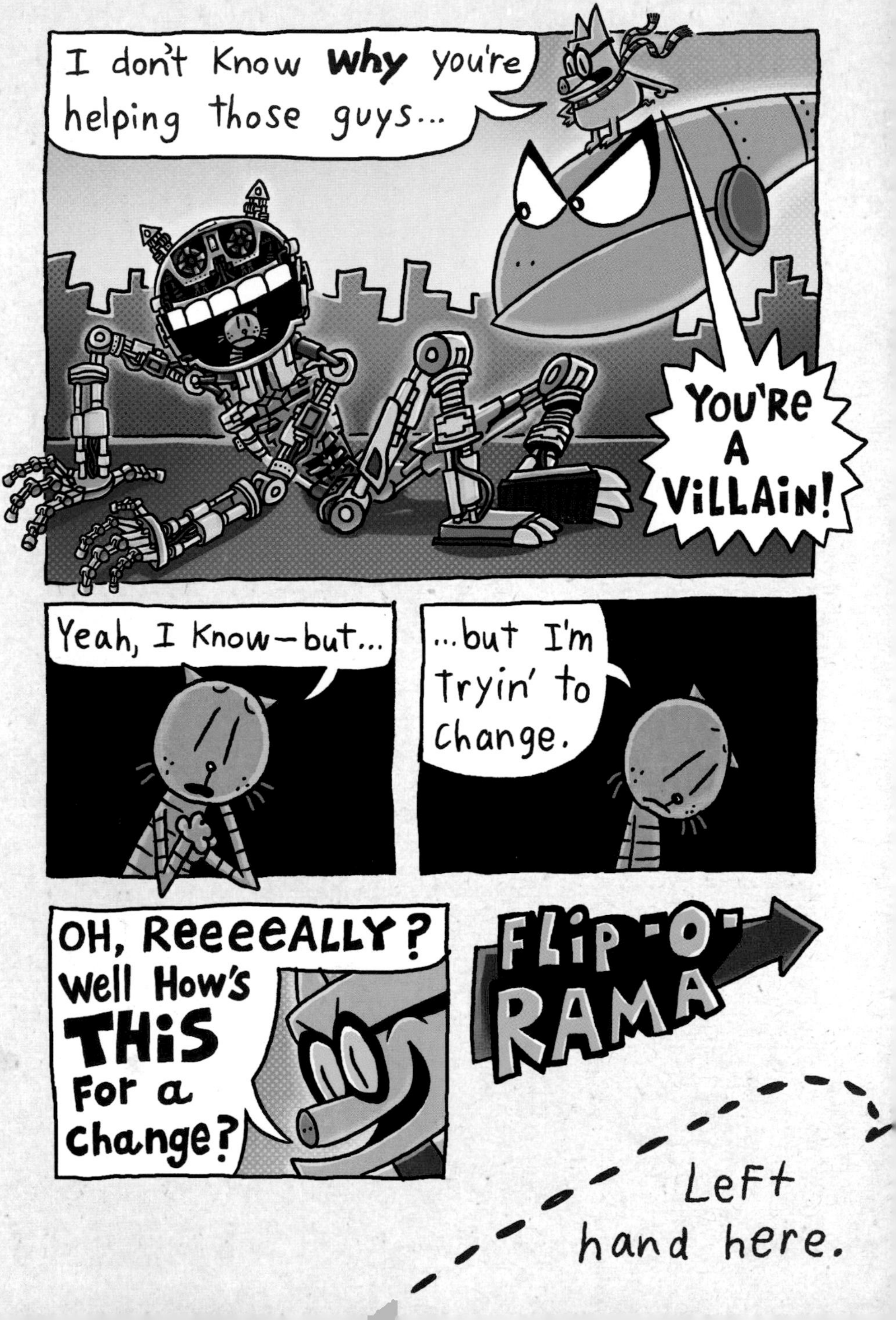
I don't Know **why** you're helping those guys...
YOU'RE A VILLAIN!
Yeah, I Know—but...
...but I'm tryin' to change.
OH, REEEEALLY? Well How's THIS For a change?
FLIP-O-RAMA
Left hand here.

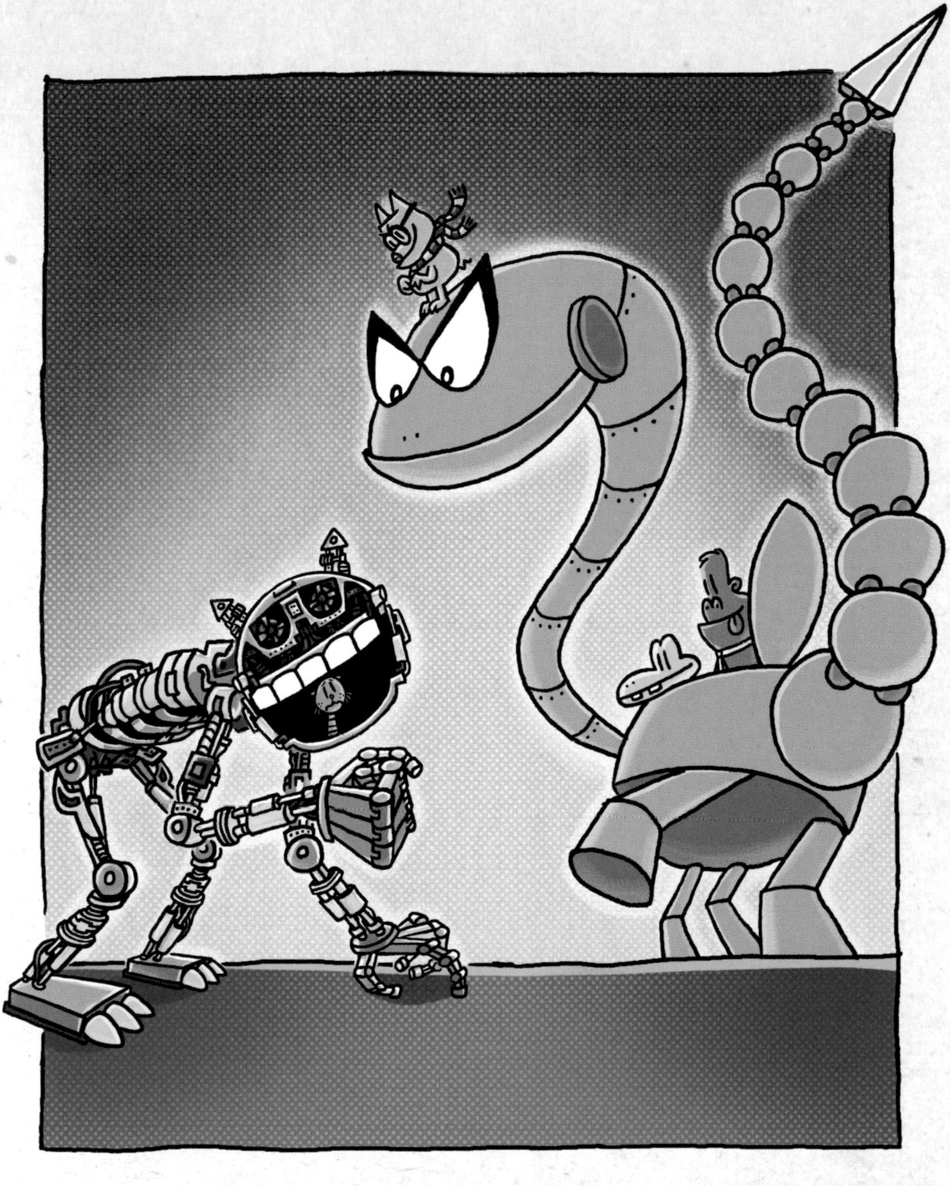

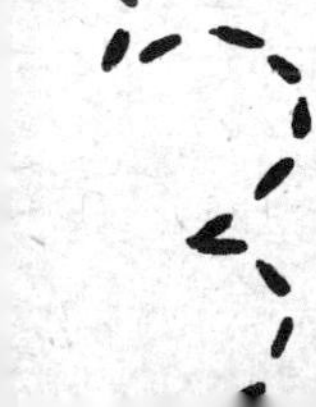

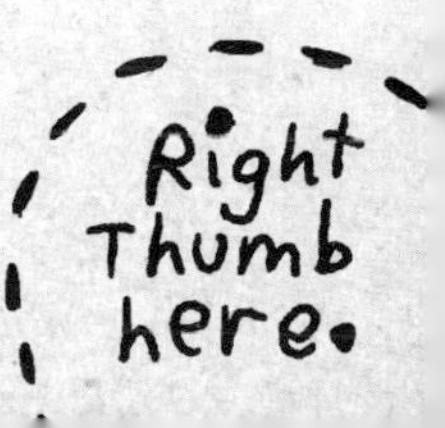
Right
Thumb
here.

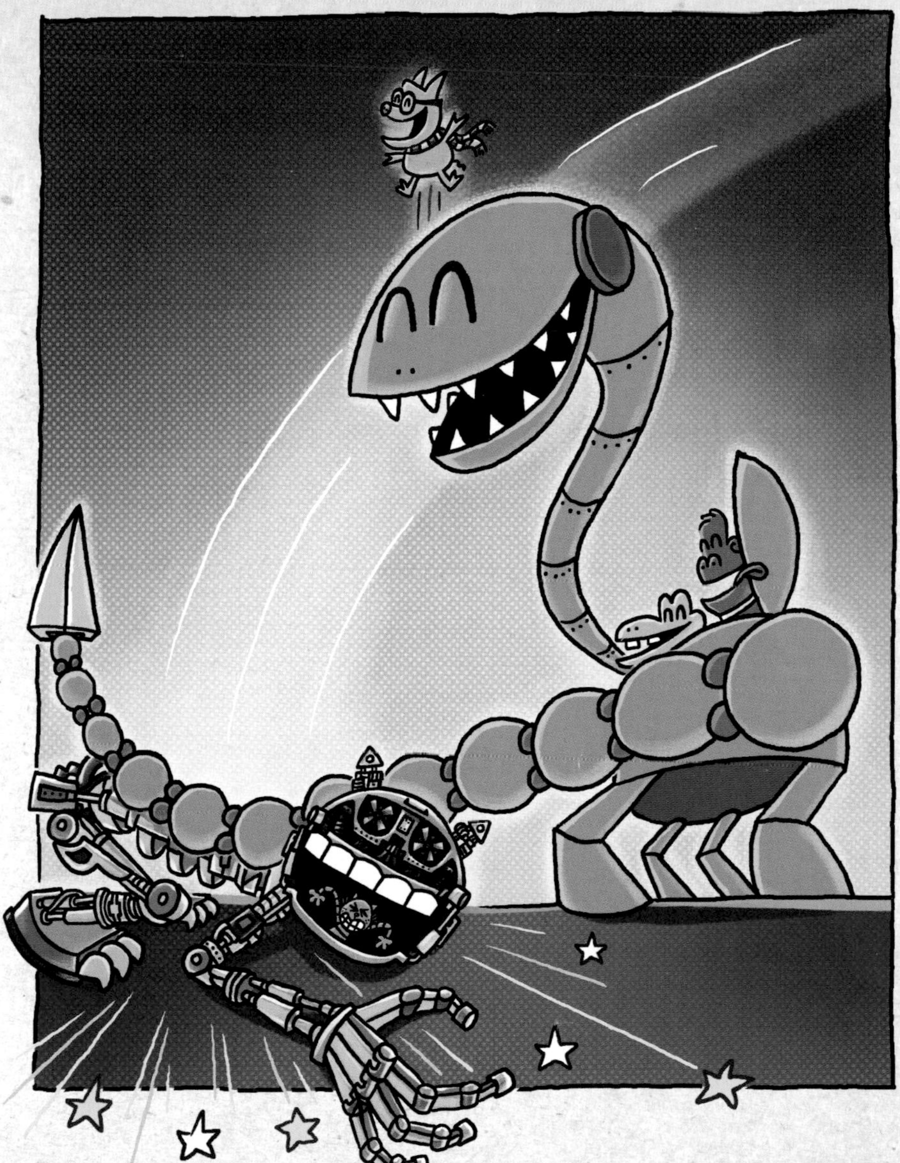

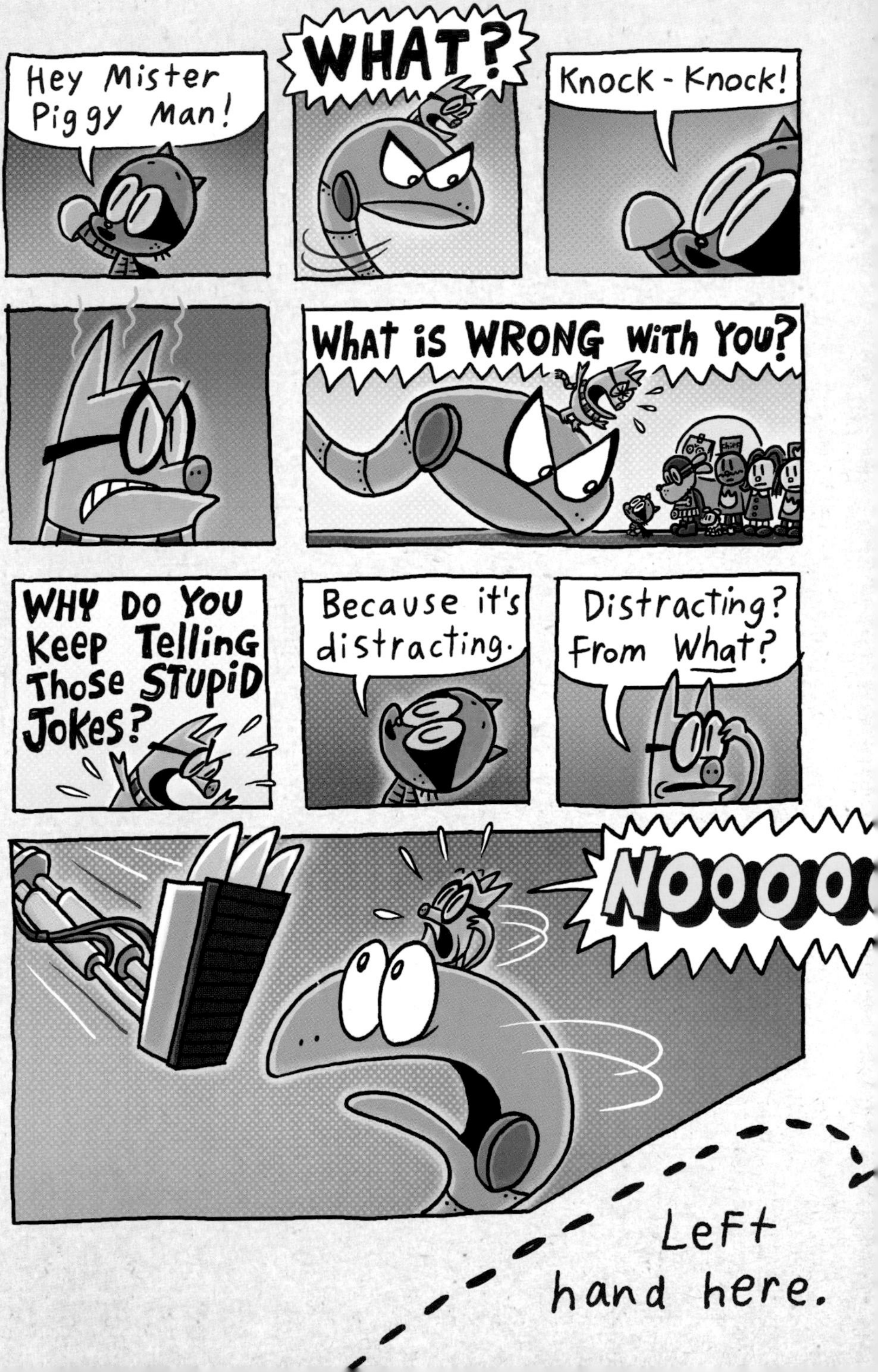
Hey Mister Piggy Man!
WHAT?
Knock-Knock!
What is WRONG With YOU?
WHY DO YOU Keep Telling Those STUPID Jokes?
Because it's distracting.
Distracting? From What?
NOOOO
Left hand here.

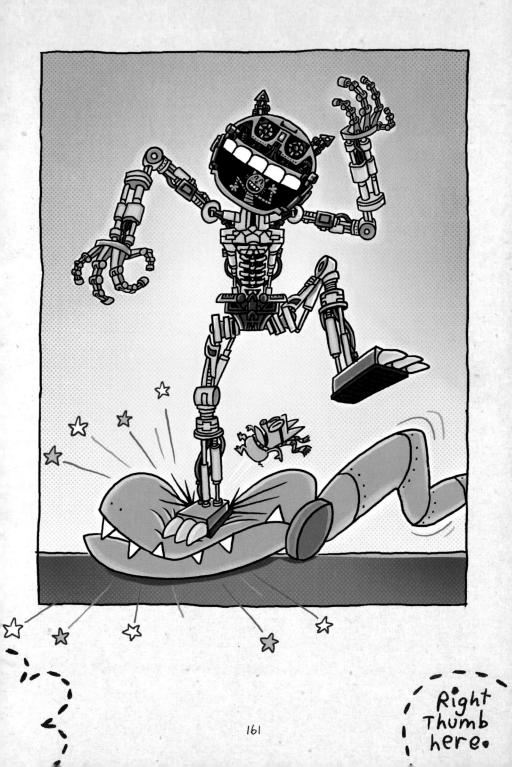

Right
Thumb
here.

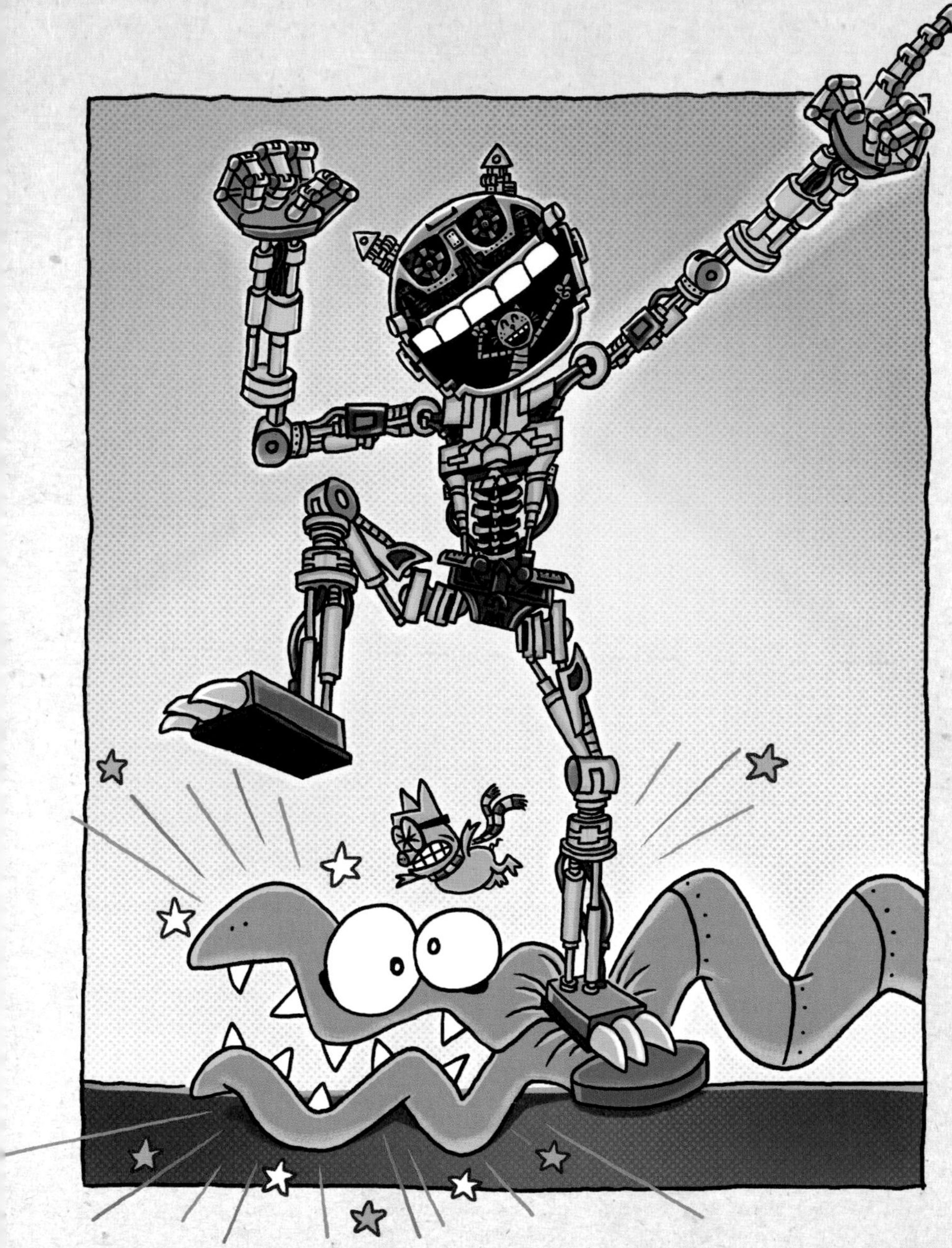

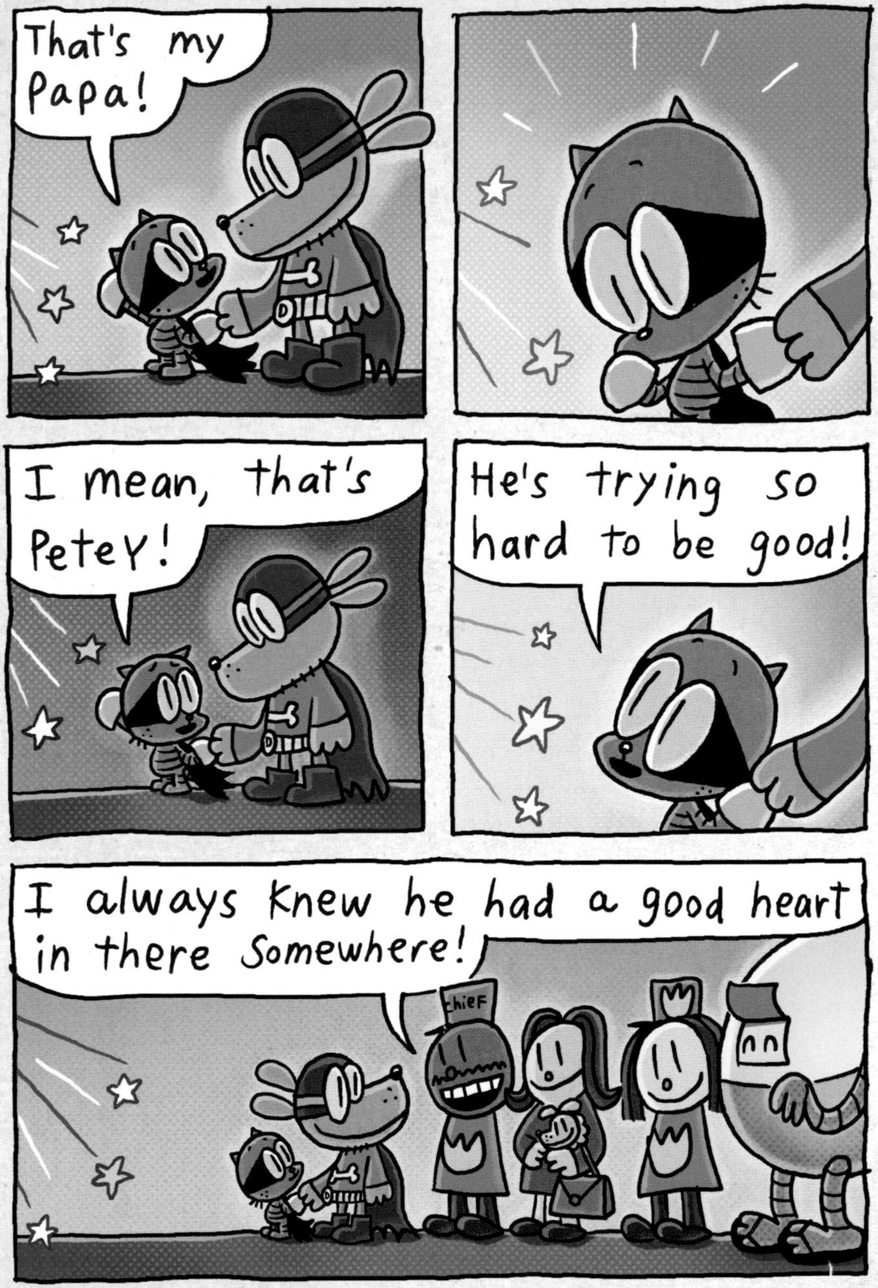

That's my Papa!
I mean, that's Petey!
He's trying so hard to be good!
I always knew he had a good heart in there somewhere!
chief

CHAPTER 7

The Darkness

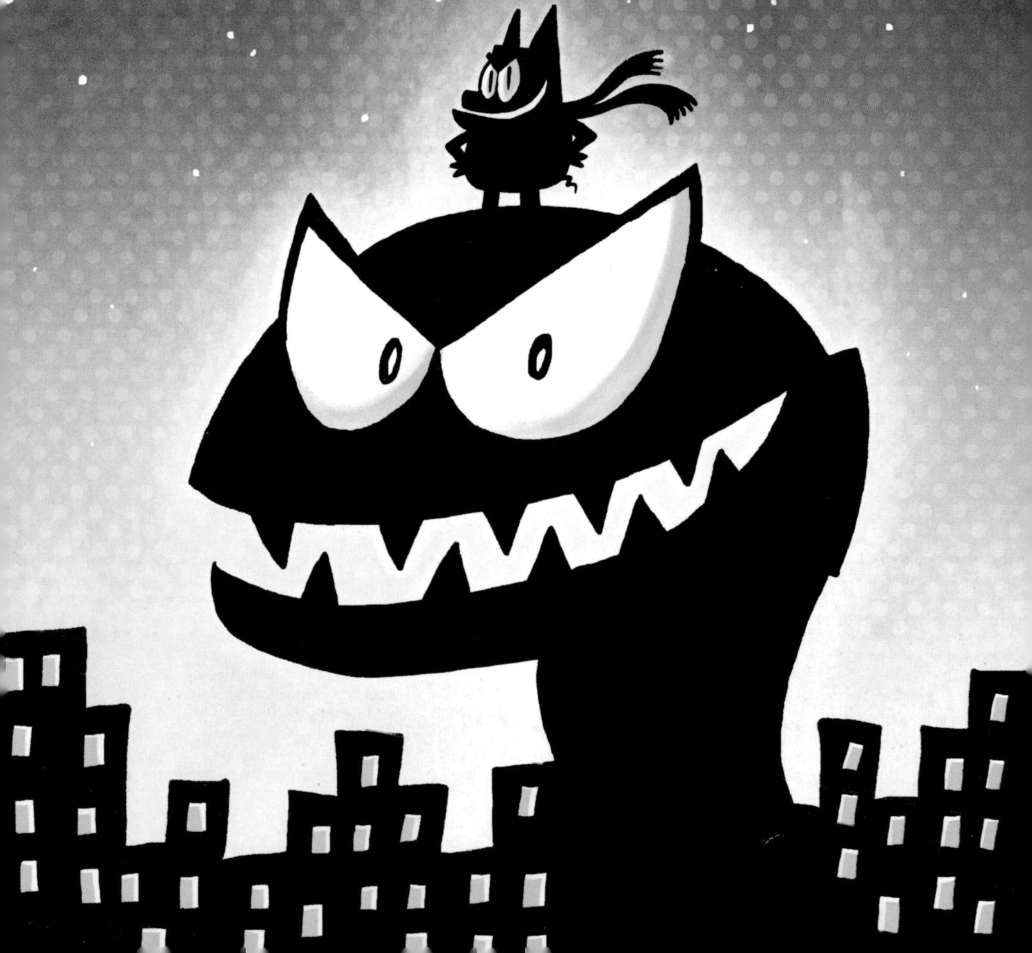

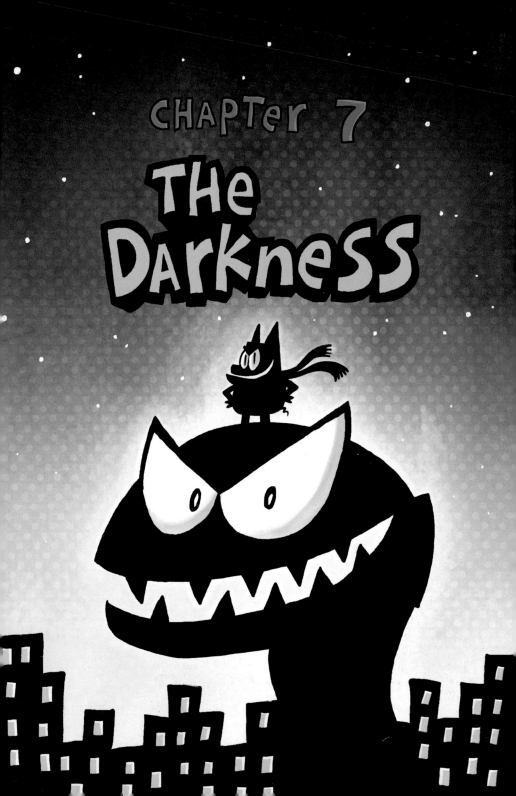

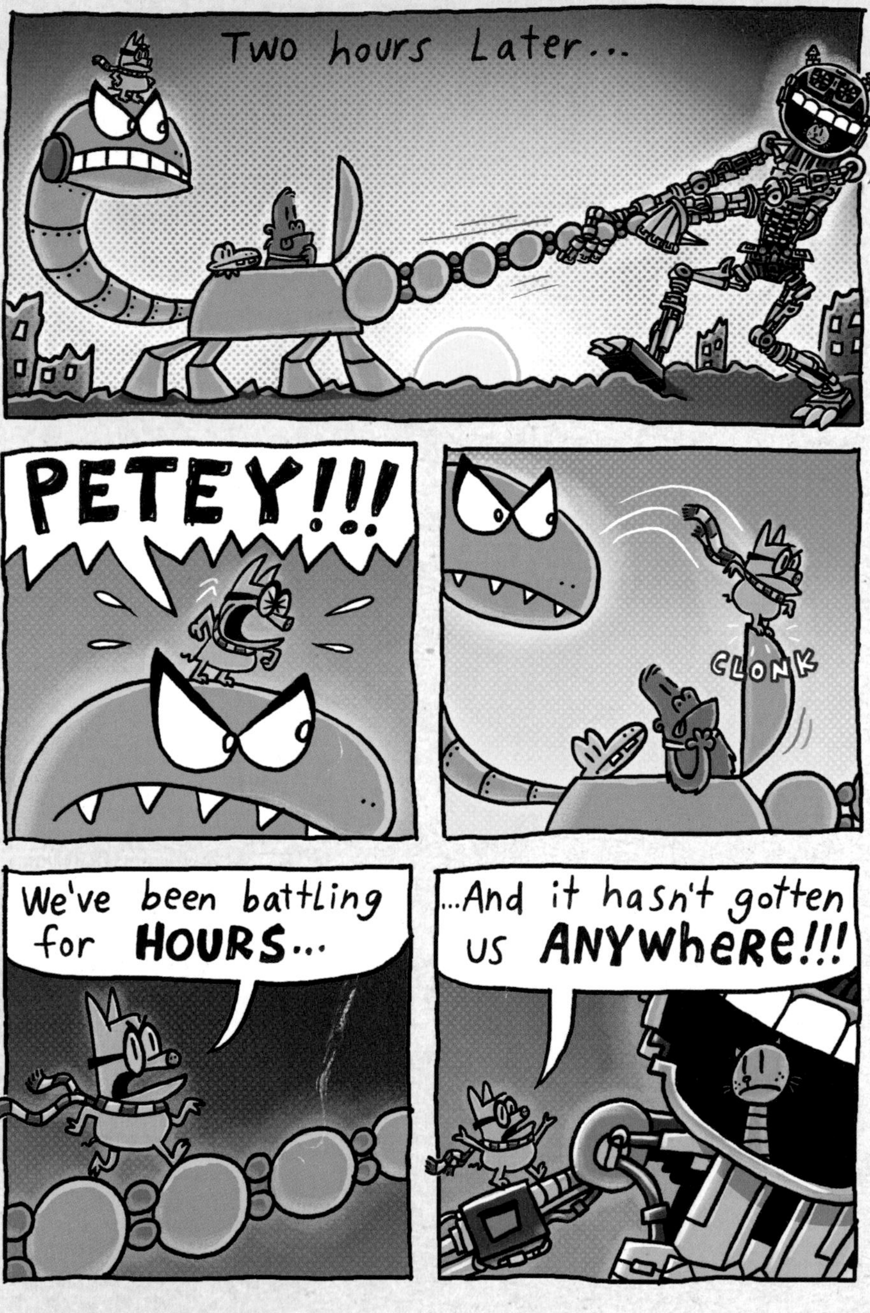

Two hours Later...
PETEY!!!
CLONK
We've been battling for HOURS...
...And it hasn't gotten us ANYWHERE!!!

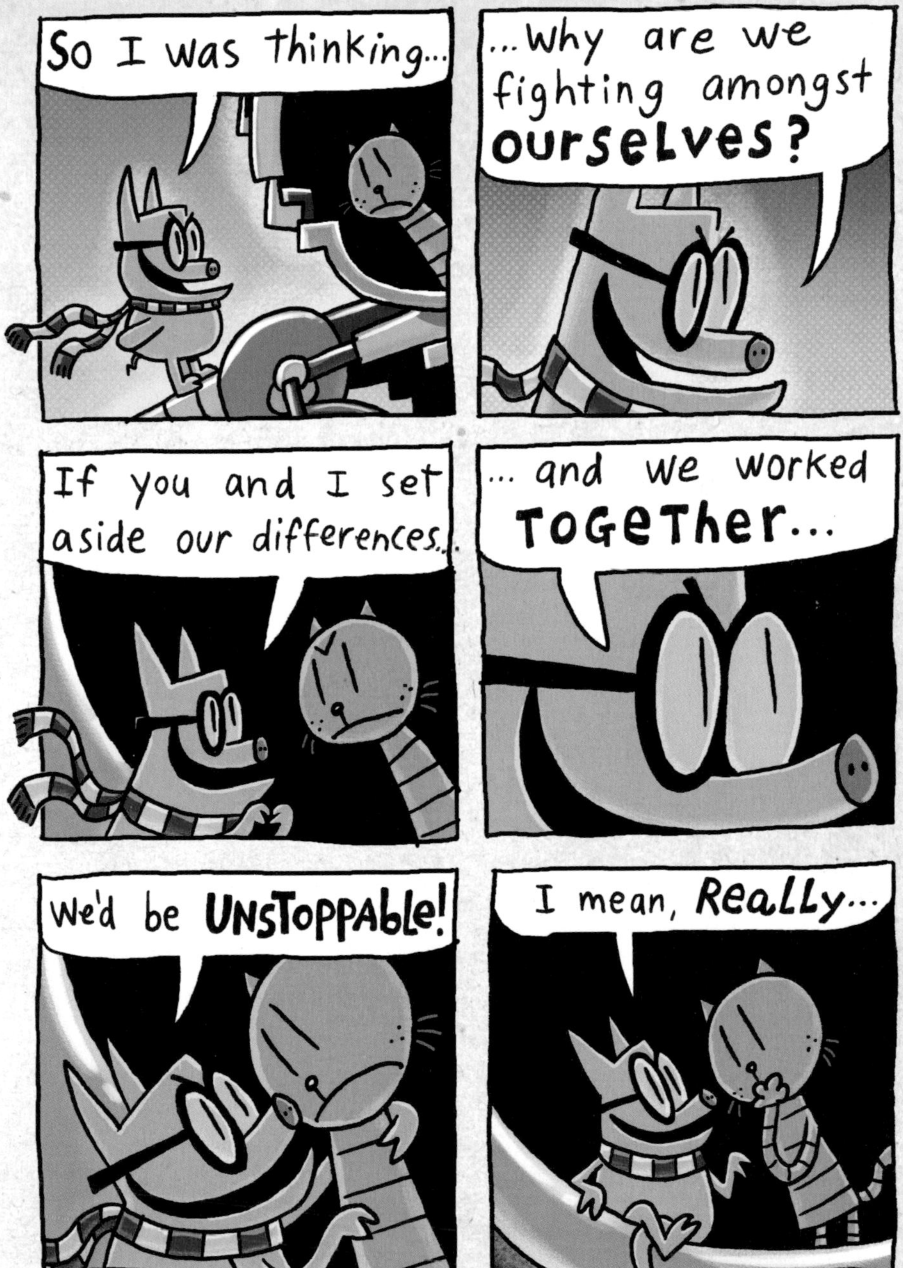

So I was thinking...
...Why are we fighting amongst OURSELVES?
If you and I set aside our differences...
... and we worked TOGETHER...
We'd be UNSTOPPABLE!
I mean, REALLY...

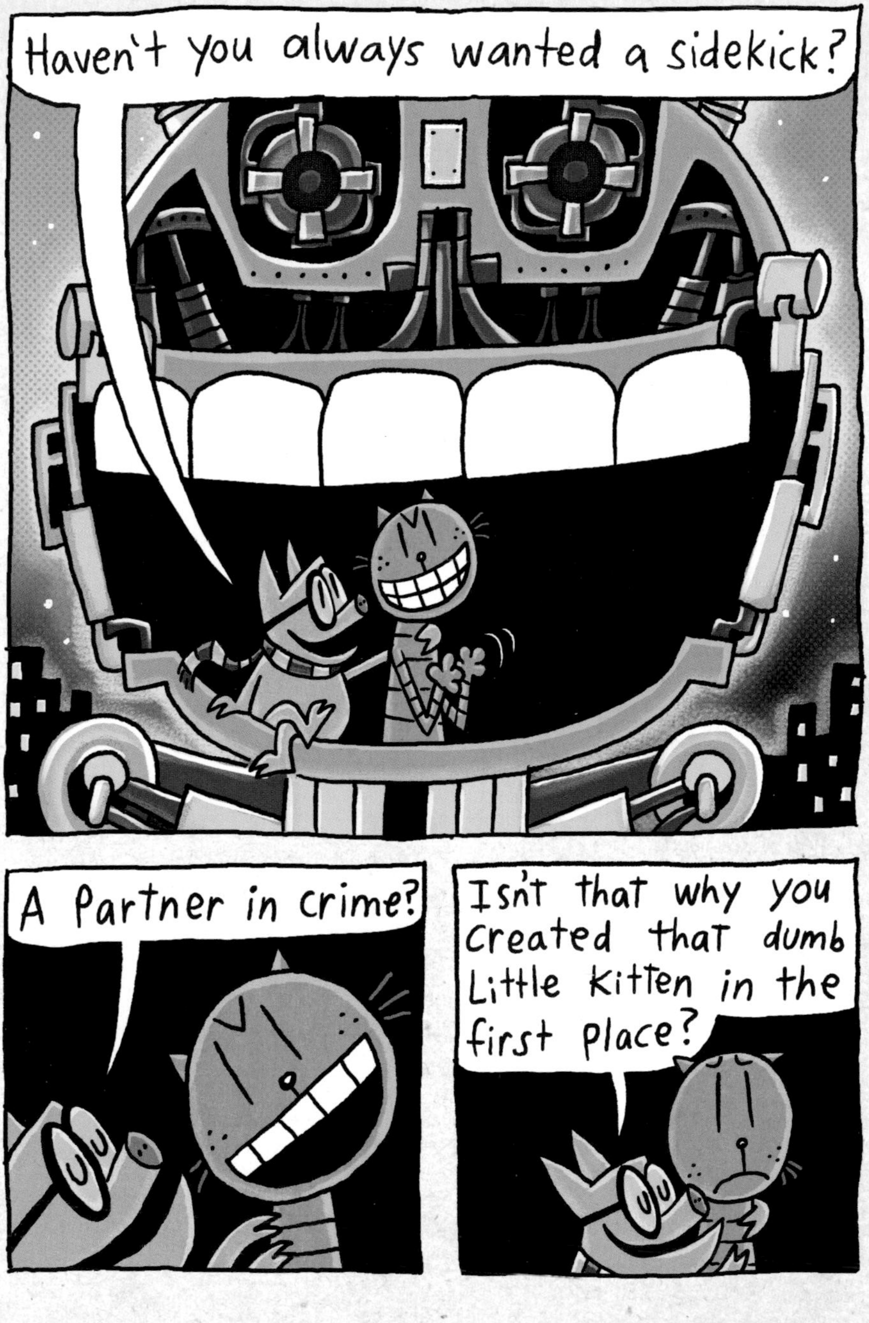
Haven't you always wanted a sidekick?
A Partner in crime?
Isn't that why you Created that dumb Little kitten in the first place?

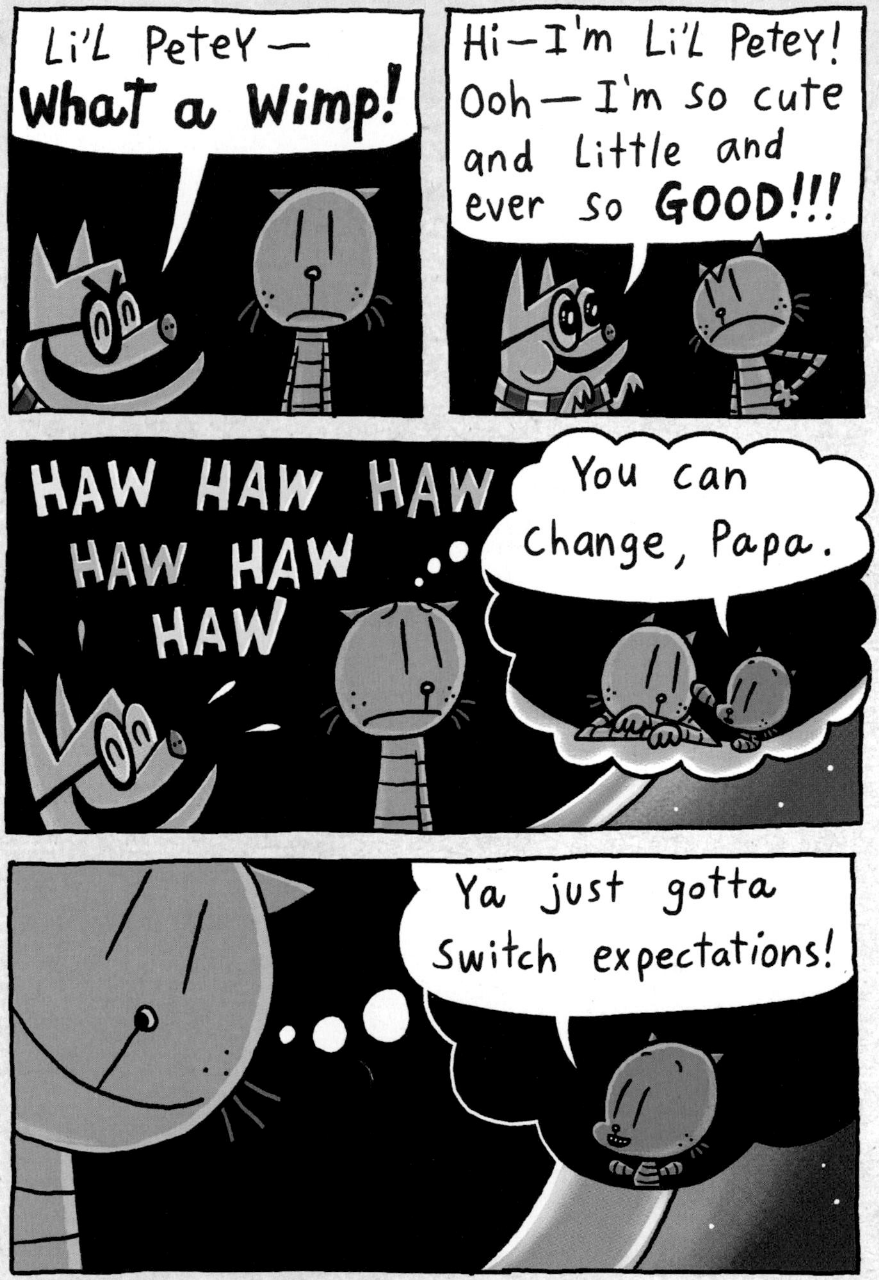
Li'L Petey—
What a Wimp!
Hi—I'm Li'L Petey! Ooh—I'm so cute and Little and ever so GOOD!!!
HAW HAW HAW HAW HAW HAW
You can change, Papa.
Ya just gotta Switch expectations!

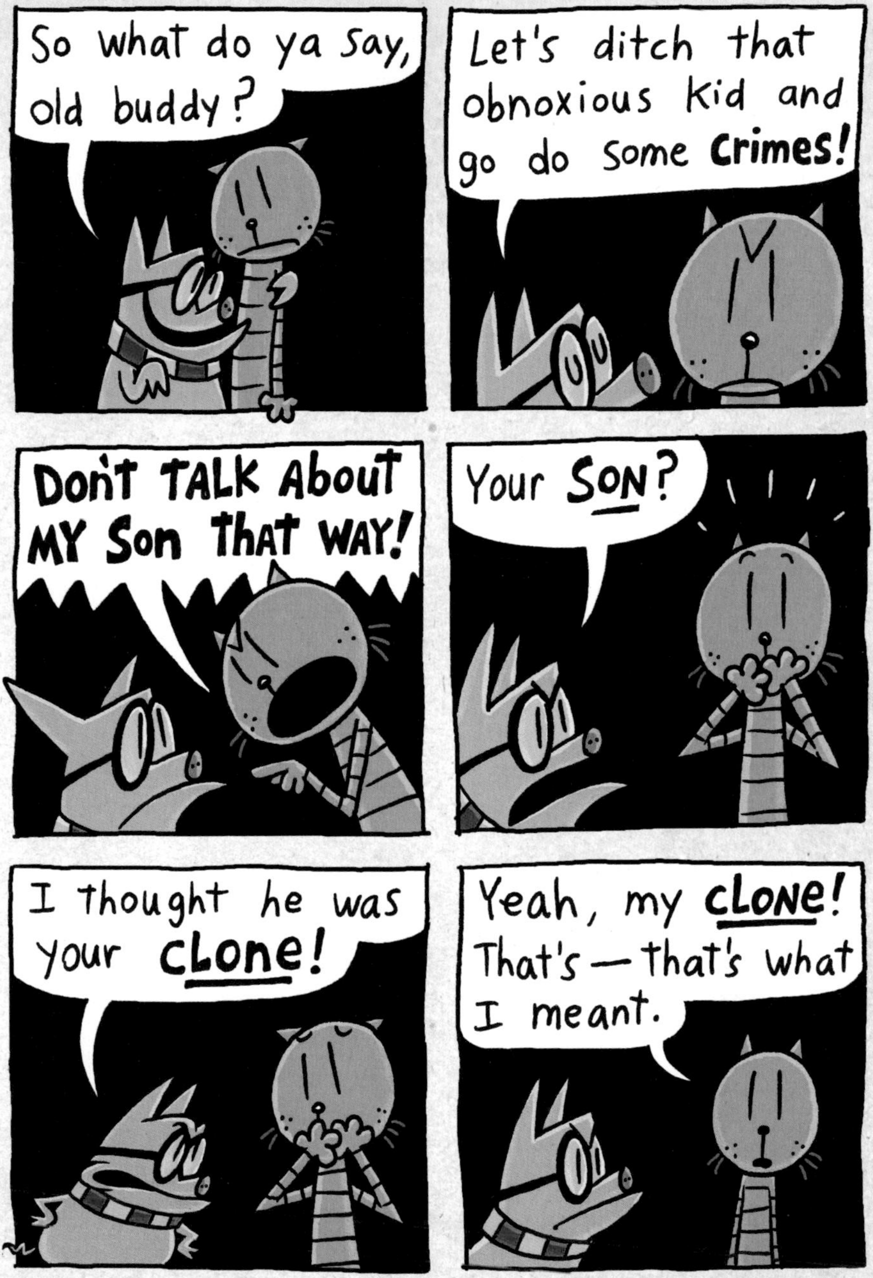
So what do ya say, old buddy?
Let's ditch that obnoxious kid and go do some **Crimes!**
DON'T TALK ABOUT MY SON THAT WAY!
Your SON?
I thought he was your CLONE!
Yeah, my CLONE! That's—that's what I meant.

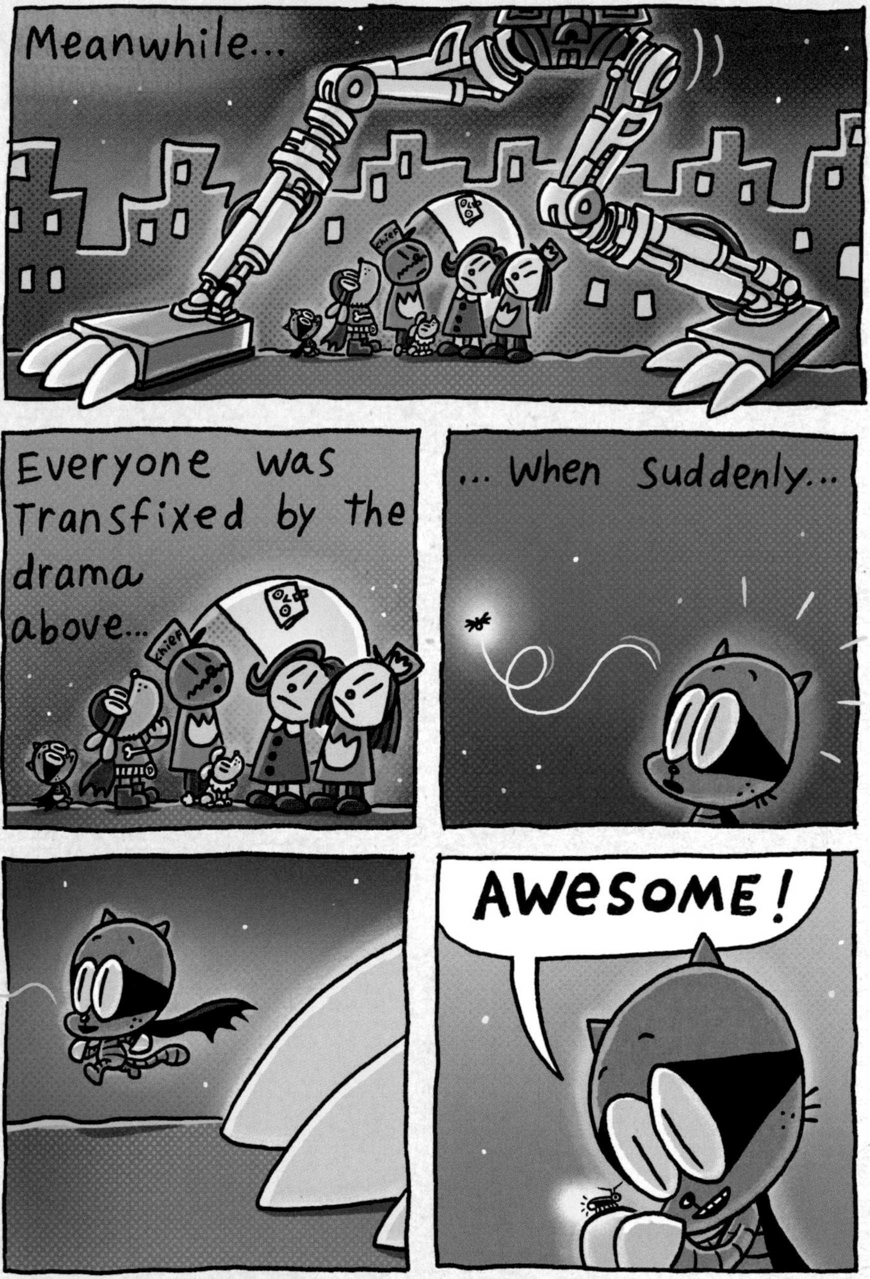
Meanwhile...
Everyone was Transfixed by the drama above...
... When suddenly...
AWESOME!

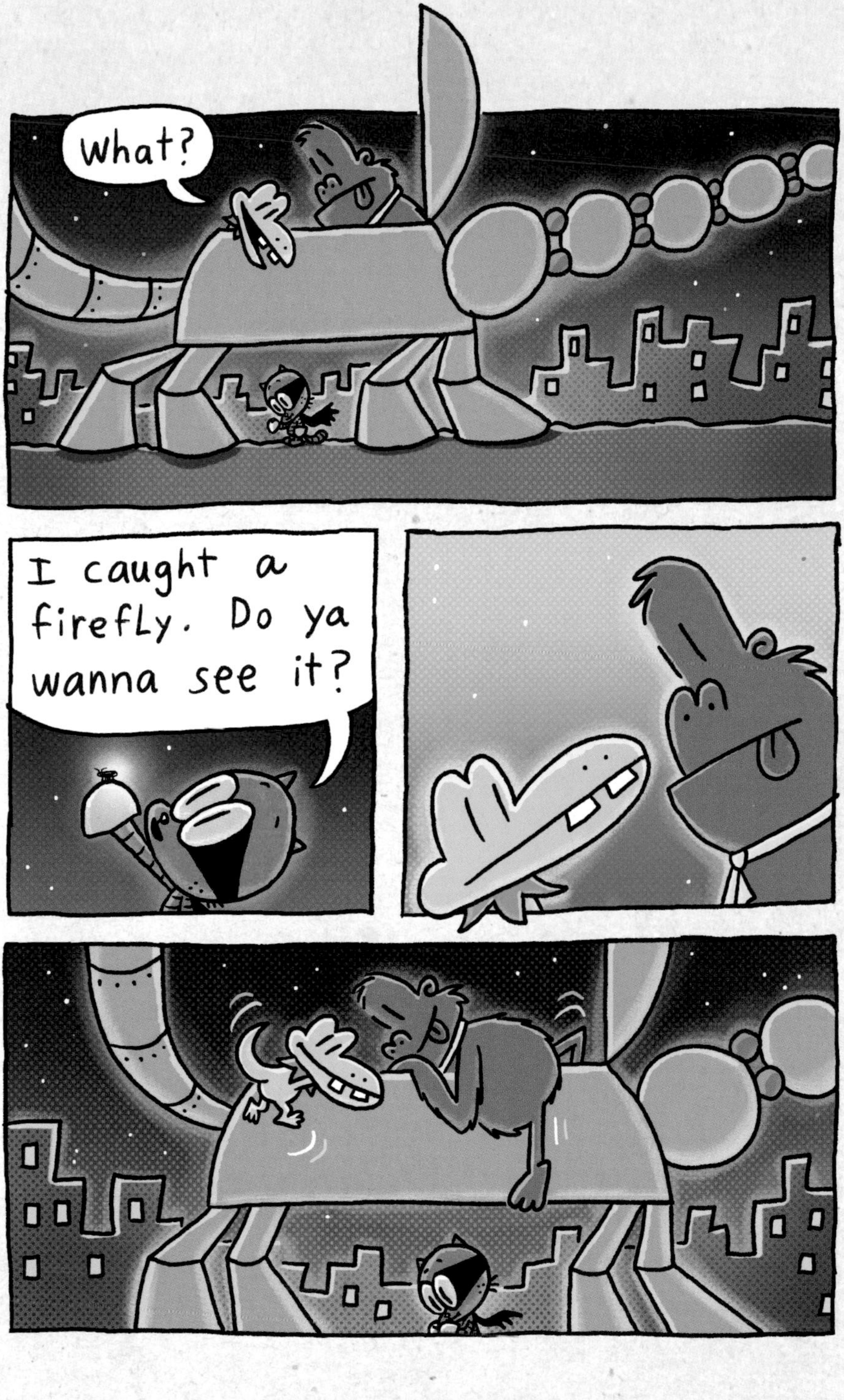
What?
I caught a firefly. Do ya wanna see it?

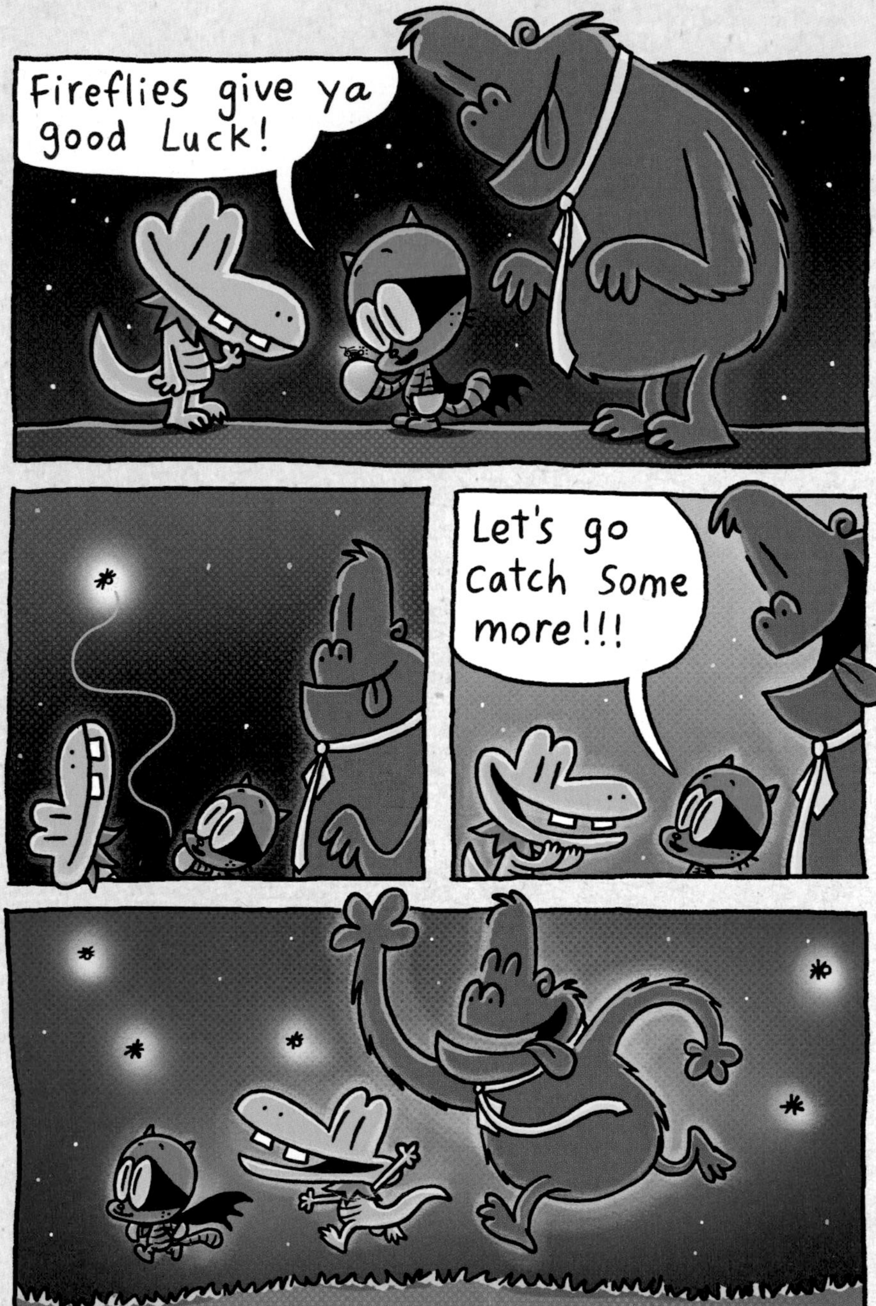
Fireflies give ya good Luck!
Let's go catch Some more!!!

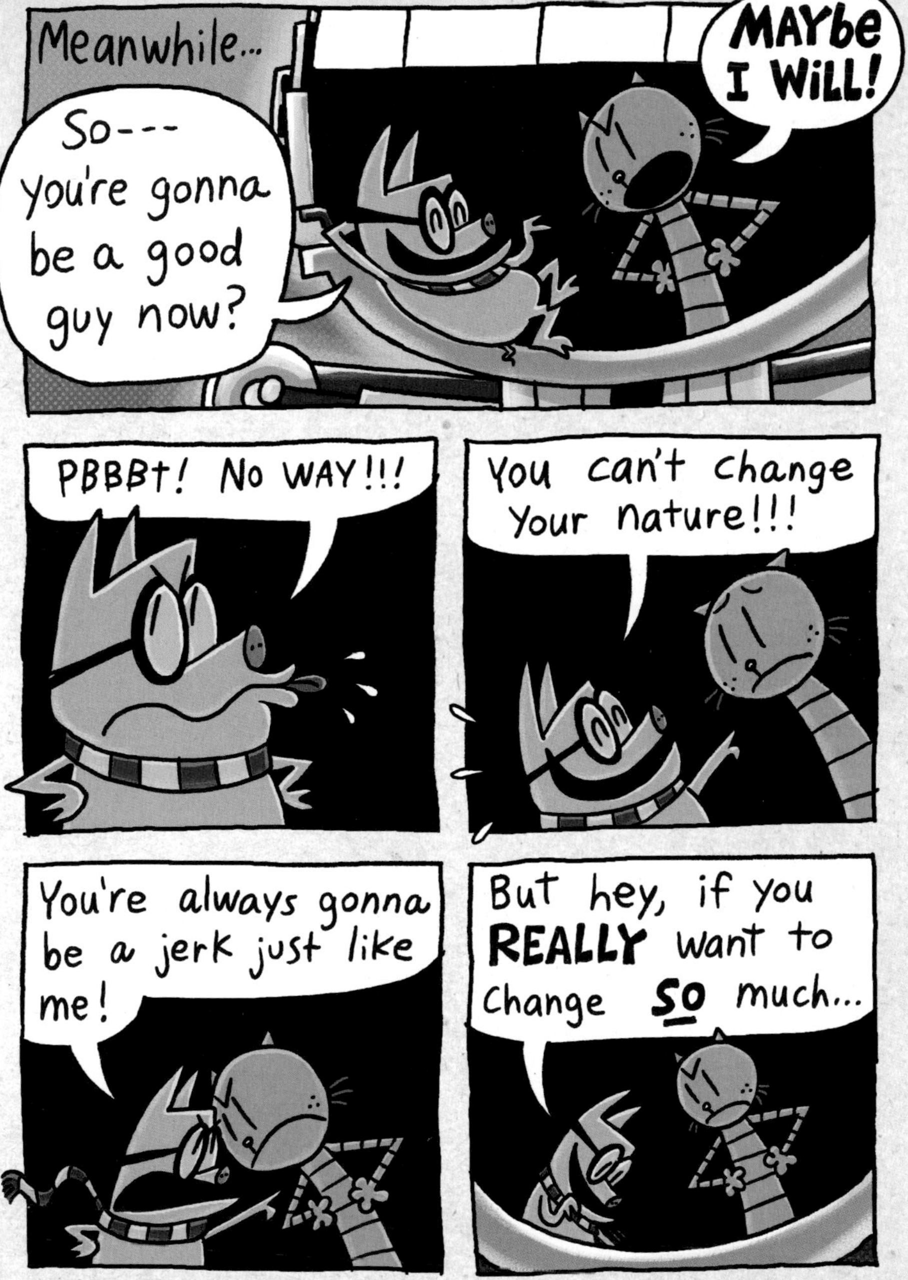
Meanwhile...
So--- you're gonna be a good guy now?
MAYbe I WiLL!
PBBBt! No WAY!!!
You can't change your nature!!!
You're always gonna be a jerk just like me!
But hey, if you **REALLY** want to change **SO** much...

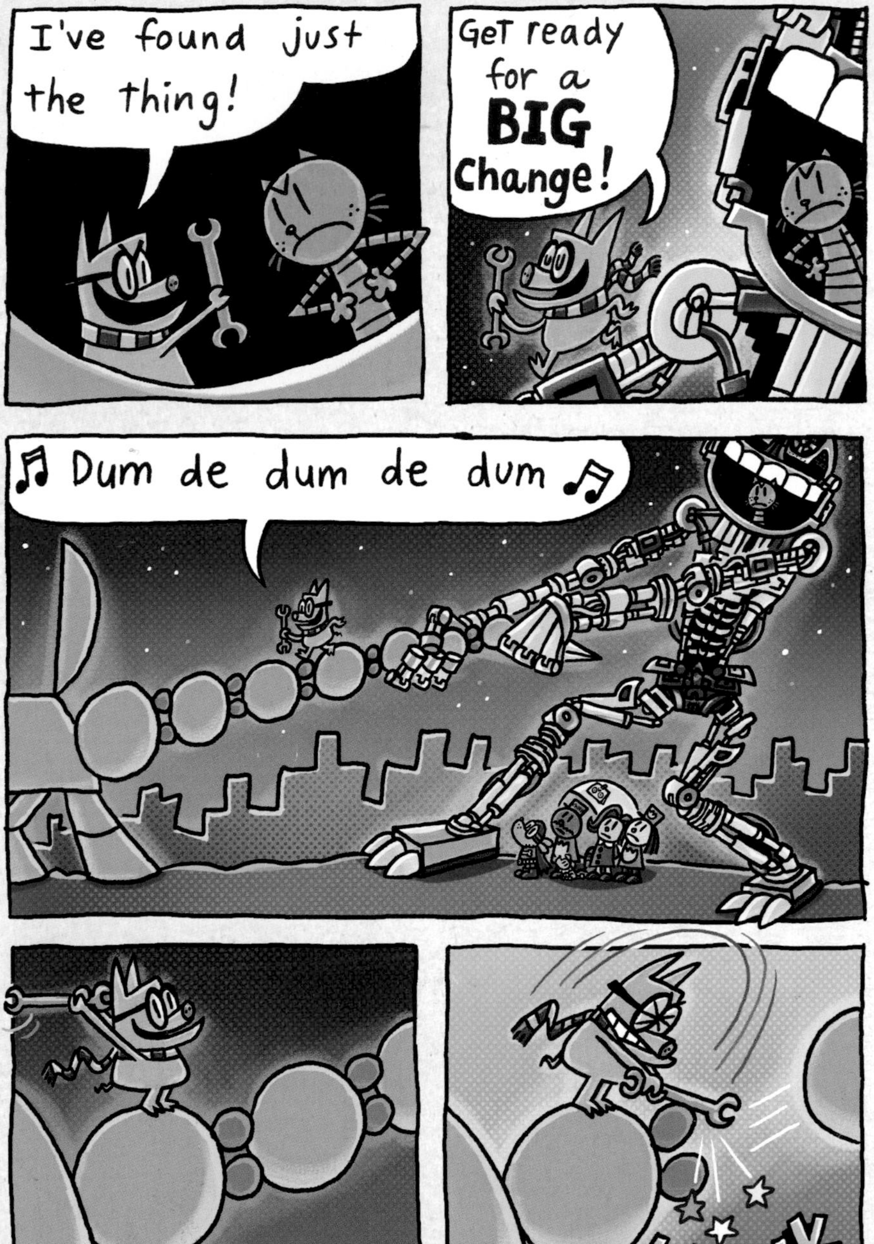
I've found just the thing!
Get ready for a BIG Change!
♫ Dum de dum de dum ♫
KLANK

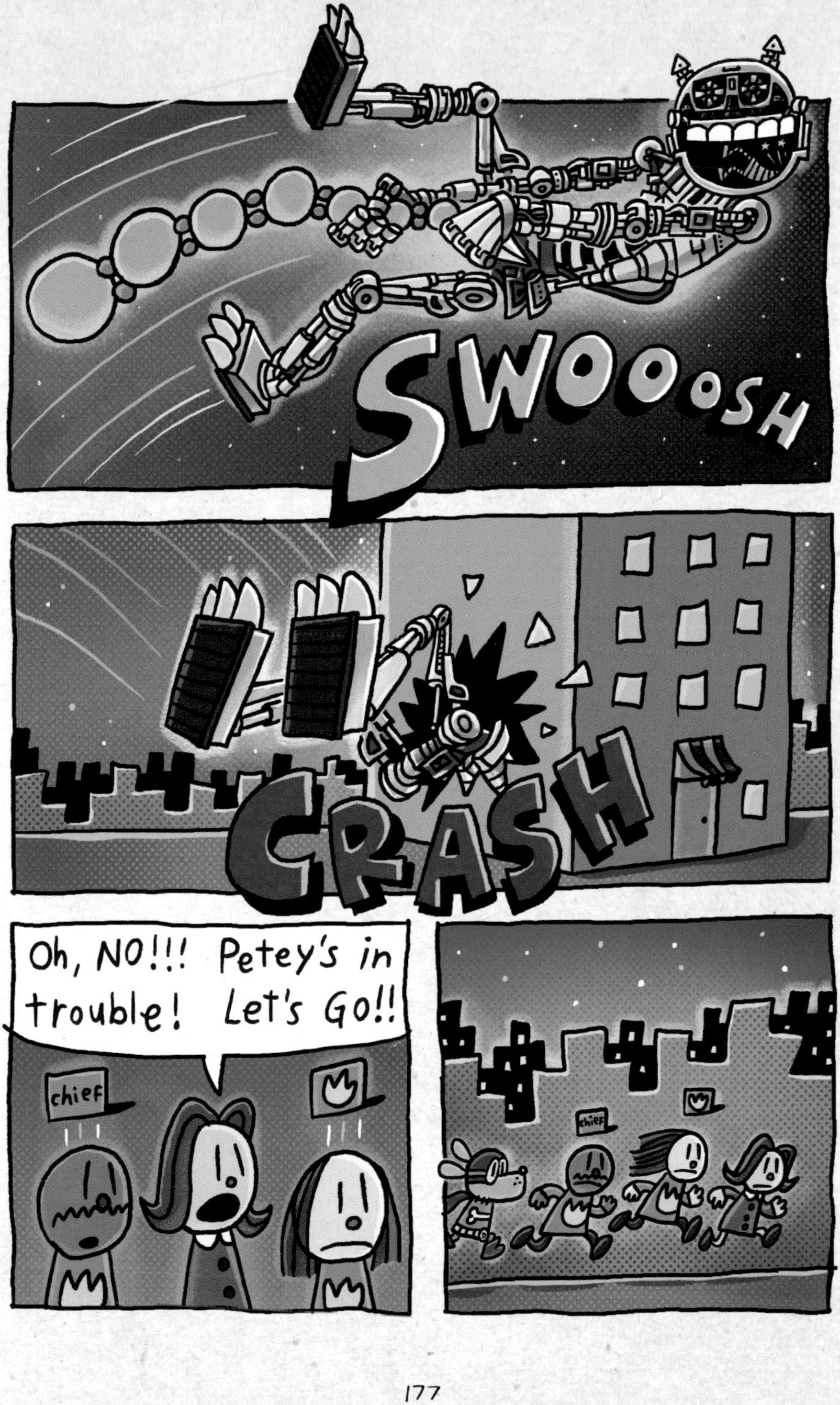
SWOOOSH
CRASH
Oh, NO!!! Petey's in trouble! Let's GO!!
chief
chief

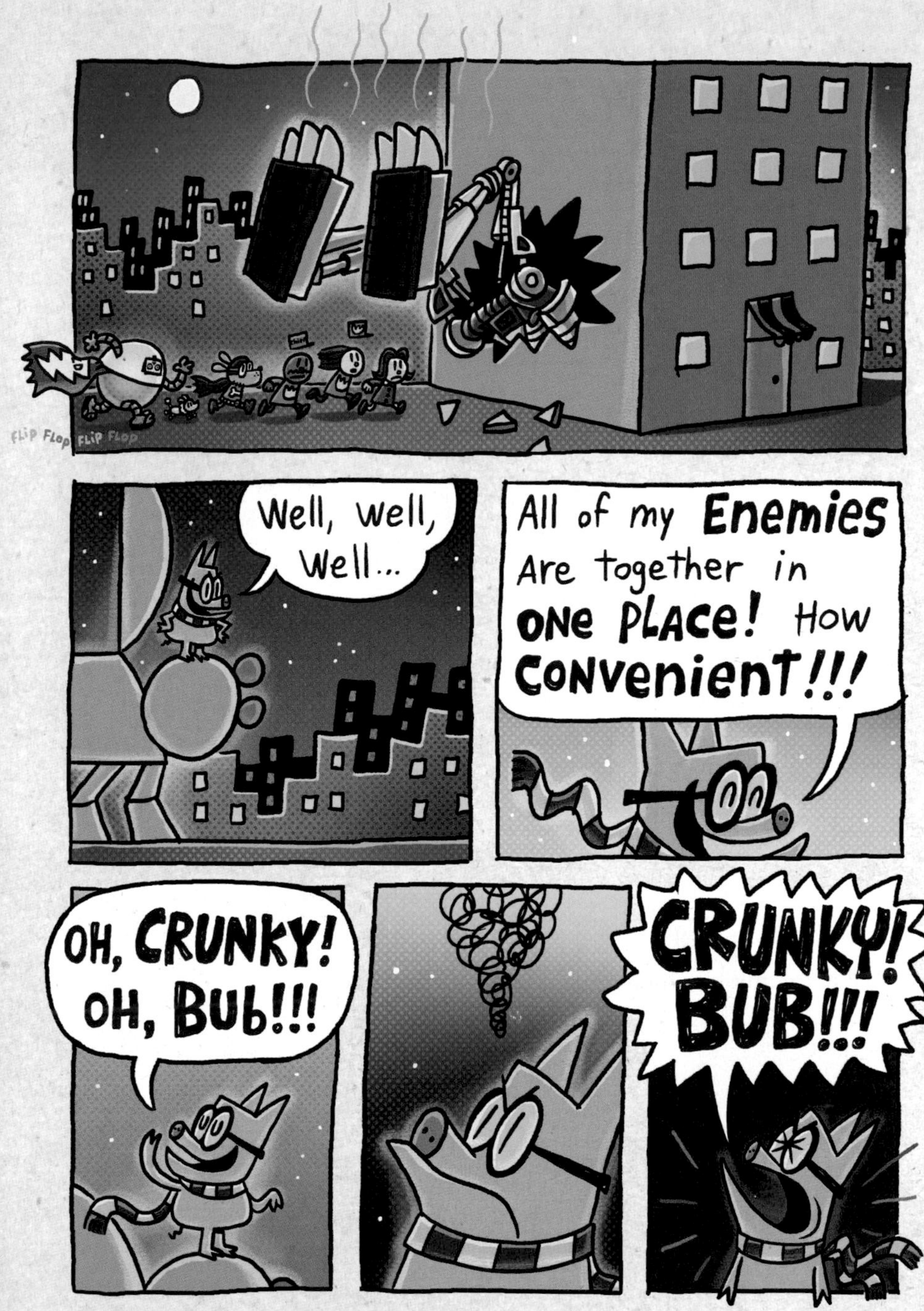
FLIP FLOP FLIP FLOP
Well, well, Well...
All of my Enemies Are together in ONE PLACE! How CONVENIENT!!!
OH, CRUNKY! OH, BUB!!!
CRUNKY! BUB!!!

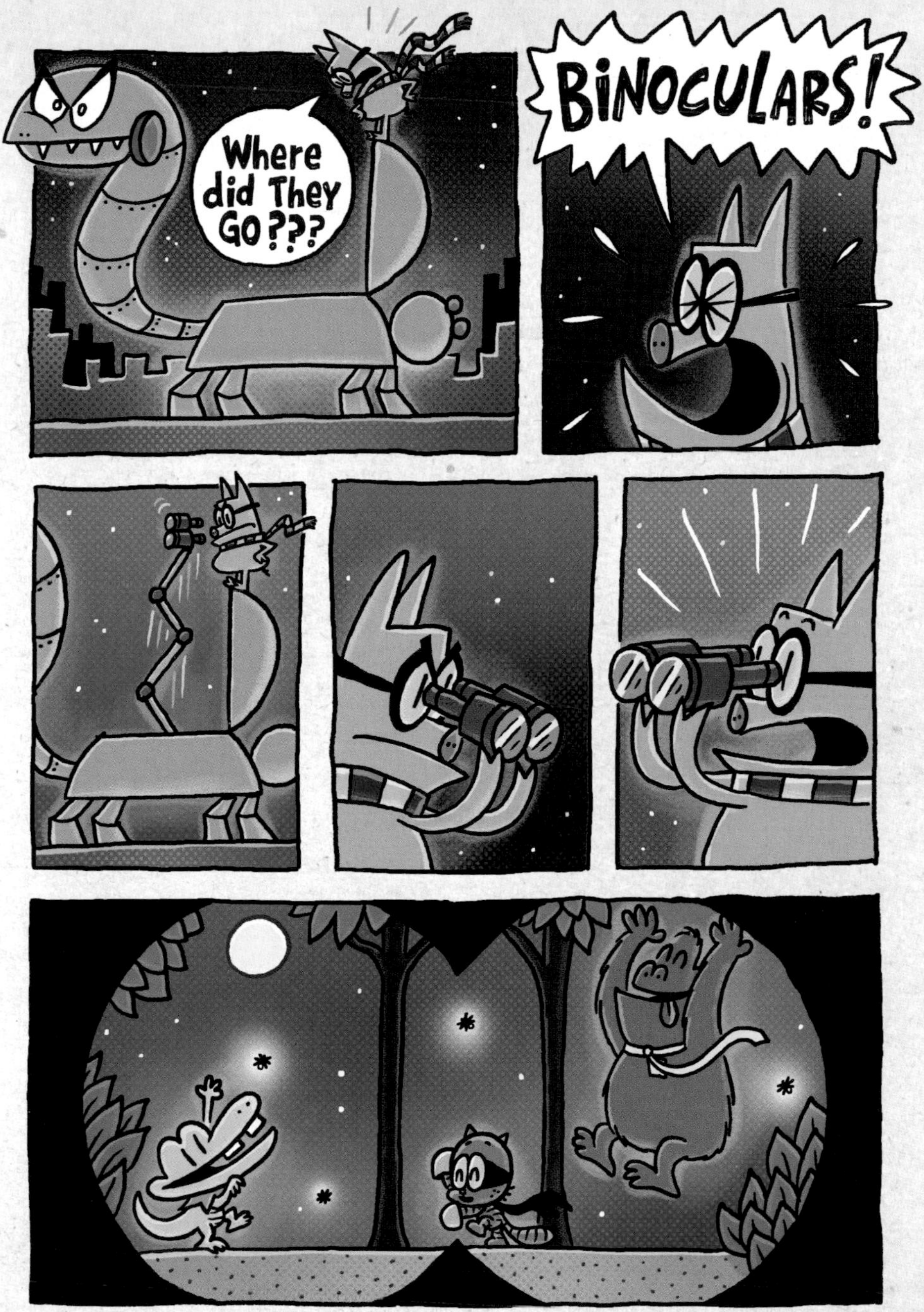
Where did They GO???
BINOCULARS!

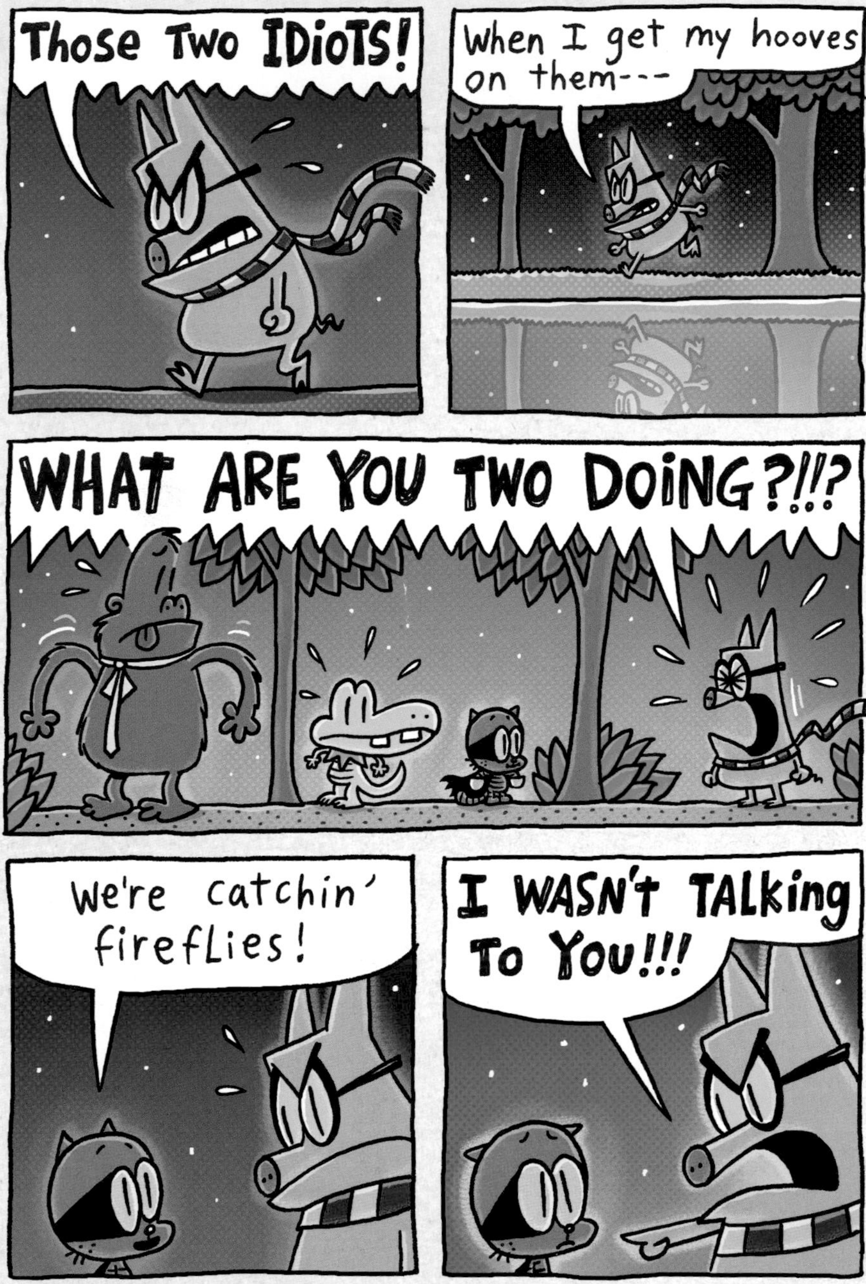
Those Two IDIOTS!
When I get my hooves on them---
WHAT ARE YOU TWO DOING?!!?
We're catchin' fireflies!
I WASN'T TALKING TO YOU!!!

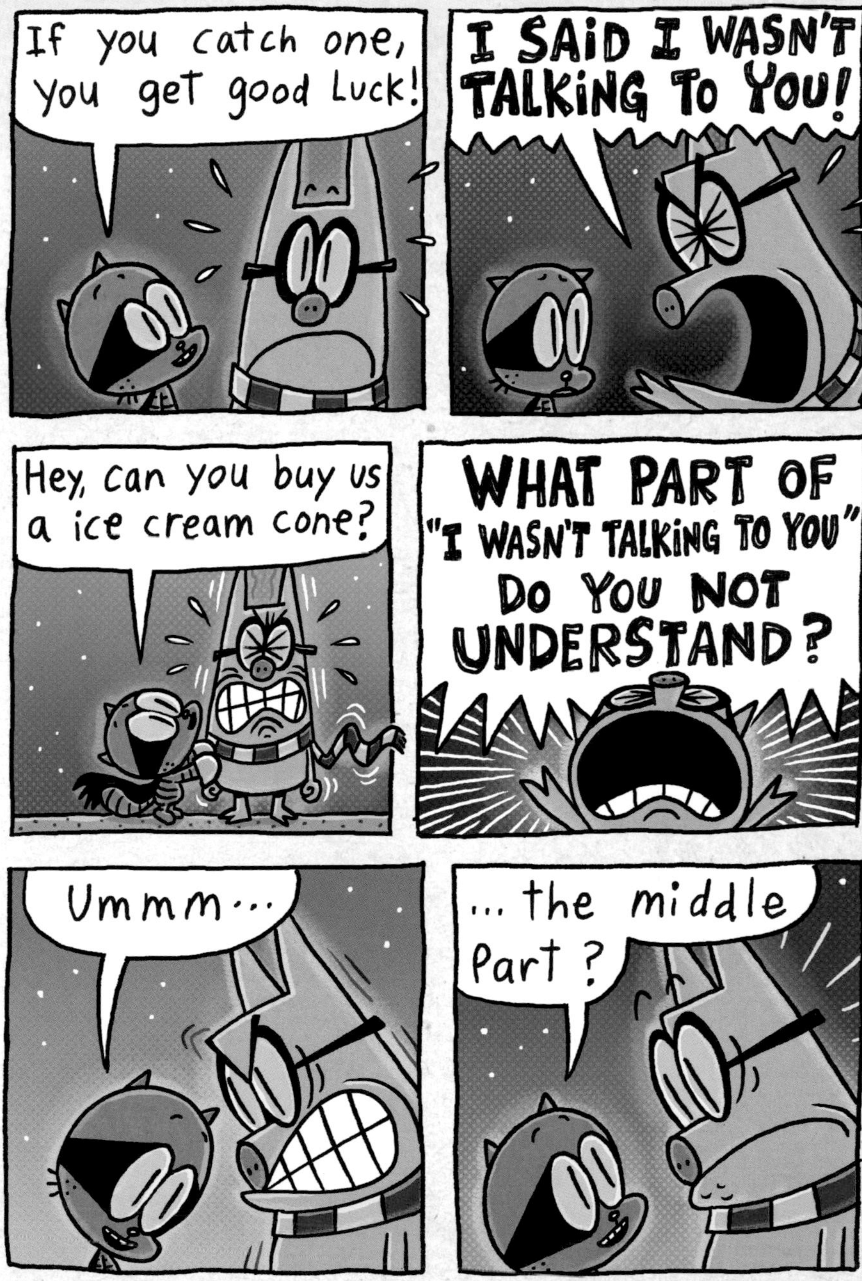
If you catch one, you get good Luck!
I SAID I WASN'T TALKING TO YOU!
Hey, can you buy us a ice cream cone?
WHAT PART OF "I WASN'T TALKING TO YOU" DO YOU NOT UNDERSTAND?
Ummm...
... the middle Part?

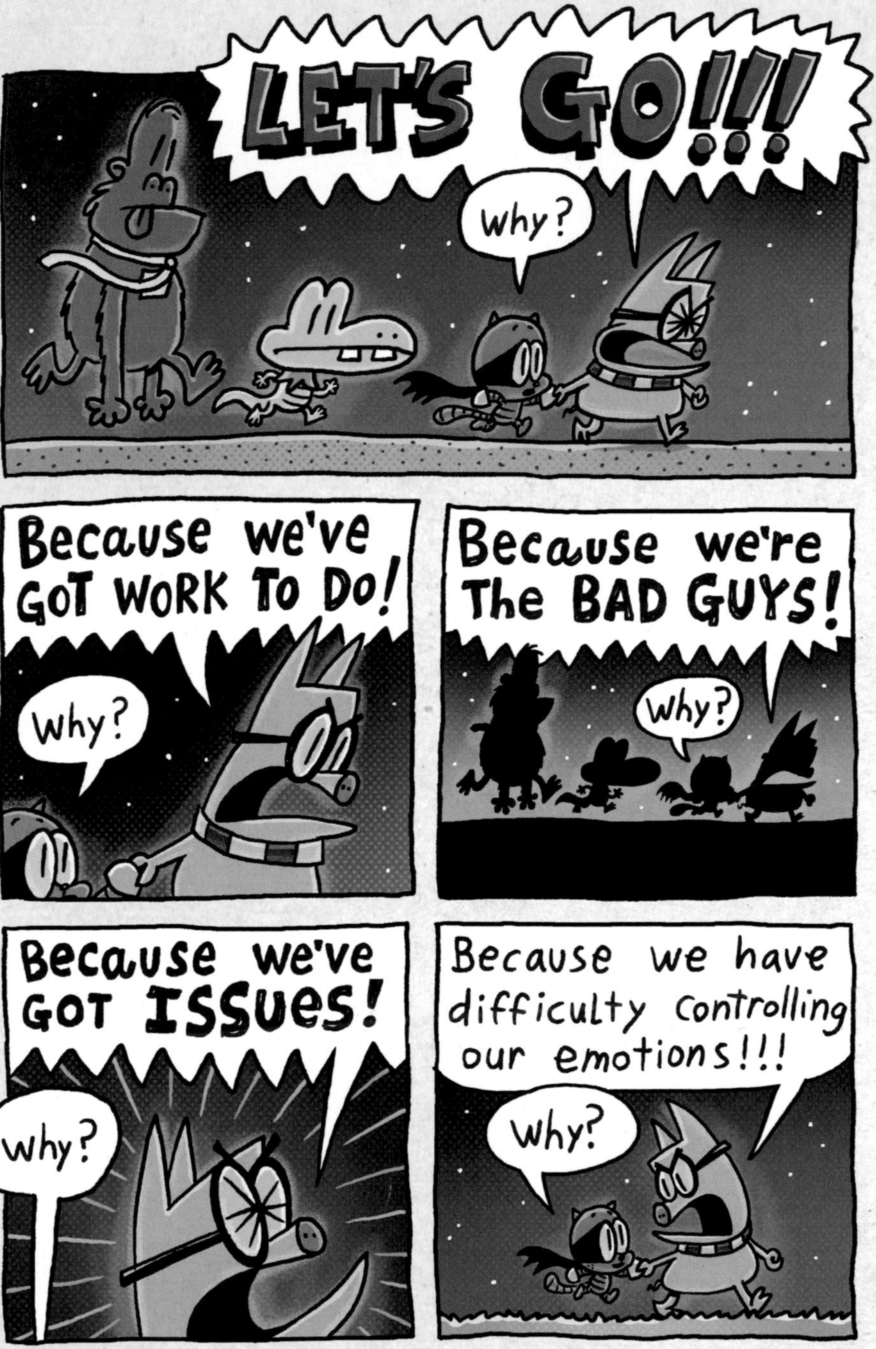
LET'S GO!!!
Why?
Because we've GOT WORK TO DO!
Why?
Because we're The BAD GUYS!
Why?
Because we've GOT ISSUES!
Why?
Because we have difficulty controlling our emotions!!!
Why?

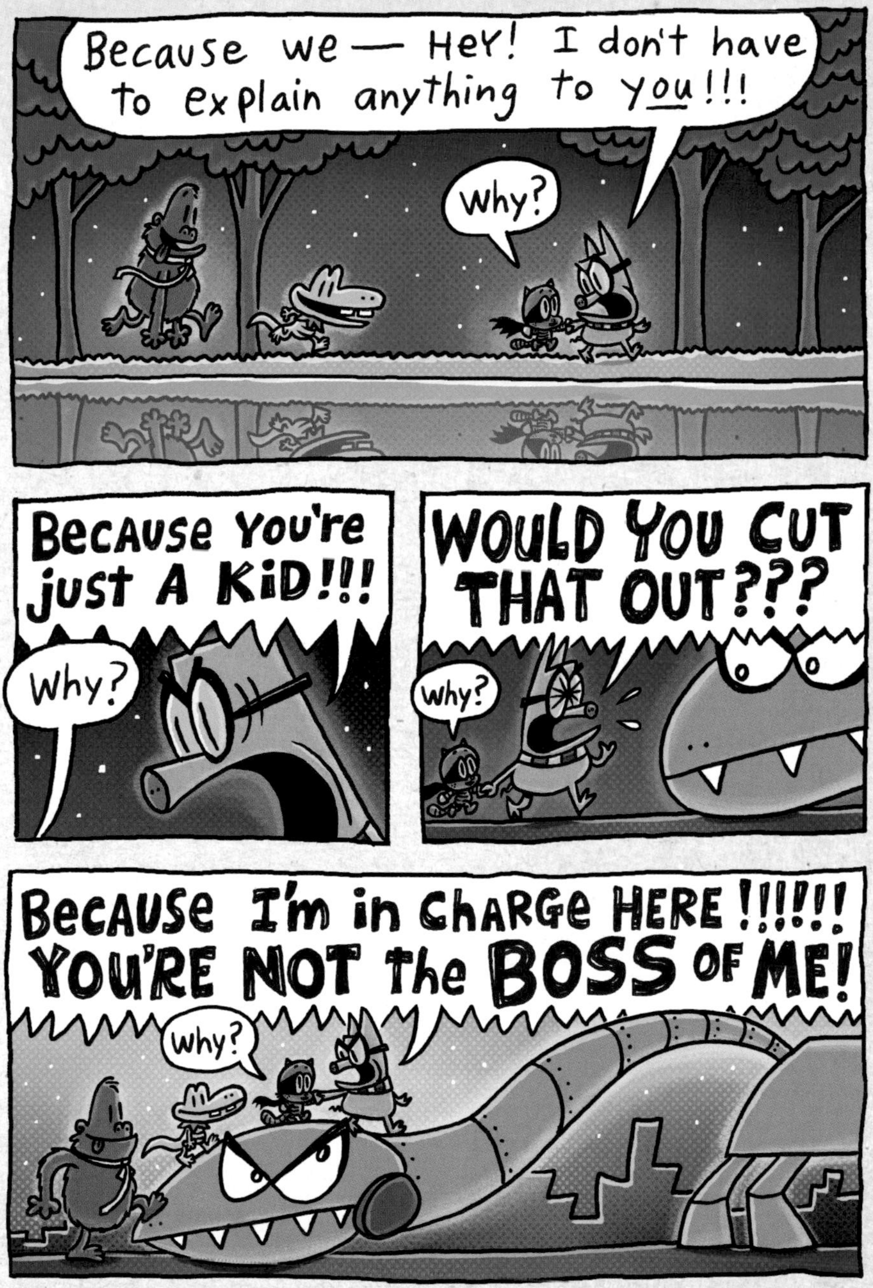
Because we— HEY! I don't have to explain anything to you!!!
Why?
Because you're just A KiD!!!
Why?
WOULD YOU CUT THAT OUT???
Why?
Because I'm in ChARGe HERE!!!!!! YOU'RE NOT the BOSS OF ME!
Why?

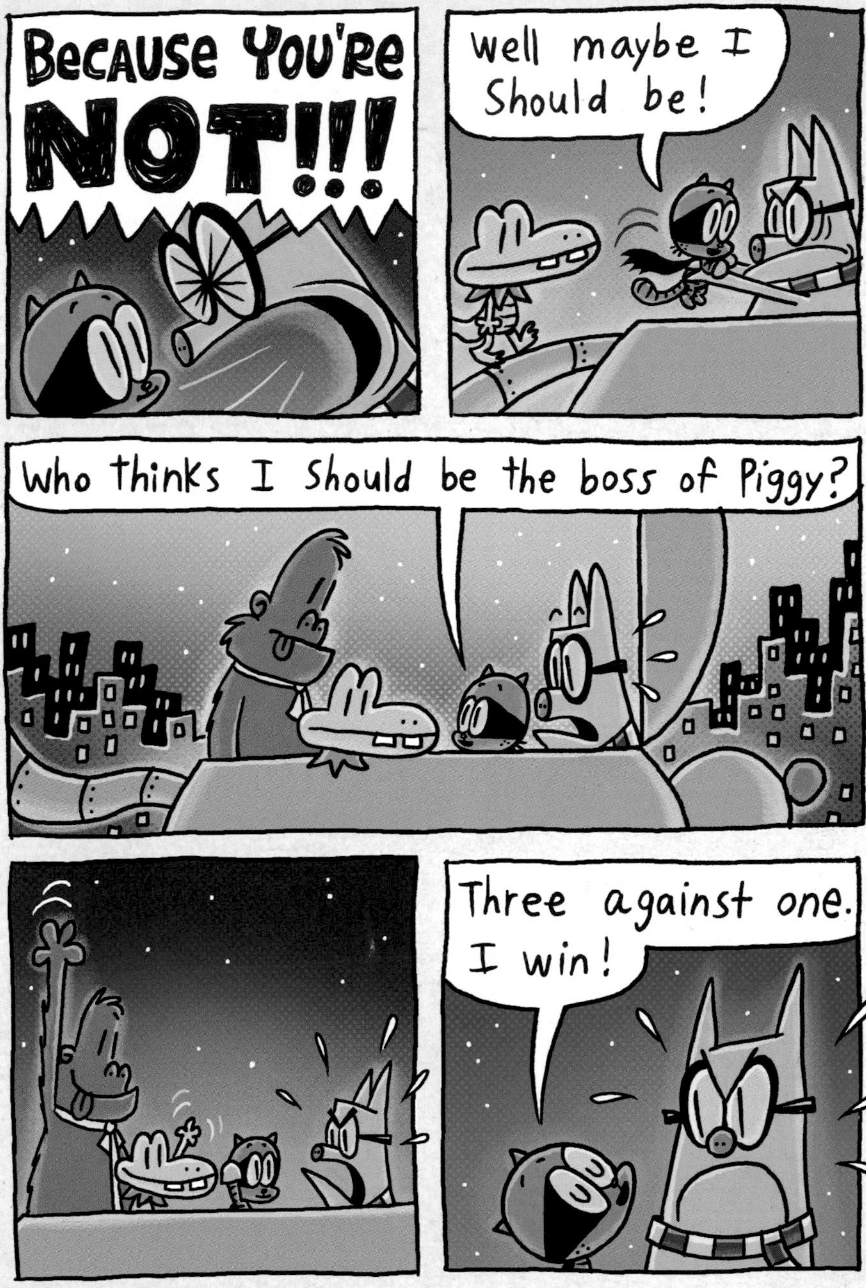
BECAUSE YOU'RE NOT!!!
well maybe I Should be!
Who thinks I Should be the boss of Piggy?
Three against one. I win!

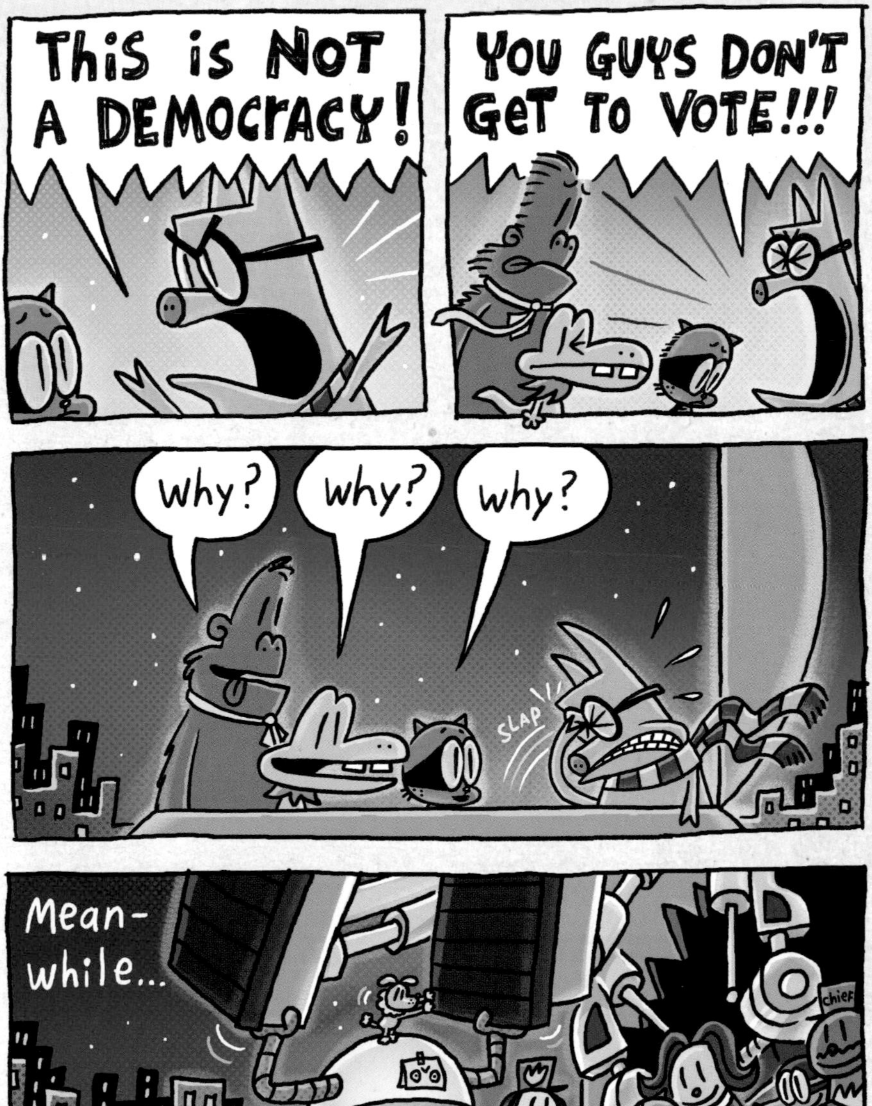
THIS is NOT A DEMOCRACY!
YOU GUYS DON'T GET TO VOTE!!!
why?
why?
why?
SLAP
Mean-while...
chief

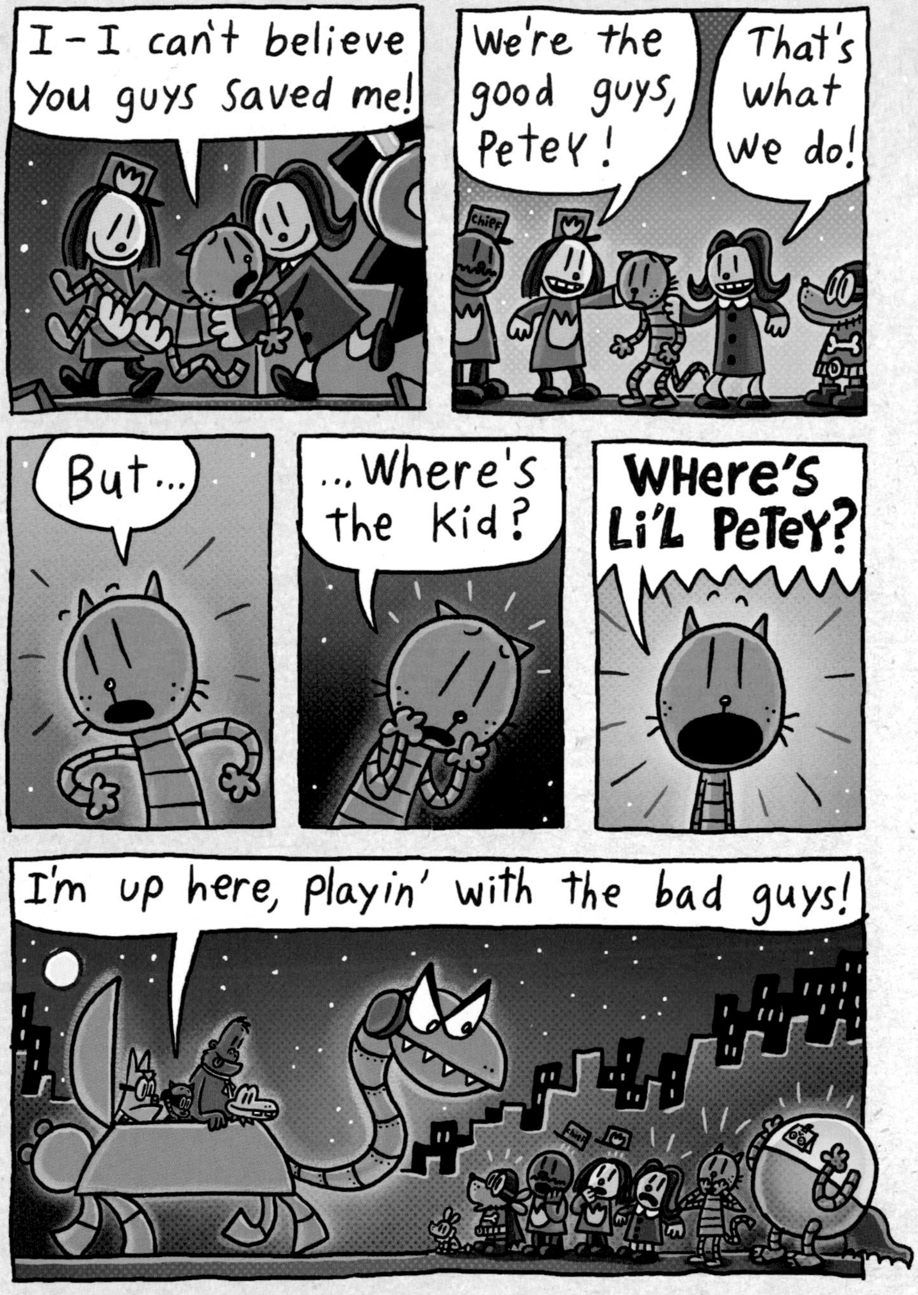

I-I can't believe you guys saved me!
We're the good guys, Petey!
That's what we do!
But...
...Where's the kid?
WHERE'S LI'L PETEY?
I'm up here, playin' with the bad guys!
CHIEF

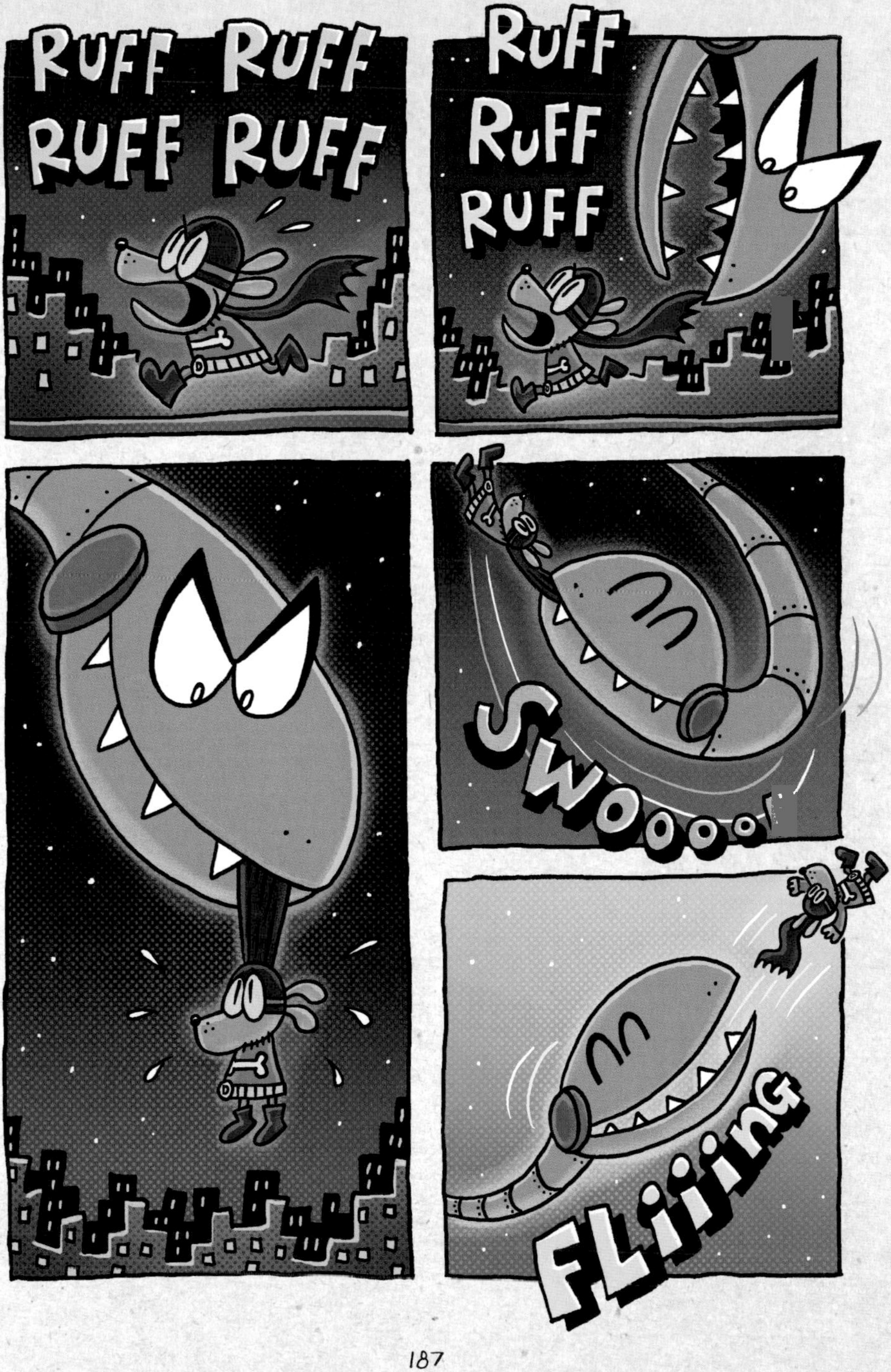
RUFF RUFF
RUFF RUFF
RUFF
RUFF
RUFF
SWOOOO
FLiiiNG

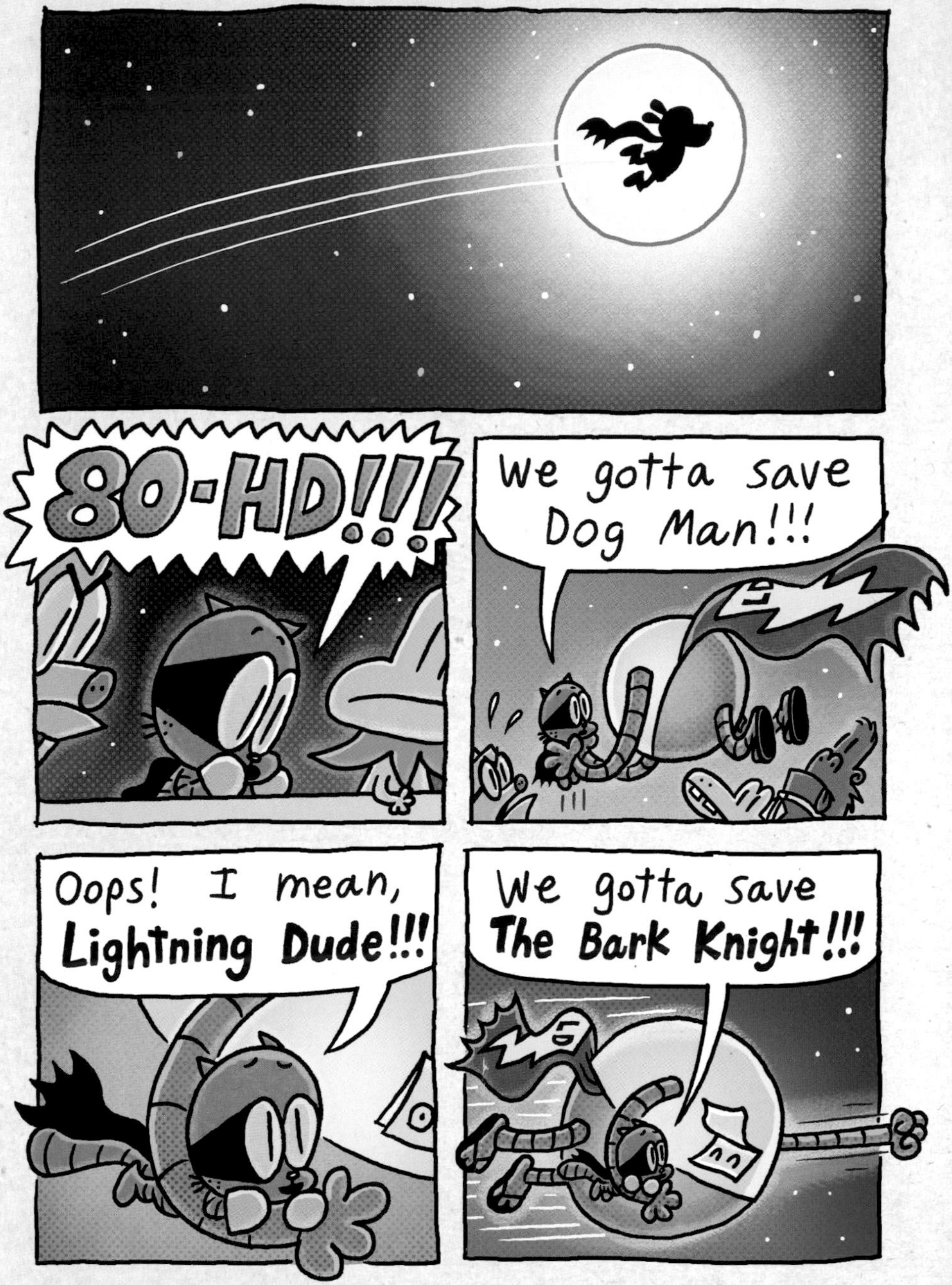
80-HD!!!
We gotta save Dog Man!!!
Oops! I mean, Lightning Dude!!!
We gotta save The Bark Knight!!!

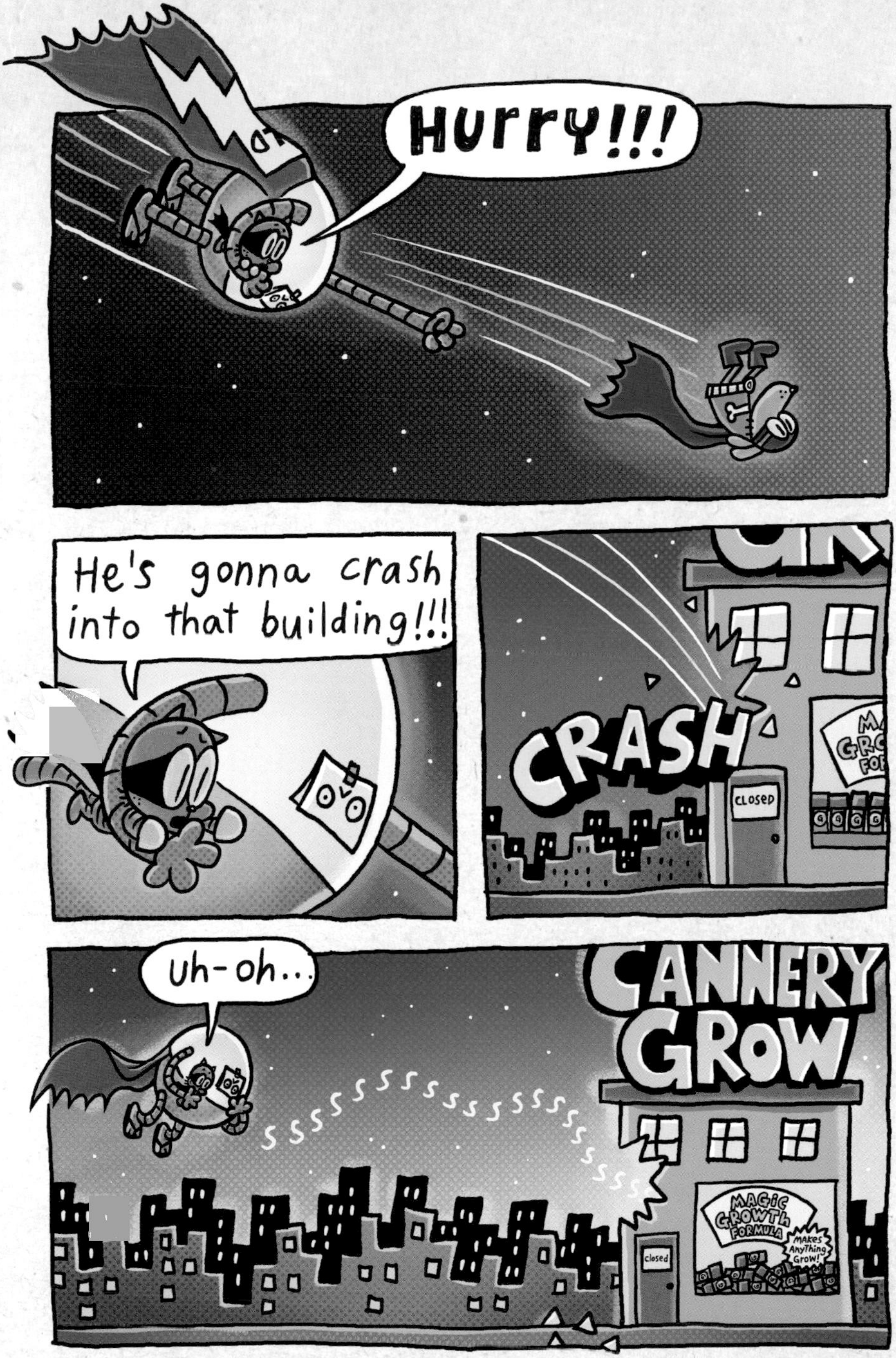
HURRY!!!
He's gonna crash into that building!!!
CRASH
CLOSED
uh-oh...
CANNERY GROW
SSSSSSSSSSSSSSSSSSSSS
MAGIC GROWTH FORMULA
MAKES AnyThing Grow!
closed

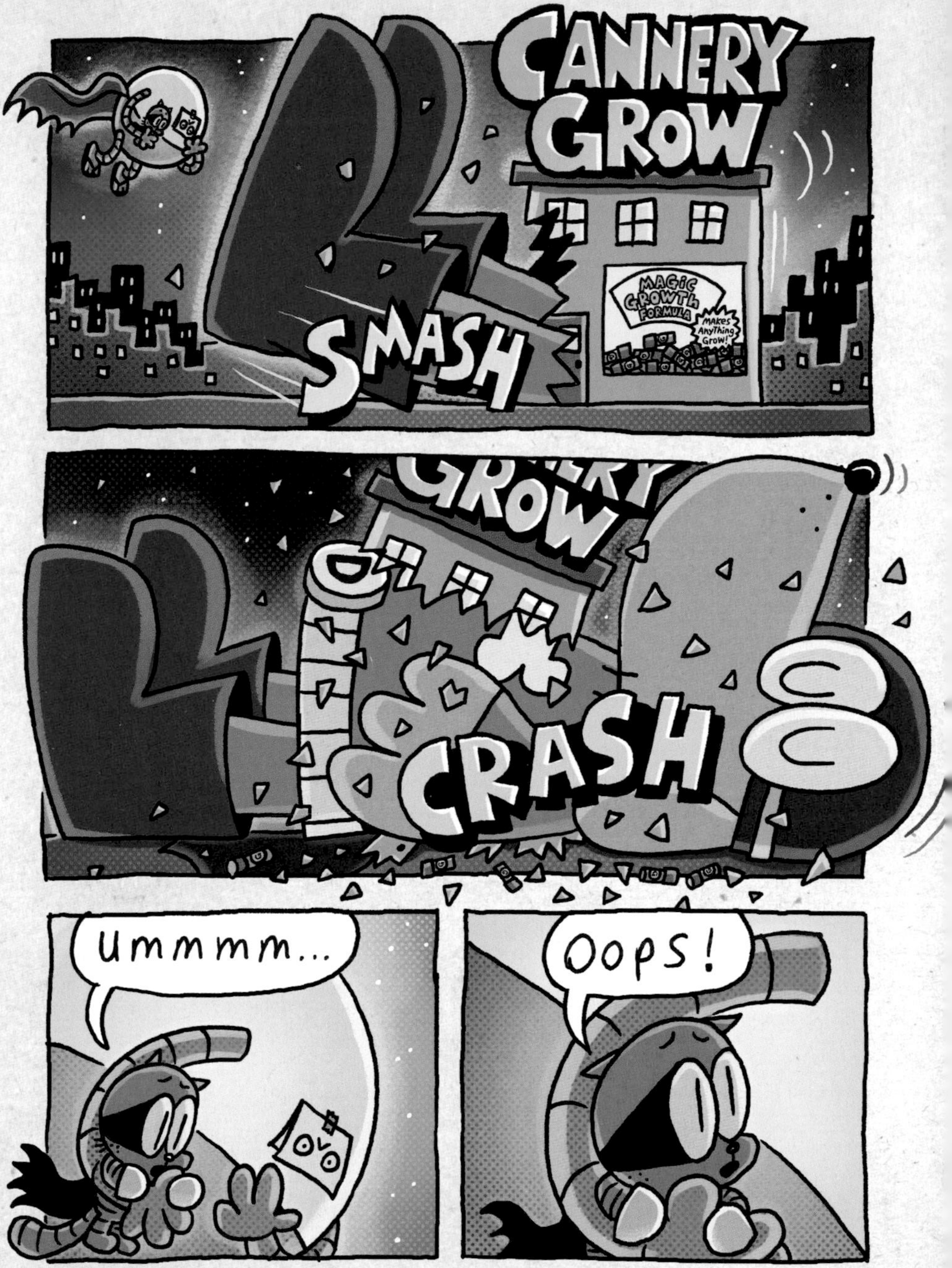
CANNERY GROW
MAGIC GROWTH FORMULA
MAKES AnyThing Grow!
SMASH
GROW
CRASH
Ummmm...
Oops!

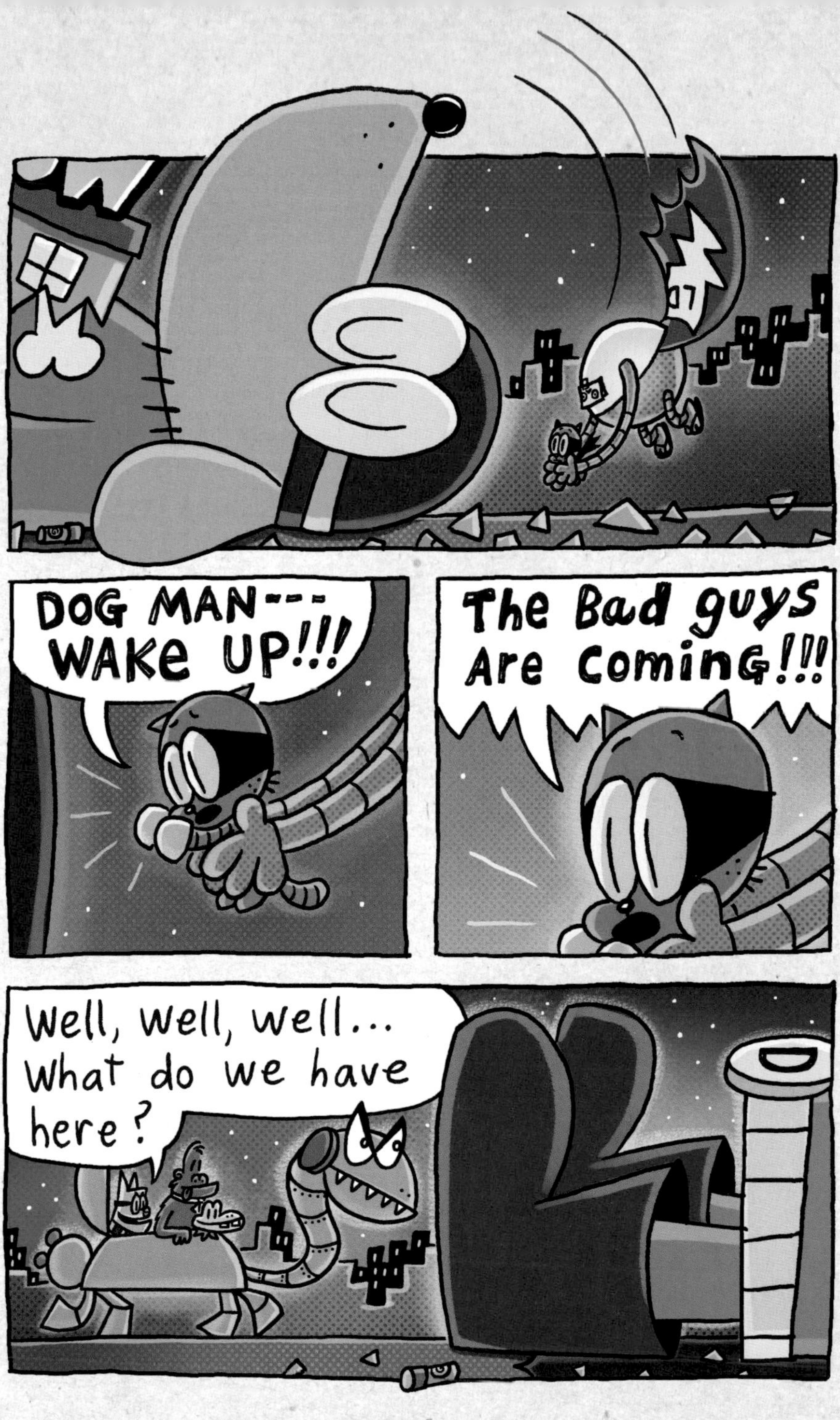
DOG MAN---
WAKE UP!!!
The Bad guys
Are Coming!!!
Well, well, well...
What do we have
here?

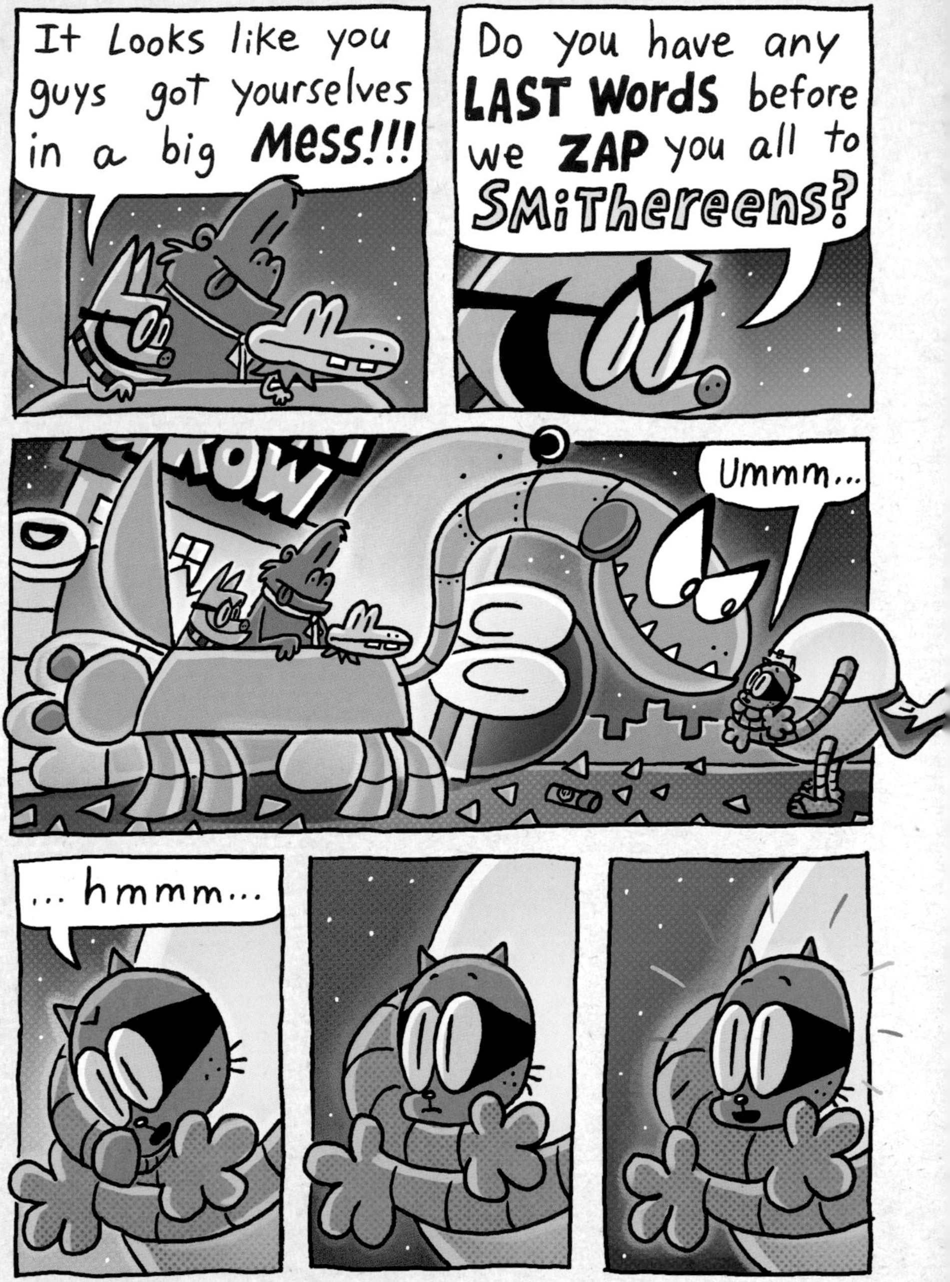
It Looks like you guys got yourselves in a big MESS!!!
Do you have any LAST WORDS before we ZAP you all to SMiThereeens?
Ummm...
...hmmm...

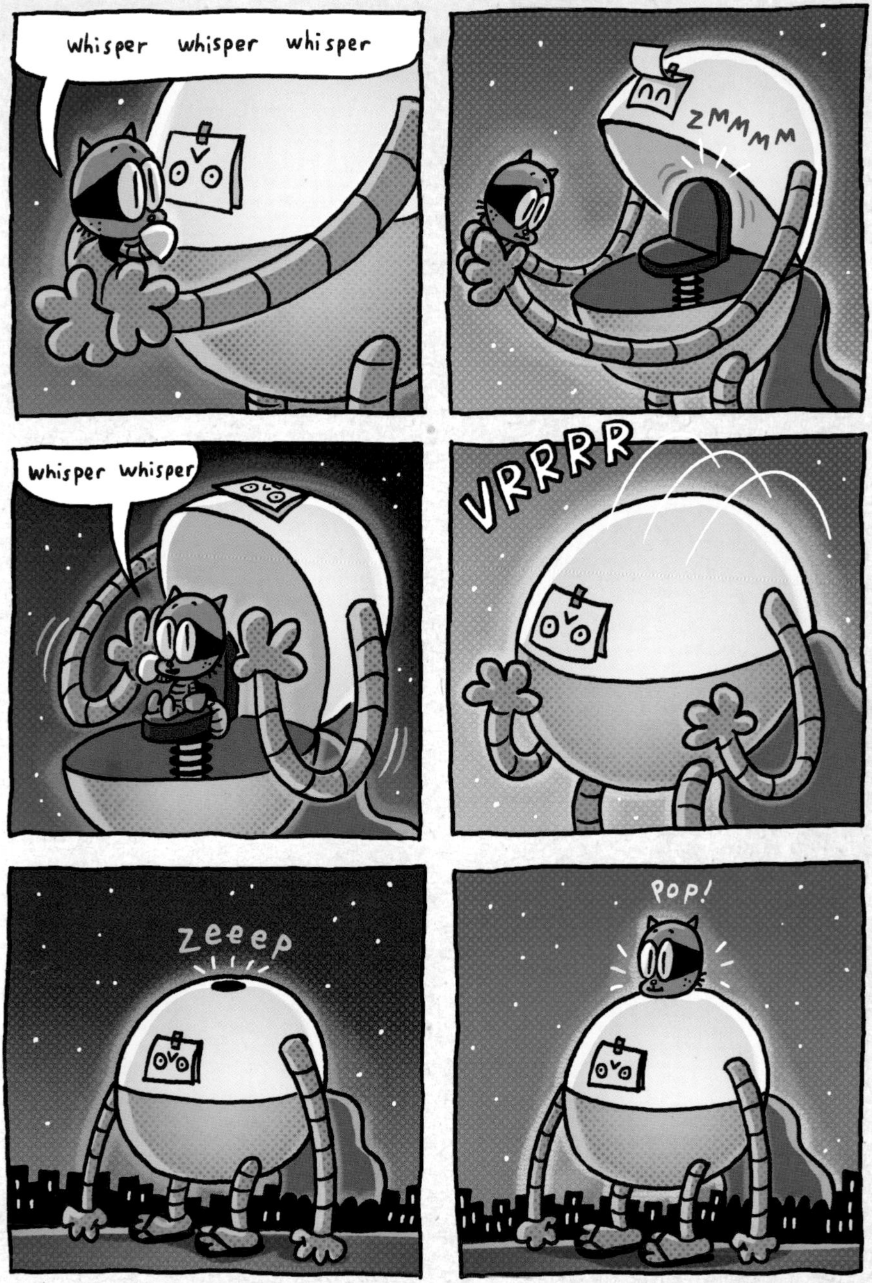
whisper whisper whisper
ZMMMM
whisper whisper
VRRRR
zeeep
POP!

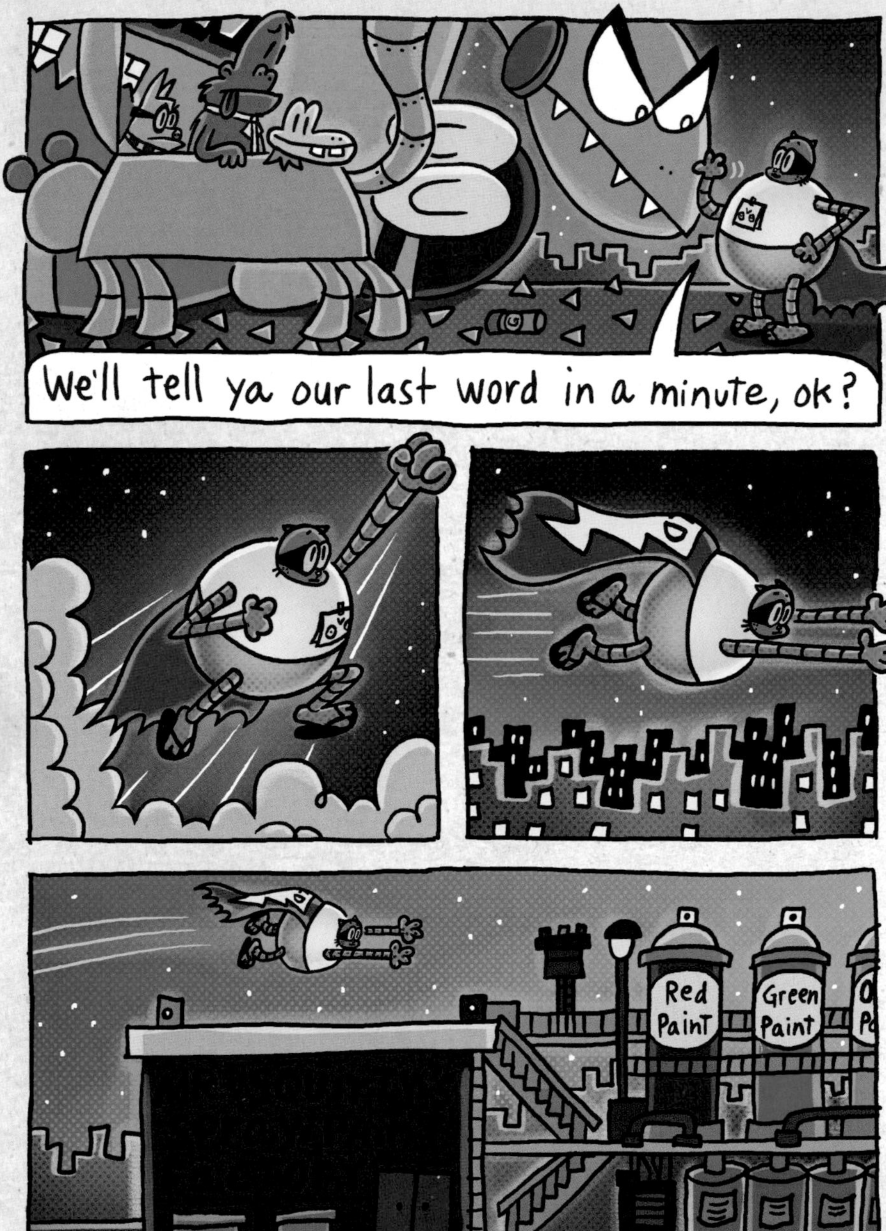
We'll tell ya our last word in a minute, ok?
Red Paint
Green Paint

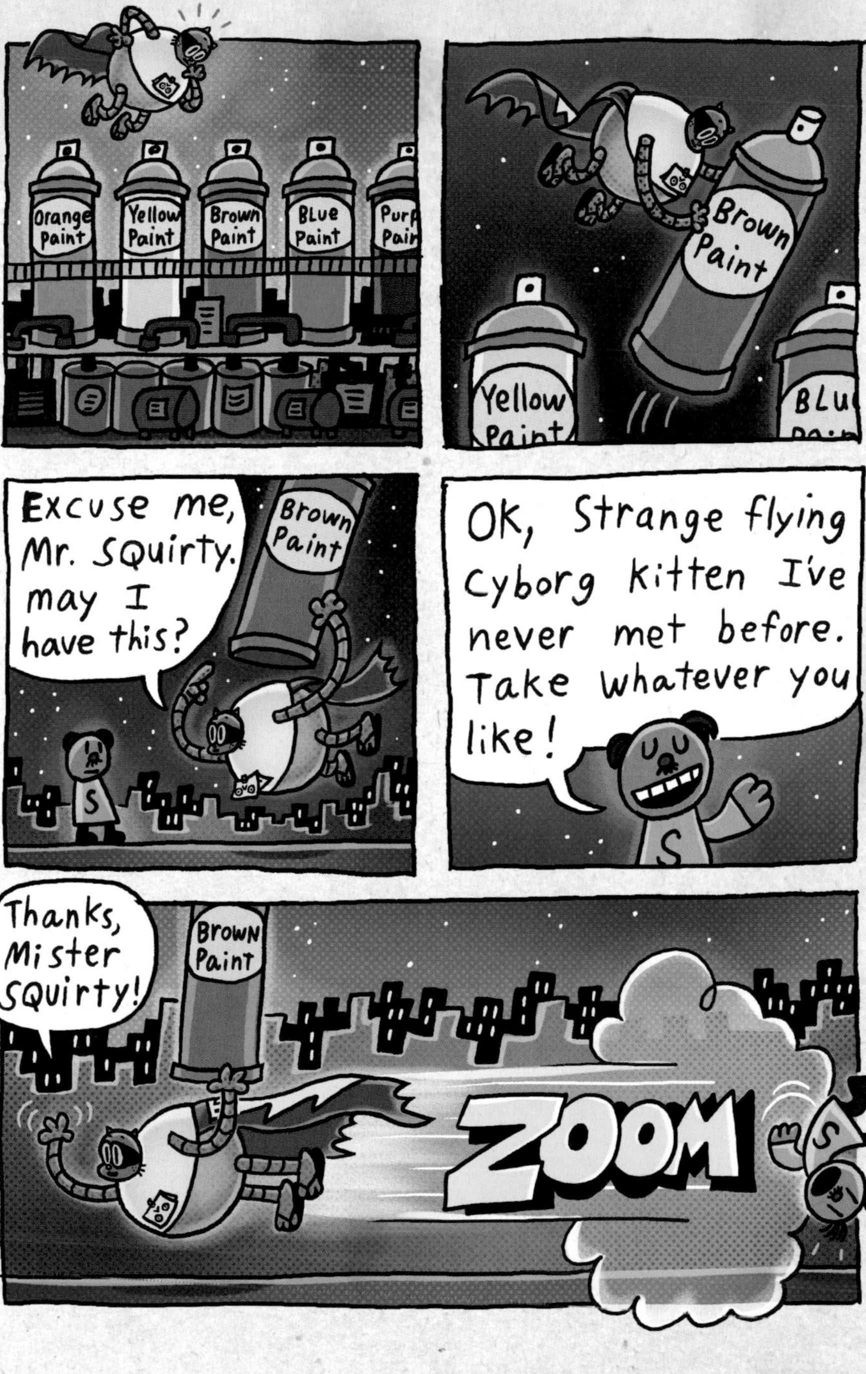
Orange Paint
Yellow Paint
Brown Paint
BLue Paint
Brown Paint
Yellow Paint
Excuse me, Mr. SQuirty. may I have this?
Brown Paint
OK, Strange flying cyborg kitten I've never met before. Take whatever you like!
Thanks, Mister SQuirty!
BROWN PaINT
ZOOM

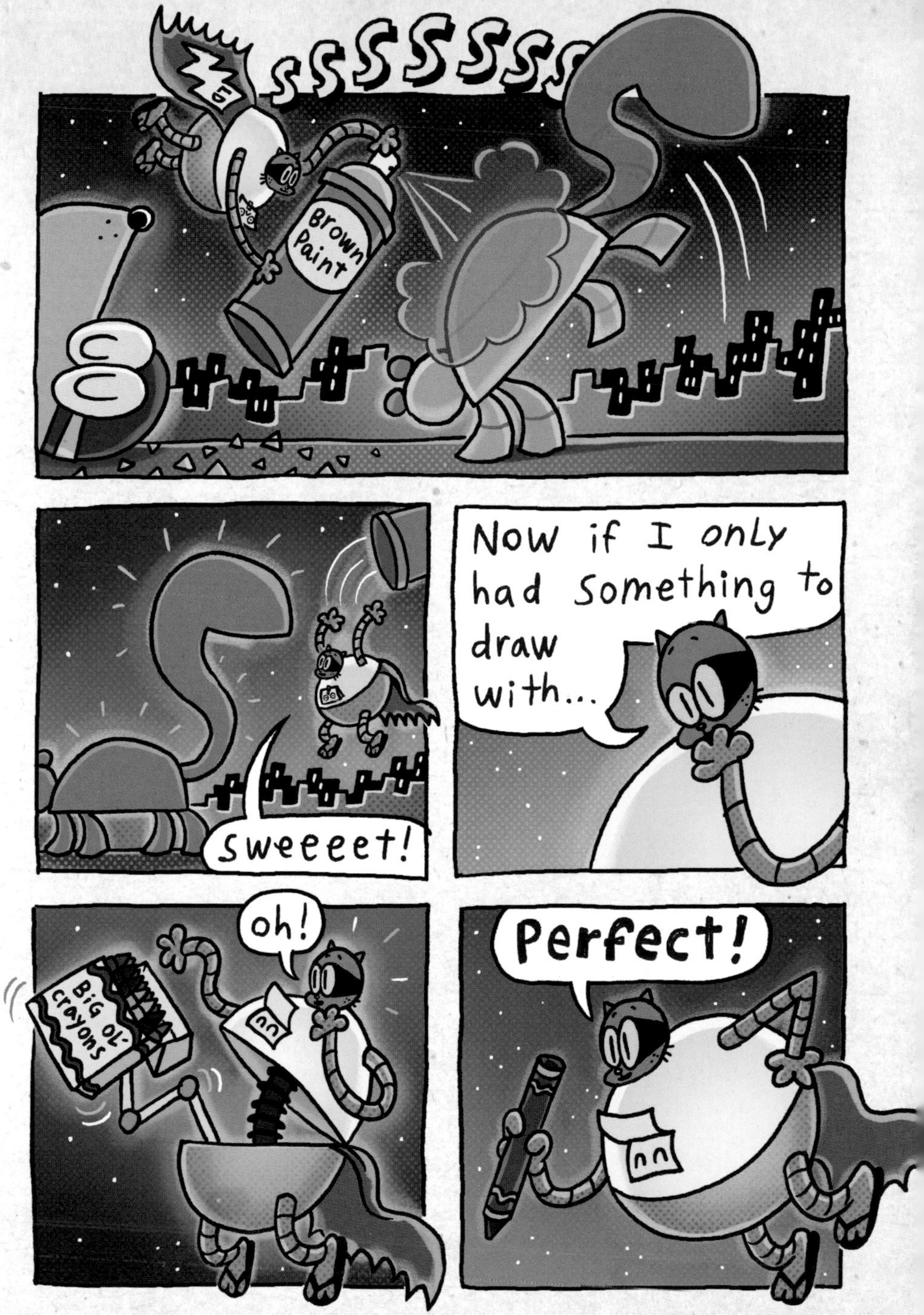
sSSSSSS
Brown Paint
sweeeet!
Now if I only had something to draw with...
oh!
BiG OL' crayons
Perfect!

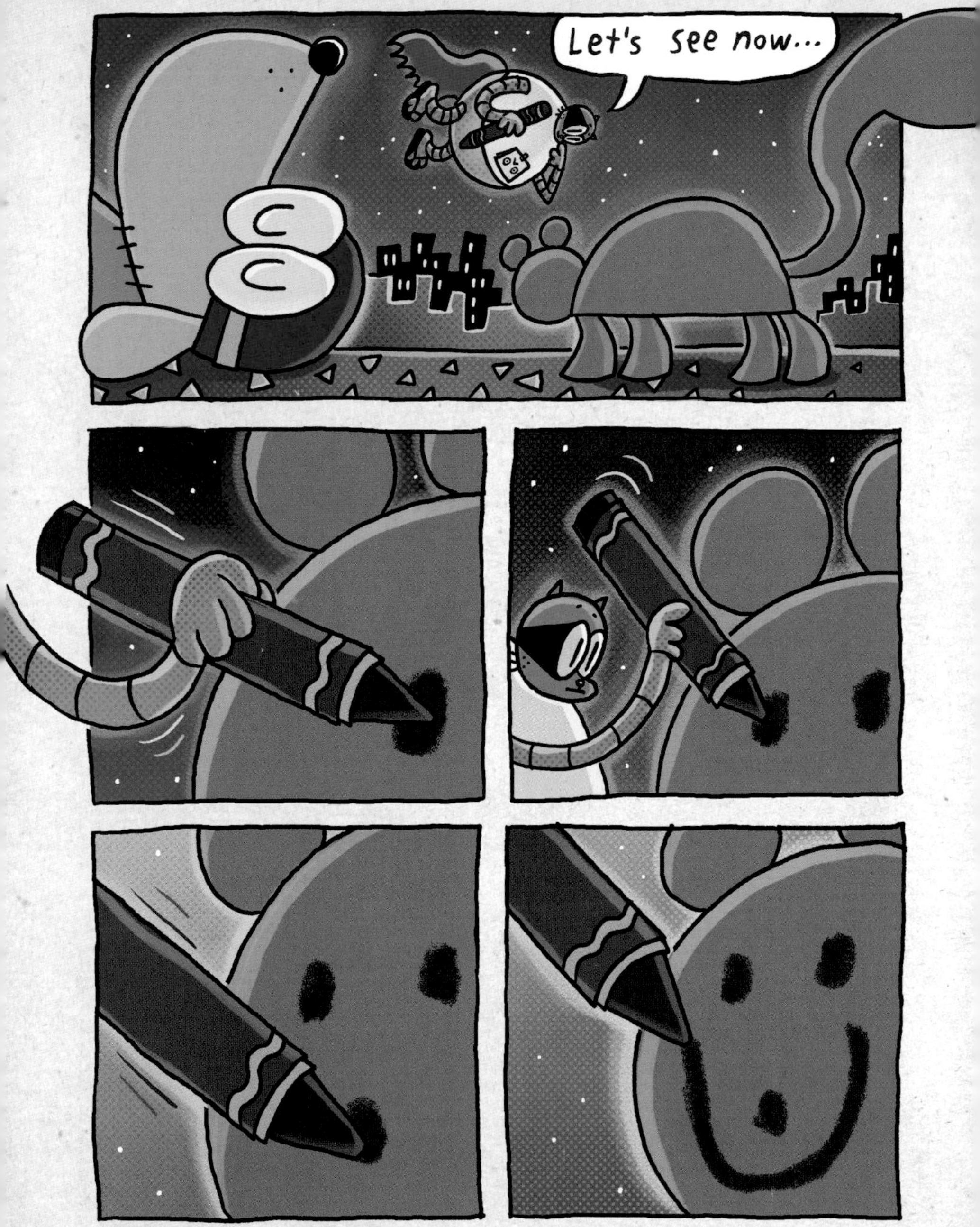
Let's see now...

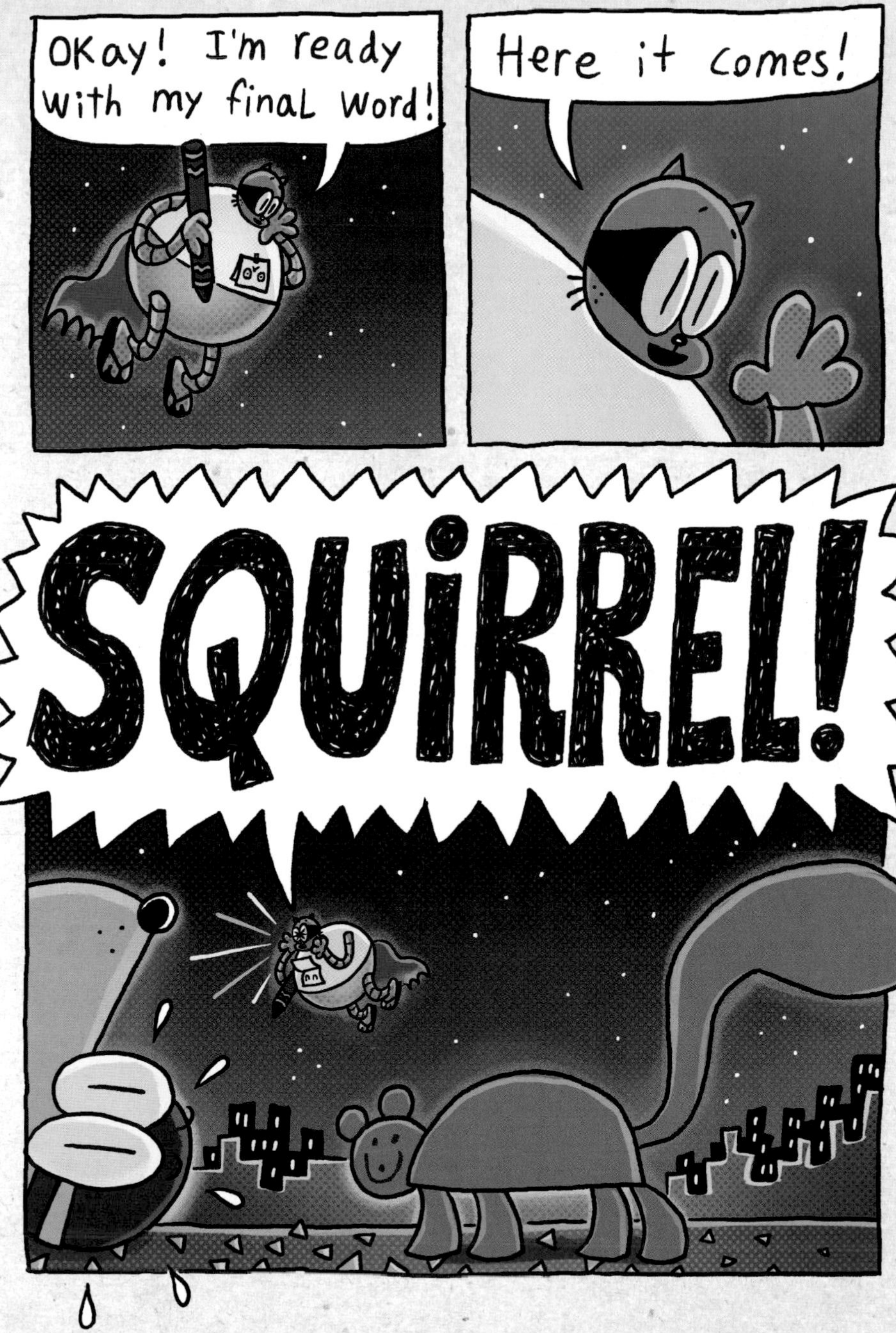
OKay! I'm ready with my final word!
Here it comes!
SQUiRREL!

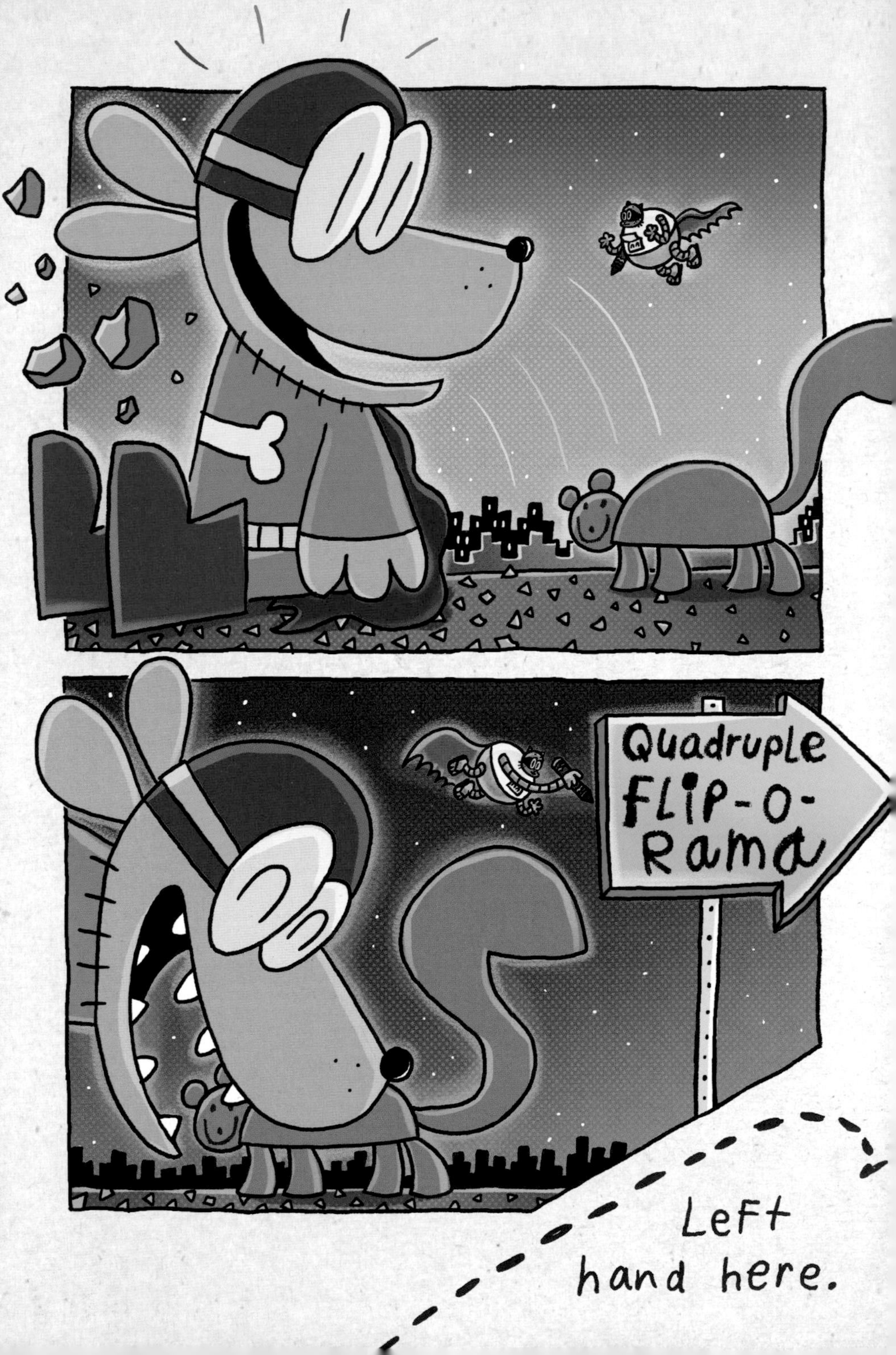
Quadruple
Flip-O-
Rama
Left
hand here.

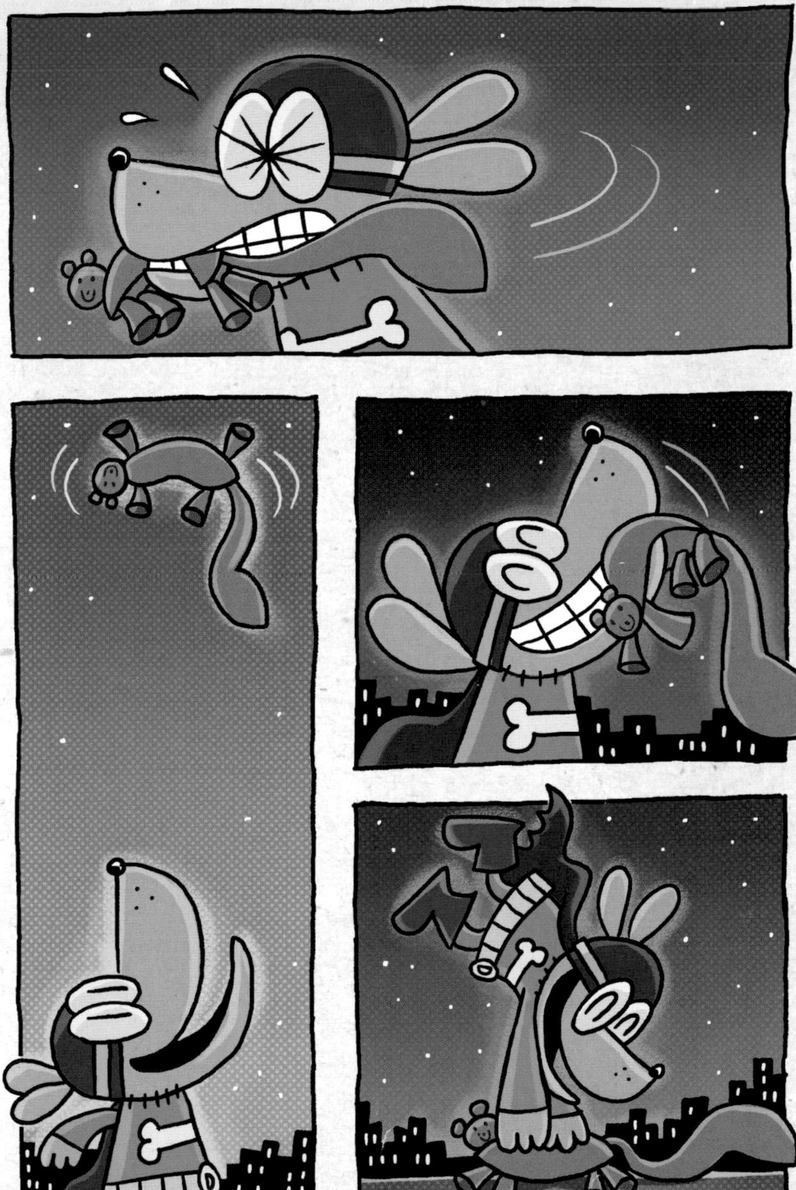

Right
Thumb
here.

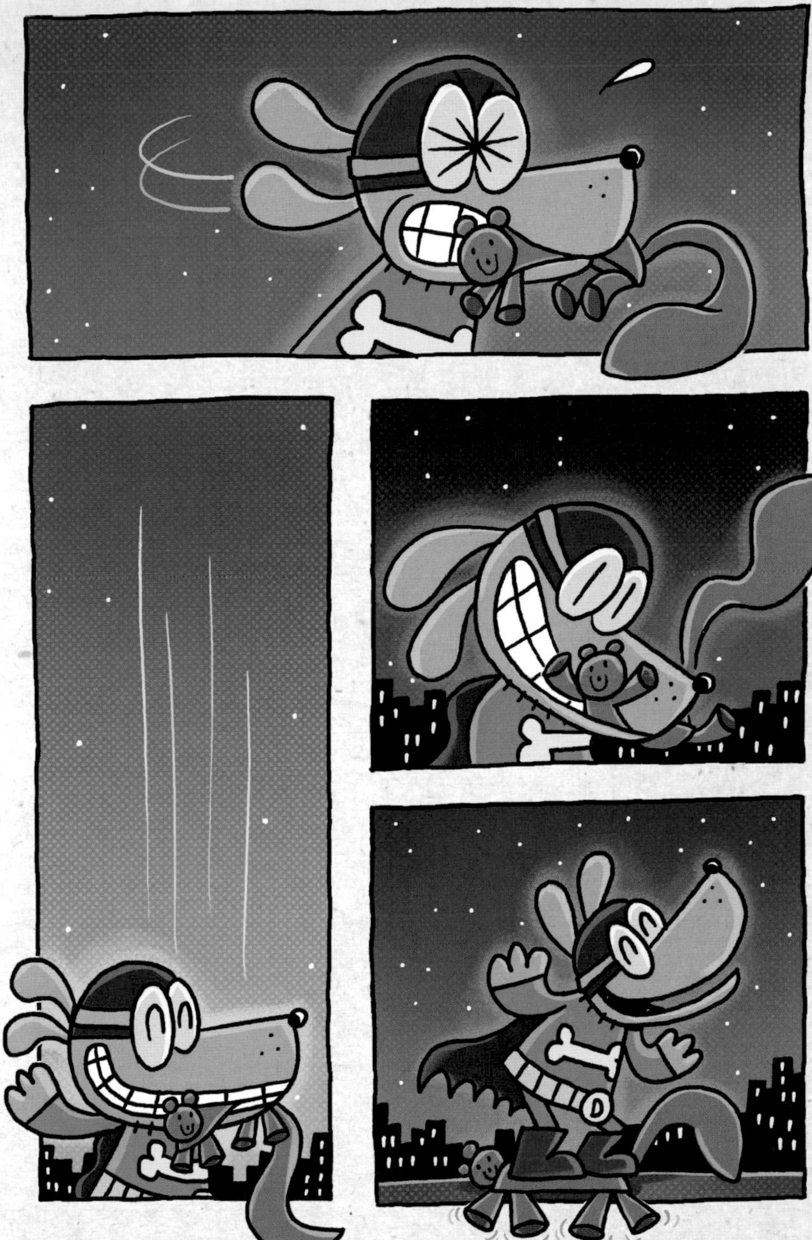

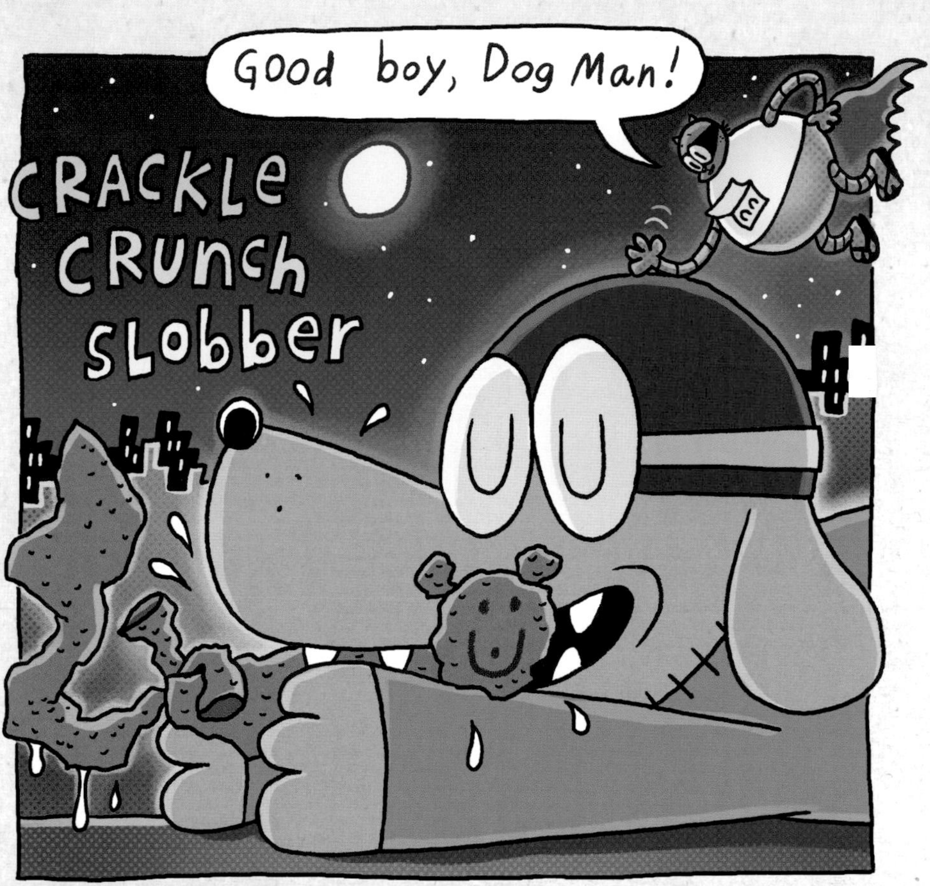
Good boy, Dog Man!
CRACKLE
CRUNCH
SLOBBER

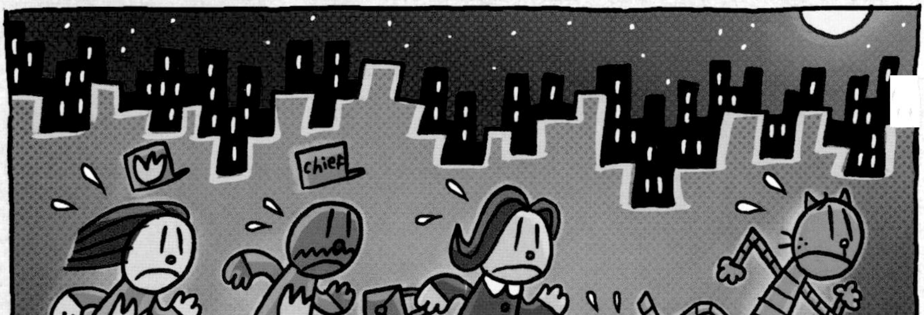
chief

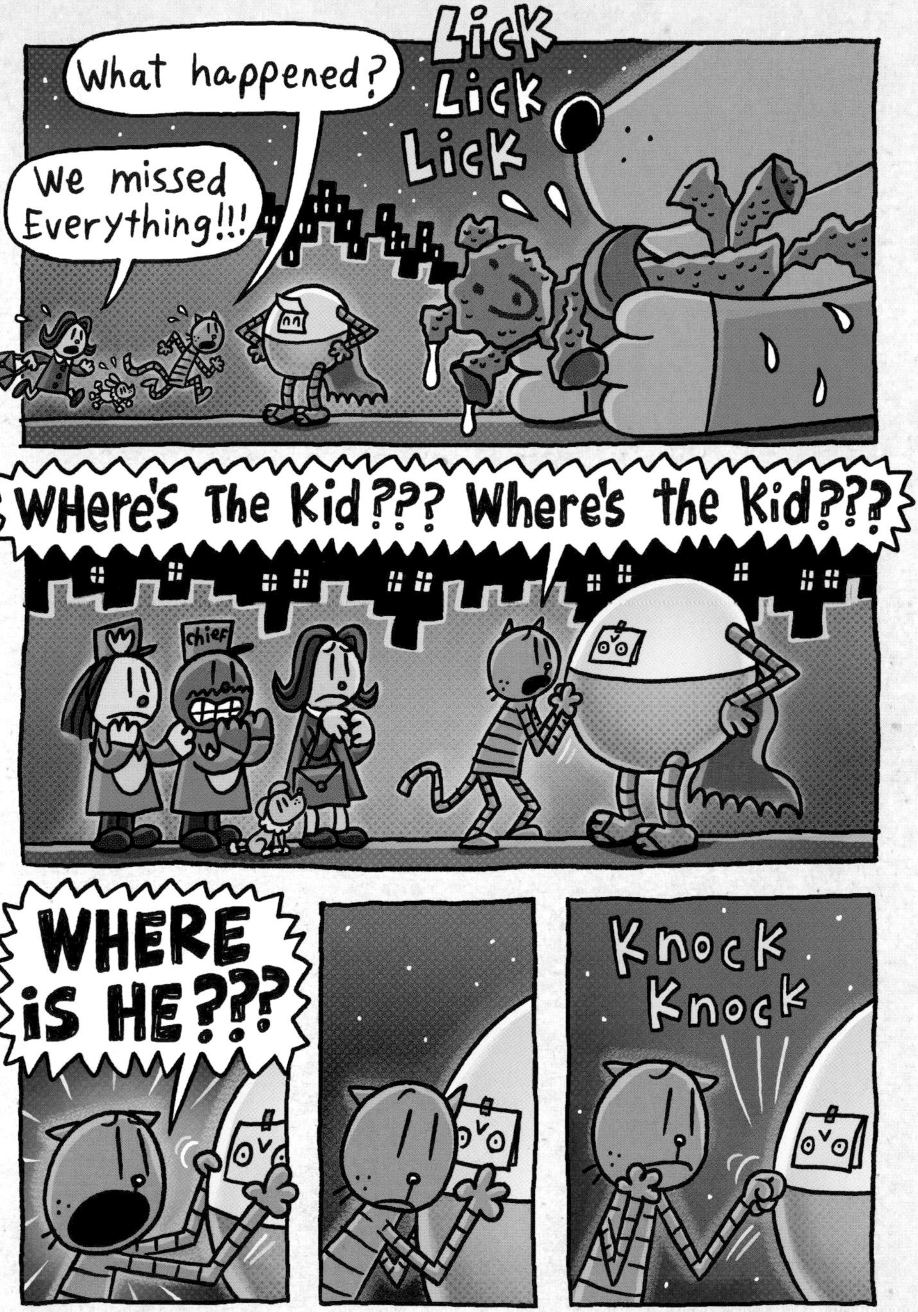
Lick
Lick
Lick
What happened?
We missed Everything!!!
WHere's The Kid??? Where's the Kid???
chief
WHERE iS HE???
Knock Knock

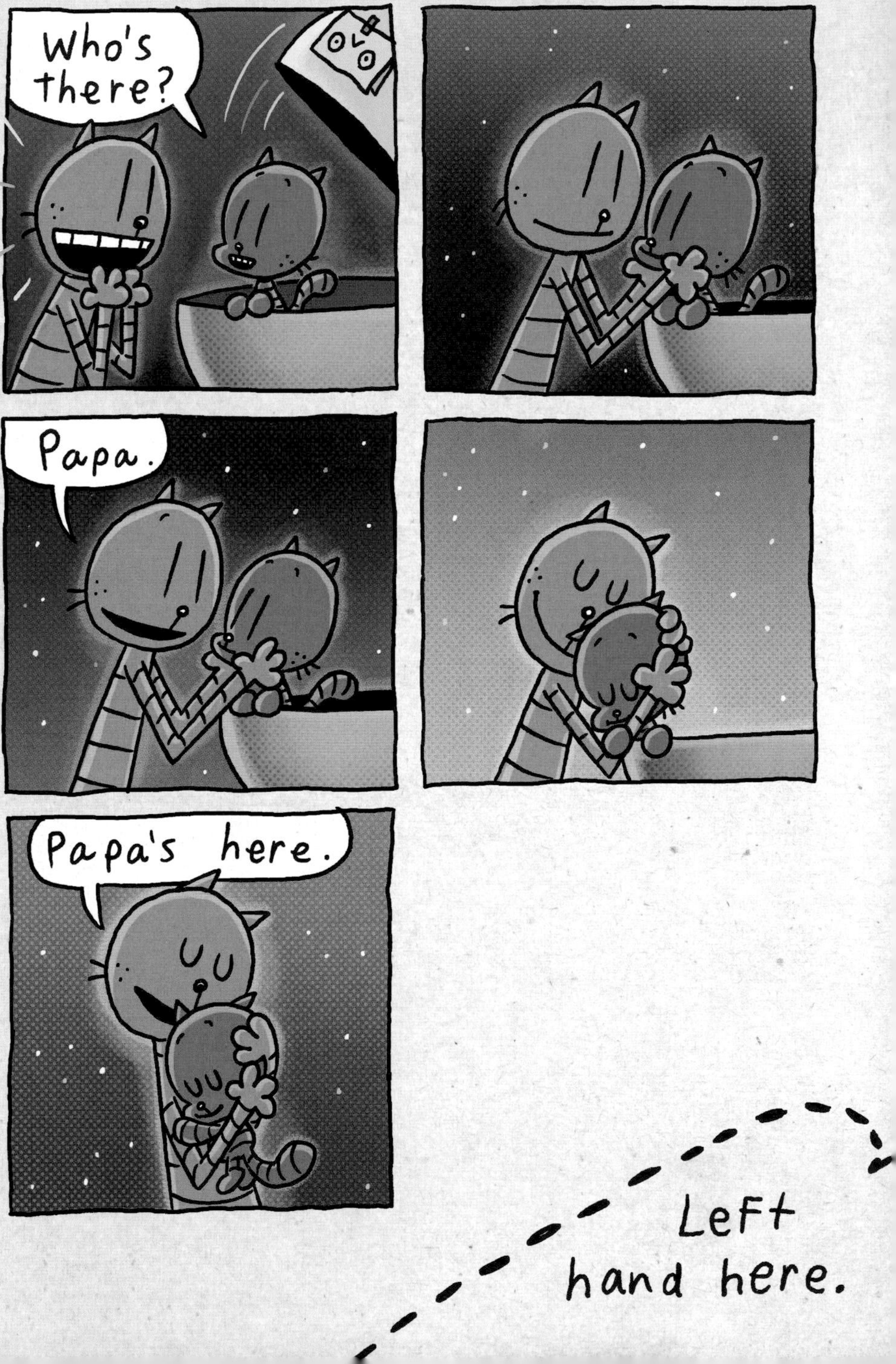
Who's there?
Papa.
Papa's here.
Left hand here.

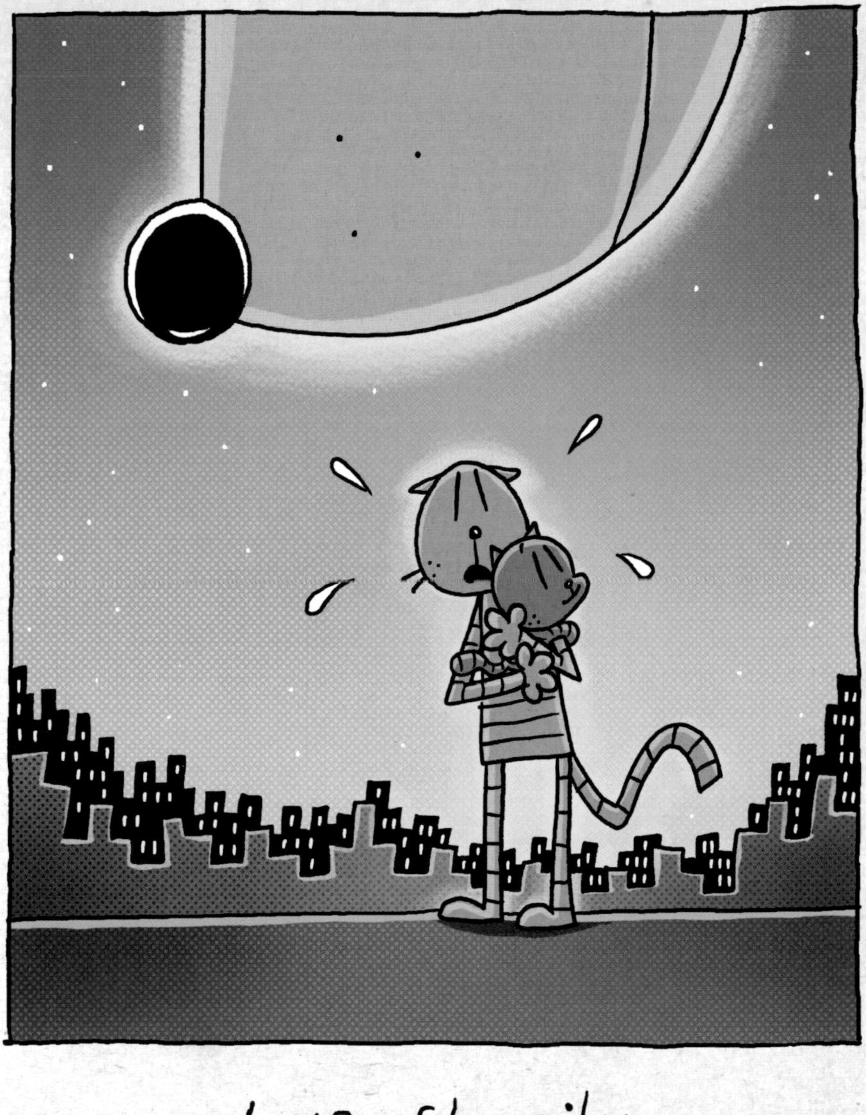

Love, Sloppily

Right Thumb here.

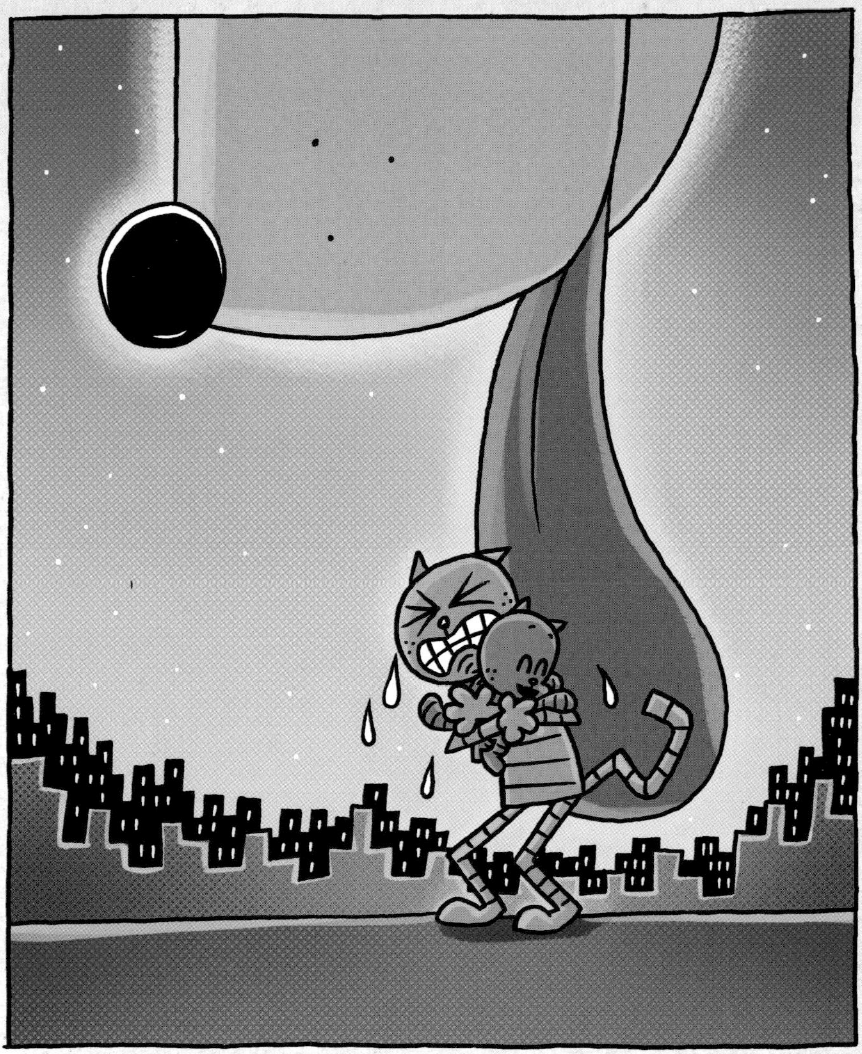

Love, Sloppily

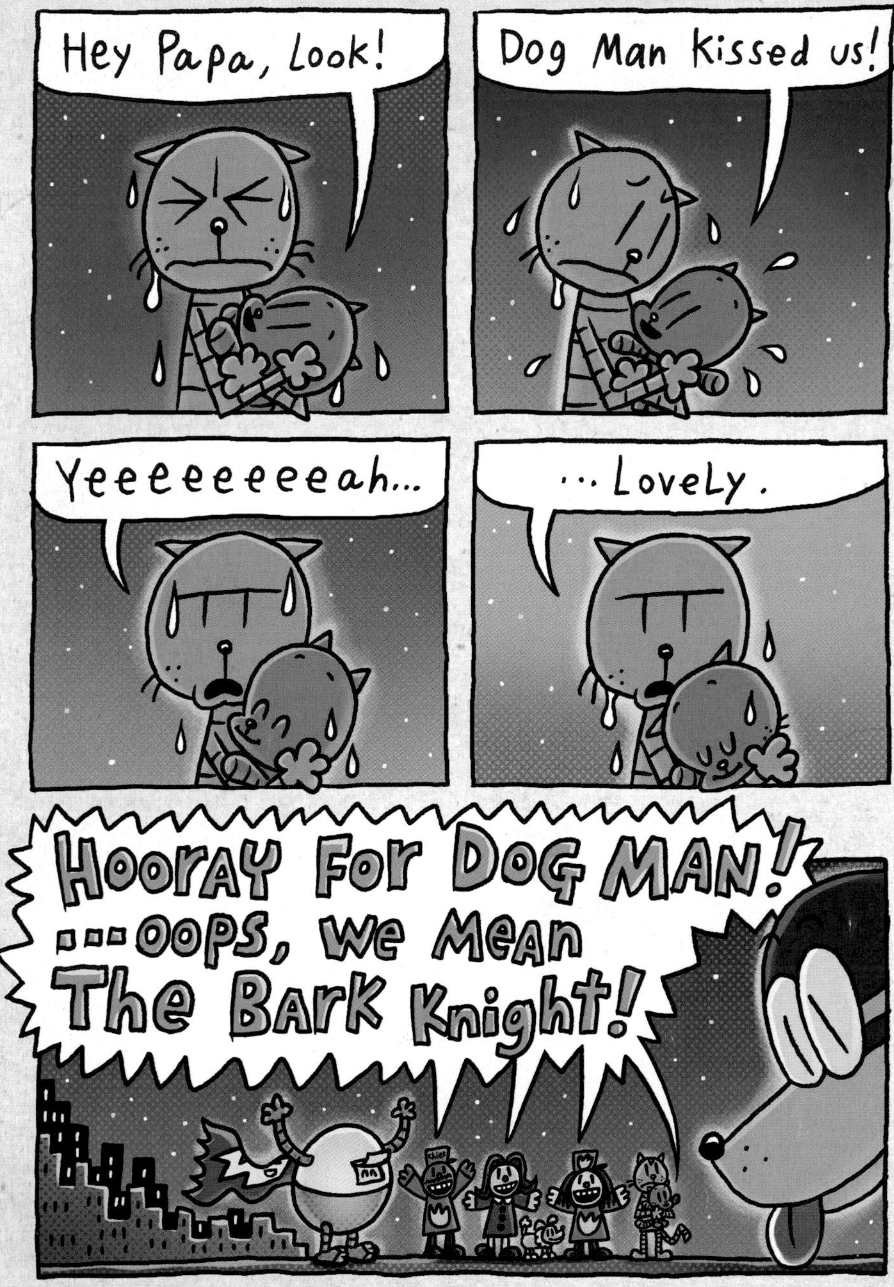
Hey Papa, Look!
Dog Man Kissed us!
Yeeeeeeeeah...
...Lovely.
HOORAY FOR DOG MAN! ...OOPS, WE MEAN THE BARK KNIGHT!
Chief

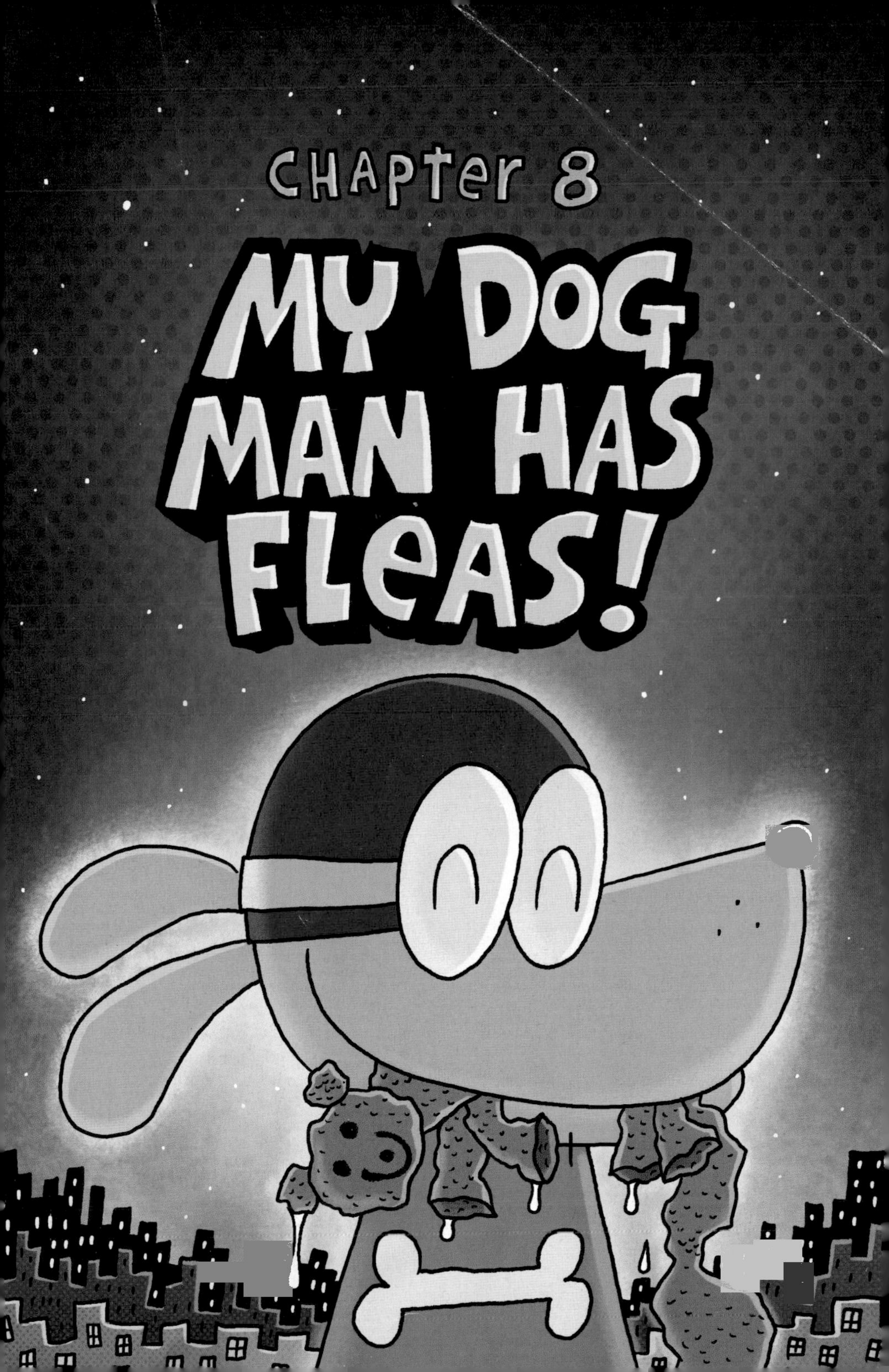
CHAPTER 8
MY DOG MAN HAS FLEAS!

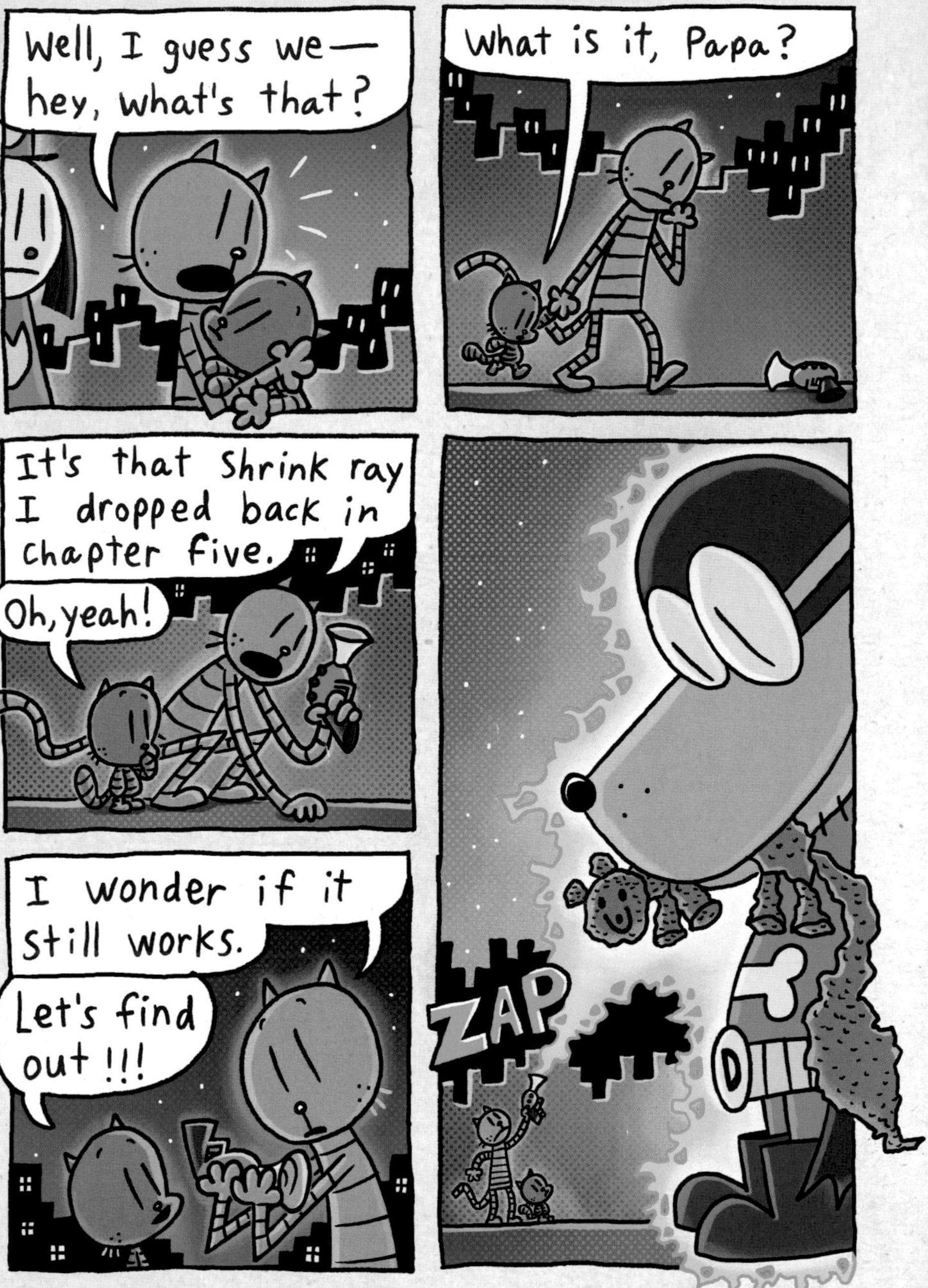
Well, I guess we—
hey, what's that?
What is it, Papa?
It's that Shrink ray I dropped back in chapter five.
Oh, yeah!
I wonder if it still works.
Let's find out!!!
ZAP

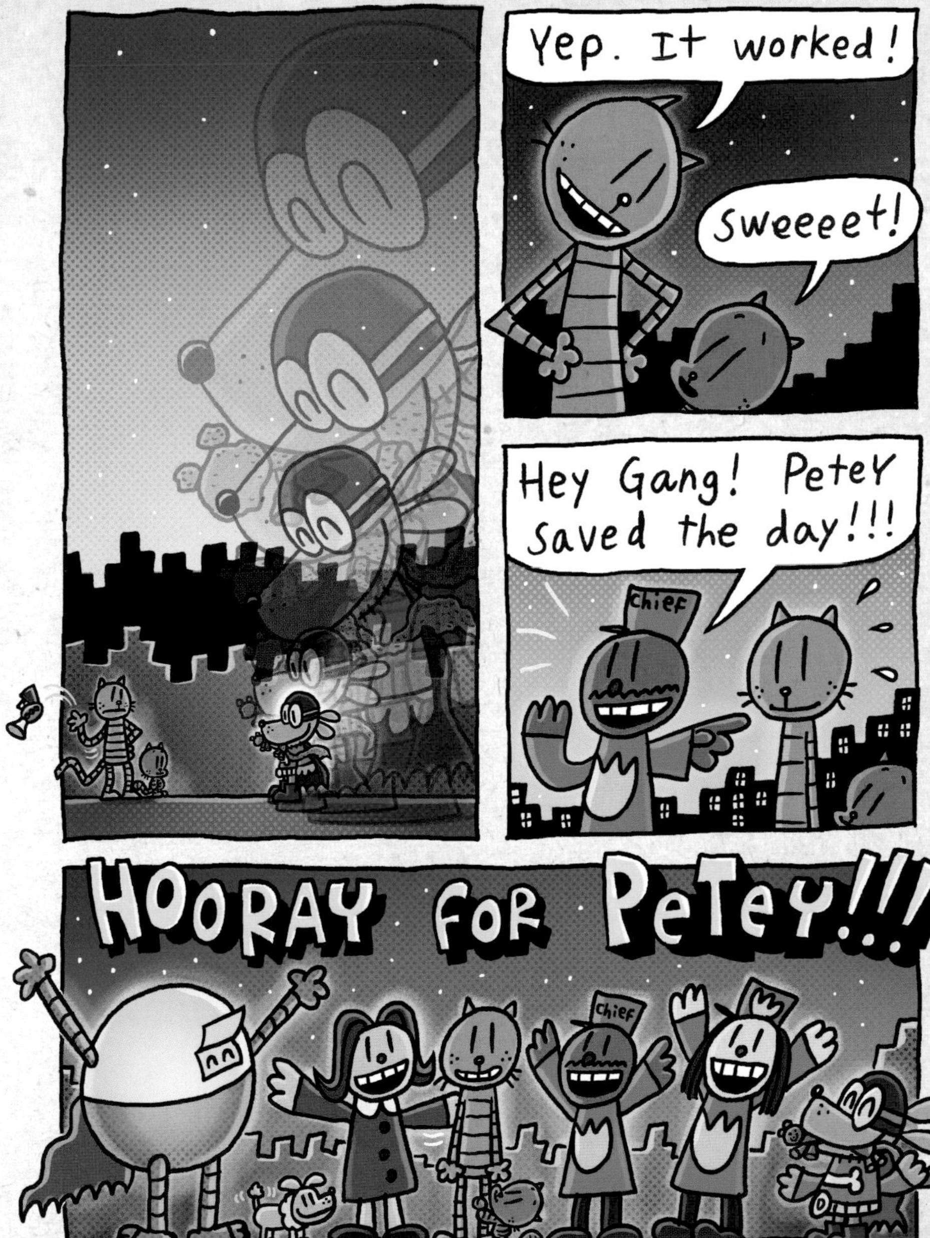

Yep. It worked!
Sweeeet!
Hey Gang! Petey saved the day!!!
chief
HOORAY FOR PETEY!!!
chief

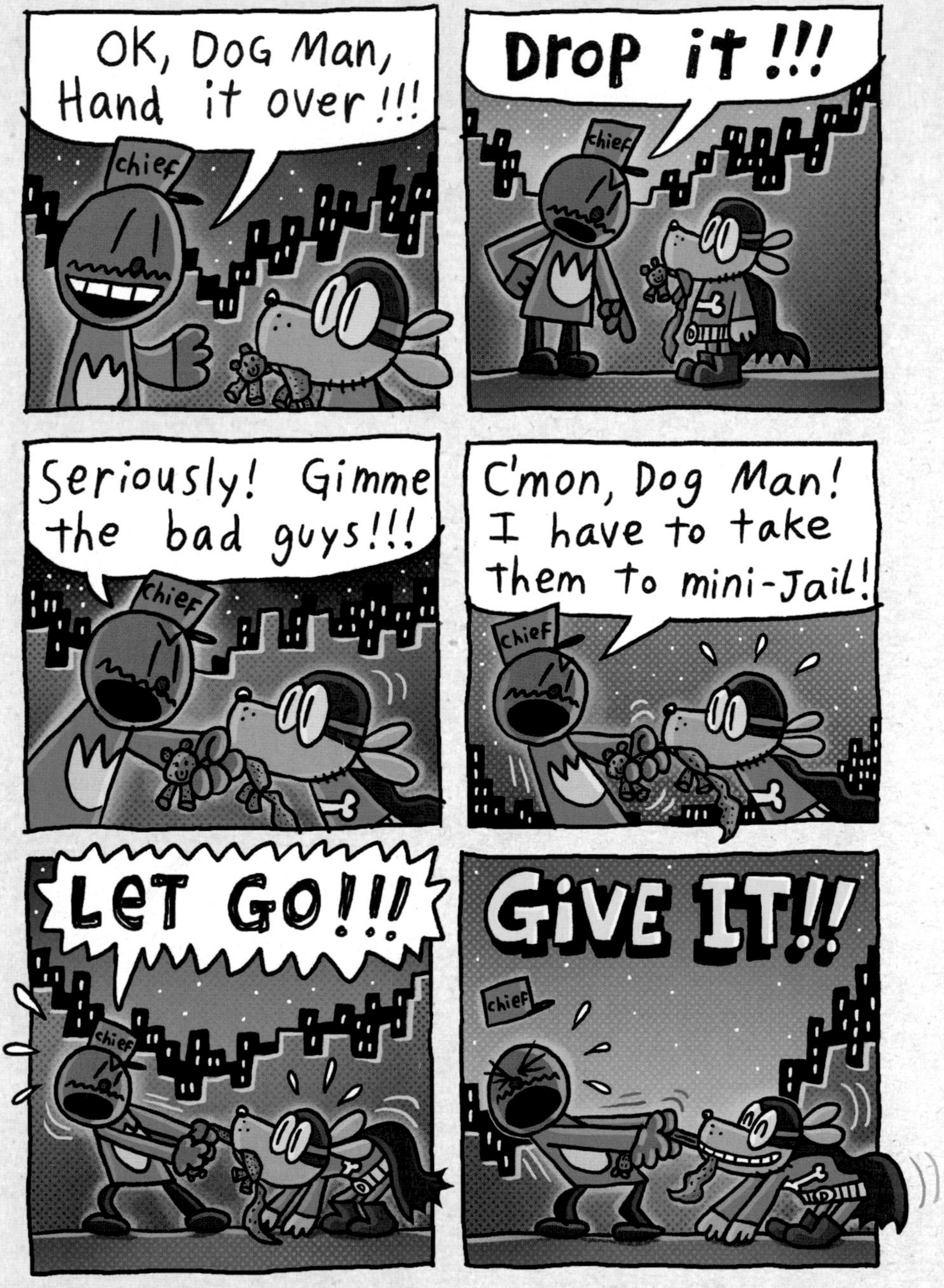
OK, DOG Man, Hand it over!!!
chief
Drop it!!!
chief
Seriously! Gimme the bad guys!!!
chief
C'mon, Dog Man! I have to take them to mini-Jail!
chief
LET GO!!!
chief
GIVE IT!!
chief

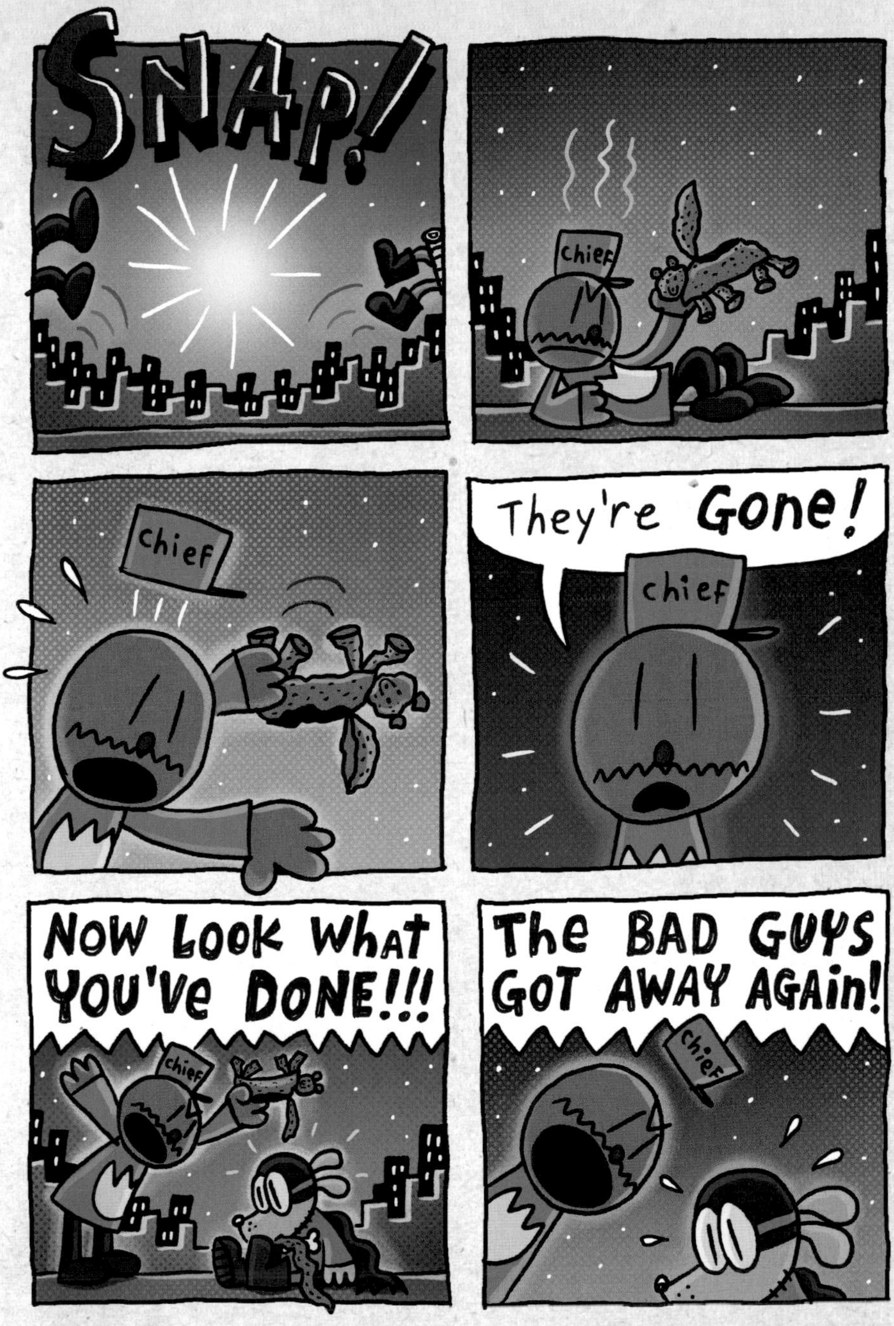
SNAP!
chief
chief
They're Gone!
chief
NOW LOOK WhAT YOU'VE DONE!!!
chief
The BAD GUYS GOT AWAY AGAIN!
chief

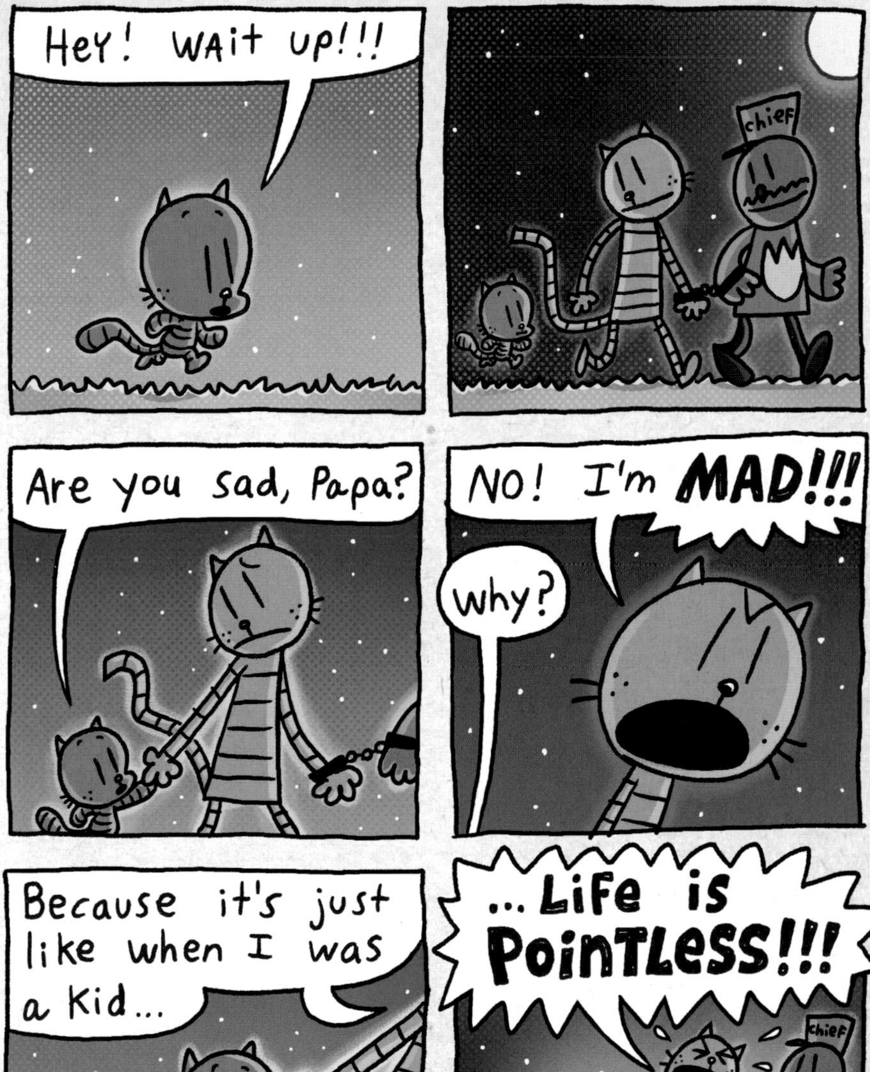
Hey! WAit up!!!
chief
Are you sad, Papa?
NO! I'm MAD!!!
why?
Because it's just like when I was a kid...
...Life is PoinTLess!!!
chief

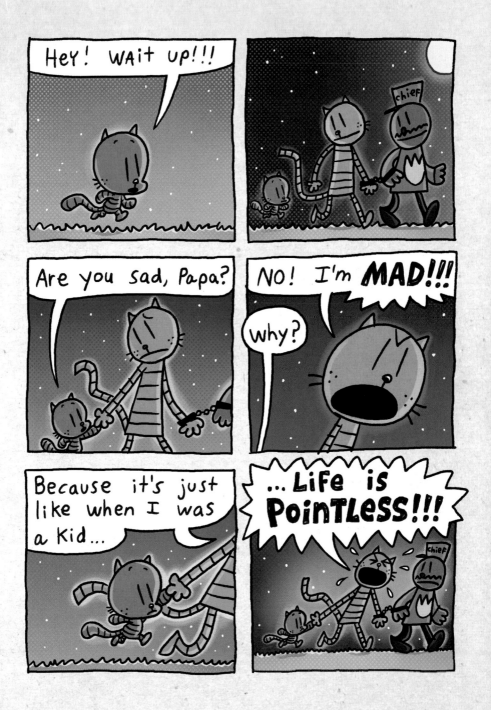

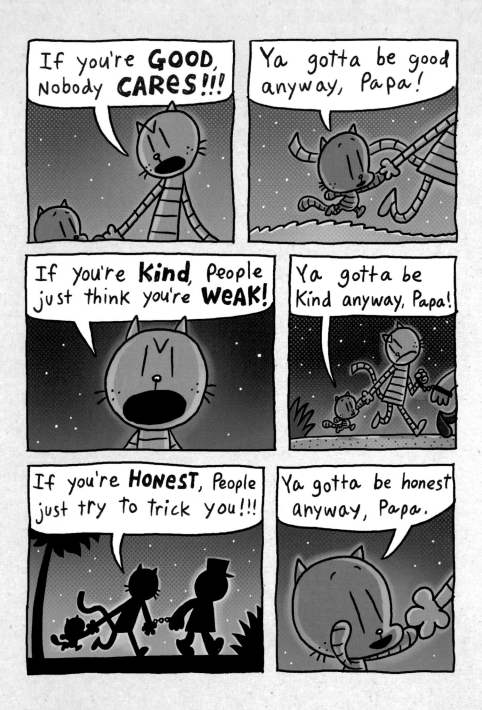

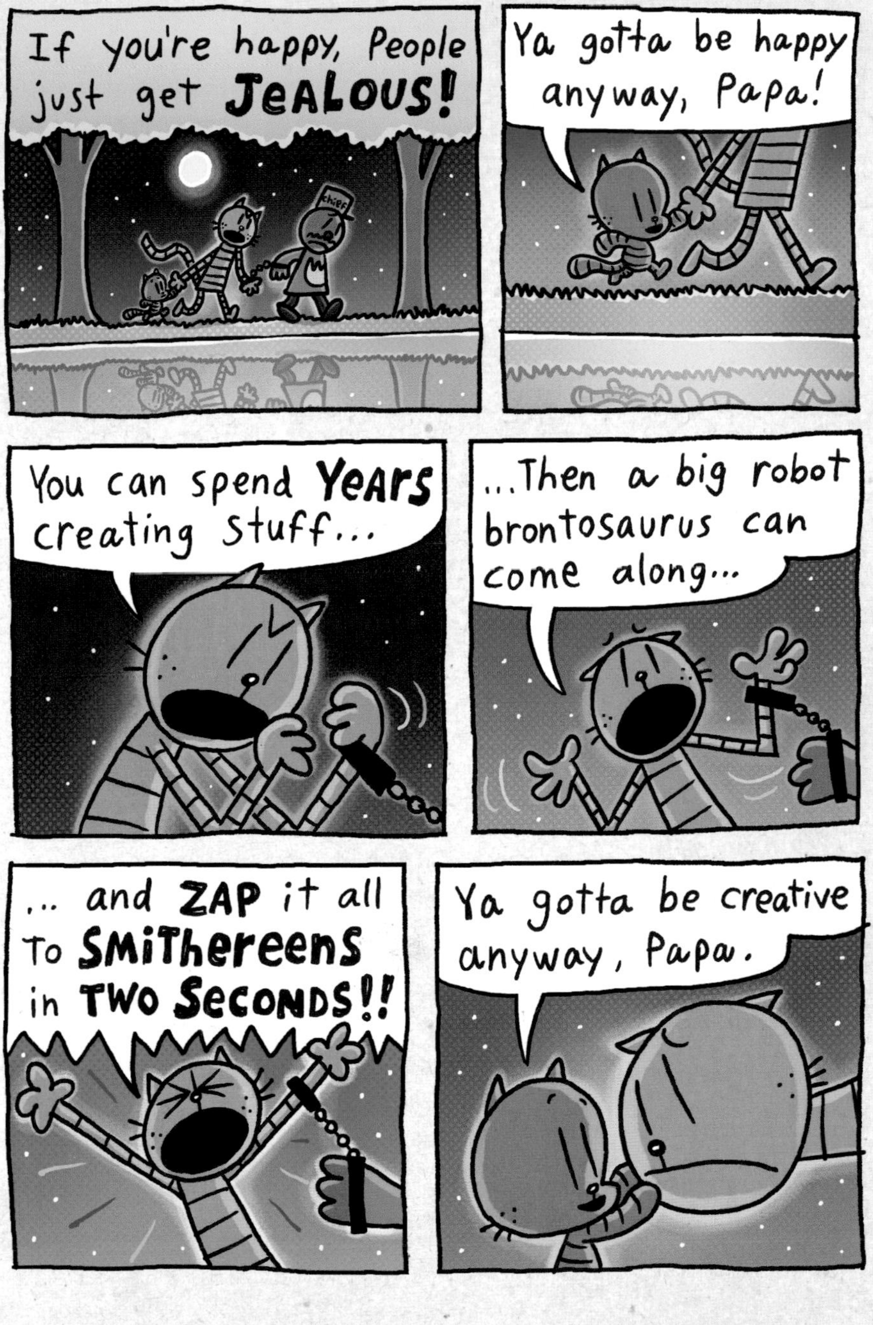
If you're happy, People just get JEALOUS!
Ya gotta be happy anyway, Papa!
You can spend YEARS creating stuff...
...Then a big robot brontosaurus can come along...
... and ZAP it all To SMIThereens in TWO SECONDS!!
Ya gotta be creative anyway, Papa.

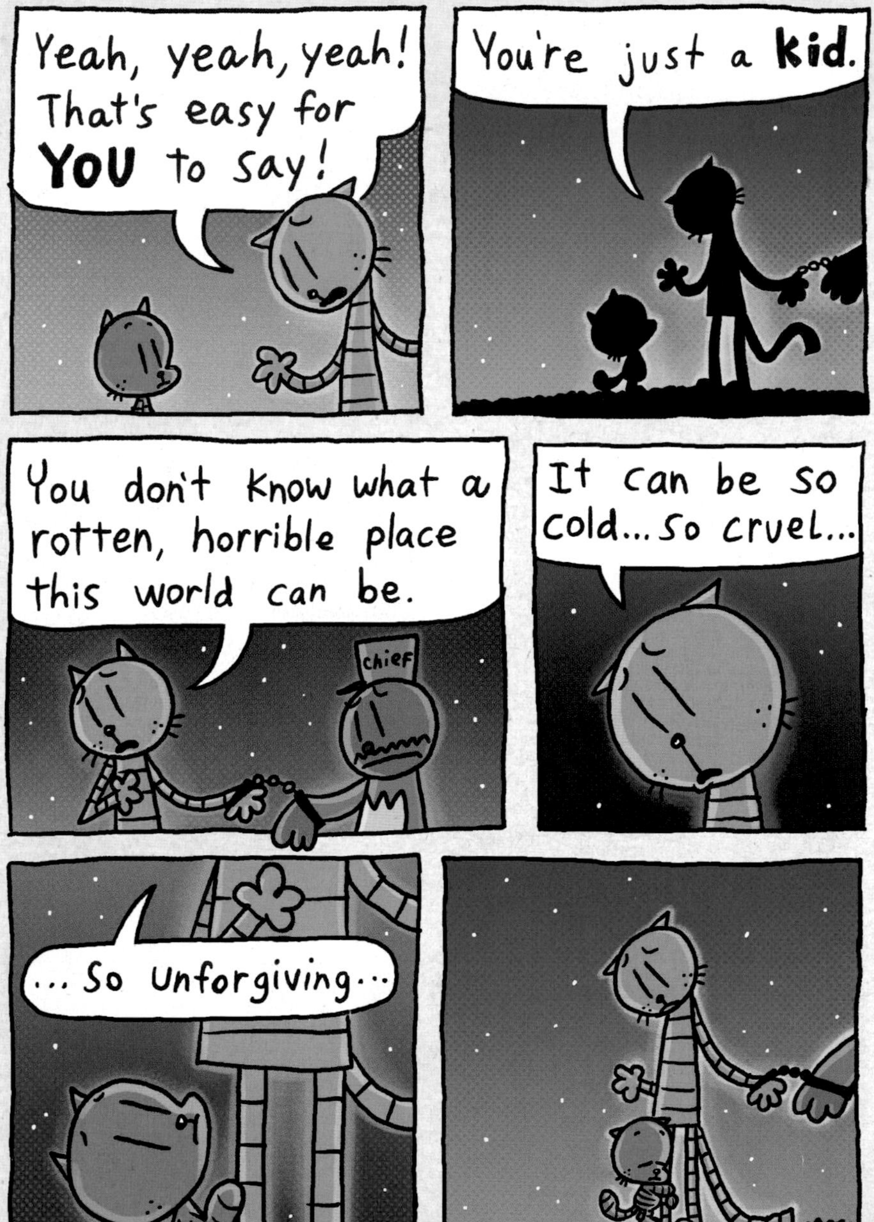
Yeah, yeah, yeah! That's easy for YOU to say!
You're just a kid.
You don't know what a rotten, horrible place this world can be.
chief
It can be so cold... so cruel...
... So unforgiving...

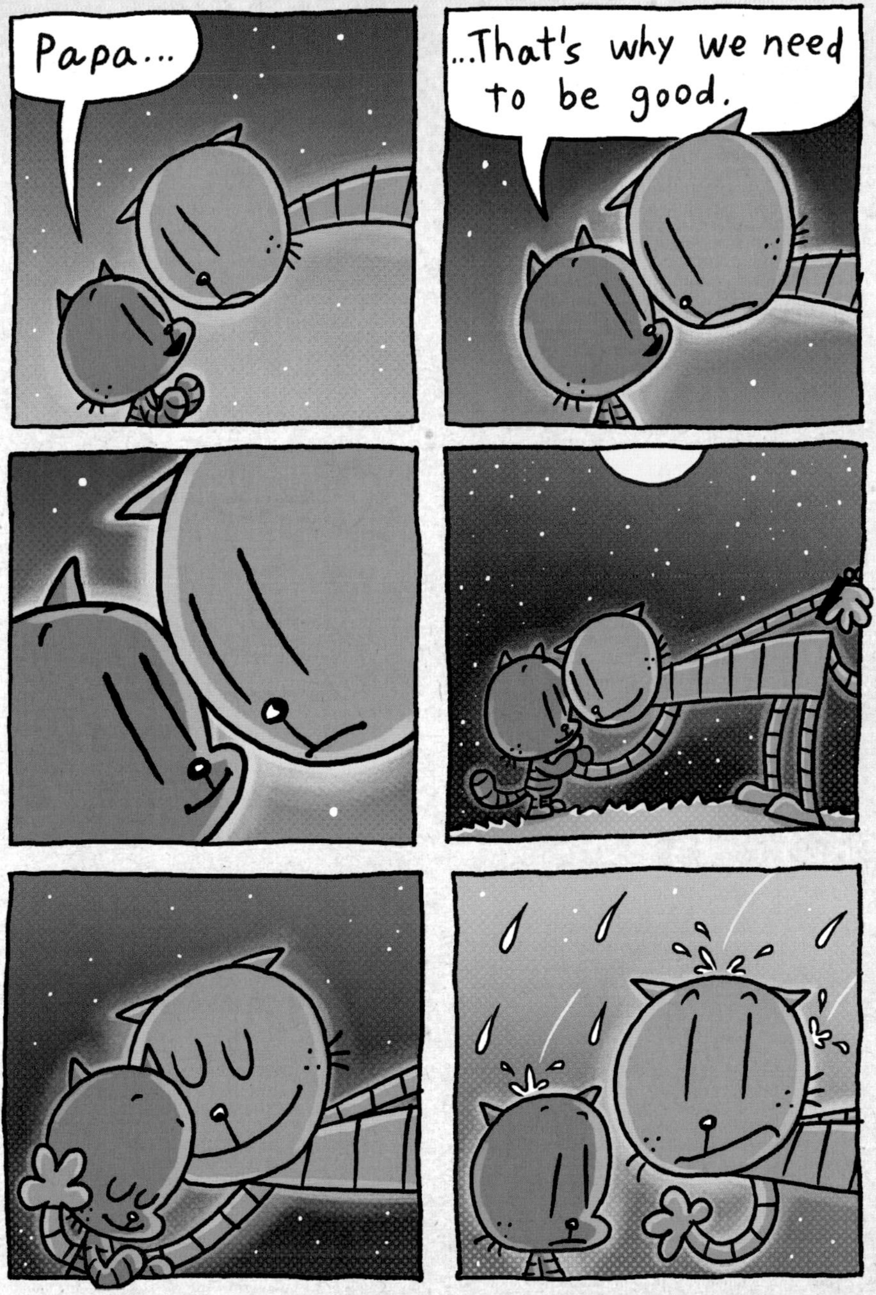
Papa...
...That's why we need to be good.

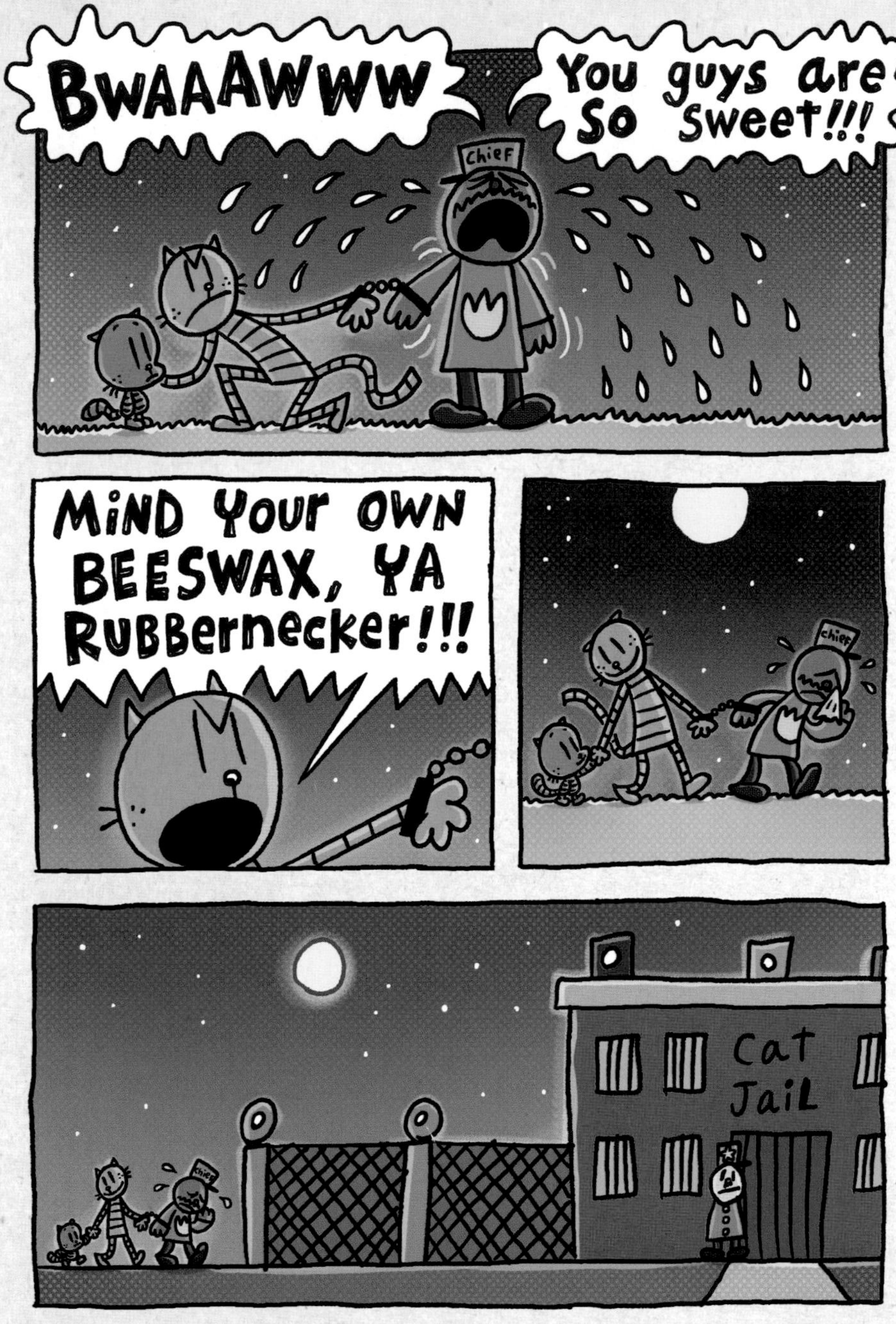
BWAAAWWW
You guys are So Sweet!!!
CHIEF
MIND YOUR OWN BEESWAX, YA RUBBERNECKER!!!
chief
chief
Cat Jail

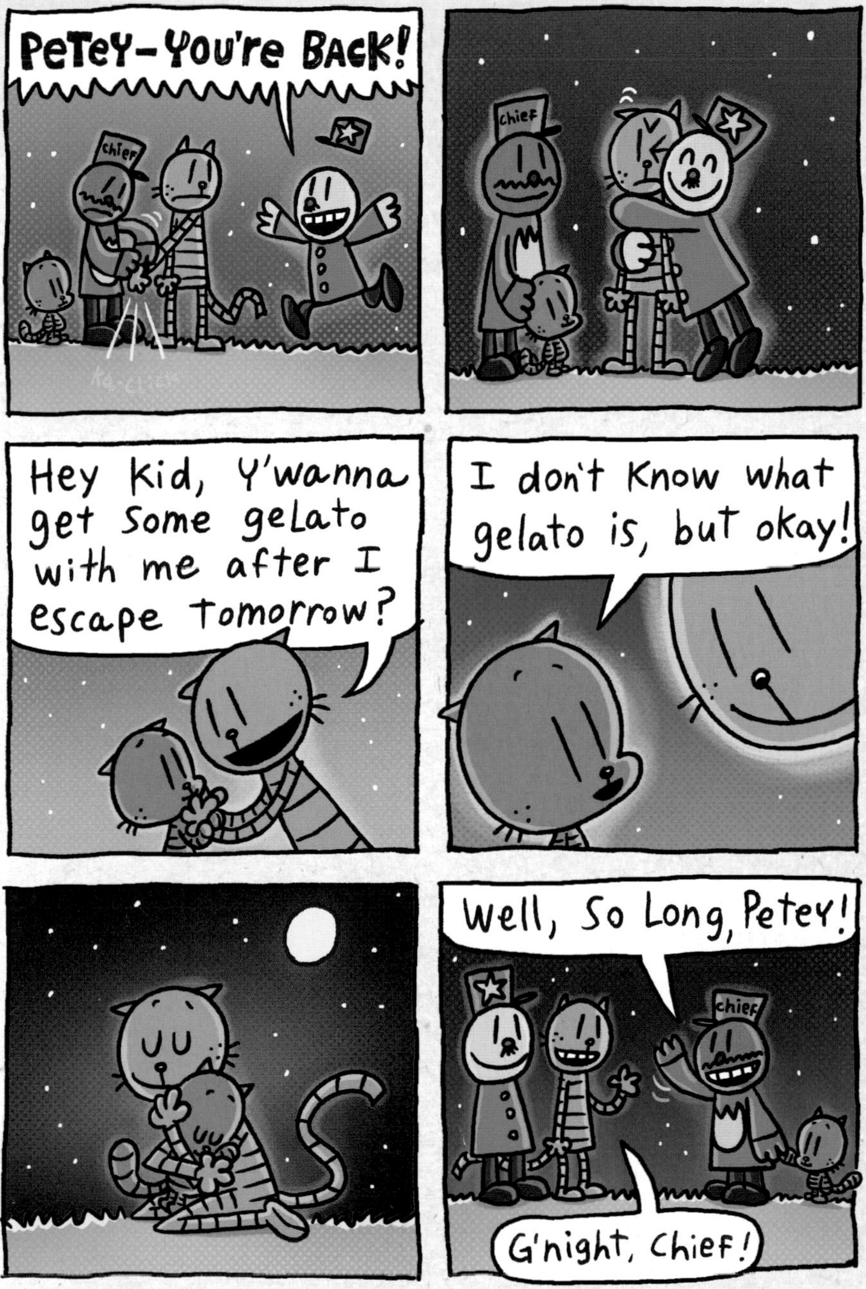
PETEY–YOU'RE BACK!
KA-CLICK
Hey Kid, Y'wanna get Some geLato with me after I escape Tomorrow?
I don't Know what gelato is, but okay!
Well, So Long, Petey!
G'night, Chief!

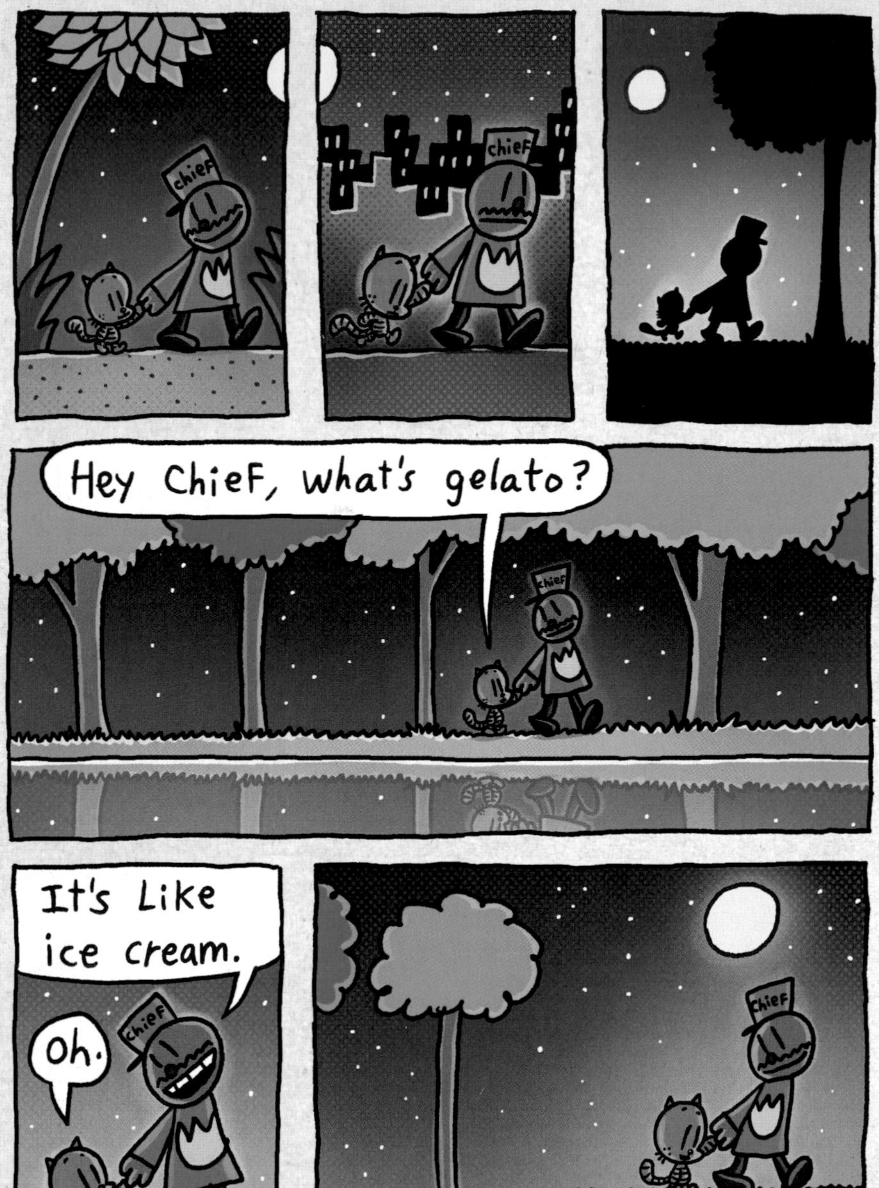
chief
chief
Hey Chief, what's gelato?
chief
It's Like ice cream.
chief
Oh.
chief
sweeeet!

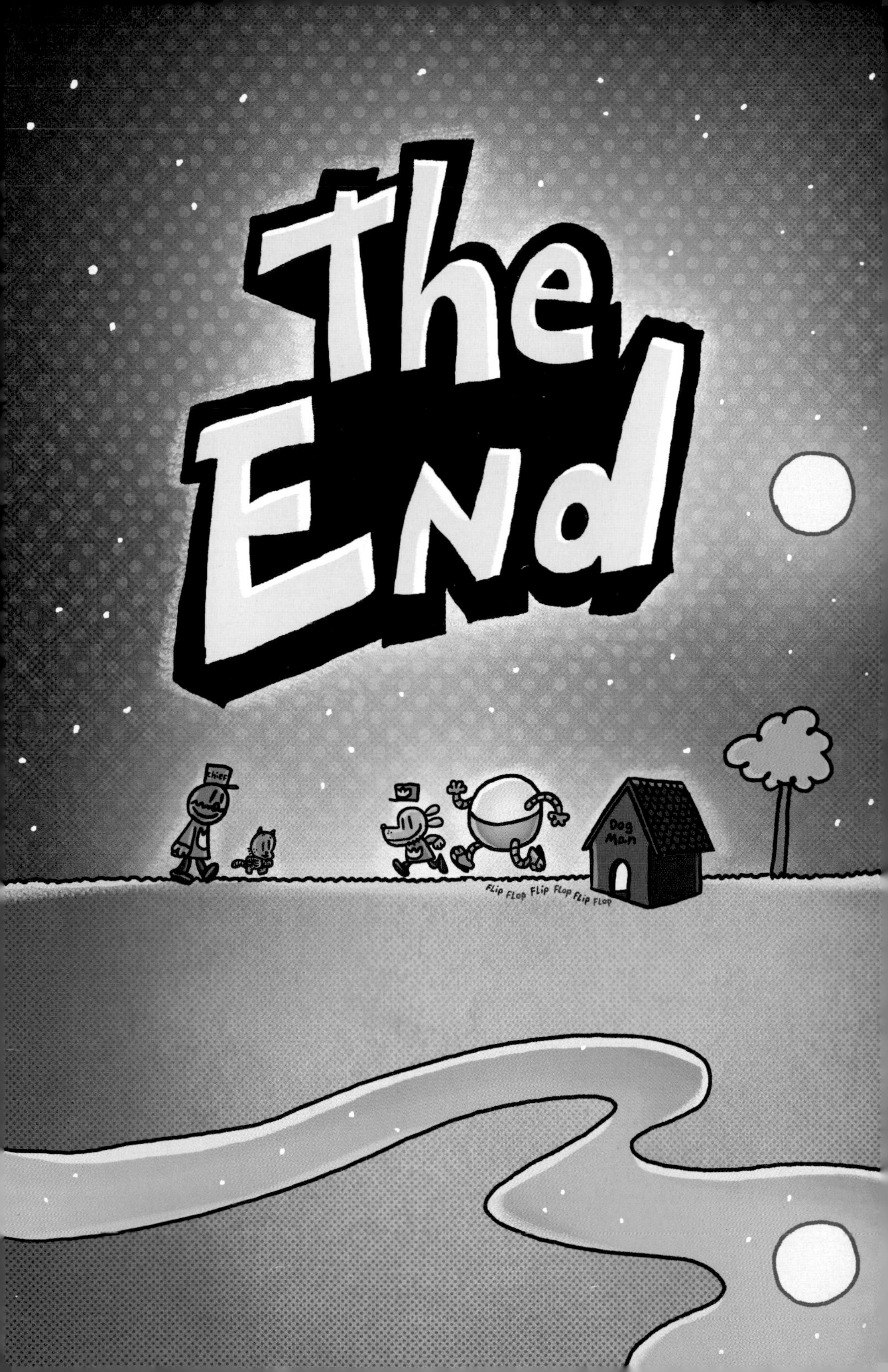

The End
Chief
Dog Man
FLip FLop FLip FLop FLip FLop

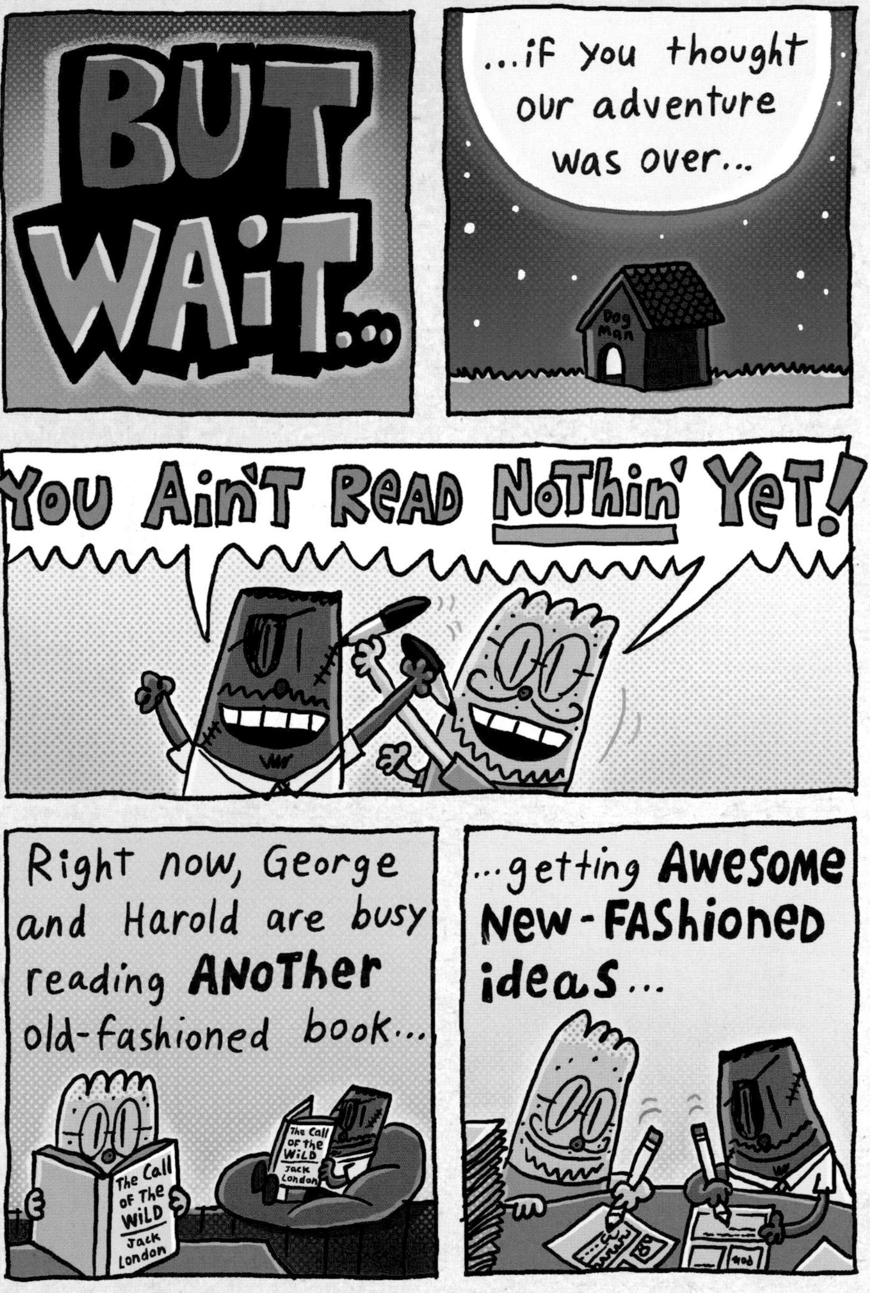
BUT WAIT...
...if you thought our adventure was over...
Dog Man
YOU AIN'T READ NOTHIN' YET!
Right now, George and Harold are busy reading ANOTHER old-fashioned book...
The Call of The WILD Jack London
The Call of the WILD Jack London
...getting AWESOME NEW-FASHIONED ideas...

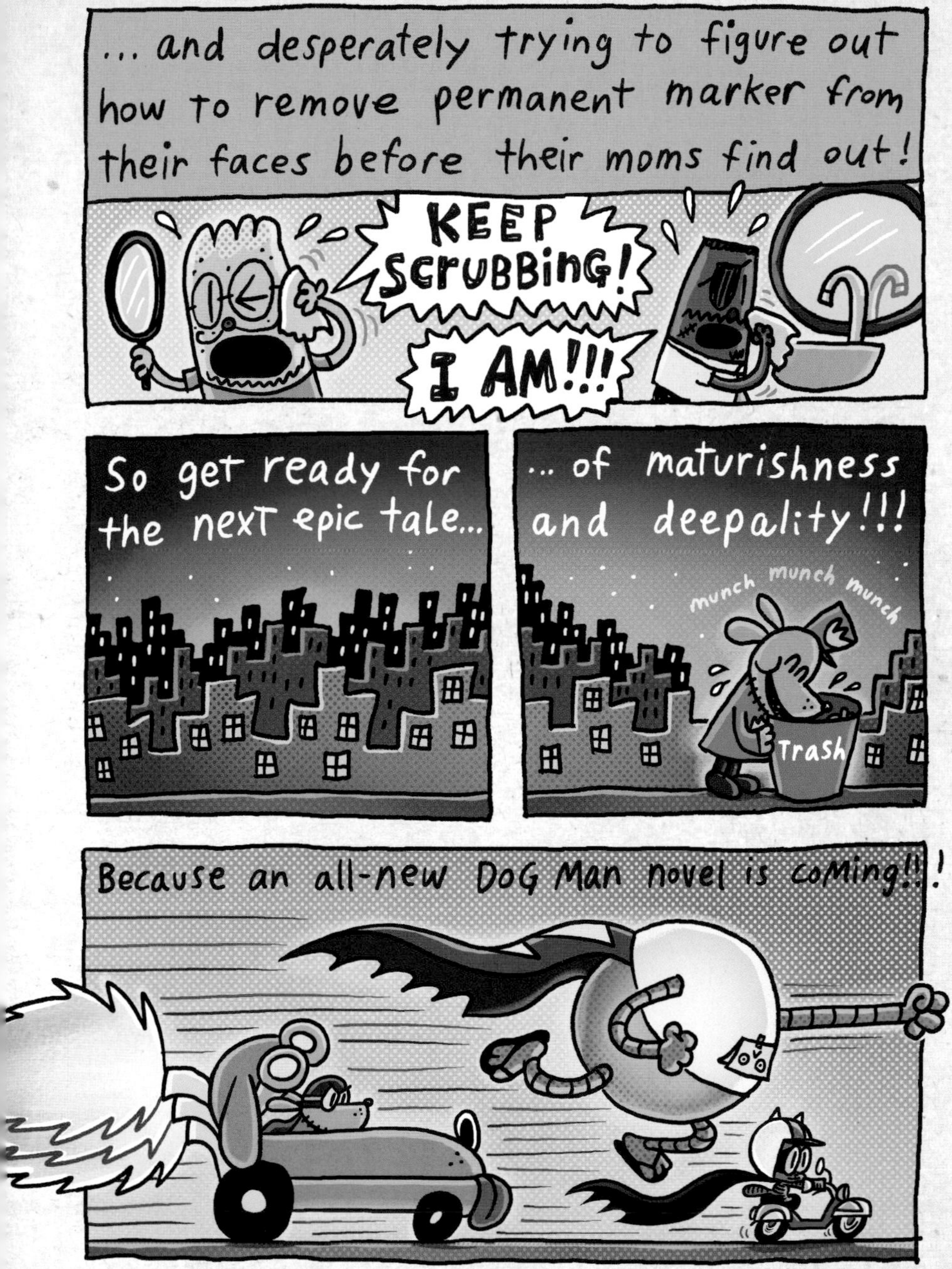
... and desperately trying to figure out how to remove permanent marker from their faces before their moms find out!
KEEP SCRUBBING!
I AM!!!
So get ready for the next epic tale...
... of maturishness and deepality!!!
munch munch munch
Trash
Because an all-new DOG MAN novel is coming!!!

HOW 2 DRAW The BARK KNIGHT in 42 Ridiculously easy steps!

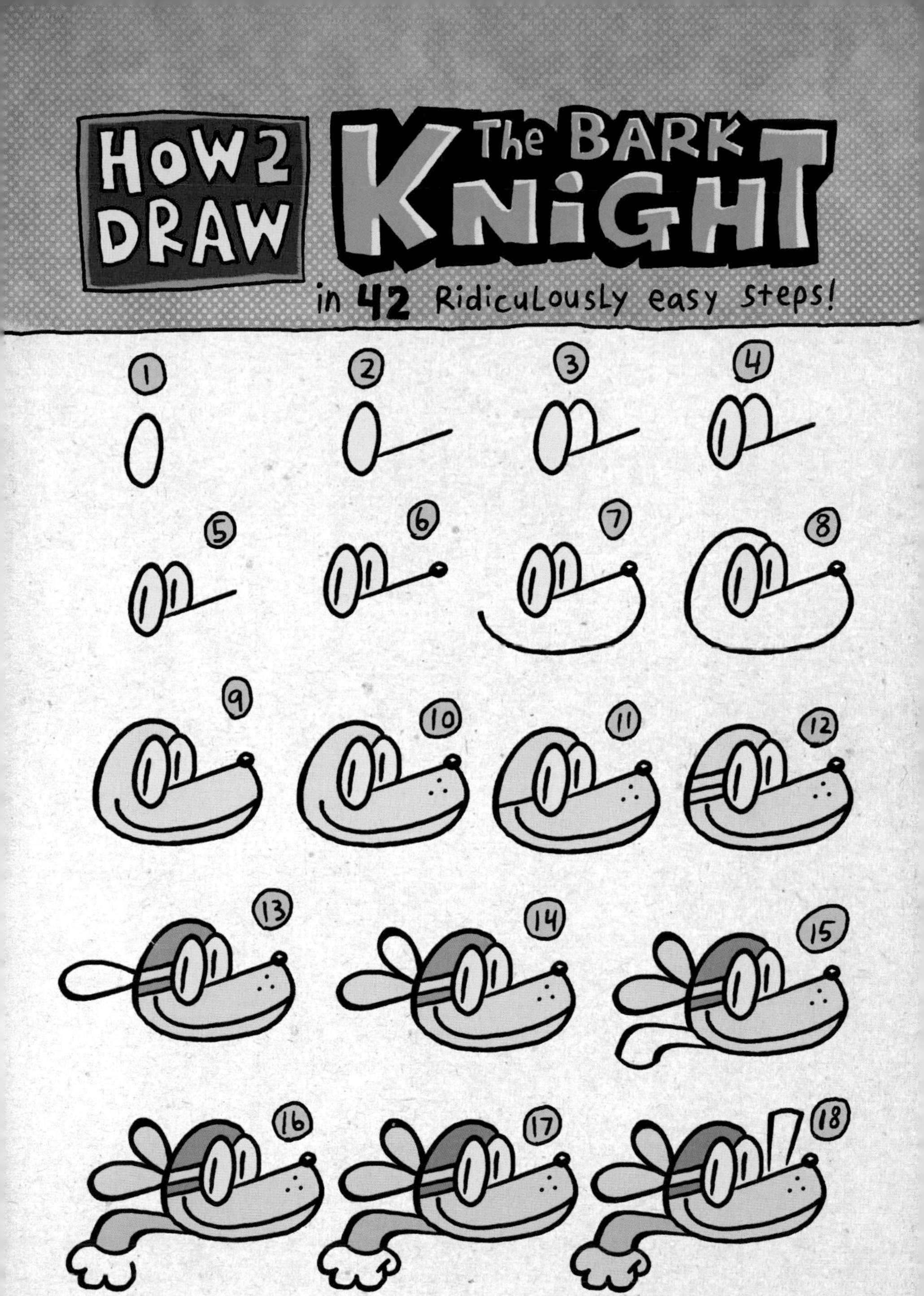
1
2
3
4
5
6
7
8
9
10
11
12
13
14
15
16
17
18

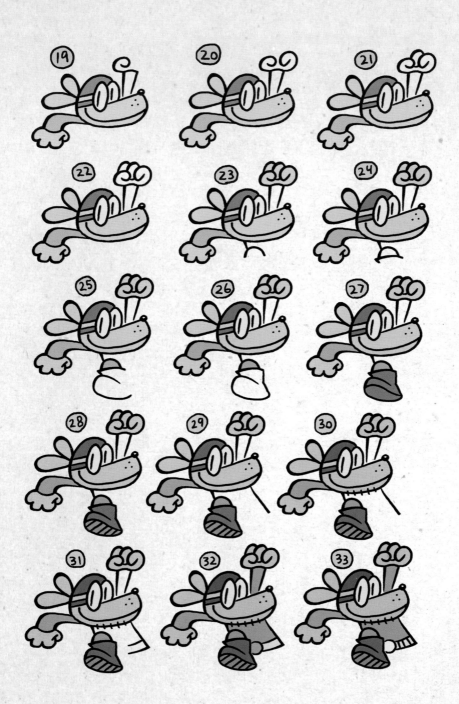

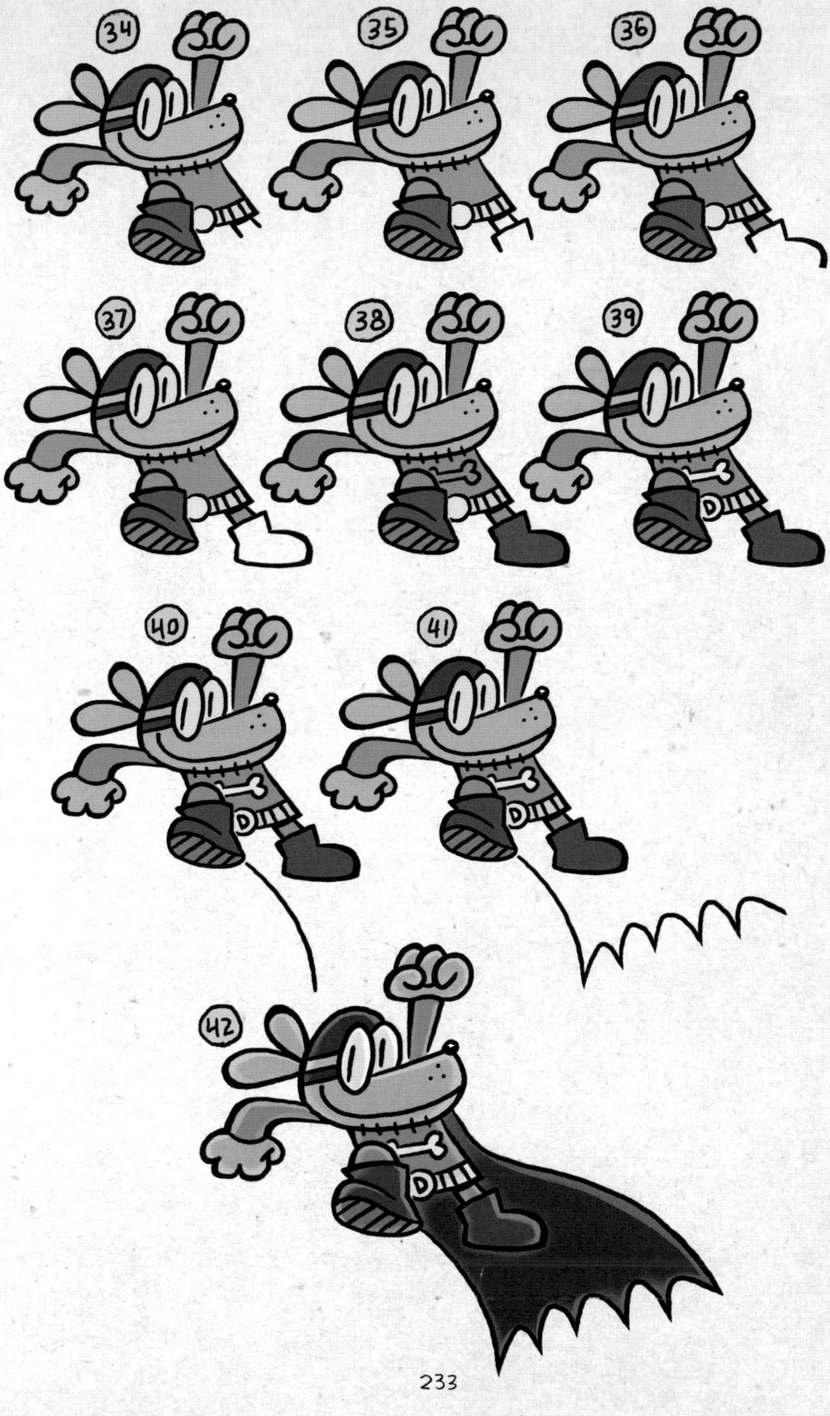
34
35
36
37
38
39
40
41
42

HOW 2 DRAW CAT KID

in 41 Ridiculously easy steps!

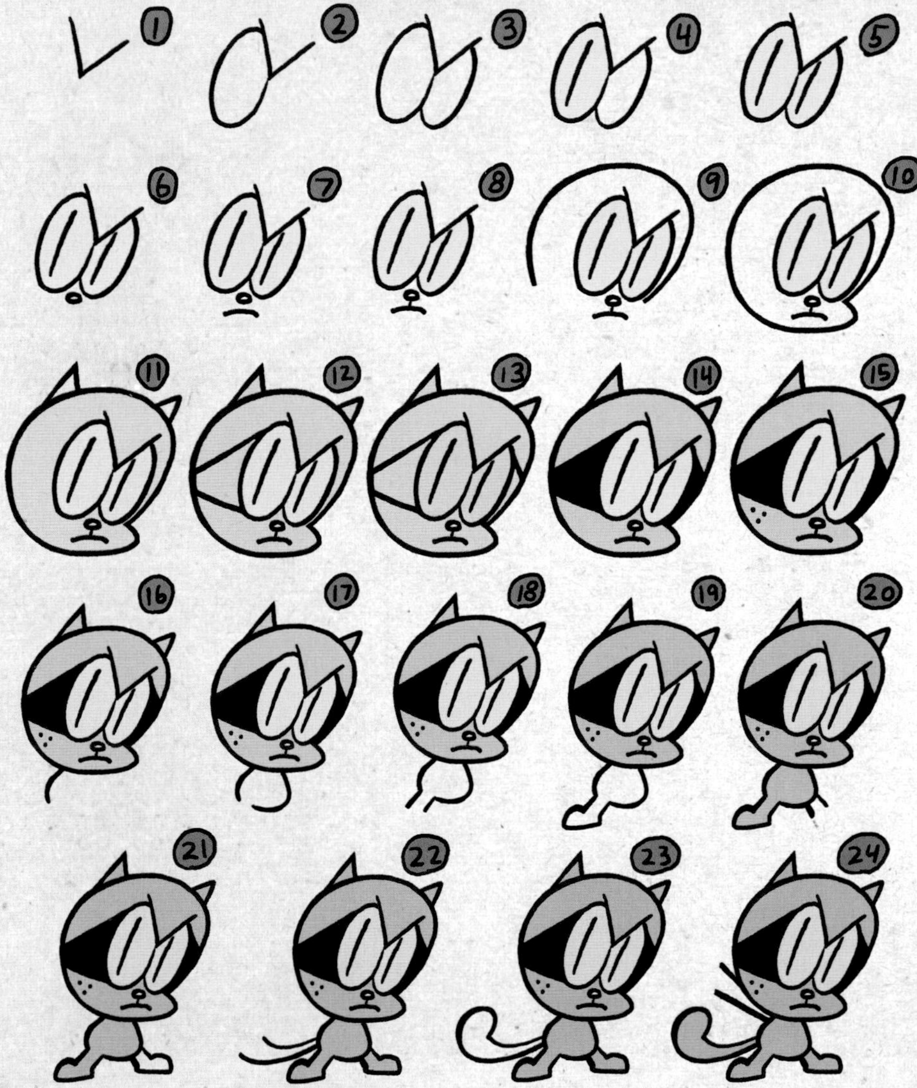

1
2
3
4
5
6
7
8
9
10
11
12
13
14
15
16
17
18
19
20
21
22
23
24

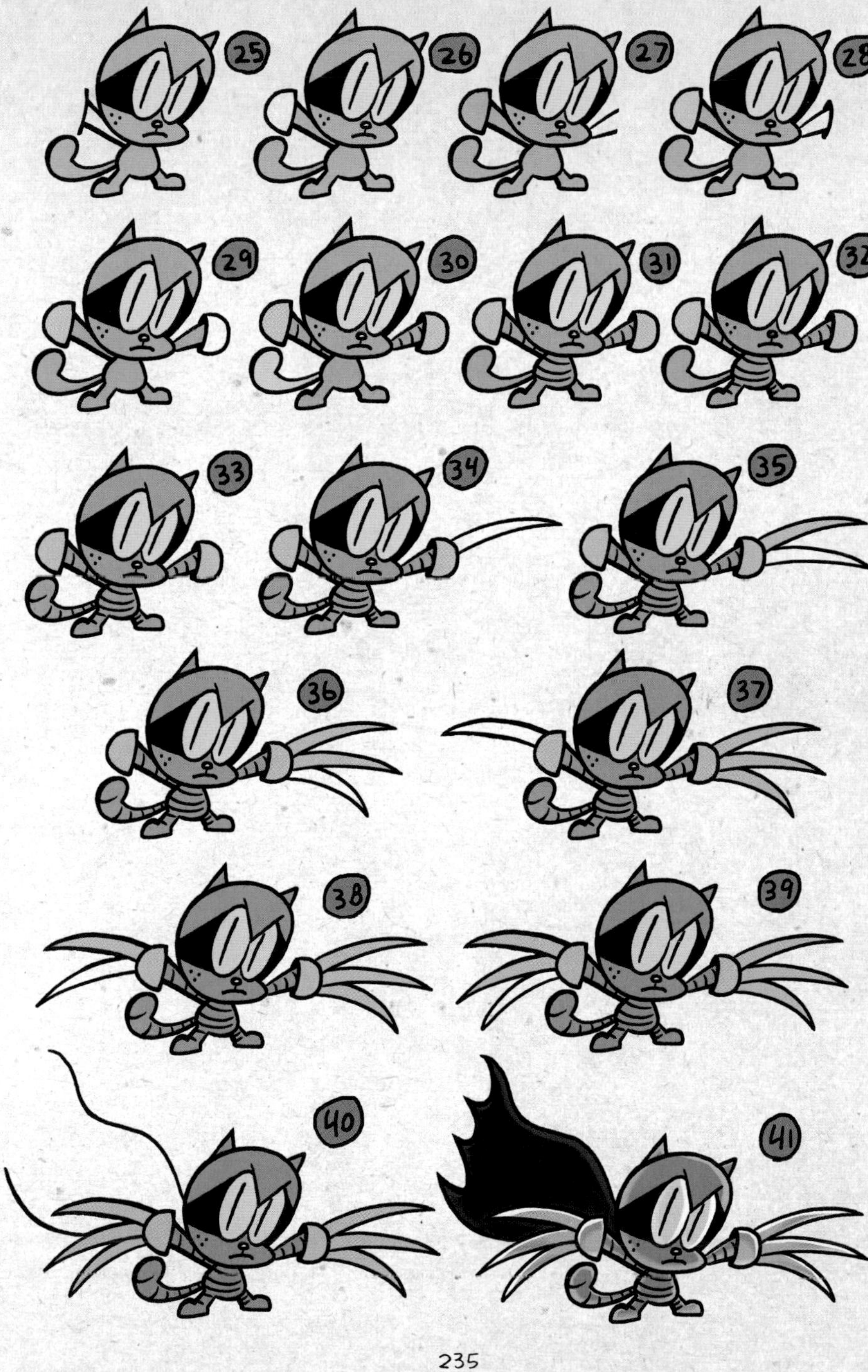
25
26
27
28
29
30
31
32
33
34
35
36
37
38
39
40
41

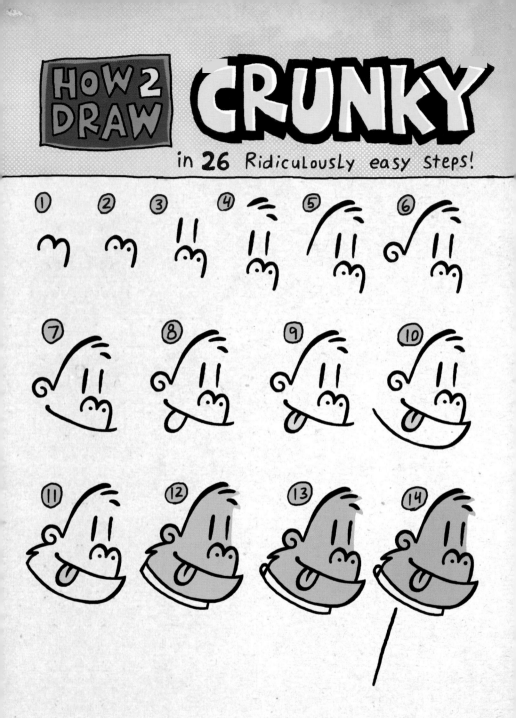

HOW 2 DRAW CRUNKY

in **26** Ridiculously easy steps!

① ② ③ ④ ⑤ ⑥
⑦ ⑧ ⑨ ⑩
⑪ ⑫ ⑬ ⑭

236

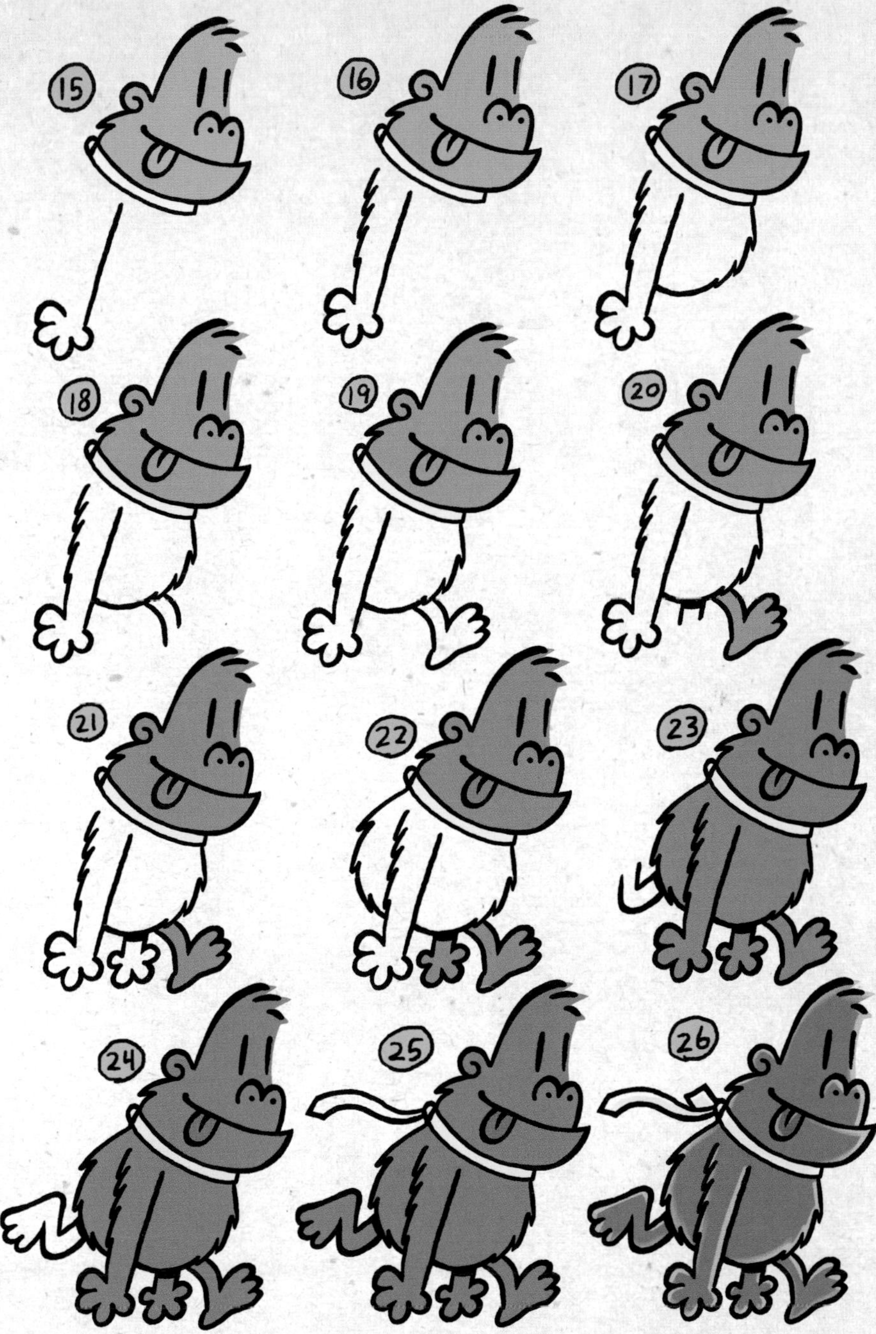
15
16
17
18
19
20
21
22
23
24
25
26

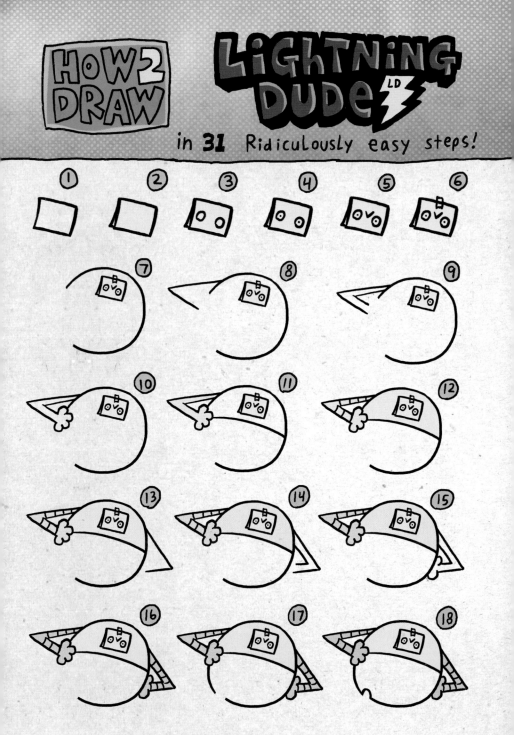

238

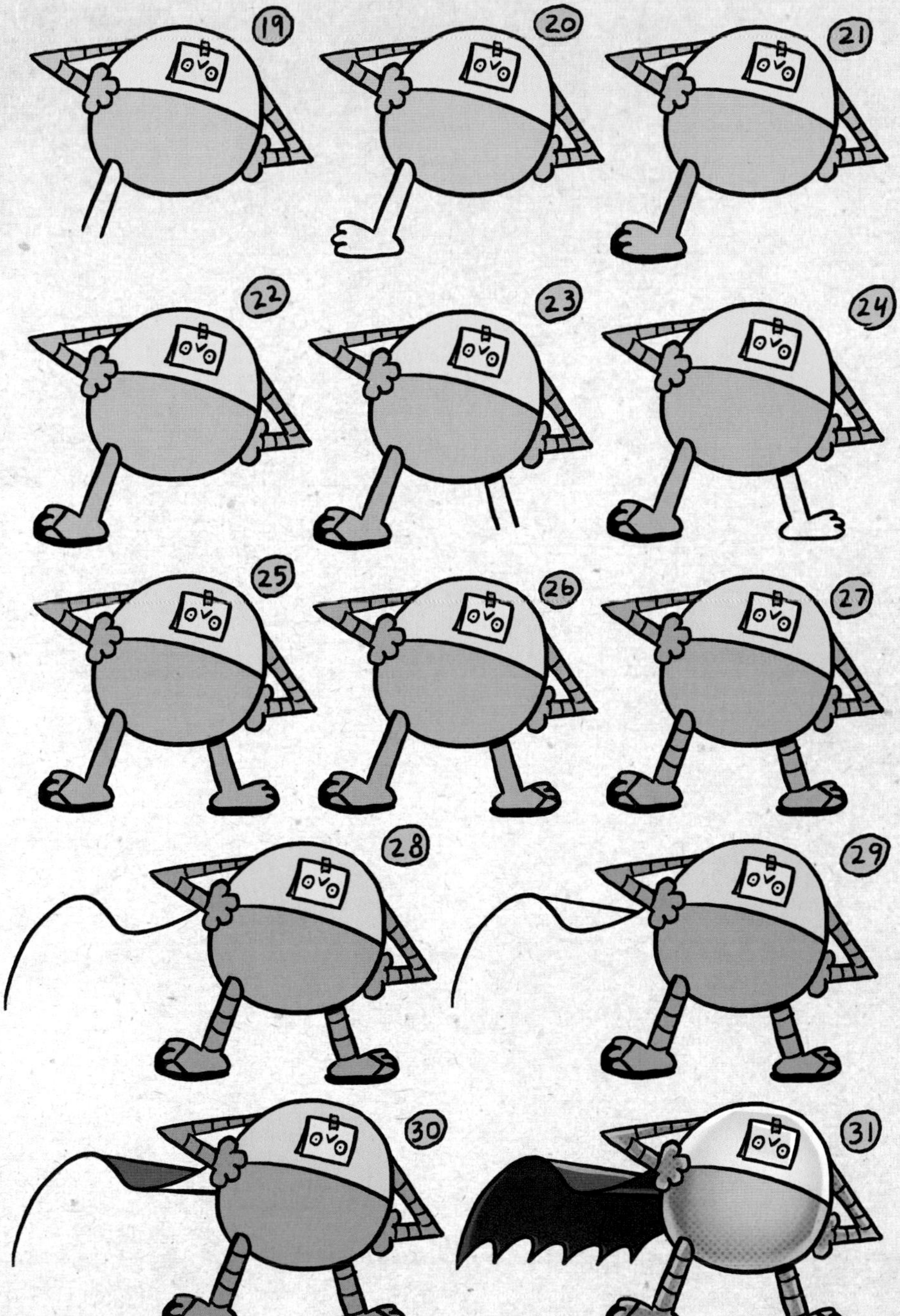
19
20
21
22
23
24
25
26
27
28
29
30
31

HOW 2 DRAW PIGGY

in 33 RIDICULOUSLY easy steps!

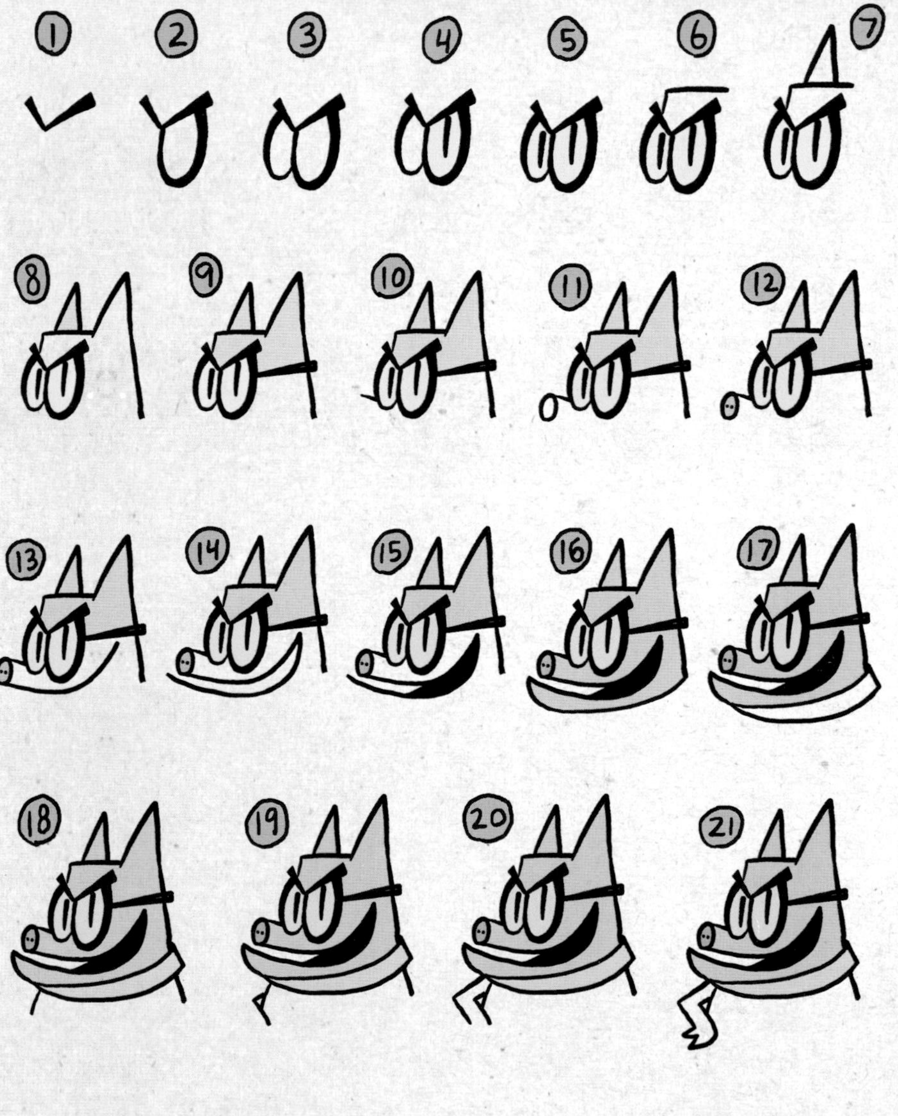

1
2
3
4
5
6
7
8
9
10
11
12
13
14
15
16
17
18
19
20
21

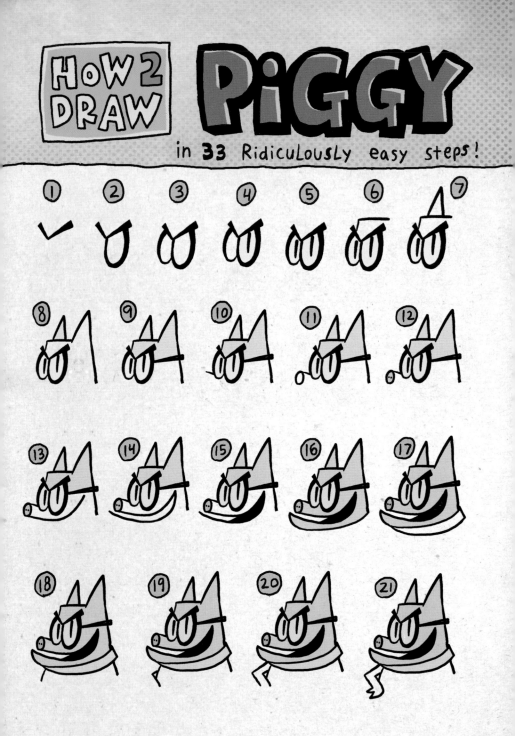

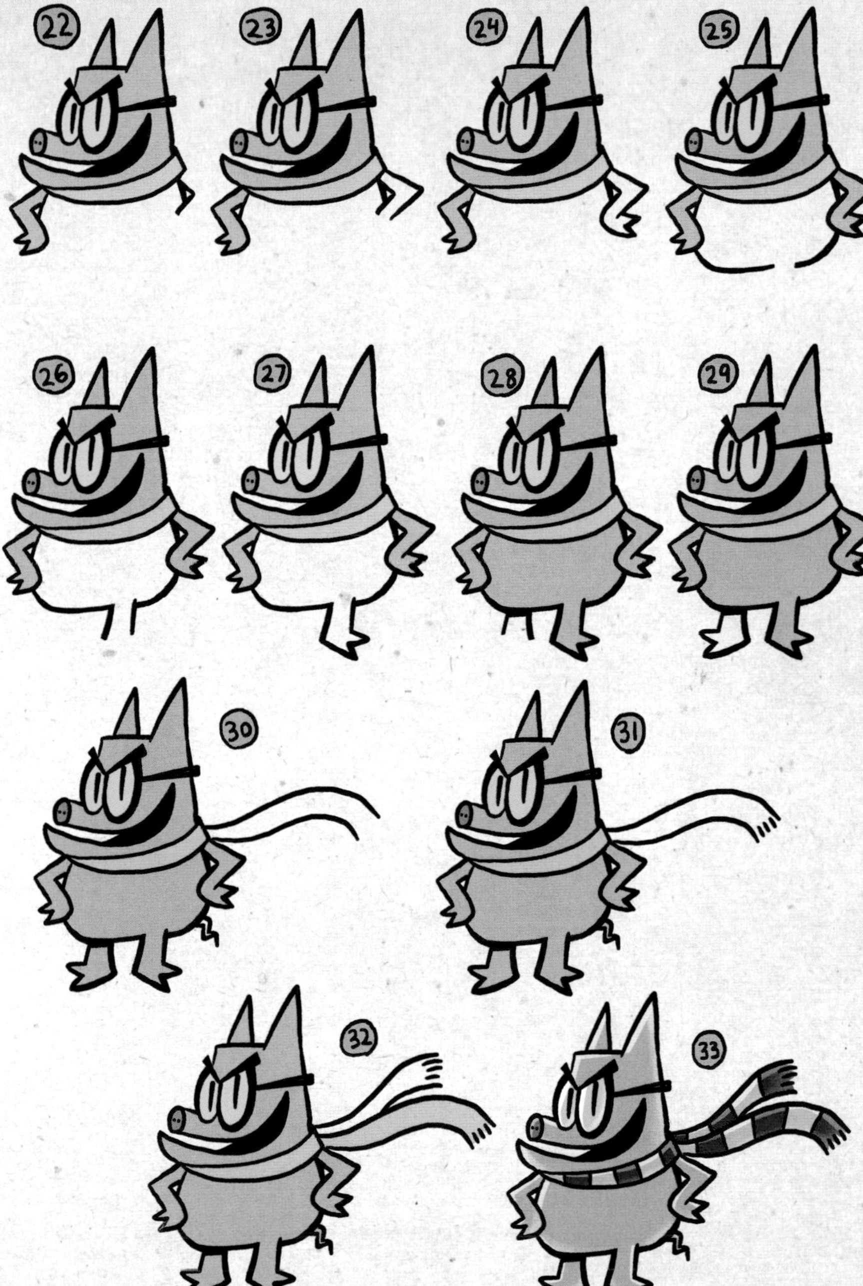
22
23
24
25
26
27
28
29
30
31
32
33

HOW 2 DRAW BUB

in **21** Ridiculously easy steps!

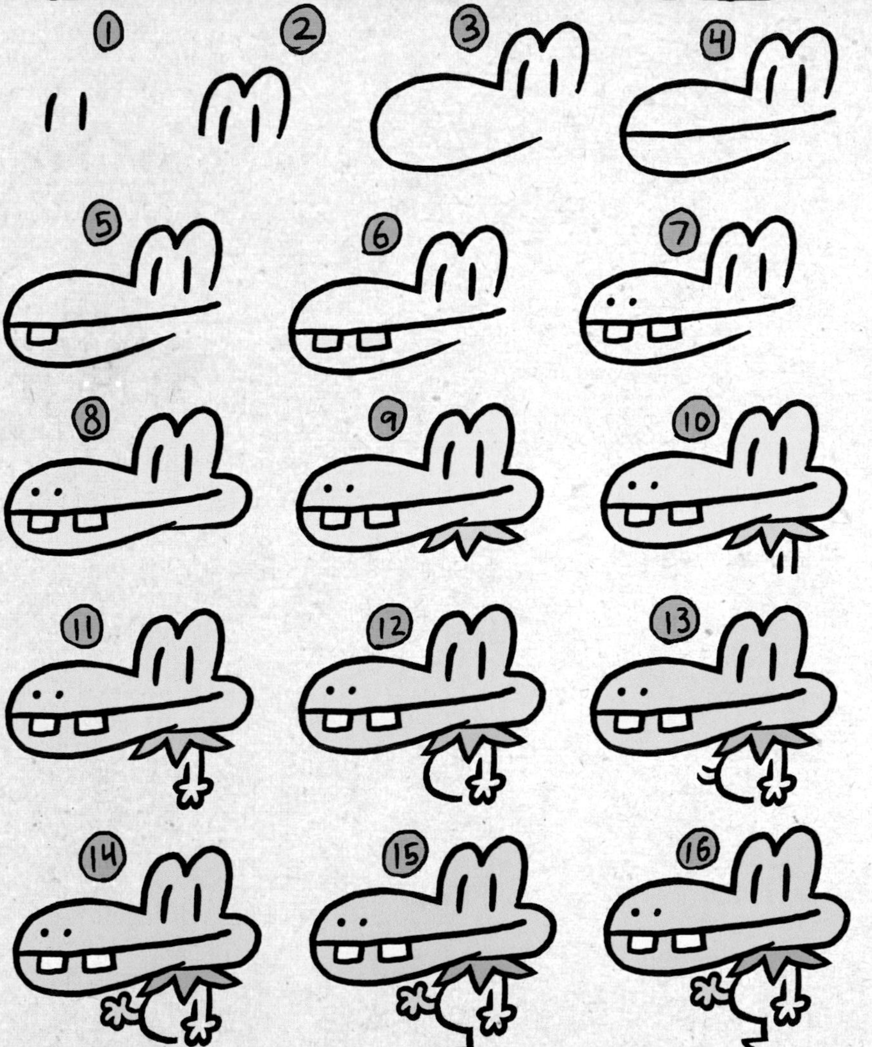
1
2
3
4
5
6
7
8
9
10
11
12
13
14
15
16

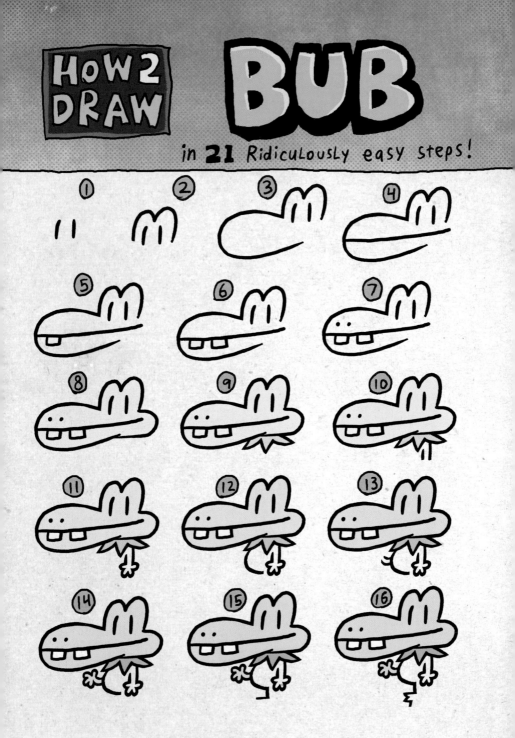

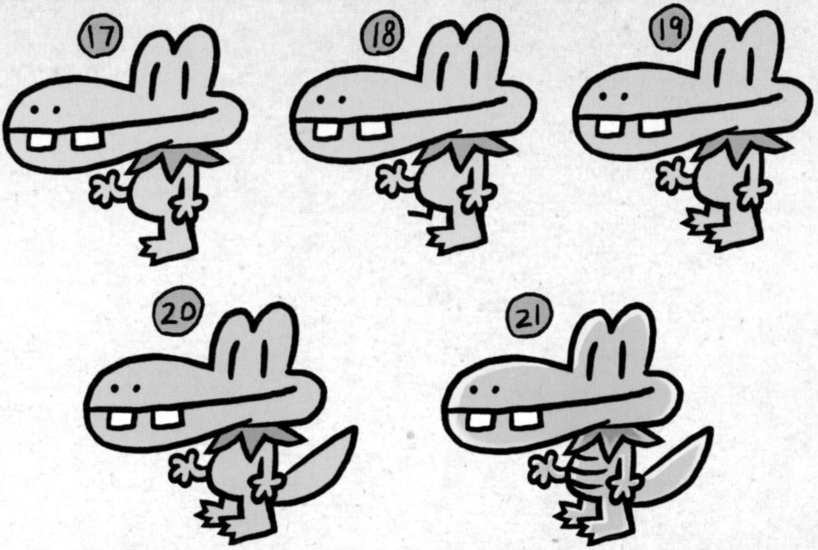
17
18
19
20
21

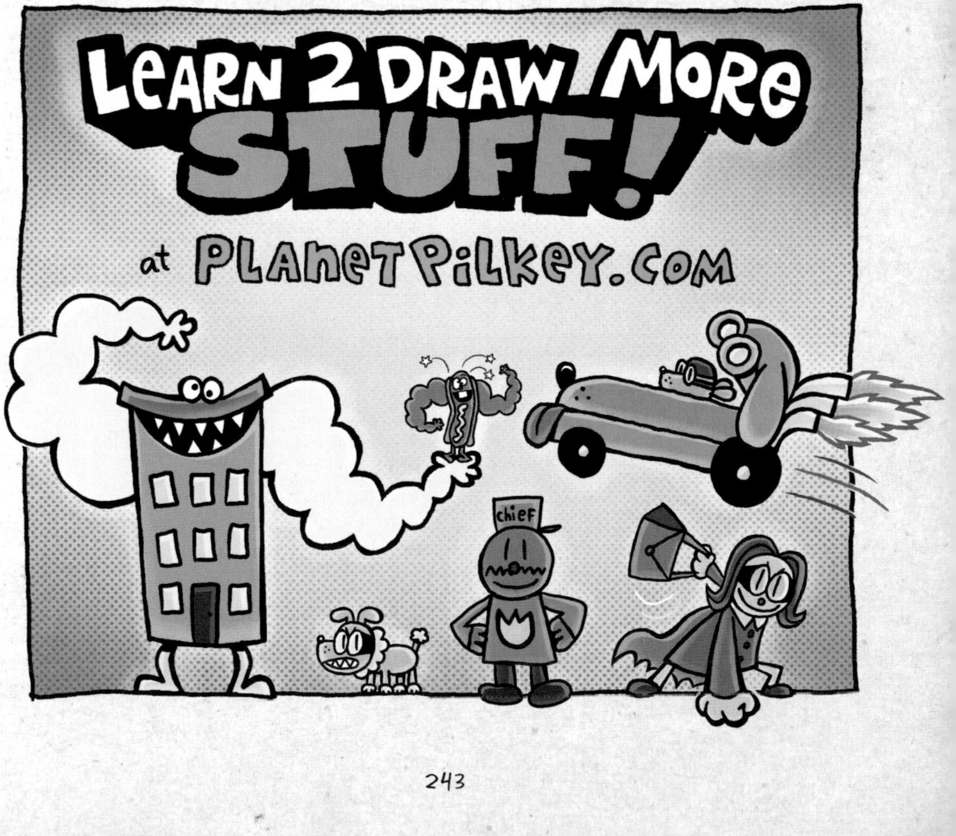
LEARN 2 DRAW MORE
STUFF!
at PLANETPILKEY.COM
chief

NOTES

by George and Harold

⭐ Our favorite character from William Golding's <u>Lord of the Flies</u> is Piggy. The Piggy in our book is a bad guy, though.

⭐ The dialogue on page 147 was inspired by quotes commonly attributed to Mark Twain and Dr. Seuss.

⭐ The conversation on pages 220-221 was inspired by the poem "Anyway," by Kent M. Keith. A version of this poem is inscribed on the wall of Mother Teresa's home for children in Calcutta, India.

⭐ "I finally finished reading <u>Lord of the Flies</u>. It WAS awesome." — Harold Hutchins

Read to Your CAT, Kid!

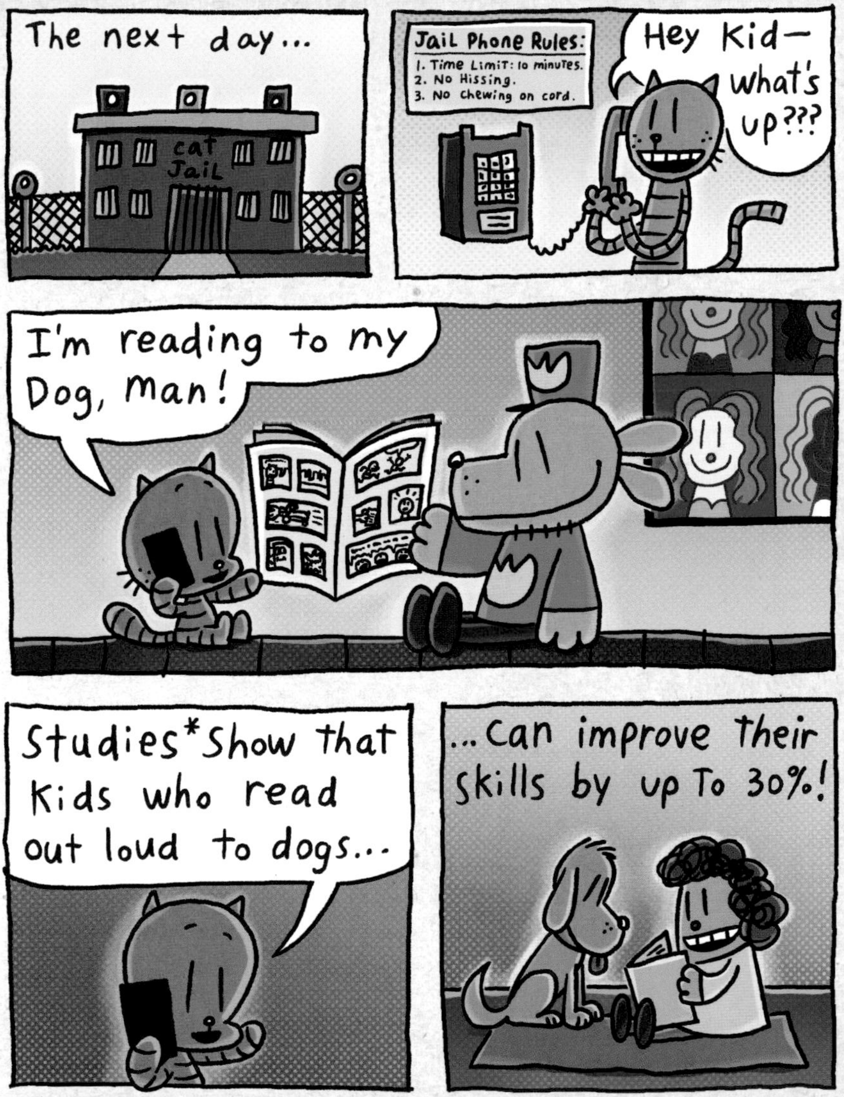

The next day...
cat Jail
Jail Phone Rules:
1. Time Limit: 10 minutes.
2. No Hissing.
3. No chewing on cord.
Hey Kid— what's up???
I'm reading to my Dog, man!
Studies* Show that Kids who read out loud to dogs...
...can improve their skills by up to 30%!

* University of California-Davis: Reading to Rover, 2010

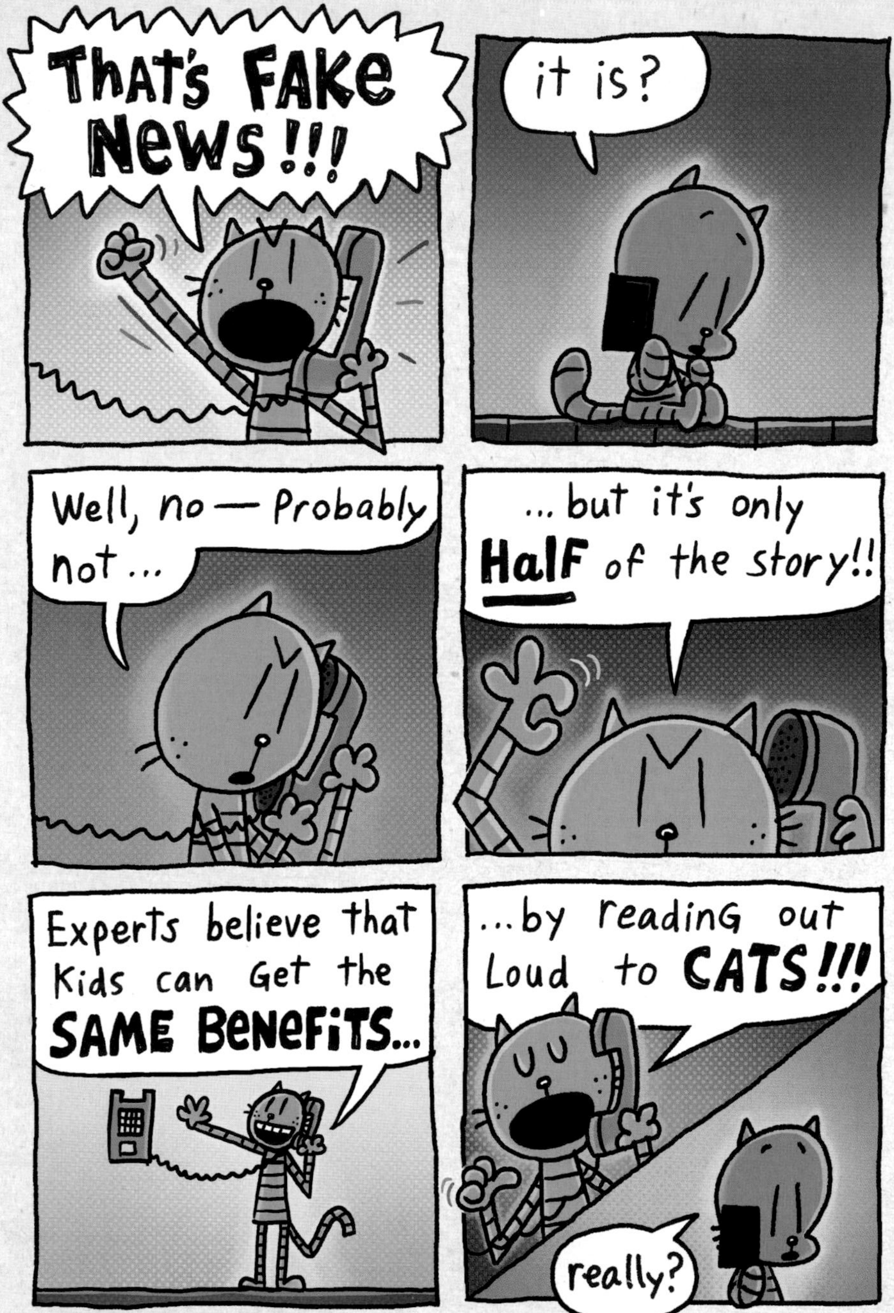
That's FAKE News!!!
it is?
Well, no — Probably not...
...but it's only HALF of the story!!
Experts believe that Kids can Get the SAME BeNeFiTS...
...by reading out Loud to CATS!!!
really?

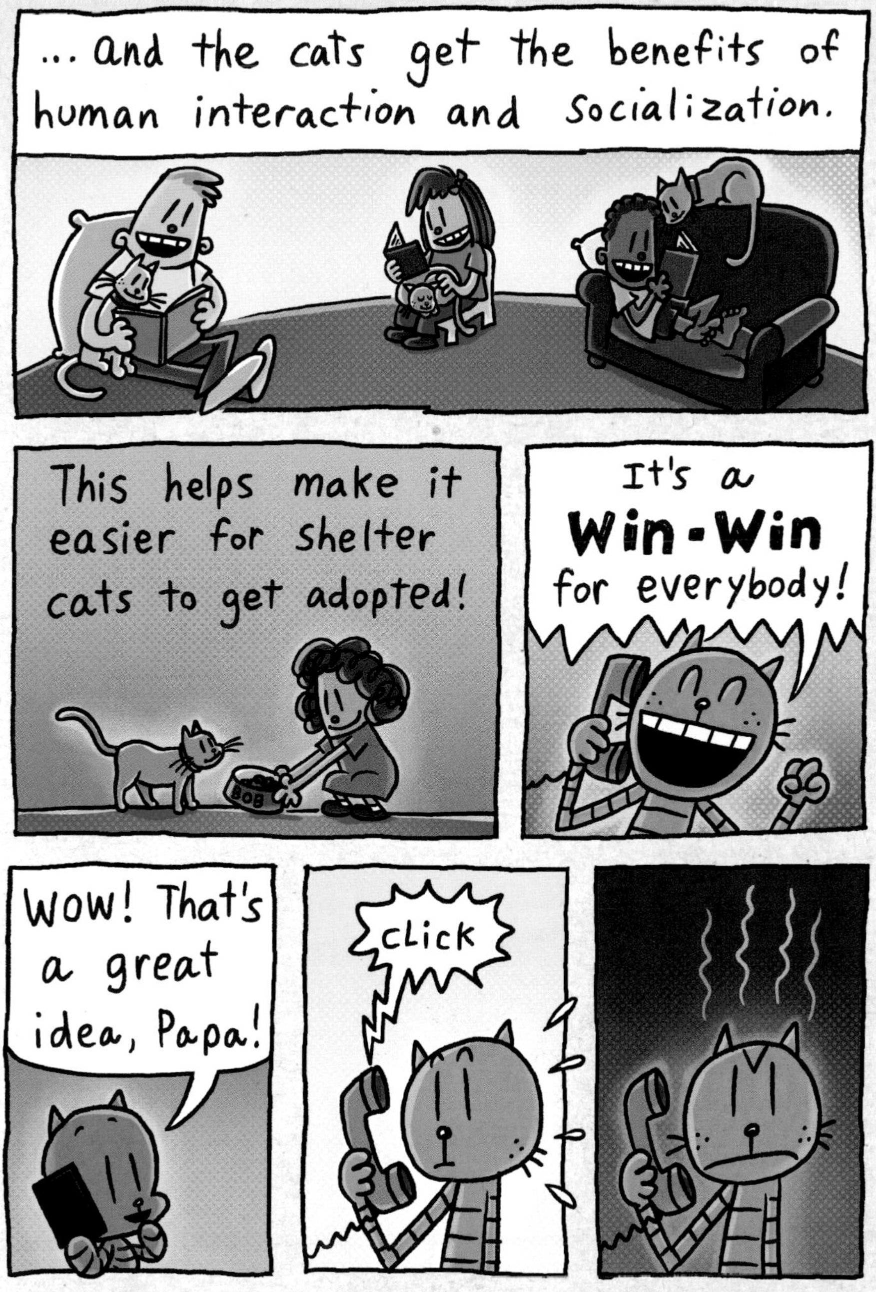
...and the cats get the benefits of human interaction and socialization.
This helps make it easier for shelter cats to get adopted!
BOB
It's a Win-Win for everybody!
WOW! That's a great idea, Papa!
click

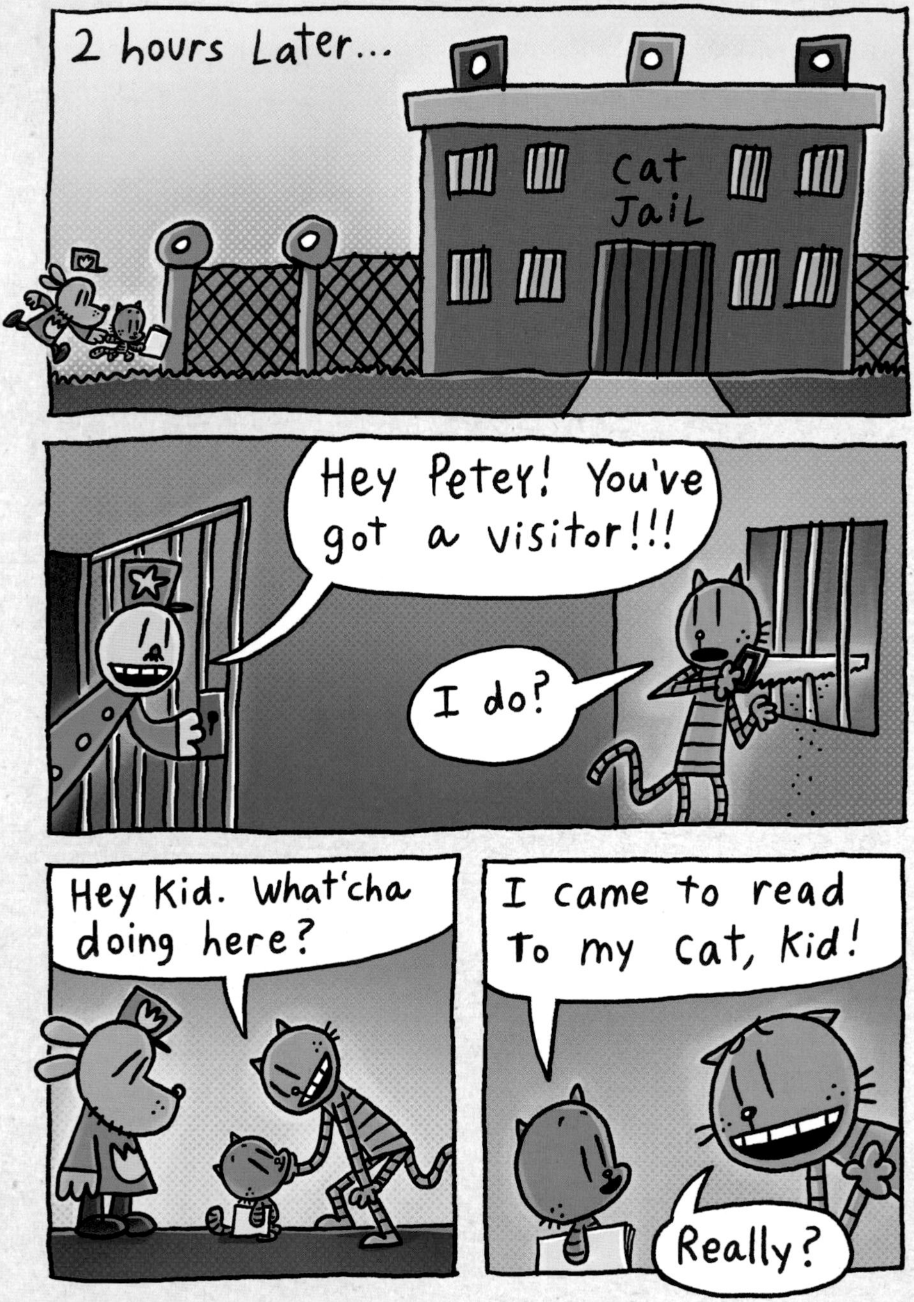
2 hours Later...
Cat Jail
Hey Petey! You've got a visitor!!!
I do?
Hey Kid. What'cha doing here?
I came to read To my cat, Kid!
Really?

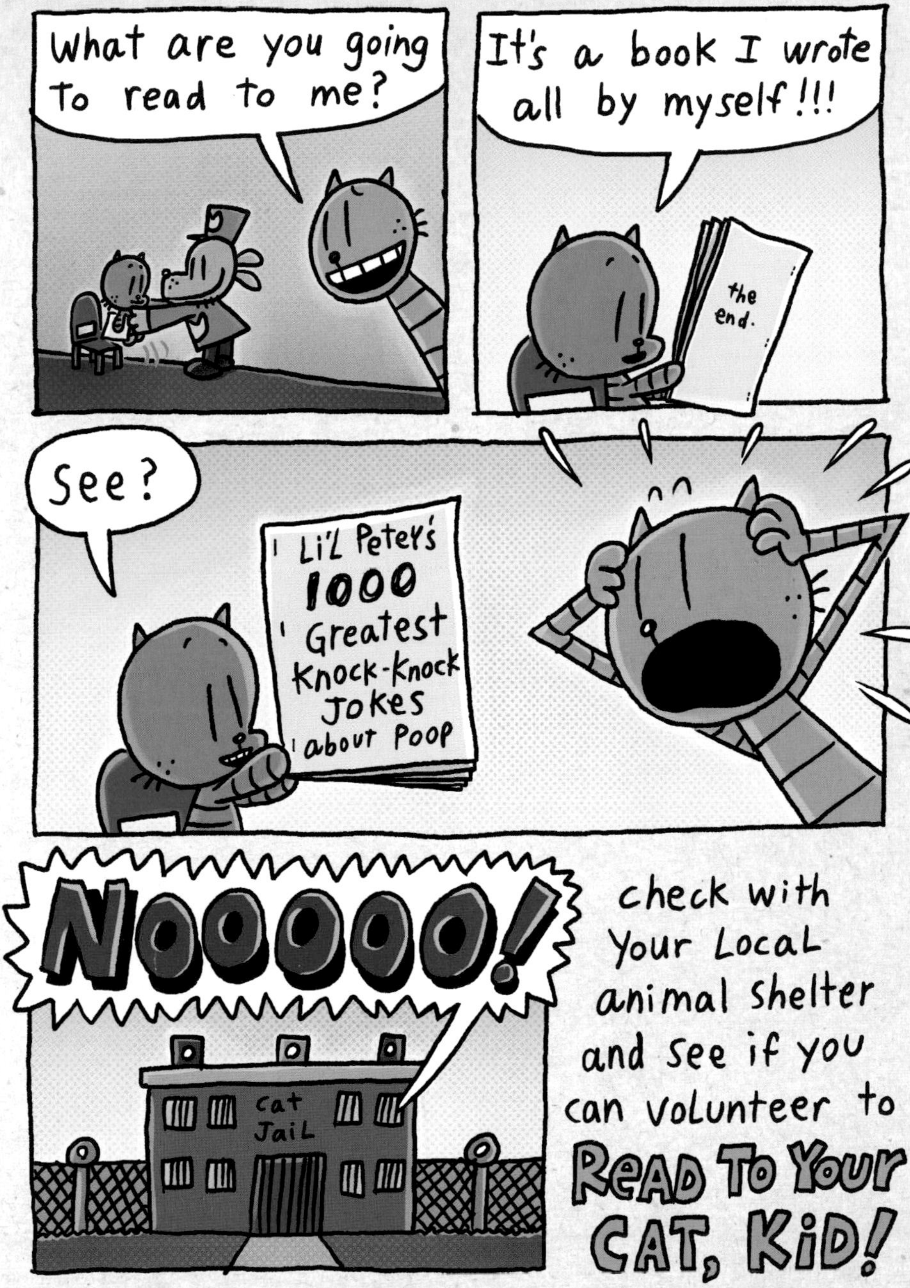
What are you going to read to me?
It's a book I wrote all by myself!!!
the end.
See?
Li'L Peter's 1000 Greatest Knock-Knock Jokes about Poop
NOOOOO!
Cat Jail
check with Your Local animal Shelter and see if you can volunteer to
READ TO YOUR CAT, KID!

READING TO YOUR CAT IS ALWAYS A PAWS-ITIVE EXPERIENCE!

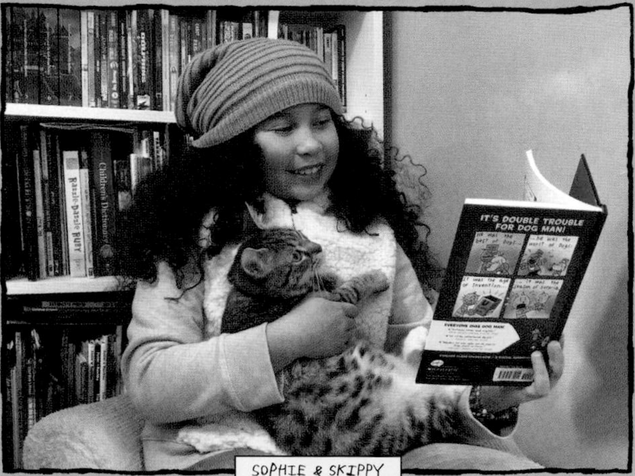
IT'S DOUBLE TROUBLE FOR DOG MAN!
SOPHIE & SKIPPY

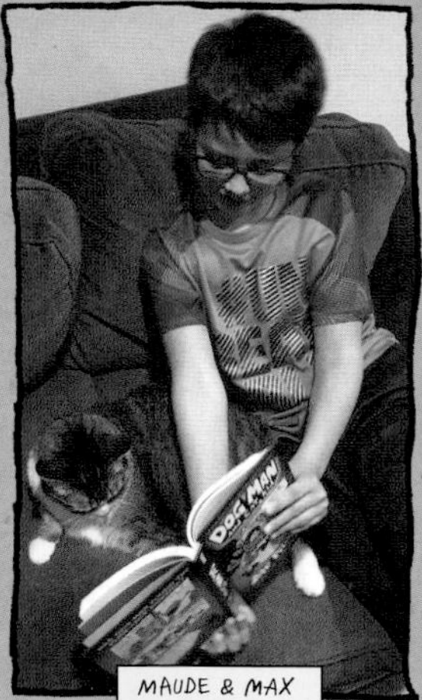
DOG MAN
MAUDE & MAX

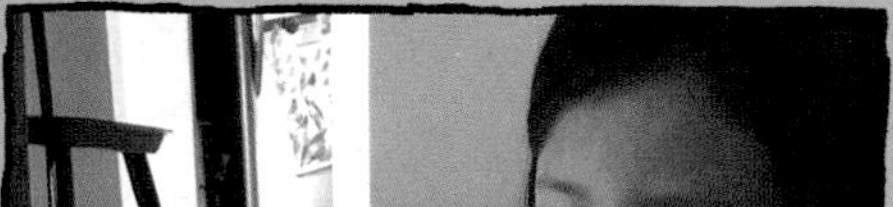
MAUDE & ABBY

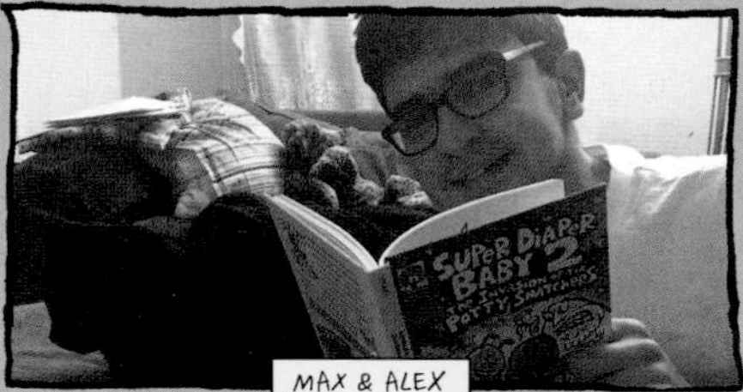
SUPER DIAPER BABY 2
MAX & ALEX

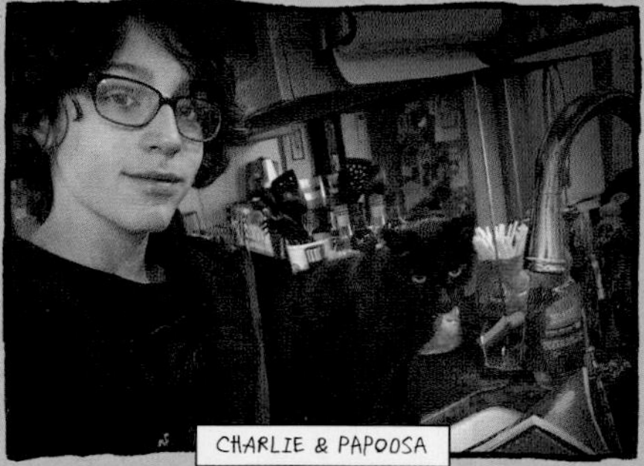
CHARLIE & PAPOOSA

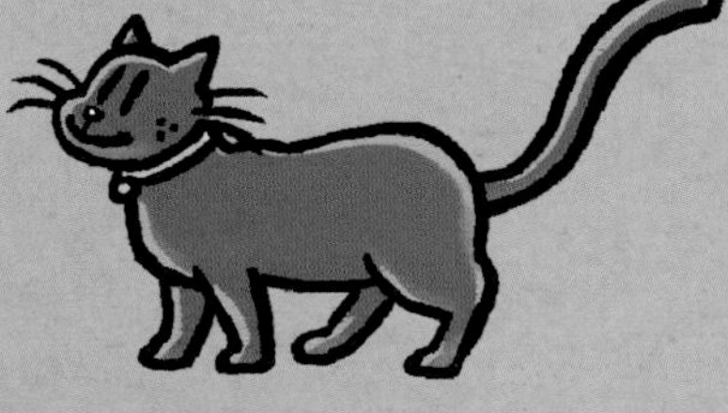

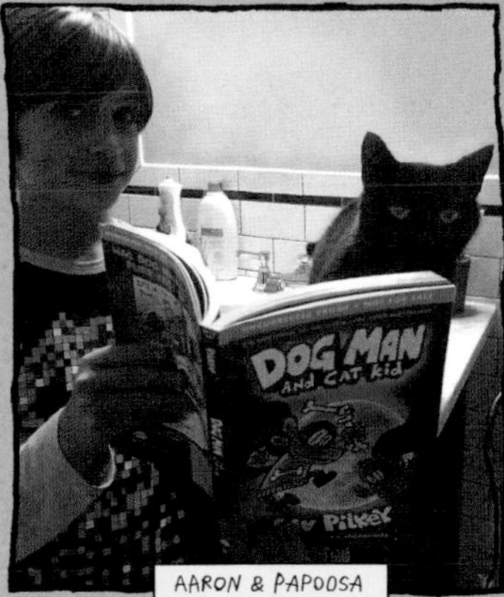
DOG MAN
And Cat Kid
Dav Pilkey

AARON & PAPOOSA

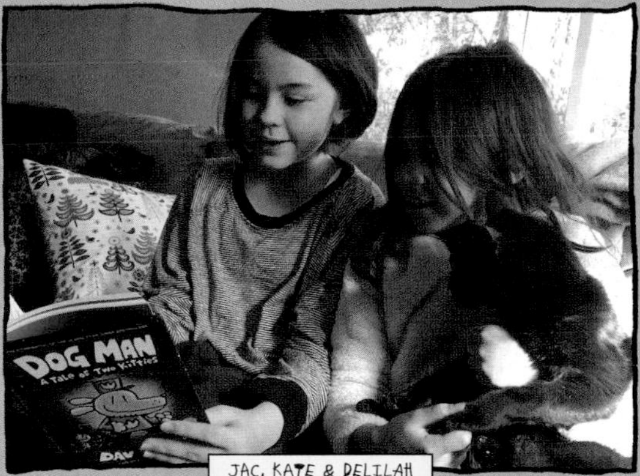
DOG MAN
A Tale of Two Kitties

JAC, KATE & DELILAH

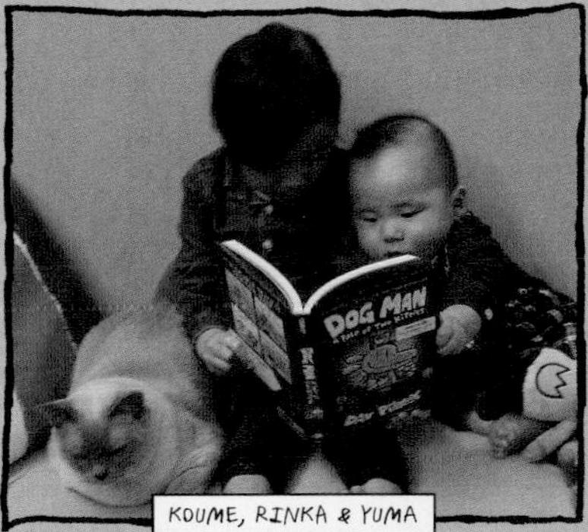
DOG MAN
A Tale of Two Kitties

KOUME, RINKA & YUMA

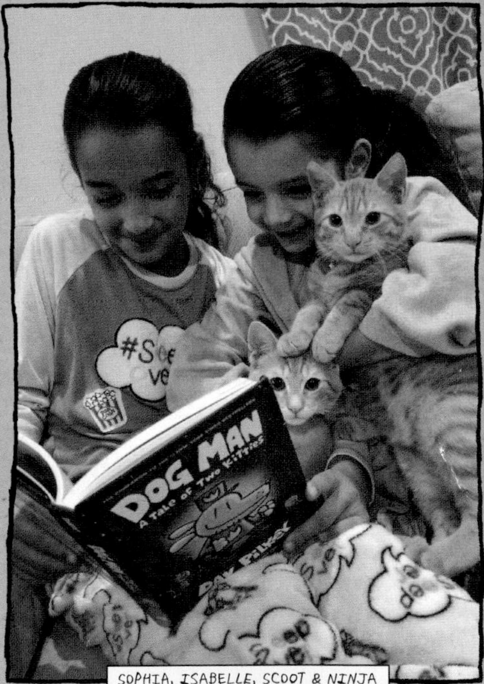
DOG MAN
A Tale of Two Kitties
Dav Pilkey

SOPHIA, ISABELLE, SCOOT & NINJA

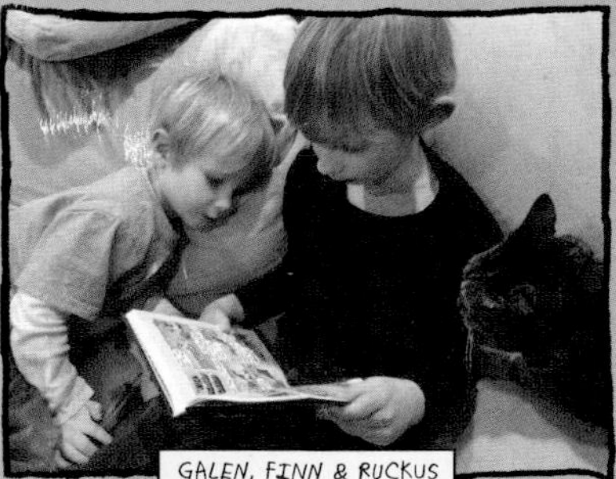

GALEN, FINN & RUCKUS

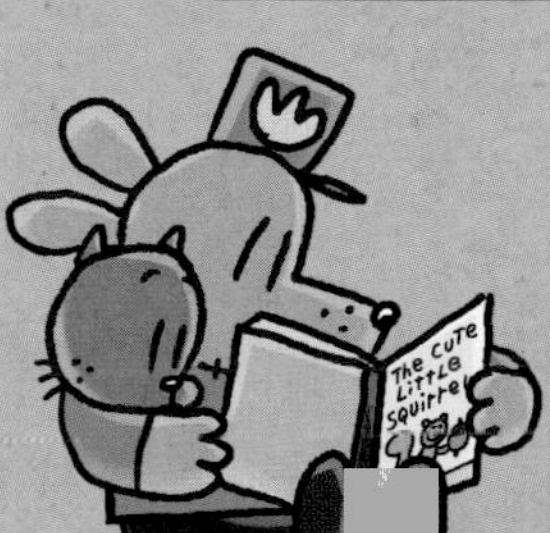
The Cute Little Squirrel

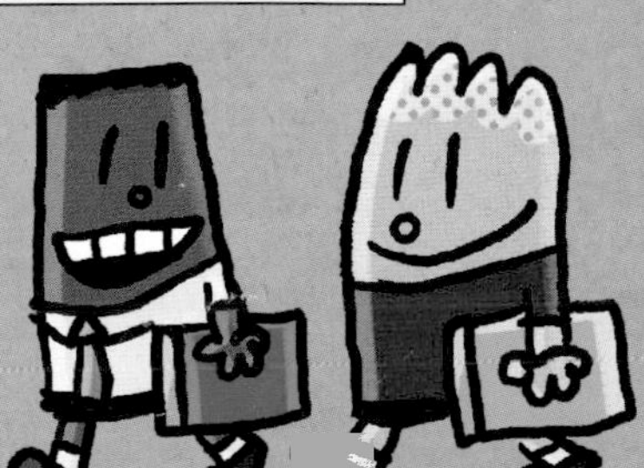

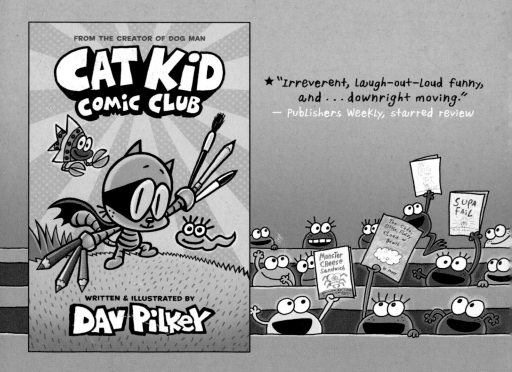

ABOUT THE
AUTHOR-ILLUSTRATOR

When Dav Pilkey was a kid, he was diagnosed with ADHD and dyslexia. Dav was so disruptive in class that his teachers made him sit out in the hallway every day. Luckily, Dav loved to draw and make up stories. He spent his time in the hallway creating his own original comic books — the very first adventures of Dog Man and Captain Underpants.

In college, Dav met a teacher who encouraged him to illustrate and write. He won a national competition in 1986 and the prize was the publication of his first book, WORLD WAR WON. He made many other books before being awarded the 1998 California Young Reader Medal for DOG BREATH, which was published in 1994, and in 1997 he won the Caldecott Honor for THE PAPERBOY.

THE ADVENTURES OF SUPER DIAPER BABY, published in 2002, was the first complete graphic novel spin-off from the Captain Underpants series and appeared at #6 on the USA Today bestseller list for all books, both adult and children's, and was also a New York Times bestseller. It was followed by THE ADVENTURES OF OOK AND GLUK: KUNG FU CAVEMEN FROM THE FUTURE and SUPER DIAPER BABY 2: THE INVASION OF THE POTTY SNATCHERS, both USA Today bestsellers. The unconventional style of these graphic novels is intended to encourage uninhibited creativity in kids.

His stories are semi-autobiographical and explore universal themes that celebrate friendship, tolerance, and the triumph of the good-hearted.

Dav loves to kayak in the Pacific Northwest with his wife.

Learn more at Pilkey.com.

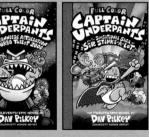